In praise of Diane Duane's works

D0964426

NOVELS

THE HARBINGER TRILOGY

Volume One:
STARRISE AT CORRIVALE

Volume Two:
STORM AT ELDALA
(March 1999)

Volume Three:
NIGHTFALL AT ALGEMRON
(October 1999)

STAR DRIVE

NOVELS

STARRISE AT CORRIVALE

Volume One of the HARBINGER TRILOGY

Diane Duane

For Martin and Julia Zurmühle,
with many thanks for making available a high place
from which the view of Corrivale was unusually clear.

STARRISE AT CORRIVALE
©1998 TSR, Inc.
All Rights Reserved.

Cover Art by rk post
First Printing: October 1998
Library of Congress Catalog Card Number:
9 8 7 6 5 4 3 2 1
ISBN: 0-7869-1179-4
2810XXX1501

U.S., CANADA,
ASIA, PACIFIC, & LATIN AMERICA
Wizards of the Coast, Inc.
P.O. Box 707
Renton, WA 98057-0707
+1-800-324-6496

EUROPEAN HEADQUARTERS
Wizards of the Coast, Belgium
P.B. 34
2300 Turnhout
Belgium
+32-14-44-30-44

Visit our web-site at **www.tsr.com**

WARNING: certainty, much-desired, gives way,
great change, great difficulty now descends.
Harbinger bows beneath the load, cries out:
cold-starréd silence says, seek no respite:
refuse the load and it will crush you still:
accept the burden and it bears you down,
though willingness may help to ease the pain:
but virtue is yet cruel: though change brings good,
beware, harbinger, how it changes you.

Stochastics, mechalus version (v28.0),
XV, 3-11

Chapter One

THE WOMAN STOOD at the window, watching the planet turn beneath her, or seem to turn. The ship's orbit was low, but not so much so that the dun and emerald curve of Ino would seem to take up the whole view that her two-meter-wide window afforded. Over the world's edge, night was approaching, one of ninety or a hundred nights that the ship would see in the course of one of Ino's genuine rotations. Under the ship, for the moment, a golden day of early summer in the planet's northern hemisphere lay drowning deep in lazy afternoon. The startling blue of the huge twin lakes of Aimara and Noumara, old meteoric impacts in the planet's equatorial continent, looked at her like eyes, round and surprised, a little hazed even at this altitude with the slowly burgeoning seasonal warmth. There would be people fishing out in little boats on those lakes right now, while overhead, water birds skimmed by uttering little lazy cries. Nothing disturbed the placid waters but the stroke of oars and the glittering golden circles of water where the fish rose into the endless brazen afternoon, daring the edge of their world for a gulp of air.

But if you raised your head only a little from the blue of the lakes and the thought of the afternoon, you could see the night coming—the blurred, shadowy edge of it sliding on toward the unsuspecting afternoon, silent, inexorable, and uncaring. And how do you stop the night? she thought, shivering, just once.

The Concord Heavy Cruiser *Falada* had been her home for nearly three years now. Although Lauren Delvecchio had grown used to life on the ship, she would be more than glad to leave it when this mission was done at last. There had indeed been times during these last few years when she had thought it would never be done—that she would spend the rest of her life circling one or the other of these globes, either the green and dun belted globe of Ino with its polar seas, or the dun and white streaked expanse of Phorcys. There were periods during which she had become heartily sick of the sight of both of them and refused to look out the window when she woke up in the morning because she would see only one or the other of them again, going through the same old dance around their primary, Thalaassa. Day succeeding night, and night succeeding day, and not a breath's worth of change ensuing as a result. *How many thousands of these "little nights" have I seen now,* Lauren had thought at such times, *and how many more am I going to see before this situation improves?*

But now it was changing. Slowly, like a real night shading moment by moment into the gray of earliest morning, the change had begun . . . no thanks to the people down below. Or rather, all thanks to them. The unquestioned, intransigent mutual hatred of the people on these two planets had finally pushed them into a position from which neither could escape without the other's assistance. Except for the inherent ironies, it was a nasty situation, but the present circumstances promised the beginning of an end to the troubles which had brought Lauren here in the first place. She would finally be able to go home to Thuldan Prime for a leave long enough to help her forget—with the utmost pleasure—what both these planets looked like. Soon enough after that she would be back at Corrivale, helping the senior staff in juggling the economic and political tensions among VoidCorp, the Hatire Community, and the Concord to which her own allegiance was given. But let a little forgetfulness come first . . . .

She turned away from the window to look around the small wood-paneled room and at her desk, which was clear for the moment. Her office was unlike any other in *Falada*'s maze of corridors. Ambassadors of her station were allowed a bit more room for personal conceit than even the higher ranking officers on board, and Delvecchio had taken eager advantage of it, for beyond the thick wooden door of her office, the majority of

Falada's inner passageways were uniform durasteel and molecularly enhanced plastics, just several thousand tons of dull metal floating in space above Ino. But within these four walls was a sanctuary that held at least the promise of warmth and solitude. Dark wood paneled the walls and ceiling, reflecting the light from the ceiling illuminators with a soft, warm glow. A large, tasseled rug covered all but the edges of the tile floor. The three high-backed chairs facing her desk were designed for both comfort and beauty. But even these small comforts had long since lost their ability to soothe her.

She paused to think about where she should start the day's preparations. Just as she turned, the knock came. *Tck, tck, tck.* For the first time that morning she smiled just a little, knowing who it was. "Lieutenant," she said, "come in."

The thick wooden door opened a crack, and the young man in the somber dark blue uniform of a Concord Marine put his head into the room and glanced at her amiably. That by itself struck Lauren as charmingly old-fashioned, but it was like Lieutenant Connor to exploit the presence of an old-fashioned non-dilating door for such a gesture. This sort of behavior was one of the things that had made him stand out for Lauren at the beginning of this long cruise and more so as time went by. The senior diplomat under whom she had trained had often said, "There's nothing wrong with old-fashioned manners," and he would pause, and get that wry look for which he had been famous, adding, "Especially since old-fashioned manners throw the people around you completely off their stride." All the more so, Lauren knew, when the manners in question were natural, not applied as a cosmetic. As far as she could tell, in Gabriel Connor they went down to the bone.

Gabriel shut the door behind him and came to stand in front of her desk, looking at it without really looking—the kind of circumspect glance intended to see whether there was something there that he should avoid looking at.

Lauren laughed. "No need yet," she said, "It's too early for paperwork. Can I give you something hot?"

"Let me do that, Ambassador."

She chuckled and sat down at her desk, knowing there was no use arguing with him when he got into one of these chivalric moods. "A throwback," she called him sometimes, teasing Connor with references to ancient times when men were afraid or unwilling to let women do anything physical. Lauren watched him go to the dispenser set in the wall between two of the oldest watercolors that hung on the dark paneling. He tapped in the code for what he knew she would want—grosgrain brew, half and half with hot milk—and his own preference, black chai, no sweetener, no anything. She shuddered at the thought of drinking such stuff, but he seemed to thrive on it.

Connor handed her the mug and sat down, sipping at the chai already, even though by the way it was steaming it looked hot enough to burn anyone's mouth.

"I thought only drill instructors had leather tongues," Lauren said, sitting down at her desk and putting the grosgrain aside for the moment. "You make me think Marines must have them installed as standard equipment."

Gabriel looked at the plain white mug, surprised, and then at Lauren again. "Sorry?"

"The heat."

"Oh. I didn't notice."

That's in character, I suppose, Lauren thought. She had seen him equally untroubled by other kinds of heat on this cruise. The way he handled pressure was another aspect of this young marine that made her interested in the further progress of his career.

"How did the spatball game go last night?" Lauren said.

Connor shrugged. "We lost to Star Force. Fifteen-eight."

"Terrible."

"It hardly came as a surprise, Ambassador," Gabriel said. "But at least we knew which way to bet." His smile was ironic. He took another sip of chai and said, "Are you all ready for the resumption of the plenary?"

"Ready?" she said, and smiled slightly. "I might look for

some other word. The lion's den has never been one of my favorite places."

"You seem to be doing all right," Gabriel said.

"Well . . ." she said. He considered her, under cover of drinking his chai. Idly, Lauren watched him do it. Just fleetingly the idea went across the front of her mind: If I were even fifty years younger . . . But Lauren suppressed the thought, not for the first time, with some amusement at herself. It was hard for anyone around here, male or female, to ignore such rugged good looks. They seemed even more attractive since Gabriel wore them completely without affectation, even apparently without seeming to be aware of them at all. He was dark with high cheek bones. His eyes were set deep so that thoughtful looks on him seemed more thoughtful than they might have on a less structured face, and angry looks seemed somehow more threatening, flashing out from underneath those eyebrows that nearly met over the nose— a feature that the old stories suggested indicated an unusual amount of blood more directly traceable to the Union of Sol. Either way, it was rare enough to see an angry look from Gabriel, but you saw a lot of the thoughtful ones, another reason why Lauren had begun making a point to invite him to work more closely with her. There were few enough career officers who had that considering look this early in their careers. It always boded well, in Lauren's opinion, and she was not above grabbing new young talent for her branch of the Services when she could. There was too much old entrenched habit and lack of talent to make up for.

In any case, she considered him an asset. Add to the physical handsomeness the size of the young man—tall, big across the shoulders—and you came up with an almost daunting package. It never hurt for an ambassador, or someone who was likely enough to be an ambassador someday, to be physically imposing as well as handsome. There were some negotiations in which brawn was still as useful as brain. And Gabriel apparently took the physical training part of his job description very seriously. A Concord Marine shall maintain himself in physical condition suitable to his role . . . to be ready for anything, anywhere, any time, was what the regs said. As in any other branch of the Services, there were always Marines who honored the regulations more in the breach than in the observance, but Connor was not one of them. *Eager to Strike*, the Marine motto went. Gabriel looked it, and though the eagerness was low-key, it was still very much there.

"Is the briefing still at nineteen?" Gabriel said, after another drink of his chai.

"Yes. You'll be there?"

"I wouldn't miss it. Fortunately I've been able to get the day's other duties handled early."

And you stayed up how late for the last couple of nights to do that? Lauren thought, obscurely pleased. Very good. Aloud she said, "Have you had a chance to review the last few weeks' transcripts?"

Gabriel nodded, suddenly looking a little weary to Lauren's eyes. "I don't usually have trouble with research," he said, "but reading that stuff made my head hurt."

"A normal reaction," Delvecchio said, leaning back in her chair.

"It's just that . . . they've been doing this for so *long*," Connor said, shaking his head. "Four, five generations now. Brush wars, flare-ups, 'hot' wars that last a year, two years, five . . . those I can understand. But the idea is that the fighting is supposed to resolve something . . . for good or ill. This has resolved *nothing*. It's as if the fighting has become a habit: something they don't dare stop, because they don't know what they would do if they didn't have a war to fall back on. And meanwhile, the basic problem—access to the resources on Eraklion—hasn't been solved. It's as if they didn't *want* to solve it."

Delvecchio tilted further back in her chair. "Well, we've been over this ground a couple of times before. I'll grant you that would be a competent enough analysis for someone who wasn't all that intimate with the problem. Maybe it passes for analysis on the upper decks." She gave him a wry look. The "upper

decks" were where the Marine forces were quartered. "And
before you accuse me of insulting your shipmates' intelligence,
let me say that you have access to more information than they
have. So tell me: why *did* the governments on Phorcys and Ino
agree to allow negotiations to start three years ago? What's
changed all of a sudden?"

"The Concord stepped in," Gabriel said. He wore a slight
smile as he said it.

"Now stop grinning like a Marine who sees the prospect of
stepping into a good fight. As doubtless you do. If I get my way,
it will need to step in no further. And your job is to help me get
my way."

"Via diplomatic channels," Connor said mildly, "or via the
barrels of our guns?"

"At the moment there is no difference," Delvecchio said,
"though if our efforts tomorrow afternoon finally fail, that will
change. Meanwhile, you and I and this whole ship are a gun
pointed at the heads of the governments of Phorcys and Ino . . .
though only a symbolic one. Sooner or later, there will be peace,
or they'll wish there had been. But you still haven't answered my
question."

"But I have. The Galactic Concord did step in. The Verge has
been forgotten territory or ignored territory for so long. Now the
Concord appears and begins asserting itself . . . ."

"More popular mythology," Delvecchio said, just a little
sharply. "This was *never* forgotten territory. But it is a major
error to intervene in an area before you have the force, both military and infrastructural, to support your intervention. Only in the
last ten years or so has such force become available, along with
the political will at the First Worlds' level to assert it. Now we're
here. We come to Phorcys and Ino at *their* reques, which by itself
is interesting and worthy of attention. We've been fact-finding in
this neighborhood for three years, making no actual decisions
about them or requirements of them . . . just finding out why they
hate each other so. The surface reasons, of course. And letting
them see, standing behind us as it were, all the reasons they

might want to pay serious attention to anything we might suggest during the actual negotiation period. Affiliations with stellar nations, with other Verge systems, military protection and development, investment packages . . . "

"And if they don't take advantage of the suggestions?" Gabriel asked.

Lauren's smile was brief and grim. " 'Eager to Strike.' Well, that *is* what you're here for should hostilities break out—hostilities aimed at *us* instead of the end of negotiation. But as for the parties involved . . . Certainly there *was* once a time when there was only one kind of negotiation: the kind where you stand over the participants and explain to them that if they don't stop fighting you'll kill them all, and that what they're going to do is *this* . . . Then rather later came the kind where you coerce the hostile parties into close quarters for an extended period and force them to recognize one another as 'human.' " She put up her eyebrows, sighing. "Can you imagine how simple it must have been when there was only one species involved in this kind of thing? Only one set of biological 'code'?"

"The ones we're working with now are all *Homo sapiens*," Gabriel said, "and they still seem to have enough trouble grasping the concept."

"Yes," Delvecchio said. "Well, the semantics are antiquated, I admit. But the ancient negotiators would try holding people together until they stopped being Us and Them, until 'They' were perceived as 'enough like Us that they should have our kind of rights and be treated with the kind of respect we accord one another.' Or, rather, 'enough like Us that we shouldn't kill them.' "

Gabriel nodded. "That kind of diplomacy must have been hard to bring off."

"Oh, sometimes it worked. There were gifted diplomats who realized that getting intelligent, hostile, and wary humans to grant one another that kind of privileged status was almost impossible to do by mere persuasion. So they used all kind of other dirty tricks, exploiting cultural 'hardwiring' that the participants had forgotten they had." She smiled: a wry, sly little look.

"No one forgets more quickly than an 'intelligent, civilized man' how different he looks while eating, for example . . . or how different his enemy looks. Or how different the kinds of conversation are that take place over dinner tables from those that happen over negotiation tables. Who cares what shape the dinner table is, as long as you can reach the salt?" She sighed. "But the problem is that, even after you've tricked both sides into seeing one another as different kinds of 'Us,' the perception requires constant reinforcement. Remembering one's *own* humanity and its requirements is something that has to happen constantly, after all. How much more complex and distasteful will you find the business of remembering your former *enemy's* humanity? Of believing in it? Of upgrading them once again, every day, to 'Us' status from 'Them'? It's easy to forget to do it. Saints would find it difficult. Sinners—" She gave Gabriel a cool look. "Those are mostly who we deal with, ordinary beings, all too representative of both the worst and the best of their species' traits. The 'sinners' take a lot of work before the upgrading of their enemies becomes routine, and a generation or two before the perception of their children's children shifts to match it. Then the trick is a trick no more, but reality."

"The older kind of diplomacy must have been a lot easier," Gabriel said. "I mean, the kind where you just tell them to stop fighting . . . or else."

"It was," Delvecchio said. "But we can no longer be so careless or so unethical. Tomorrow afternoon the negotiating teams from the two planets will arrive, and they'll leave either with a peace or our implicit blessing on the final destruction of one another's planets. I trust that the spectre of the second will overshadow the feast, as it were, quite effectively. If not, we must let them get on with working out their own destruction, though I don't think it's going to happen that way—which is why we both have a briefing to prepare for." She stood up.

Gabriel stood up too, looking thoughtful. After a moment he said, "So what *is* the answer to the question?"

"About why the two parties have consented to negotiations?"

Delvecchio gave him a dry look. "I don't know."

"*What?* I mean, I beg your pardon?"

"I have no idea. I hope to have one over the next few years. Sooner or later, after peace in this system starts to become a reality, someone will slip and let out the truth about what's really been going on here. My replacement will be alert to that occurrence, believe me."

"Replacement? You think they're going to just ship you out? Just like that?" Connor looked rather more shocked than Delvecchio had expected.

"It's nearly inevitable," Lauren said. "The diplomat who brokers an unpopular peace agreement immediately becomes a liability in that neighborhood, a reminder to both sides of what they gave up—excuse me—'were forced to give up.' The sooner I get out of here—the sooner this ship and all its personnel get out of here, as well—the sooner the illusion has the chance to start setting in that the peace was their idea. Five years from now I'll be nothing but a bad memory in this system. Ten years from now I'll be a footnote to the end of a bad stretch in history. Thirty years from now I will be forgotten. And that is the way I want it." She smiled. "The diplomats who make history are usually the ones who messed up badly along the way. The best ones are invisible."

Lauren watched his reaction to that, carefully keeping in place the poker face that had worked on petty kings and religious leaders and trade union representatives. She watched Gabriel's face work for a moment, and then he looked at her in something like dismay.

"That is either the most purely self-sacrificing sentiment I've ever heard, Ambassador," he said, "or the most purely cynical one."

She chuckled, then. "You *definitely* are diplomatic material," she said. "No question how you came by those stripes, Lieutenant. Nor that you'll get the new ones you're aiming for."

He looked at her in slight surprise and some concern. "Is it that obvious?"

"No more than usual," Delvecchio said. "Even if it were,

ambition has its uses. And there's nothing intrinsically evil about it, except as it interferes with the basic implementation of your humanity."

Gabriel's look of concern was fading, which suited her. "I'd say you're in no great danger of that," Lauren said, "and I'd also say you'll have no trouble piling on the stripes and bars over time, once you find what it is you really want to do. For my own service's sake, I hope you get tired of the rank game after a while and put it aside for more worthwhile work. You have talents worthy of better, I think."

"Uh, thank you, Ambassador."

"You're welcome. Now, I have things to do, so I'll see you later in the briefing. Keep your eyes open. I'll be wanting to talk to you later about what reactions you see in the other participants and how they may interact with the negotiating teams tomorrow. This would be something you would be doing anyway, of course, for other reasons."

Gabriel blinked at the slight emphasis on *other.*

"And you can just lose that nothing-to-do-with-me look," Delvecchio said mildly. "Do you think I would have taken such an interest without knowing about your other 'affiliation'? Now go on, get your breakfast. Don't think I don't know you haven't had it. You're standing there wasting away in front of me."

He saluted her, as he had not done on coming in, and went out.

Lauren Delvecchio, Ambassador Plenipotentiary without Portfolio to the Verge from the Galactic Concord, turned and looked out the window again, where over the edge of Ino a long, blinding streak of rainbow was coming up over the edge of the world, a harbinger of dawn. She smiled to see it come, then lifted her eyes to see above it, waiting, as it always waited, the dark.

* * * * *

Gabriel Connor made his way down *Falada*'s white-walled corridors from the ambassador's quarters toward the forward senior wardroom in a rather more somber mood than usual. Normally he was fairly cheerful about his life and the events that filled him . . . enough so that other marines sometimes commented on it, suggesting either that he had a chip loose somewhere to take things so easily, or that it was a sure sign that sooner or later something terrible would happen and take him down a rung or three. Gabriel let them think what they liked. There was no point in trying to change their minds, and anyway, by and large, life was too interesting for him to bother wasting his time.

Putting aside the questions running through his mind, Gabriel was still glowing slightly from his pre-breakfast meeting and was doing his best to make sure it didn't show. Delvecchio was a succinct old codger at the best of times, and you didn't routinely get language out of her of the kind she'd just used. In fact he could never remember her praising anything or anyone outright like that. She was much more likely to show either approval or disapproval, to her own species anyway, with silence and a look. And the look could warm you or scorch you crisp, depending on the circumstances.

Yet there was also something else to consider: that she knew about his "security"connections. Yes, well, she's right to say that she should have known. Yet at the same time, Concord Intelligence was very disapproving of people knowing where its operatives were placed. That is, about people knowing operatives' locations when Intelligence hasn't told them itself. His immediate superiors on the Intelligence side could very well come to the conclusion that Gabriel had somehow let something slip that had put Delvecchio onto him. That idea would be bad enough. Or they might think that he had told her himself, which would be far, far worse.

He breathed in, breathed out. *No point in worrying about it*, he thought, heading down the hall for the lift that would take him updecks toward the Marine part of the ship. Either it'll happen, and they'll cashier you, or it won't, and you'll have wasted precious heartbeats on worrying. He smiled, just a little grimly. The

Marines had a saying: It might never happen. Meanwhile, go
clean your weapon.

Yet it niggled at him. He had not been entirely comfortable
when, just before he graduated from Academy five years ago, an
Intelligence operative approached him and asked if he would like
to serve the Concord "with something besides a gun." The work
would be neither difficult nor obvious. He was simply being
asked to keep his eyes and ears open to what was going on
around him, in barracks or on assignment, space-side or planet-
side, and to report to other Concord Intelligence operatives who
might identify themselves to him from time to time. "Network-
ing," the operative had called it. The man's ID had been
genuine—Gabriel had checked that carefully—and after thinking the matter over for a few days, Gabriel had agreed. In the five
years that followed he had been asked to volunteer information
or to look into a situation, exactly twice. In both cases the
requested information had been so minor and seemingly unimportant that Gabriel wondered if he was being made the butt of a
very involved practical joke. Was he simply being tested somehow, or was the information genuinely useful? He still had no
idea. *And maybe I never will. One of life's little mysteries.*

Gabriel got into an empty lift. Its shining steel door slid shut,
and it hummed off sideways toward the main lift tubes, then
upward. His stomach growled. *Was it doing that when I was in
with Delvecchio?* he wondered. *Hope not.* The old lady had been
polite enough to him, but sometimes he got a very clear sense
that she was humoring him, that she considered him—despite
her praise—to be seriously in need of education in many important ways. *Well, maybe she's right. I can hardly be expected to
have absorbed all the wisdom of the universe when I'm not even
twenty-six yet.* He grinned. *But when I have absorbed it all, will
it be enough for* her?

The lift doors opened. Before him was a wall, not merely
white durasteel for once, but emblazoned with the Concord
Marine arms and a banner beneath that said, *1st, 2nd, 3rd Diplomatic Service Squadrons*, with two smaller banners to either side

of the shield bearing the words *READY TO TALK* and *READY TO FIGHT.* Gabriel swung to the right, past the shield and down a side corridor toward the wardroom. The door slid aside for him as he neared it.

The room was empty, as he had mostly expected, and the place was in shakedown mode—tables pushed off to one side and stacked, chairs hung on the gold-hued walls. A team must have been in here this morning cleaning the place. Naturally there were machines and robots whose business was to keep the ship clean and in order, but it was a matter of tradition and pride that nothing was ever clean enough for a Concord Marine. Every inch of every room that was detailed as marine quarters in a Concord ship had its turn, in rotation, to receive personal attention from the Scrod Squad. Gabriel had never met any marine who actually knew what a Scrod was—there were a lot of jokes about it, all suggesting impossible or at least highly improbable explanations—but any marine worth his collar tabs fought to be on the squad at least once a month, just to prove that dirt was no safer from his or her proud kind than any other designated enemy.

He stood there in the doorway for a moment and sighed. Anyone who disturbed this perfect cleanliness before lunch would not make friends. *I'll go get something from the galley.*

Gabriel turned to go—then, just briefly, since there was no one there, he paused to look himself up and down in the full-length steel mirror mounted on the wall just inside the wardroom door.

His uniform was in order: the sharp upstanding collar in place, the dark tunic and tight breeches and the dark matte-leather boots all in proper trim. But he knew they were. No marine made it to a position such as assignment on board a diplomatic vessel without having the very minor matter of uniform under perfect control. Gabriel's problem was that even now, more than a year after the fact, he just couldn't stop looking at the small enamel band on his left breast—three stripes, white, green, blue, and centered on the green, the old Greek letter M, "epsilon." Epsedra. He swallowed hard and blocked the memories fast.

"Aw, he's admiring it again," came the voice from behind him. "Isn't that cute?"

Gabriel knew the voice perfectly well. He turned, frowning, but immediately lightened up, since no one else was in earshot. It was just Hal standing there, giving him one of those sardonic looks in which he specialized. "Just Hal" was how he always introduced himself. Marines in their squadron who felt like tempting fate might refer to him as Halforth Quentin, those being only the first two of the numerous names with which he had somehow come equipped. Apparently he had some obscure tie to ancient royalty back in the Union of Sol or on some other planet too far away in time and space to matter (to anyone except his family at least). He was as unroyal-looking a creature as Gabriel could imagine, a blocky, beetle-browed, bent-nosed young man with massive shoulders and a neck so broad that it was hard to think how to describe it except that it was between his head and his shoulders so it *had* to be a neck. There he stood in his usual immaculate uniform, astonishingly straight up by even marine standards, towering over Gabriel and grinning his usual ugly and amiable grin.

"Do you have to sneak around like that?" Gabriel said. "You're a menace."

"You should have heard me coming," said Hal. "Anyway, if you keep picking at it, Gabe, it's never gonna get better." He peered over Gabriel's shoulder at the ribbon.

Gabriel blew out an annoyed breath. Hal was one of the few people from whom he would tolerate such an assessment on the subject, for Hal had been in the fighting on Epsedra, and *knew* . . . knew, especially, about that last desperate night out on the glacier, down in the crevasses in the ice with the fire raining down all around. Too few marines had come away from their desperate holding action on that planet. About a third of them had come away with the valor decoration. Hal, for his own part, was completely unselfconscious about teasing Gabriel for having cheated in some obscure way, since Gabriel had the decoration and Hal did not.

"It's a good thing I like you," Gabriel said, "because otherwise I'd take you up to the gym and decorate the walls with you."

"I'm serious," Hal said. "You ought to stop dwelling on it. It's going to make you unbalanced."

"Thank you so much for your concern," Gabriel said. "Just the kind of psychoanalysis you could expect from an engineer." The very idea of a marine engineer was one which many of the more weapons-oriented marines found at least potentially oxymoronic, it being gospel among most of them that marines had more important things to do than fix recalcitrant machinery. Nonetheless, their transport shuttles and powered suits and weaponry needed service and repair, and since their lives depended on the equipment, the marines preferred to do it themselves. The engineer-marines responded to their brothers' and sisters' raillery by explaining that only truly superior fighting talent coupled with sublime intelligence could make a machine behave, and that naturally their less gifted shipmates couldn't help but misunderstand the relationship between engineer and engineered.

"Think nothing of it," Hal said.

"Believe me, I will." Gabriel thumped Hal hard in the shoulder as he turned away.

"Not like you to miss breakfast," Hal observed, as they walked away together from the empty wardroom into the white-walled corridor. "You'll have to scrounge in the galley. Didn't see you all yesterday."

"Nope, I was busy. Haven't seen you for a day or so, either."

"Been re-equipping the shuttles for the diplomatic transport tomorrow," Hal said. "Putting in the posh seats, the drinks dispensers . . . upgrading the toilets." He made a face. "Can you believe that the vips actually think diplomats deserve softer—"

"Spare me the details," Gabriel said, rolling his eyes. "When'll you be done?"

"Tonight sometime. There are four shuttles in all, and a fifth and sixth have to be held on standby in case one of them goes south. It's a nuisance, but the Mighty One Above Us likes redundancy." This was a veiled reference to Lieutenant Colonel

Arends, their marine senior commanding officer, who was a short colonel in both rank and size—not that he couldn't throw you right over the horizon any time he pleased in unarmed training.

"Yeah," Gabriel said. "You busy this evening? We've got to get the spat team together and talk strategy. We can *not* let the Starfies walk all over us again the way they did last night."

"Okay. After suit drill?"

"Okay, but I won't be at drill. I did it yesterday with beta shift."

They passed a trio of marines headed in the opposite direction, all three in fatigues and looking a bit disheveled. Hal nodded a greeting to the sole female of the trio, then he looked at Gabriel in bemusement. "What *is* it with you lately? No one knows where you are half the time." Then he grinned. "Or rather, everyone does."

"What now?"

"You're sucking up to the Gray Lady. Bucking for some soft job, I bet."

"Not right now," Gabriel said, "believe me."

"Not sure I do. But look, after that—" his friend glanced at the ribbon—"nobody could blame you. Or any of us."

Gabriel flushed hot. "I was just doing my job, same as you. And I like it just fine right here, thanks. Don't go jumping to conclusions."

"Oh really? Not a soft job, then. Something closer to home?"

Gabriel scowled at his friend. "What are you naffing on about?"

"It has not been ignored the way certain officerial eyes are turned toward you," Hal said. "Quite high in ship's rank. About as high as it gets, in fact—"

"You spoo-brain," Gabriel said, "are you *completely* nuts? She and Lem are tight as ticks. If anyone tried to get between the two of them, Lem would pull the frivolities off him. And anyway, it's not that way with her."

"That's not what I hear. Rike said that he heard her say to—"

"Rike has methane between his ears," Gabriel said, starting to get annoyed now. "Just clamp it down. I don't want to hear it."

Hal shrugged. "They're all saying it . . . you'll hear it from Them, if you don't hear it from me. The Group Mind."

"If 'mind' is the word we're looking for," Gabriel muttered. The "Group Mind" was local slang for what elsewhere would be called "the rumor mill."

"So what happens now?" Hal said, more quietly, as they turned a corner down the long crosswise corridor which led toward the galley.

"Happens?"

"The Group Mind says that these might be the last few days of this mission," Hal said even more quietly.

"Hard to say," said Gabriel, and there at least he felt he was giving nothing away. "There are some pretty hard nuts to crack down there."

"Nuts," Hal said, and snorted. *"That's* to the point. Why can't they just get along?"

It was a fair question. "Brother, I wish I had the slightest fracking idea," Gabriel said, thinking with some pain of his long slog through the transcripts of the last month's negotiating sessions. At times the hatred that constantly broke out in the interminable dialogues seemed so sheerly stupid that it started to become unreal, and Gabriel had found himself half believing that he was reading some extremely neurotic work of fiction. The two chief negotiators in particular were almost ceremonial in their loathing of one another. They could barely bring themselves to be in the same room and left it whenever diplomacy offered them a chance. "They sure make it look like they just love to fight, though."

"Well, if they want a good one, let 'em start one with us," Hal said as they came to the galley. "Meanwhile, I've got to get back down there. We're only halfway through the equipment refit."

Gabriel shook his head. "Six shuttles," he said. "Doesn't it seem like a lot?"

"Yeah, but these people are scattered all over two planets,

after all. Some of the pickups have to start at oh-dark-thirty
tomorrow morning, to get everyone here for fourteen." Hal
shrugged again. "The one for that first head of delegation,
anyway, the Inoan, that's the worst. Oh-four-something, that
goes out. You should hear the pilots groaning on about it."

"Yeah, well they weren't groaning when they collected on
their bets last night," Gabriel said. "And if I have anything to say
about it, they'll have reason to groan the next time we play. Pass
the word and make sure the team's all together tonight. We've
got to get this sorted out before the game next week."

Hal saluted a lot more sharply than he needed to. "Later,
boss," he said, and headed down off the stark white hall toward
the lifts for the shuttle bays.

Gabriel paused just long enough to watch him go.

Rike said he heard her say what? he thought—

—and then, before that line of thought took him farther down
one particular path than he cared to venture, he sighed and went
into the galley to get something to eat.

Chapter Two

THE MEAT-STUFFED rolls Gabriel liberated from the galley vanished down him almost without his noticing after he took them back to his quarters. As a lieutenant, Gabriel had the privilege of his own quarters, if one counted such a small cubicle as a privilege. Once fed, he got started on the last stint of his scheduled reading, the last few days' worth of transcripts. He had had them printed, since he had to keep referring back and forth to issues handled or not handled earlier in order to tell what was going on, and the little screen on the desk built into the wall of his small bare cubby was simply not equal to the task of so much display—at least not without giving him a blinding headache from trying to read words scaled down so small. The spread-out paper almost made a second blanket for his bunk when he folded it down from between the cabinets built into the walls. Pieces of this messy "blanket" kept falling down onto the hard dark carpet on the floor. The print on the glossy paper looked neat enough, but the words were eloquent of much death, much pain, a lot of blood spilled.

The soft hoot of the alarm went off before he was expecting it. Ten minutes until the afternoon briefing session. Gabriel got up hurriedly, stacked the papers up neatly on his desk and folded his bunk away again. Just before going out, he straightened his uniform and glanced in the mirror. The glint of the room light on the bar: green, white, blue, epsilon—Oh, stop it, he told himself, pulled his tunic down straigh, and headed out, touching the door panel so that it locked behind him.

As he got out of the lift on the deck below bridge level, the

deck where the main briefing room was located, he could catch
a faint buzz of conversation coming from ahead of him, the
sound of other people heading that way. There was more to it
than that, though. There was an edge of excitement there, a
change that he'd heard in the commonplace daily murmur of the
ship's complement before. It was the edge that meant something
was about to happen. *Action* . . . of the only kind that mattered to
a marine. Gabriel's hair stood up on the back of his neck at that
sound, and he actually had to stop briefly in the hall and calm
himself as he felt his pulse pick up. It was not time for racing
pulses and adrenaline, not just yet. But maybe soon.

It took him only a couple of minutes more to get to the briefing room, a rather plusher kind of room than the wardroom or
other marine quarters. The room was windowless, and the walls
were bare of any ornament, but soft lighting shone down from
around the ceiling, glowing on a long gleaming black table. The
room was already three-quarters full of Star Force personnel, as
well as other marines—his immediate superior Captain Urrizh,
and her superior Major T'teka. The short colonel was missing,
and T'teka was probably standing in for him. That started
Gabriel wondering a little. It was not like Arends to miss one of
these briefings.

Is something up? Gabriel wondered.

Gabriel sat down in an empty chair near the end of the table
where he knew the ambassador would be by preference. Not too
near, though, since his main business today (besides noting
whatever strategy she had planned) was to notice others' reactions. He was distracted from this for the moment as the ambassador herself came in. Everyone stood. Theoretically, of course,
she outranked everyone here, even the commanding officer of
the ship. But Gabriel suspected that the gesture had more to do
simply with the way Lauren Delvecchio carried herself. Someone unfamiliar with anything but the dry facts of her career
record might have thought that a woman of a hundred and thirty-
three might look dangerously ordinary in the plain gray uniform
of her service. But that, and the white hair braided up tight, and

the lean little body with the fierce sharp little eyes that now glanced around her, all joined to communicate a dangerous sense of control and power. She looked like a sword, even to the slight curve of her back, which the surgery after her flitter crash had not been able to correct. Seeing her in full official array rather than in civvies and leaning back behind an empty desk, Gabriel once more felt very sorry for the governments of Phorcys and Ino. Things were plainly about to start moving somehow, and they would never know what had hit them.

She acknowledged the standing Star Force and marine crew. "Please, sit," she said. "We have a lot to cover."

They did. People sorted themselves out into the few remaining seats, including a latecomer who plunked herself down on Gabriel's left, nearer the ambassador. Delvecchio sat down and put a printout and a couple of datacarts down on the table before her, dropping one on the "read" plate for the projection system.

"I want to thank all you ladies and gentlemen for joining me," Delvecchio said. "Such attention to ongoing business is appreciated, since a chance look or word from any of us could have the potential to influence what's going to happen here tomorrow afternoon. Particularly, I want to welcome those of you from *Callirhoë* and *Wanasha* who made starfall in this system such a short time ago and still have gone out of your way to be here on time. Shall we get started?"

She reached out and touched the read plate before her. Above the middle of the table a holographic schematic appeared, not to scale: the bright spark of the sun Thalaassa at the center of its system, and highlighted, the third and fourth planets out in its six planet system, Phorcys and Ino.

Gabriel leaned over toward the blonde-haired shape in the chair next to his and said, very softly, "Captain, do you think we can sneak out and come back in later? We've already seen this part."

Captain Elinke Dareyev barely moved her eyes sideways to meet his, a slightly wicked look, and said almost inaudibly and nearly without moving her mouth, "One of these days I'm going to remember to bring a discipline stick in here with me." But the side of her mouth nearest him curved up just slightly as she turned to face the ambassador more fully.

Gabriel erased his own grin and did his best to look attentive, but his attention was still mostly on the woman sitting beside him. They met for the first time the week after Gabriel had been assigned to *Falada*, a bit more than a year ago, as just one more of the standard coterie of Concord Marines put aboard diplomatic vessels to assist in missions that were deemed likely to require a show of force. The Captain's Mess at which they had all been introduced to her had been one of the usual slightly ritualistic, formal affairs that shipside protocol required "to introduce the new officers to one another": full mess dress, tea-party manners, everything very much on the up and up . . . for the time being. No matter how stiff the manners were, a lot of sizing up happened at such functions. Instant likes or dislikes were formed, and afterward the word got around as to who was likely to be all right to work with and who was likely to be a pain.

Gabriel would have normally classed Elinke Dareyev as "pain" at first sight. She was not merely good-looking, but downright beautiful. Her features were very chiseled and perfect, the eyes a wonderful and peculiar blue-green that nonetheless could not distract from the proud angle at which Elinke's head was carried. And the way she seemed to look coolly and graciously down at you even though you were half a meter taller than she never left anyone any room for doubt as to who was in charge of her ship. The overall effect was that of a petite ice maiden who had stumbled into Star Force and made good. Not stumbled, as it happened. The supreme self-confidence with which she bore herself was a symptom of three generations of space service or Star Force on her mother's side of the family. Practically her first words to Gabriel had been "Yes *those* Dareyevs"—actually a remark made to Hal as Gabriel came up beside him, the words drawled rather genteelly over the rim of a tiny glass of something clear and deadly looking. But from the sidelong look she had given him, the shot had been intended as much to go over

Gabriel's bow as over Hal's. Hal had backed off after a few completely unconvincing pleasantries, but Gabriel had stayed, waiting for a particular reaction. And when Captain Dareyev had
asked him what his secondment was—all the marines aboard had
a secondary duty assignment, something to "keep them busy"
improving themselves and their career prospects while they were
not attending to fitness issues—and when he had said, very off-
handedly, "Security," Gabriel had seen what he had wanted to
see: those blue-green eyes looking, just for a flash, intent rather
than politely bored. Dareyev had covered the reaction up immediately, as she would have been bound to do, but she took leave
of him for the next group of marines with a little more interest
than the situation absolutely required.

When the two of them had met again in the joint-use wardroom a couple of weeks later, accidentally as it seemed, there
had been considerably more conversation. It had started out as
business, a conversation that would have had to happen sooner
rather than later: where one of the Intelligence officers assigned
to her ship is involved, a captain must routinely have enough
contact with him to be sure she trusts what he's up to and his way
of working—to let her own intuition warn her of any agendas
that might conflict with her ship's present business or other business yet to come among the stellar nations to which marines may
routinely be deployed. Captain Dareyev had grilled Gabriel thoroughly. He could hardly remember when anyone had more casually or vigorously wrung him dry. Yet all through the
interrogation, he received a constantly recurring sense of
approval. By the end of the grilling, when they had moved from
official to casual conversation, she was "Elinke," and he was
"Gabe," and the friendship was fast already.

It was one of the stranger things about shipboard life, the way
that seemingly accidental scheduling and career moves could
throw you together with people whom you either utterly detest-
ed, or whom it seemed you had been waiting to meet all your
life. People with whom you fell in effortlessly, as if picking up a
conversation that you had broken off a few hours or days ago—

when you had never met the person before. That this should have happened between a first lieutenant of the Concord Marines and a Star Force captain was bizarre and amusing, but that was all. It continued to be a source of amusement to both of them as the ensuing weeks of the cruise passed by and *Falada* went on about her business. There had been gossip about it, of course, but that was all it was. Elinke had a lover, crazy young Lemke David in Navigation, and no matter how beautiful Elinke was, Gabriel would never have considered trying to cut in. The two of them were too perfect together, Lem's cheerful lunacy balanced perfectly by Elinke's ironic and self-conscious cool. But even so, there were other reasons not to meddle. Elinke in friendly mode was one thing. Elinke offended would simply turn around suddenly, smile at you, and walk off, and you would find yourself clutching a bloody stump and wondering what had happened.

Gabriel sighed and wrenched his attention back where it belonged, even though much of the present discussion was old news to him.

". . . Thalaassa," the ambassador was saying, "which is the system primary, is unremarkable, an F2. Overtly, the two inner planets are equally unremarkable. Ino, as you can see from the schematic, is the innermost of the two. It holds a much more favorable position climactically, with median temperatures within the subtropical spread. Phorcys, in the next orbit out, is colder, but not too much so. Its distance is balanced by a very benign axial tilt of 1.3 degrees, which evens out the seasonal differences considerably and generally improves the climactic picture. The other two planets in the system are worthless for colonization—either 'light' bodies that couldn't hold their atmospheres, or in the case of the heavier worlds, too cold.

"These two worlds were settled by a single colonization effort in 2280. There was a problem when they got here, in that not everyone was going to be able to settle on the choicer of the two planets. The colonization contract stated that the colonists must divide equally between the two 'target' planets, and should divide other system resources equally between them."

"Uh oh," someone said from the back of the room.

"Exactly," said Delvecchio, with an expression like that of a tired mother hearing the kids getting ready to start an old familiar fight. "Out in the Verge, policing such an argument was hardly going to be a simple or routine matter if both parties involved did not show good faith. In this case, both sides not only immediately started to show bad faith, but each automatically presumed it in the other side. An ugly situation. The actual business of settlement, of who went to which planet, was finally decided by lottery—but the great majority of the people who wound up settling Phorcys felt that they had been cheated. Opinion divided widely on exactly by whom. The people who wound up on Ino, the Company with whom they contracted, some other unknown force—all were blamed at one point or another. You'll understand that this kind of thinggives conspiracy theories fertile soil in which to flourish. And they did. Tensions built, and either no one in a position to intervene noticed the way things were going, or the problem was deprioritized in error. But the result was that within twenty years of colonization, the two planets were at war. It started small—raids and skirmishes were all either side could afford while they were building up their respective industrial bases. But soon enough they could afford to do better, as they started manufacturing their own system craft. Both of them had their eyes on an additional prize."

She pointed at the hologram, indicating the fifth planet out in the system. "This is Eraklion. It doesn't look like much: small, light gravity, unsuitable for colonization at this distance from the primary because of the temperature and the reducing atmosphere. But what it does have in plenty are fissionables and metal ores, both light and heavy. This planet is a prize for the planet that controls it, and Phorcys and Ino have been fighting over it for well over a hundred years. They have not yet damaged each other's planets too severely, but the conflict has been escalating in that direction. Neither side has been willing to use anything more dangerous than conventional weapons . . . yet. But that may change soon if we don't succeed in getting them to make an accommodation. Populations may suffer. And leaving aside the not inconsiderable questions of human suffering and death if the war between these worlds breaks out in earnest, if that *does* happen, and they wipe each other out, a hundred years' worth of not unsuccessful colonization of this system will be lost."

She looked around at the slightly troubled faces around her. "Ladies and gentlemen," she said, "you must not mistake my meaning. The death of one child on Phorcys or Ino is one death too many for me. There have been enough such deaths in the past. It must stop. But as representatives of the Galactic Concord, we have other responsibilities as well: to the long view, to the ongoing history and development of the Verge. This part of space has had a difficult and terrible recent history. Every star system that is colonized successfully and *stays* that way helps every other that comes after it. Each single system exerts on all others in its area a civilizing influence that we cannot afford to ignore. The loss of one system spreads an influence too, a dark one. The ripples of unease and fear spread out, affecting worlds and relationships many light-years away, shaking the stellar nations themselves in time. There are enough things going on in this part of space that we do not now understand and may not for many years . . . things that desperately need investigation." For a moment she looked unusually somber: Gabriel found himself, not for the first time, wondering what she was thinking about. "But every system that succeeds out here in the Verge brings us closer to the kind of stability that will lead to increased understanding of the forces moving in these spaces. In the long term, we must come to *understand* . . . and immediate as they may seem to us, the life-and-death motives of the moment must be held and examined in the larger context before we act."

The room was very quiet. "So," Delvecchio said, "the first part of this mission, as those of you who have sat in on these briefings before know, has been taken up mostly with fact-finding. My representatives and I have spent considerable amounts of time on both Phorcys and Ino and more time than any of us wanted on Eraklion. We then started the second phase of the operation, which was to bring the disagreeing parties together." A small sound that might have been a groan, suppressed, came from one of her assistants down the length of the table. "This," said Delvecchio, "was about as easy as taking the sunglasses away from a sesheyan. These people hate each other with a pure intensity that bids fair to take your breath away."

"I take it," said one of *Falada's* Star Force officers, "that there was no chance to do a standard 'detoxification' period on the negotiating teams."

Delvecchio laughed ruefully. "How do you detoxify pure poison? No, I'm afraid not. If we had ten or twenty years to spare, we could start such a program and start getting each planet's people used to the idea that the others are human. But there's no time for that. The arms situation has deteriorated much too far. We have had to offer extensive economic incentives just to get their attention."

Looks were exchanged around the table. Gabriel looked wry at the ambassador's expression. "The carrot and the stick, as they used to say," Delvecchio said. "We've had no choice. If this effort fails, we will have to fall back on much more robust measures. And I would prefer the lesser form of failure, however inelegant it is, to the greater."

She raised her eyebrows and looked resigned. "There have been numerous false starts. At first, just after the two sides invited us in, it was plain that they intended no rapprochement with each other at all. They wanted us to come along and make them nice trade and support offers, and then they would possibly consider beginning to talk to each other. Well, they didn't get very far with that, and the Concord was quite prepared to just drop the whole matter at that point. Yet even the news that we had responded at all to their initial overtures heated their local economy up so substantially that they weren't able to simply let us turn their backs on them. They had to offer us something so that we would stay around and talk some more."

"And lure in more investment from the stellar nations," a young male Star Force officer down the table said.

"Oh yes," said the ambassador. "Notice was taken immediately, as you might imagine. This system is only a starfall from Corrivale, very convenient indeed to other trade traffic in the Verge. Numerous commercial concerns started to become interested in metals and fissionables mined on Eraklion. But not too interested, mind you, since after all the system is at war, and in wartime, you can't guarantee a steady 'cargo chain.' Both worlds knew that something had to be seen to be done first."

Delvecchio smiled. "So the formal negotiations began three years ago. The two planets declared a truce for the period of negotiation, because naturally they couldn't be shooting at each other while Concord ships were in the neighborhood. There might have been an accident. And naturally some further investment started to come in as the situation stabilized somewhat. Nearly all the politicians and the business conglomerates on both planets were very pleased by this. The 'peace dividend' . . ."

"The carrot," said Captain Dareyev.

"Another carrot, yes," said Ambassador Delvecchio. "Nice, wasn't it, that it seemed to come from somewhere besides us? But then came the stick. The negotiations themselves. And there the representatives dug in their heels and made it plain they could never deal with one another, never give in to one another's demands."

"You'd think that after such a long time they'd be willing to compromise a little, for the sake of all the benefits that would follow," said another of the Star Force commanders down the table.

"Well, for one thing," Delvecchio said, "compromise isn't a word we could ever have used in a negotiation like this. To people arguing over territory or economic advantage, the word 'compromise' coming from a third party is code for 'We're going to help the other side get the better of you.' You can try to produce the *symptoms* of compromise: a settlement in which each of the participating parties goes away secretly feeling that they've given up too much and the other side has given up hardly anything. But the word itself must never be mentioned. Nor must you allow any situation to arise in which one side starts looking too satisfied. The other side will immediately suspect betrayal— or even worse, that the side opposite is going to get more of what it wants than your own side might. In these long hate cases, that's tantamount to winning. There must never be a winner in a negotiation. Or at least, there must never be a *perception* that there is a winner on either side."

Major T'teka was shaking his slender dark head. "Ambassador, their behavior simply doesn't seem rational."

She smiled, a thin tired look. "Of course not, Major. If they were being rational about this, *any* of them, we wouldn't have had to come Space knows how many starfalls and half a million kilometers past that to stop this old war. If you treat the various sides in a given negotiation as essentially crazy as bedbugs, you'll do a lot better . . . and this one is no different."

Captain Dareyev blinked at that. "Excuse me, Ambassador, but what's a bedbug?"

Delvecchio put her eyebrows up then laughed. "You know, I have no idea! It's something my mother used to say. I assume it's some kind of bug that gets in bed with you, a nasty enough prospect. Makes me itch just thinking of it. At any rate," Delvecchio said, "matters have been deteriorating over the last six months. Various power blocs in the governments of both planets have been pressing for either quick results, in terms of a massive investment package from outside-the-Verge interests, or a walk-out and the end of the negotiations, followed by an immediate return to war."

"Old habits," Gabriel said softly, "die hard."

"Yes," the ambassador said. "And planetary elections are due shortly on Ino. The politicians there are quite aware of the galvanizing effect of a good war on the populace. They intend to use this to consolidate their own position and then come back to the negotiating table stronger than the other side." She looked wry. "At the same time, they are aware that if they break the present truce or if I catch them stalling, I will dissolve the negotiations, leave, and tell the Concord Administrator that this particular disagreement is

to be classified as 'intractable' with further intervention to be
attempted no sooner than seventy-five years from now."

The faces around the table went very quiet. "You mean, after
everyone presently negotiating is dead," said Gabriel.

"That is language that must not leave this room," Delvecchio
said. "But you're correct. If war breaks out, there will be no
action except to keep it quarantined here. If the two parties wish
to continue in that vein, they will be allowed to do so, and in
seventy-five years my distant successor will come back and try
again with the next generation. The rest of the Verge will have
gone ahead with its own military and economic development, of
course, with the Concord's assistance, and Phorcys and Ino will
not have. You may imagine the results. I assure you, the delegations will have been doing so. That is, if the more intelligent
members of the delegations have gotten a whiff of the Concord's
intentions."

"Which you will have seen to it that they have," Captain
Dareyev said.

Delvecchio threw her an expression of utter innocence.
"Well," she said, "in a roundabout sort of way. In our non-joint
sessions four days ago, I let each side know that I had been
authorized to make them both offers that far surpassed earlier
levels of assistance that had been mooted. Both sides were
amazed and understandably suspicious as to why this had happened just now. Neither of them knew, nor was I about to tell
them, that I had been authorized to make offers at these levels
nearly a year ago. At that time, though, had I made such offers,
they would have either been too easily accepted with no promise
of change forthcoming, or they would have been rejected in a bid
to improve either party's negotiating position.

"Now both parties have gone off with the new offers in hand.
Many members of both governments have turned right around in
their skins and are hot to accept these offers, even though it
means much closer cooperation with the other side than they
would normally ever have been willing to admit. But both negotiating teams, for differing sets of largely personal reasons, are

intent on rejecting the offers. Their problem is that the offer is too *good* to reject. The pressure on both planets for acceptance has been rising. If I have judged the situation correctly, each side will arrive here tomorrow with the covert intention of sabotaging not the other side's deal, but its own—by revelation of elements of improper behavior, or behavior that can be construed as improper, from the side hostile to them. This then will give them an excuse to cry 'bad faith' and break off negotiations. And then, in the fullness of time, they will go back to war."

Someone down the table swore under her breath. Someone else said, "Ambassador, don't they even care about their own people?"

"Oh, absolutely they do," Delvecchio said dryly. "They care about them enough to see them dead rather than allow them to betray their principles. Their *masters'* principles, at least."

An uncomfortable silence fell all around. "No matter," Ambassador Delvecchio said. "If what I have planned works out, none of this will come to pass. And if it does, it won't be for lack of our trying to stop them. Here is the order of business." She touched the table again. The holographs vanished, to be replaced by a scrolling list of political points to be handled.

Gabriel leaned over and said to Captain Dareyev, "What are the odds at the moment?"

Elinke gave him one of those sidelong, potential-bloody-stump looks. "Lieutenant," she said under her breath, "you know regulations strictly forbid betting of any kind aboard ship."

"I heard seven to four against the ambassador last night."

Elinke made a very demure and nearly inaudible snort down her perfect nose. "If you were such an idiot as to lay money down before the odds lengthened," she breathed, not taking her eyes off the text scrolling up into the air from the tabletop, "I'd gladly take it off you, and *then* chuck you into stir. It was nine to five against after breakfast, which you would doubtless know if you had been there. You need to stop skiving off. People are beginning to notice. Not officially yet, lucky for *you*. Now pay attention."

Gabriel did, though not entirely to the text. He had read it all last night, anyway. "Here," Delvecchio was saying, indicating one subsection of the text. "Here is what I'm counting on to set it off. Rallet, the head of the Phorcyn delegation, is furious about the potential Eraklion heavy metal allotments. He thinks they give Ino much too much potential to get their breeder program into high production—especially the secret one, the 'dirty breeder' that neither we or Phorcys are supposed to know about. So Rallet will blow the secret program's cover. On the Inoan side, once this happens, their own senior negotiator, ErDaishan, will riposte by informing us of Phorcys's sabotage and destruction of the Eraklian open-cast heavy metal workings at Ordinen." She shot a quick glance at Elinke.

Captain Dareyev nodded, just once. "Which has been successfully averted," Delvecchio said. "And without loss of life—congratulations, Captain, and please pass the congratulations to Captain Devereaux on *Callirhoë*. The Phorcyn delegation is presently in a state of shock. They will be looking for some other way to respond, but they won't be able to find anything in time, by my reckoning. And I shall remove the possibility of any such intervention by confronting *them* with the information about both these matters, immediately, up front. Both sets of actions are in direct contravention to both parties' agreements with us as 'honest brokers,' and that contravention will derail the negotiation process immediately without either the Phorcyn or Inoan delegations gaining the pleasure or the political advantage of having caused it themselves. Instead they will have mutually pulled the roof right down on their own heads, and they will beg us to get them out of the situation."

Delvecchio smiled, ever so gently. "And, of course, we will."

There was a somewhat breathless silence. Finally Commander T'teka said, "Ambassador, *how do you find all these things out?*"

She looked very calm. "I have my sources," Delvecchio said, "and it might surprise you where they are. 'Discovery' on that can wait a few years—at least until the people involved are out of office—or it otherwise doesn't matter any more. What matters now is that tomorrow afternoon the Inoan and Phorcyn delegations will arrive here prepared to destroy these talks. They will instead find themselves engaging in what will be the first of many unpleasant but useful rapprochements: a genuine agreement, a treaty, to which they are both going to have to sign their names. It will take most of the day and the night. There will be a lot of noise. There may be violence."

"Not on *my* ship," said Captain Dareyev.

"Attempted violence, I should say," said the ambassador, nodding at the captain in courteous acknowledgment. "But neither side will be willing to leave without bringing some kind of resolution about because neither trusts the other as far as any of them can spit. Trust." She looked rueful. "It will be decades before we see that from these people. But a settlement, yes, by quite late tomorrow night, I'd say. And if not, we return the delegations, break orbit, and make starfall back to Corrivale where reports will be filed for the various authorities involved, and where informal quarantine will be invoked on the Thalaassa system. After that . . ." she shrugged. "Further business will be in the hands of the local Concord Administrator. Any questions?"

Falada's protocol chief, Lieutenant Ferdinand, had some queries about the setup of the formal meeting room for the next day, which Delvecchio handled. Then she looked down the table again and said, "Ladies and gentlemen, thank you for your help. I know you will all do your best to forward this process without revealing any details to non-cleared personnel."

"Especially the negotiating teams," said Captain Dareyev.

Delvecchio gave her a particularly dry smile. "Especially. They will be brought to different docking bays, as usual, and all precautions should be taken to have them avoid seeing one another even at a distance until they actually enter the meeting room. All right? Then thank you, all. And wish us luck."

All stood as the Ambassador did. Slowly people began to head out. Elinke, standing up and stretching, looked around her casually, then glanced over at Gabriel and said, very softly, "Fourteen to one, at best."

"Think so?" Gabriel said and gave her what was meant to be a noncommittal look.

She flashed him a grin and left, heading back up to her Bridge. Gabriel let the room empty in front of him, then drifted up to Delvecchio. She looked at him, still wearing that dry smile.

"Disappointed?" she said. "You'd really like it if the warring parties turned on us, wouldn't you?"

"I'm a marine," Gabriel said. "Whichever answer I give you in this context could be the wrong one. But—"

"Don't be concerned," the ambassador said. "I understand you. But I don't think we have to worry about them threatening us. There are much worse problems to avoid."

Gabriel nodded. After a moment, he said, "Do you really think you can pull all this off?"

"Oh, I know I can," Delvecchio said, looking down at the paperwork and the datacarts. "My part of it, anyway. Everything now rests with the two negotiating teams. As long as human nature doesn't change before tomorrow afternoon, and they don't stop hating each other before then, we'll be just fine."

Gabriel shook his head in bemusement at the sheer cheerfulness of her cynicism. *And she thinks I might be good at this kind of work? I think I've got a long way to go.* "And will they stop hating each other after that?" he said.

Delvecchio looked up at him mildly as she gathered up her papers. "*I* won't live long enough to find out," she said, "but that's hardly an issue. I'll see you in the morning."

She went out, and a few moments later Gabriel went after her, suddenly very eager indeed to see the "bloodshed" begin the next afternoon.

Chapter Three

THE REST OF the day's schedule went haywire, which gave Gabriel the hint he needed that things were indeed in the air. For one thing, many marine staff under Hal's supervision were pulled back from other duties to be run over to *Callirhoë* to assist in maintenance work secondary to the mission she had just completed. The swearing started in earnest when word spread among *Falada*'s marine complement of the action that the other ship had seen not six hours ago. It had not been hand-to-hand work—just shipboard stuff, the Star Force ship going in low to preempt the little Phorcys-based raiders who had attacked Ordinen, Eraklion's biggest open-cast mine—but the marines assigned to *Callirhoë* managed to make it sound like the Second Galactic War when they came aboard that night for the usual "two-ships" social.

All this meant that Gabriel's spatball team's meeting had to be postponed, and the idea of doing any further reading of transcripts that night went right out the airlock. Suit drill, though conducted as professionally as always—after all, there was no treating casually the only thing that stood between you and space—had more than the usual buzz about it. Crew morale was always a major concern for Star Force. They knew what made their ships effective—not machines, but people. So any time two Concord Star Force vessels met for the first time in a system, especially when they were carrying complements of marines, there would be a social get-together as soon as circumstances permitted it. The two captains, having conferred at some length, were fairly certain that there would be no further antics from the

local system-based ships—especially with one Star Force vessel
in orbit around each of the two "offending" planets keeping an
eye on them and (via a few clandestinely sown surveillance satellites) on Eraklion as well.

By 2000, the temporary walls separating the main briefing
room from its twin next door had been opened out so that one
big space was available. By 2030, alternating panels of white-
silver and midnight-velvet curtains had been hung up to soften
the feel of the place, the lights had been lowered, and the room
was full of tables and chairs and food. Lots of food. If there
was anything anyone knew about marines, it was that they ate
their weight in protein every day, just to prove they could. The
other thing that everyone knew about marines—that they could
talk the tusks off a weren—was also being proven all over the
room.

"You shoulda seen it," someone was saying to Hal as Gabriel
came up beside him. "It was just like a dirg's nest when you
knock it down off the rocks. They came in real low over Eraklion's spaceward side. The Phorcyns thought they were under the
radar, and maybe they were, of the ground-based stuff . . . but not
ours. There were maybe two hundred of them—little ships, not
even military, some of them—just hoppers, just private craft with
guns. Are these people *crazy?* What kind of line are their bosses
selling them that they'll go up against a cruiser with nothing but
the family in-system flitter with a couple of grenade cannons
strapped to it?"

"Phorcyn fanatics," someone said. Laughter rippled through
the group as they caught the play on words.

The guy who was talking, a tall thin red-haired man, shook
his head. "I don't know," he said. "I'll tell you this: fanatic or not,
they knew how to fly, that bunch. We were watching them on the
repeaters in the landing craft, and they were right down and dirty
with the mountain chain around that place. Thought they were
going to do themselves permanent damage, some of them. But
they seemed to know those mountains pretty well."

"A little too well," said another of the marines nearby, a

slender little dark-haired woman with big dark brown eyes. "If they'd gotten down there to take the attack to a second stage, we would have had to root them out, and *that* would have been entertaining."

The man who had been talking first shrugged. "It didn't happen," he said, "and our weapons were clean, anyway, if it had. I would've given a lot to see their faces, though, when they came in close on the mine and saw the ship rising up out of that big ol' hole in the ground with all her guns hot. Never tell me that Captain Devereaux can't make her boat sit up and beg! And as for all those little ships—" He broke out laughing. "Just like a dirg's nest. They went scattering in every direction that God sent and took themselves away before something a lot worse than they were expecting happened to them."

"Meaning us," said the dark-haired woman, grinning.

"Yeah, well, every now and then you have to sit one out," said the marine who had been speaking. "We'll get the next dance, somewhere else. Hey, look—"

Noisy whistles and shrieks went up as two shapely forms walked in, in full Star Force dress black, everything from the full-length skirts to the wound sashes to the optional rakish hats. Captain Dareyev and Captain Devereaux, the latter looking somewhat abashed by the deafening welcome. She looked over at Elinke. Elinke shrugged and led her over to the first refreshment table to get her a glass of wine, but they never had a chance, being well mobbed by every nearby marine before more than a few steps had been taken. The marines always appreciated their captains even when they weren't women. A sharp set of reflexes in the center seat could save your life and those of all your teammates. But female captains had a special mystique—not entirely, Gabriel thought, having anything to do with their superior reflexes.

Even more marines arrived to congratulate the captains, and the two women smiled and let them get on with it, glancing at each other resignedly. Gabriel smiled a little too and turned back to the marine who had been talking, the one from *Callirhoë*. He was still talking to the brown-eyed marine, but he was slowing down somewhat. Not exactly running out of steam, perhaps, but he and a lot of his buddies, to Gabriel's eye, had that about-to-fall-over look that he had seen more than enough times in his career so far. Men who had been sitting in their shuttles, suited up, ready to be delivered to some godforsaken spot that they had never seen before, ready to take it and hold it as if it were their own, as if they would shed their last drop of blood for it—and indeed they would. Waiting for that to happen for hours on end, sometimes days. The men and women who went through that on a regular basis showed changes in their faces that Gabriel had learned to recognize without being able to describe. Tonight it looked most like weariness to him. And fear, too. But that was not something you would say out loud to a marine, not until you knew him or her very well indeed. For the meantime, these were brothers and sisters, but not yet brothers in blood, except in the abstract. Sooner or later, it might happen . . . probably would. But you didn't force the pace.

The tiredness in those eyes faded for a moment. "Hey, brother," the marine said, "nice place you have here."

"We like it," Gabriel said. "You're welcome! Gabriel Connor."

"Mil Wyens."

"Where are you from when you're not from a ship?"

"Orion League. Damrak."

"Hey, we're neighbors!" Gabriel grinned a little. Neighborhood was something Orions took seriously, even if it was spread over many light-years. "I was born on Jaeger, and then we moved to Bluefall. My folks moved there on a colonization contract."

"Long way back there," Mil said. "You must not see 'em often."

"Not my dad, anyway. Not since I enlisted. Dad's still on Bluefall; he's retired. Mom died a few years ago," Gabriel added, knowing from too much experience that if he didn't add it, someone would most likely ask. Better to get it over with.

Mil's green eyes looked troubled. "Hey, I'm sorry."

The usual response, *it's all right, it was a release, finally,* came up. But for some reason Gabriel rejected it and just nodded. He said, "You guys did a great job out there today."

"We didn't do much of anything," Mil said, sounding rather disappointed.

"You did, though," Gabriel said. "Waiting. Waiting's hard."

He thought of the long hours down in the ice on Epsedra. The explosions overhead. And down in the crevasses, the slow drip and trickle of melting ice and the bright brittle sound when a bomb came down too close, shattering the ice into spears and shrapnel. In some ways, that seemed like another lifetime, ages ago. Some ways it seemed like a matter of minutes. And it could sneak up on you at other times when you were waiting, sometimes for something much more mundane and make itself a nuisance.

Mil looked at him without much expression for a moment or so and then made half a smile and said, "Had enough of it for today."

"Let me get you something," Gabriel said. "How much 'something' do you want in it?"

"Normal dosage," Mil said after a moment. "No point in replacing palpitations with a headache."

Gabriel went off to fetch a couple of Pink Deaths. When he came back and handed one of them to Mil, the brown-eyed marine who had also drifted away in search of something liquid, now came back and leaned over Mil's shoulder. This was something of an accomplishment. She had to stand on tiptoe to do it, and she nearly spilled her drink down Mil's back in the process.

"Mil, what about you-know-who's commcode?"

"Huh?"

"You remember. You were going to give me his commcode. You said you wrote it down."

"I did. Now where did I leave it?" Mil started going through his pockets.

"In the go-down boat," said the brown-eyed marine to Gabriel, and the various others who were gathered around, "he was sitting next to someone whom I would—someone in whom

I am extremely interested. Tell me you didn't lose it," she said, poking Mil meaningfully in the ribs, "or you are going to have a *bad* weapons drill in a few days. *Very* bad."

"No, I *know* I have it, it's—" Mil kept going through his pockets, coming up with the usual clutter: cardkey for his quarters, cardkey for the secure locker in his wardrobe, and a little dark something. But the darkness didn't last. It flashed dully as Gabriel looked at it. He glanced away, wondering if the room lighting had something to do with it, but it didn't.

"What *is* that?" he asked.

Mil was concentrating on going through his other pocket now, and looked up, slightly confused at being distracted from this. "Oh, this? It's a luck stone. I got it on . . ." He frowned, bemused, until his eyebrows threatened to bang into each other. "Dilemma, I think it was."

"You couldn't have gotten it on Dilemma," the brown-eyed marine said. "We didn't get leave there. *Where is that comm code?*"

"Not the last time. The time before last."

"You didn't have this thing then," the brown-eyed marine said. "I didn't see it until we'd been to Tractate. Stop stalling."

"There wasn't anything on Tractate. I got it on . . ." He stopped going through the other pocket, looking annoyed. "Never mind."

Curious, Gabriel watched the little smooth thing in Mil's hand. It was vaguely oval and more flat than spherical. It had an odd metallic sheen to it, almost like brushed metal. But the color was black, except when it glowed from inside, a little diffuse light like a coal being blown to life and fading, blown bright and fading again. "How does it do that?" Gabriel said.

"I don't know," said the man, turning the little object over in his hand. "Batteries? No, I don't know at all; some guy in the daily market in the city we were in—I know," he said triumphantly to the brown-haired marine. "It was Dorring."

"It wasn't Dorring. You weren't *on* Dorring. Where did you *put* it?"

"She's right," said another she-marine who had come up behind Mil, a tall blonde woman. "You were in medical stir for nearly a week that starfall. Remember the—"

"Ow," said Mil, "yeah, did you have to remind me?" He pocketed the "luck piece" and turned around. "What are *you* doing here anyway? I thought you had duty this shift."

"I did," she said, "but some schedules have been changed. Better check *yours.*"

"Not before he gives me that comm code!"

That small knot of marines saluted Gabriel with their glasses and wandered off toward the food, leaving Gabriel looking after them while one of his floor mates, Mick Roscinzsky, came up beside him, carrying a couple of drinks. "Here," he said as he handed one to Gabriel.

"What is it?"

"How should I know? All I know is you were standing there with your two arms the same length."

Gabriel took an experimental sip of one of the drinks and made a face. "Did it occur to anyone to put anything in this *but* alcohol?"

Mick looked shocked. "Oh, this is one of the guest drinks. Sorry." He took it away from Gabriel and gave him his own.

Gabriel sipped it, looking suspiciously at Mick. This drink was mostly fizzy water. "Better," he said, realizing that he had nearly been on the receiving end of a hoary old trick intended for *Falada*'s guests but not her own marine complement. "Are they buying it?"

" 'Fraid so. I feel sorry for their tiny heads tomorrow."

Gabriel grinned and wandered along behind Mick toward the bar. One of his other floor mates, Charles Redpath, was tending bar. He saw Dawn Steilin, a second lieutenant of his acquaintance, come moseying along and say to Charles, "I'll have a Squadron Special."

Charles reached down, chose a glass, filled it from one of the clear flasks nearby. Dawn took the glass from him, raised it, said, "Up the Concord, boys!" and knocked it back in three long gulps.

A few of the marines from *Callirhoë* looked at her in appreciation or astonishment. One of them leaned close to whiff at the glass, or possibly her breath—or possibly just because Dawn was pleasant to lean close to—then said in some surprise, "Austrin gin?"

Dawn nodded, gave the guy a bright and completely unaddled look, and wandered away again. "I'll have one of those," said the marine who'd spoken to Dawn, and Charles, with a slight smile, handed him a glass the size of the one Dawn had downed.

Gabriel kept his own smile out of sight. The glass from which Dawn had been drinking, he knew, had been behind the bar, rimdown in a saucer of that Austrin gin. The flask from which it had been filled, though, the flask identical to the one from which Charles was now pouring, was full of plain old water. The *present* flask, though, was full of straight Austrin. Their guests would go away from this party with the belief that their hosts were supermen, at least insofar as their ability to hold their drink was involved.

Gabriel turned away, half afraid he would lose control of that smile, and found Jake Ricel standing behind him, apparently watching the show at the bar. The dark-haired man was near Gabriel's height but less broad in the shoulders and leaner. His fair-skinned face was altogether unremarkable, one of those people who blended easily into any crowd without being noticed. Jake caught Gabriel's eye and glanced off to one side.

Now what the hell, Gabriel thought. Of all the times to— For this was his shipboard Intelligence contact, the man whom he had seen only once or twice, and that accidentally, in the last whole year. Jake was Star Force and worked up in Drive Engineering. From a marine's point of view, this would normally make him suspect regardless of any possible Intelligence connections, since people who could actually understand the gravity induction engine were assumed to be, as the saying went, "a hundred and twenty-one hours from a nervous breakdown." But he seemed otherwise overtly normal according to people Gabriel knew who had worked with him.

Gabriel said, "Oh, hi, Jake," as casually as he could. "Drink?"

"What you're having," said Jake, glancing idly over to where the two captains were unsuccessfully attempting to fend off another wave of marines.

Gabriel turned back to the bar and said, "Charles? Two Squadron Specials."

Charles looked over at them, eyed Jake, recognized him as inship but not marine, and handed Gabriel two drinks that looked the same but differed significantly in composition. "Thanks," Gabriel said.

"We take care of our own," Charles said and turned around to take another order.

Gabriel and Jake walked away slowly from the bar, sipping their drinks. Jake's was very full. "How do you people *drink* this stuff like you do?" he said.

"Genetic engineering," said Gabriel. "Haven't seen you for a while."

"No need," said Jake, "until now. Something needs to be looked into."

"Oh?"

Jake nodded, making a face as he took another drink. " 'Upabove' is a little curious about some things that might or might not have been seen in this system."

"Well, that's real definite," Gabriel said. "If you mean people from Phorcys and Ino shooting at each other, there's plenty of *that* to be curious about."

"No," Jake said, "not that, specifically." His voice got lower, and he turned to look toward the doorway. " 'Upabove' is wondering whether any of the diplomatic staffs from Phorcys or Ino have mentioned anything about . . . trouble in the system. Trouble that's not of their own making."

"There's more than enough of the kind they make themselves to keep them busy," Gabriel said. "What kind of things are 'Upabove' curious about?" He was mystified.

Jake shrugged, looking around him again, so that Gabriel wondered exactly what or who he was looking for. Anyone close enough to stand a chance of eavesdropping seemed intent on their own conversations. "Aliens, especially aliens that aren't usually seen in these parts."

Gabriel shook his head. "For creep's sake, this is the *Verge*," he said. "You might run into any one of thirty alien races out here and never think anything of it."

"It might not be one of the recognized ones," said Jake, even more softly. Gabriel could hardly hear him now. "Making trouble somewhere in the system . . . trying to keep it quiet. Star Force might not know about it, but possibly the diplomatic types coming and going might drop a line or two on the subject."

"Not usually where we can hear," Gabriel said. "They think we're spies half the time as it is."

"But some of you they get used to looking at," Jake said. "You've been seen helping out in high places a lot lately." He gave Gabriel a slightly quizzical look.

Gabriel shrugged. "The ambassador's preference," he said. "I don't understand it myself." But Jake was looking at him, waiting for an answer. Then he looked at the doorway again, as if unusually eager to get out of there.

"All right, sure," Gabriel said. "I'll see what I can find out. But I don't know if I'm going to be able to help you all that much. I've been shipboard, mostly, and I think I'm supposed to be that way for the next couple of days anyway."

"Well," Jake said, "don't worry about that. Just keep your eyes and ears open and see what you can find out."

"Sure." But privately Gabriel felt sure he would find out almost nothing. "I'll leave a message on your computer if I need to talk to you."

"No!" Jake said, with surprising vehemence. "Just find me. Make an excuse to get up my way or have someone bring me a message by hand." Gabriel shrugged again, agreeing. Even now, there were times when an officer might prefer to have a message hand carried rather than put in the system. "If you do hear anything, I'll have a message for you to take back to the source. Not a word to anyone of who gave it to you—you'll have to find a way to slip it to the target without revealing the source."

Gabriel nodded. Jake pushed his unfinished drink back into Gabriel's free hand, turned, and disappeared through the nearest passageway. Just like that, he was gone.

Gabriel shook his head, bemused, and turned his attention back to the stir in the room, the laughter of relief and release, the sight of people drifting around, eating and drinking and unwinding. The captains had finally been able to break away from their myriad admirers and sit down off to one side by themselves. Their heads were bent close together and their drinks were forgotten as they conferred. Gabriel caught Elinke's eye just briefly as she looked up and around, and he saluted her with his empty glass. She looked at him, grinned slightly, lifted both hands as if holding something in them, and put her eyebrows up. Gabriel realized he was still holding two glasses and went off hurriedly to put one of them down.

As he was making his way to one of the buffet tables, Hal came lounging along toward Gabriel. Hal eyed the second glass disapprovingly. "Bad day?"

"Not mine," Gabriel said, just slightly nettled.

"Oh. Good, because schedules have been shuffled," said Hal. "Have you seen?"

"I haven't looked since this afternoon, no."

"Better go check. I had a word with the computer and got a few little surprises. You will too. Among other things, you're on shuttle duty tomorrow."

"*What?* That's impossible! The am—" Gabriel stopped himself. "I was told I was going to be shipboard. The negotiations."

"Look again," Hal said, not entirely without sympathy. "Oh-dark-forty, you poor thing. And here you thought you were going to have six whole hours to sleep this off."

Reading, reading something for pleasure for a change, instead of the never-ending bad fairy tale of the negotiation transcripts, had been more on Gabriel's mind, at least enough of it to lull him gently to sleep. Now there was going to be little enough chance of that. "Well, frack," he said. "What fun."

"Better turn in early," Hal said. "I know I am. Shame to miss the rest of the party."

Gabriel looked around at a room full of relatively happy marines and Star Force people. It had been a good day for most of them in that none of them had died. "Yeah," he said. "But there'll be others. Meanwhile . . ."

"Yup, me too. See you in the morning," Hal said, "or what comes all too soon before it." He finished his own drink, put it down, and headed out the door.

Gabriel got rid of the glasses, paused to snaffle a couple of small meatrolls and devour them, and then slowly went the same way Hal had.

Schedule changes. He was willing enough to believe that the ambassador might have been behind them. Keep your eyes and ears open, she had said.

But so had Jake, just now, in almost the same words. And he hadn't seemed concerned that Gabriel thought he was going to be stuck shipside.

Did Jake know that my schedule was going to be changed this way? Gabriel thought. And if he did know that, how did he know that?

But after a moment Gabriel put the thought out of his mind. There was probably no point in him wasting consideration on it. He had long since gotten a feeling that as regarded Intelligence, the less you seemed to stop and think about the things you found out, the better the upper ups liked it. And it was likely enough that the ambassador was involved somehow in that as well. The Diplomatic service and the Intelligence people were well known to work closely together. The briefing earlier in the day suggested that just that kind of thing might have been going on.

Gabriel took himself off to his quarters, dropped a sober pill, and immediately turned in. He was a little uneasy, but still excited about what the next day might bring. It wasn't that many more hours, anyway, until he would find out.

Chapter Four

H E WAS UP even earlier than he thought he would be. Even though he was on shuttle duty, it was diplomatic shuttle duty and thus required the dress blues rather than fatigues. As soon as he was in a fresh uniform, Gabriel went down to the great echoing steel-arched barn of the cargo/shuttle deck that held a half-dozen of the long wedge-shaped spacecraft. He immediately made himself useful, talking to the dispatch chief about which shuttles were scheduled in and out and when. He found out who they were carrying and where they were going. Partly it was gossip, for the shuttle chief was half beside himself with the hours his pilots were having to keep and the kind of work they were having to do. But Gabriel had a half-formed idea that it would be a good idea if he could be on as many of the shuttles as he could today, at least without attracting undue notice. Being eyes and ears was all very well, but not so obviously that no one would say anything in front of you.

The next five hours were desperately wearing for Gabriel. Most of a marine's duty when doing diplomatic escort duty involved standing very still and looking like you might be useful at any moment, but not *this* moment. It was one of the reasons that marines learned the kind of mind-control exercise that helped them to keep perfectly still and blank-faced without twitching, yet still allowed the mind to roam at least moderately free. The trick worked, helping Gabriel to keep enough attention on the business around him while preventing him from falling asleep where he stood.

He was on that first shuttle at oh-dark-forty, the one that went

down to Phorcys to fetch Rallet, the chief investigator for the
Phorcys government. Gabriel had no problem with the run down,
which was enjoyable enough. He always liked near-planet work,
and the view over the planet's peculiar bands of north-south-
running mountains intrigued him, leaving him wondering about
the tectonic forces that might have formed them. But the enjoyment ceased as soon as they grounded at a small private airfield
near Endwith, the main city in the planet's northern hemisphere,
and picked up Rallet.

Gabriel resigned himself to the problem he'd gotten himself
into. He would have preferred to escort almost anyone else, for
he had done escort duty for Rallet once before. He therefore had
a much more intimate and unpleasant knowledge of the man than
the interminable transcripts contained. Rallet climbed onto the
shuttle as if he owned it and never even glanced at Gabriel's
salute, offered from the spot by the inner airlock that Gabriel
would occupy during the trip to *Falada*. Well, it was Rallet's
privilege to treat Gabriel like furniture if he pleased to, at least as
far as protocol went. And so Rallet did, stalking past Gabriel
without so much as a blink and sinking into the ridiculously lux-
urious bench seat the likes of which Hal and his people had spent
the whole previous day installing in the shuttles.

"Tat," Rallet muttered under his breath to his aide, who was
busily opening a case and going through paperwork.

"Pardon, sir?" said the aide, though Gabriel guessed that the
aide knew well enough what his master had said.

"Tat," Rallet said, more forcefully. "Look at these disgusting
interiors. It's an insult, a calculated insult. This vehicle cannot
have been maintained for months. Look at the stains! I shall
speak to the ambassador about it when we arrive."

He went on in that vein for a long while, and Gabriel, true to
his request from the ambassador and his thinly veiled orders
from Jake, listened to every word. It was unpleasant work. The
man's arrogance was apparently incorrigible, and his ego was the
size of a planet to judge by his conversation, for everything that
happened in his immediate vicinity was inevitably pointed

directly at him as a carefully crafted insult to his position, his dignity, his political affiliations, his planet's sovereignty. He complained about the unsatisfactory course of the negotiations, about Star Force's unwelcome presence in his system, about the inequity of the agreement they were trying to foist on his free and proud people, about the covert intentions of the Concord toward his world. Gabriel had seen much of this material in the transcripts, and it gained nothing by being delivered live. But it's odd, Gabriel thought, he almost sounds like . . . The thought trailed off in another withering attack by Rallet, this time on why it took so ridiculously long for the shuttle to merely get from the planet's surface to *Falada*. Gabriel turned his mind away from the idea of how pleasant it would be to tie this bloated warmongering bureaucrat into a chair and lecture him for several hours on the specifics of low-fuel-high-decay tangential orbits. Then the thought he had been chasing abruptly clarified itself. He sounds like he's reading from a script, like it's an act. Like he really wants to stop.

But why? came the ambassador's question again. Why now?

Gabriel listened and heard nothing that suggested an answer.

After twenty minutes or so the ship began its final approach to *Falada,* and she took them inboard. Rallet's poor assistant, who had been trying to get a word in here or there during the tirade, finally said, "What do you wish to be carrying as we go in, sir? The last offer?"

"No," Rallet said, "the order of business."

"Which one, sir?"

"Ours, you idiot," Rallet said, and started fussing with his restraining belts long before they were far enough inside for it to be safe for him to do so.

Gabriel blinked, but did no more. So the ambassador had been right about this, at least. Rallet had an "order of business" that differed, possibly radically, from the one which Delvecchio openly intended. Might be something, might not. Better than nothing, though. He made a note to get word to the ambassador about this any way he could, well before the proceedings began.

The shuttle door was opened from outside, and ceremonial pipes were blown as usual. Rallet got off, actually bumping into Gabriel on the way out, jostling him. Gabriel gave way and caught his balance without looking as if he were doing so. Then when the man was away and well out of sight, Gabriel let himself have one grimace of pure rage before getting off the shuttle and looking around to see where the next one was.

The rest of the morning, to his annoyance, was not even as interesting as riding with the detestable Rallet. There were two more shuttle runs to Phorcys, once to pick up the secondary Phorcyn negotiator, Rallet's chief assistant, and once for the delegation's "support team"—ten quiet men and women who seemed to spend most of their time repeating the spoken proceedings near-silently into tiny repeaters held to their throats. They had no equivalent on the Inoan side. Gabriel knew that Phorcys had several major languages, but he didn't think these people were translators. Maybe they were record keepers? There was no telling. At least they tended to chat freely with one another on the way up to *Falada,* and the talk was at least vaguely interesting, as eavesdropping often is. But they said nothing about anything going on elsewhere in the system, overt or covert; and since Gabriel's position, in terms of protocol, forbade him to speak except when spoken to, he was unable to draw them out.

That shuttle in turn came home to *Falada* and discharged its passengers. Gabriel wearily got out, looked around to see which shuttle was the next to go out, and boarded it. This one went to a small military airfield near Ino's planetary capital. It returned with the Inoan secondary negotiator—who had a terrible cold—and his four staff, all of whom were trying desperately to avoid being too near their superior while equally trying not to *look* like they were trying to avoid him. The poor man himself, all wrapped up in the voluminous silken formal robes that Inoans favored, hardly noticed his staff at all. He was too busy sneezing and coughing as if he was trying to dislodge a thrutch that had somehow become lodged in one of his lungs. Gabriel escaped from that shuttle and found himself briefly standing off to one side of the hangar and brushing his uniform as if it were possible to get the germs off it that way. I'd better take an antiviral before the session this afternoon, he thought with resignation, and just stood where he was for the moment, wishing duty didn't require him to get on another shuttle as soon as one presented itself.

One did within a matter of minutes. It was delightful, in a way, to have a few moments to admire the grace with which a shuttle could come sailing in through the hangar's force curtain and settle itself in place. This one did so with no wasted motions, came down, and sat there ticking gently to itself for a little while, the metal of its wings still shedding residual heat from the escape from atmosphere.

The shuttle's hatch cracked open, top and bottom. A delay, and then after a few moments, another marine guard debarked and walked away from it, a woman who looked at least as tired of this kind of duty as Gabriel was. From inside the door of the grounded shuttle came a voice, which Gabriel was positioned fairly well to hear, saying, "—to know anything about that business, it's not my affair."

Gabriel took a few steps backward, into the shadow of the shuttle's starboard airfoil. There was a reply from inside, but too far inside the shuttle for Gabriel to make it out as anything but a mutter.

"I don't care," said the voice nearer the door in answer, "maybe she *is* cleared for it, but *I've* no orders to tell her, and if these people can't detect their ships out that far either, then it's not a problem for us, is it?"

More muttering came from inside. The voice near the door suddenly became less distinct, but much more vehement. "—want to," it said, "you go ahead and tell them . . . kidnappings and . . . vanishing, but . . . mind being dismissed for fantasies about outsystem ghouls and . . ." The voice went low, too low to hear any more. Then just two words were audible: ". . . ghost ships . . ."

The other voice, nearer the door, said, "Ridiculous."

A man stepped out, an Inoan, one of the other secondary negotiators. Behind him another human walked down the carpeted walkway. She was not an Inoan, but a woman in the plain grays of the Diplomatic service—Delvecchio's assistant ambassador, Areh Wuhain. She went after the man, who looked unconcerned. Her own expression was extremely annoyed, but Gabriel watched her smooth it out as they headed for the airlock leading to the main corridors of *Falada*.

Now *that*, Gabriel thought, was something. Certainly something bizarre that he didn't understand terribly well, but possibly useful. He rehearsed the dialogue in his mind and locked it in place with the short-term memory technique he'd been taught and then looked for another shuttle to board.

"Are you crazy? Nothing's left, thank heaven," came Hal's voice from across the hangar. Hal was looking wearily at the last shuttle down, leaning against the second-to-last shuttle with his arms folded. "No, I tell a lie. One more, but that's not for another hour. Some hold up down on Ino."

"So they're all here now?" Gabriel said, strolling over to lean beside him briefly.

"All the important ones. Gods, what a waste," Hal said and breathed out. "I saw you getting off after Old Flat Face this morning. What a treat he must have been. You looked like you wanted to throw up."

"Duty before comfort," Gabriel said.

"For this kind of duty? You are sick," Hal said. "*Sick.* Your blood sugar must be off somehow. Did you take a pill before you went to bed?"

"Of course I did, you bollix," Gabriel said and shoved him amiably.

"Something else must be wrong with you, then. It's not normal for a marine to actively seek any duty except fighting."

"Well," Gabriel said, "maybe, but there's one I'm damned well going to actively seek out—the meeting this afternoon."

"Fireworks?" Hal said. "That 'violence' I heard mentioned?"

"I wish I could sell tickets," Gabriel said. He sighed, stood up straight again. "Never mind. I've got to go take an anti-cold nostrum."

"Did we catch a little chill?" Hal said, teasing, as Gabriel headed for the airlock back to the ship.

"More than that," Gabriel said, and added to himself: A whole lot more than that, I think.

* * * * *

Three hours later it began in the large room that had been set aside aboard *Falada* as more or less neutral territory for the Ambassador and the negotiating parties to use. It was plush and beautifully decorated, looking like a drawing room one might find in a castle on some ancient Solar Union world. Wood paneling graced the walls. A suavely polished table gleamed beneath the non-glaring, soothing light. Graceful abstract art hung on the walls or stood in the corners on demure pedestals. Any normal person would have found the effect restful, calming, but these were not normal people. Gabriel stood in his "guard" position by the door and waited, aware that his pulse rate was starting to rise.

The negotiating teams filed in, their leaders coming last. Rallet came first, with his oddly shaped head that made Gabriel think that at some point in his life his mother had lost patience with him and hit him in the face with a shovel. Then came ErDaishan, with a face that had long since fixed itself into deep and permanent lines of dissatisfaction with everything around her, from the lighting and the shape of the table to the fact that she had to breathe the same air as her opponent across the table did. They looked at each other with animated loathing. It occurred to Gabriel suddenly that what he was seeing here was a marriage . . . one into which the ambassador had unwelcomely intruded, bearing an olive branch instead of what each of the parties wanted: a stick to beat the other one with. Gabriel, meanwhile, held his breath to see what they would make of the stick that the ambassador was about to produce.

"Thank you all for your promptness," Delvecchio said. "Before we resume the proceedings, I must take your excellencies into my confidence and ask you both a question that will determine much of the direction of what remains for us all to do today."

They looked at her attentively, with loathing only a little less than that they reserved for each other. Their respective civil servants shuffled and muttered and rustled paperwork, bound and unbound, and sorted carts, already uneasy with the breach in the order of the day.

"Did you really think you could get away with it?" said the ambassador.

Those two faces went from loathing to the beginnings of outrage. Gabriel had seen this before, the how-dare-you-speak-that-way-to-me expression. But it was reflex in these two, and now it was edged with something much more noticeable: fear.

"I must inform you that this will be our last meeting," said the ambassador, "one way or the other—except for the very minor tidying up, which your assistants will manage. Since we last met, conditions have changed."

"Ambassador, this is outrageous. We are not children to be scolded by a mere—"

"Ordinen," said Delvecchio. "Mashan."

Both their mouths fell open, even ErDaishan's mouth, that mouth whose lips never moved while its owner spoke. *Now* it worked, that mouth, and words tried to make it out, but couldn't.

"Ordinen is safe," said Delvecchio, "and we have holo, lots of it, of your ships attempting the attack. And Mashan. Yes, Mashan is not just the name of a small town in the dust any more. We have holo of that too. Dirty breeding," and the ambassador shook her head like a mother tut-tutting over a child's dirty playclothes. "What will your investors think? And what about Ordinen, which you had guaranteed could produce eight thousand tons of refined ores per week? Not after all those tunnels had been blown into one great crater, it wouldn't."

The two stood up slowly, from either side of the table, with expressions of terrible rage on their faces, and they began to scream at each other.

The *Crack!* that came from the middle of the table stopped them. It was the cane, the one the ambassador had used to come aboard for the first few meetings, the long black cane she walked with or made show of walking with sometimes. Now, though, Gabriel finally understood what it was really for.

"Don't bother," said the ambassador, very softly. "Collusion. It has been heavy in the air for the last few weeks. You two thought you were quite circumspect. No one knew about this, not even your own people, just the very few in your own defense forces whom you suborned to this business. Here, on this matter only, just this once, you were able to agree."

The silence that fell had weight. First it pushed ErDaishan back down into her seat, then Rallet.

"So many other things you might have agreed on," said the ambassador, "but no. *This,* though, you thought you could get away with. I am sorry to interfere with your perception of your control over of the scheme of things, sir, madam. But now you have pulled the forces of the world around you a little too far out of shape. And like gravity and the other forces, the response is immediate. The talks are dissolved by cause of concrete proof of bad faith on both sides, and I must report my failure to the Concord."

The two Thalaassan delegates sitting opposite one another went ashen. They did not start screaming, but they did start talking. Slowly at first, then faster. One of them, then the other, and then both together. They became two matching portions of an incoherent babble, and Gabriel finally had to stop trying to make sense of it. The ambassador said nothing at all, just let them talk, let them run down. It took nearly half an hour.

Finally that heavy silence fell again. The ambassador leaned back in her chair and waited.

"Madam," said ErDaishan finally, "you do not understand. It cannot end like this—"

"It *has* ended," said Delvecchio. Was that just the shadow of a smile on her face, Gabriel wondered?

"If there was something that we could do—"

"If there was just some way that—"

"I await your suggestions with interest," said Delvecchio, "but I have no idea what can possibly restore the *status quo* that your acts have shattered."

She sat there and listened to them for another hour. During this period Gabriel had to revert to mind-control again, using the routine that helps keep the body from twitching while the brain is wishing it was somewhere else, *anywhere* else. The mitigating factor, the only thing helping Gabriel feel less than completely twitchy, was that the two negotiators—helped eventually by their teams—slowly began to suggest the very series of face-saving maneuvers that Delvecchio had described to him and written up for her team three days before. It occurred to Rallet and ErDaishan in fits and starts, in pieces that had to be rearranged, and some of those pieces caused screaming nearly as vehement as that which had begun the session. But slowly they created the solution that Delvecchio had predicted, almost paragraph for paragraph as the writing up began, as if they had genuinely thought of it all themselves.

Gabriel had often enough wondered if the ambassador had a little mindwalker in her somewhere. Now he was less sure. What he was seeing was certainly something that could pass for predicting the future or mind reading, but it was neither of these. It was an understanding of people in general and these two people in particular and the circumstances that surrounded them—and it was so profound that once or twice it made Gabriel shiver. Also once or twice he saw ErDaishan or Rallet look up from the documents wearing an expression that was a terrible mixture of anger and, not fear, but now (toward the end of it all) disgust. Disgust at having been caught, at the unfairness of it. Gabriel looked at the ambassador, but no reaction to their expressions revealed itself on her face. She was like a statue, one that occasionally spoke to approve something and otherwise caused people to make notes very fast as they worked to produce the approving result again.

This process ran at least another three hours. Gabriel lost track of the time. His inner clock had for the time being been badly skewed by having to keep himself still. He was actually jarred back to consciousness—not that he had been sleeping, just elsewhere in mind—by the ambassador's voice saying, very simply, "No."

"I don't *want* to call it an agreement," ErDaishan was saying. "To imply that we agree on—"

"It has to be called *something* that will suggest to your respective peoples that there is some hope of the war stopping," said the ambassador, "and since you will not allow it to be called a treaty, because you refuse to agree not to go back to war again later, or a settlement, because you claim nothing is settled, then agreement it must be. No lesser term will produce the stabilizing effect on the markets that you require for this whole process to bear fruit."

They stared at her. Until now, all her interjections had been fairly gentle, leading them in the direction she had predicted for them, and in which they now intended, however unwillingly, to go. There was still a little fight left in them, though.

Rallet said, "Naturally we will require time to prepare our people for—"

"Sir, I think not," said the ambassador. "There are many eyes watching this affair, and delay will be seen as uncertainty. The stock markets are watching, and you all know how little time it takes the commodities and futures markets, in particular, to start becoming nervous. For all our sakes, it would be well if the formalities were concluded within no more than the next twenty-four hours. And the news of the actual settlement must be made public immediately." There, just for a moment, the voice lost its kid-glove quality. "Besides, your people are well prepared for this moment. They have been most intent on these proceedings. The commentators on both worlds' Grids, and some of those outside, have been predicting something very like this outcome—though it remains for you to stun them with the details. A few of them, of course, you will be delighted to prove very *wrong* about those details. Doubtless you will want to start arranging the interviews."

The man looked in one direction and the woman in another, toward their respective staffs. Gabriel saw the hungry glint of eyes in one face, the set mouth, hard and vengeful, in the other. Both expressions frightened him, for they were wholly about personal pleasure, personal point-scoring, nothing better. Lives of thousands of millions of people would be affected by what had happened here today. Thousands (Gabriel thought, Gabriel hoped) would now not have to die. But neither of these two cared, not really. They were much more interested at this particular moment in getting back at people who had called them names or embarrassed them in public. And how many of their other moments are like this? Gabriel thought, trying hard to keep the look out of his face. How many of my brothers and sisters might have to die protecting the ambassador if these two should suddenly decide that *she* has embarrassed them?

"These proceedings are therefore complete," said Delvecchio, "and the only detail remaining is your signature, sir, and yours, madam, on the instrument of agreement. And I congratulate you on becoming so notable a part of your worlds' history."

The two bowed to Delvecchio across the table and reached out to their assistants for styli. Just a little hesitation there? Gabriel thought, but he could not be certain he had seen it. The two cart-based copies of the document were inserted into pad readers and pushed across to each of the signatories by one of their assistants. Each of them signed. That hesitation again. It was there.

And then it was over.

Delvecchio stood. The two seated delegations looked at her.

"Thank you," she said. "This is of course the informal version of the ceremony. If you would be so kind as to inform me when you have had a chance to discuss this with your governments, I will be pleased to be at the ceremony tomorrow where this accommodation is made public. In time for the opening of the markets in the most closely involved systems, of course."

"Certainly, ambassador. But as for the formal signing, it will take time to arrange, and in a few days we can—"

"The fine print," said the ambassador, "says 'tomorrow.' "

The signatories looked at her. Then silently they both bowed to her again and made their way out.

Gabriel watched them go, ErDaishan and Rallet, each with his or her little soberly dressed entourage, each walking rather ostentatiously next to the other. It seemed to Gabriel as he watched them go that he had never seen two people be so far apart who had only a meter of space between them. They were entirely aware of the watching eyes, the listening ears. They were practicing their act. They would have to have it right by tomorrow after all.

The room emptied rather quickly, as if something unpleasant hung in the air, a scent that people were anxious to be rid of in a hurry. Finally, it was as it had been the other morning: Gabriel and the ambassador—she slowly gathering up her papers and carts, he watching her, and after a moment, moving to help.

For some minutes she said nothing, ordering her papers, looking at some of them more carefully than others, holding up one cart—the one with the rewritten agreement on it—and placing it carefully on the top of the pile. Then she breathed out, just once, a weary sound.

When she looked up again, some of the tiredness was gone from her eyes, but not all of it. "So how did that look to you?" she said.

"Ugly," Gabriel said after a moment.

Delvecchio nodded. "Ours is the stepchild of the military arts," she said. "Guns are faster. Cruisers are prettier." She straightened and looked at Gabriel. "But sometimes we win the fight, and people don't die. Sometimes."

She picked up the one last thing, her cane, and went out the door. Gabriel swallowed, for she was actually using it. She walked out carefully, looking not like a sword or a banner, but like a woman of a hundred and thirty-three. Victory, Gabriel thought, not winged, but hobbling.

It was all very strange. He took a long breath and decided that after he was finished piling up the stripes and the bars, the Diplomatic service would have first call.

Chapter Five

THE PARTY STARTED fairly early that night. Normally shipboard protocol would have forbidden two parties one right after the other. But this situation was a little different, and the relief aboard—among both Star Force and marine staff—was so palpable that the captain gave her approval with very little trouble.

Gabriel had one stop to make before the party. After giving it some consideration, he felt that the way to attract the least attention was to do exactly what he was supposed to be doing: delivering a message to someone in Engineering. Torine Meldrum down there was on his spatball team. He wrote her a note about the rescheduling of practice and then wrote eleven more notes to other teammates, slipping them into message boxes outside people's rooms or delivering them by hand to those he knew to be on duty. Additionally, he wrote one note not to a teammate, and as he passed by Jake on the way out of Engineering, he saw that Jake got it without anyone seeing.

Then he changed into his most formal uniform, getting ready to go to the signing celebration. When he came out of his room, there was a folded note in his own message box. He opened it.

For the one who mentioned ghosts, said the note. *Deliver unlabeled.* Out of the note fell a little datachip: another message, encoded.

Gabriel, suddenly apprehensive, looked at it for a moment. All of this covert moving in the shadows and keeping secrets made him very uneasy, but he decided that he was only a low link on a long chain of authority. Surely his superiors knew what they were doing. So he went back to his desk, found an envelope into which he slipped the chip, then folded it down and activated the seal. The paper melted into itself, seamless. It was a matter of a few minutes to make his way downdecks to the second ambassador's quarters. She was not there, so Gabriel slipped the envelope into the slot of her message box and went off to the party, wondering what it had all been about.

The partying down in the reconverted main briefing room was unusually wild, at least by shipboard standards. There was a lot more singing than usual—at least what passed for singing—and the jokes were louder than normal. Everything, movement, talk, even the eating and drinking, had a slight edge about it. The edge of the sword just sheathed, Gabriel thought. Relief. He was feeling it himself. He was a marine and liked to fight, but there was something about this particular fight that he would have found distasteful. *Maybe because I've become too familiar with the details.* One part of his mind immediately resolved not to get involved with the details any more. Another part denounced the first one as a coward. To shut them both up, he headed over toward the bar where he heard at least one familiar voice.

Big Mil from *Callirhoë* was standing there having a talk with Charles, who was in front of the bar for a change. Mil was looking very amused and slightly outraged, enough so that Gabriel suspected Charles had told Mil about the Squadron Special. Some of the spatball team began to appear as well when they saw Gabriel there. All had an eye to telling their team captain that he was a little too intense about what was supposed to be a sport.

"This is the second time you've rescheduled the meeting," Torine said, having arrived a little after coming off duty. "Can't we just sort this out when we do our normal five on five game at the weekend? Don't you think some of us have *other* concerns?"

"Of course he doesn't," Dietmar said, looming his blond self up from behind the bar. "In his own mind, we are all as conscientious and duty-struck as our little Gabe."

The others made various disgusting choking noises. Gabriel rolled his eyes. "All right, all right, all of you, it can wait until the weekend! But don't you want to beat the Starfies?"

"Depends on how the money goes," someone muttered.

From around them, applause started. The group looked up and saw Delvecchio standing in the doorway—a little hesitant, almost shy. She wore a loose wine-colored robe of simple cut rather than the elegant attire she favored during the delegations. She came in, and the applause got louder. The marines and Star Force people assembled all clapped and cheered for her as they would have for a victorious captain newly returned from a successful campaign.

She took it graciously then went to sit down. A Star Force officer brought her a drink, and the partying started to get back into its normal mode. Gabriel, though, looked at Delvecchio, looked at her face, and was not entirely sure he liked what he saw.

Somebody tapped Gabriel on the shoulder. He turned, surprised. It was just Mil. He held out his hand.

"What?"

"Here."

Confused, Gabriel put his hand out. Mil dropped something black into it.

"It's your luck thing," Gabriel said.

"I know. I want you to have it."

"Huh?"

"No, seriously, take it. I saw you were interested in it yesterday."

"I can't take that; it's yours! Mil, really, don't. Tomorrow you'll be sorry."

"No, I won't. Oh, go on! I'm getting tired of the thing. It keeps getting in my way, and I've almost lost it a couple times this month anyway. Doesn't matter." He grinned. "The news just came through. I'm being discharged in a month. Back to home sweet Damrak. Gonna go home and pile me up some cash. No, really, Gabriel! Take it. Every ounce I have to ship home is going to cost me big credits. I'm letting almost everything go but my discharge clothes and a sack to carry home my back pay."

"But—"

Mil just shook his head, closed Gabriel's hand around the black stone, grinned at him, and walked off. Gabriel looked after him, opened his mouth to say something, and then was surprised and distracted by the flush of heat coming from the little thing. The faint glow was coming from inside the stone again, pulsing gently, and as he opened his hand again he saw that the warmth kept time with the light.

"Isn't that pretty," said the little soft voice from off to one side. He looked up in surprise to see the ambassador standing beside him, looking curiously at what he held. "It's a life crystal of some kind, isn't it? I've heard of them, but I've never actually seen one." She poked it gently. He offered it to her, and Delvecchio took it and cupped it in her hand, looking at the way it echoed her pulse. "Where did you get it?"

"Another of the marines gave it to me. Mil, over there. The big red-headed guy."

Delvecchio nodded. "A few of the Verge worlds have these," the ambassador said. "It's some kind of slightly electroactive silicate, a natural 'chip,' apparently. There are beaches where you can pick them up by the thousands. Must be lovely at night."

"But it only glows when you hold it."

"So it does," Delvecchio said and glanced around, handing the stone back to Gabriel without really looking. "Well, isn't everyone having a good time?"

Except you, Gabriel thought, but kept his peace as regarded that, even though the ambassador herself was obviously making no particular attempt to look cheerful. "Yes, ma'am," Gabriel said.

She gave him a slightly sharp look. "You know," she said, "sometimes it's possible to be more observant than is good for you. Well, not that I haven't been tempting you to that blessed state as it is," she sighed.

"I still wish I knew *why* this has happened now," Delvecchio said, very softly.

"What?" Gabriel said after a moment. He was still recovering from the odd little episode with Mil.

"Collusion," she said. "I said they had been talking to each other."

"You didn't tell me that."

"I wanted to see if you might pick it up yourself."

Gabriel looked away in embarrassment.

"No," she said, very lightly touching his arm, "don't feel bad that you didn't. I wasn't too sure myself until someone very fortuitously brought me proof. It would have been a lucky guess, no more, until about an hour before we started. And there were other pieces of information that helped me." Her eyes glinted at him. "Anyway, you did very well today. Don't stop tomorrow when they have to go back."

"I won't."

"And as for me," Delvecchio said, "very early this morning we'll be returning for the signing ceremony." She sighed. "I'm sorry you won't be able to be there. It is likely to be too high-powered an event for me to indulge myself with your presence. Notice would be taken, which at the moment would be unwise. But after it's all over, I'll be coming back aboard to be ferried home again, and we'll have time to achieve closure on all this. I'll want to give you contact information for some people who'll be interested in, shall we say, this informal training period, when you get out of the service at last."

Gabriel shook his head, a little in disbelief, a little in gratitude. "Ma'am, you've gone to a lot of trouble for me."

"It's been mutual," Delvecchio said. "And people took this same kind of trouble for me once upon a time, when my career was new. This is my chance to pay the favor forward. I'll talk to you later in the week, then."

She walked away.

* * * * *

The rest of the party was not much different from the one that had preceded it. Gabriel left about midnight, headed for his quarters, stripped off, took a sober pill just in case—even though he had had very little to drink—and went to sleep.

Then there was thunder. The bombs falling, ending in a sudden flash of light. But they were not the usual bombs. Or rather, there was only one explosion instead of what had become almost a monotony of crashes and rumbles, and only one light. The screams he knew, but the voices were different, and the sound faded away almost immediately so that one irrationally calm and detached part of his mind said, air first, then vacuum: explosive decompression—

One voice he heard that he recognized, though not from Epsedra. As the vacuum swallowed it he thought how strange it was to hear that serene, sedate voice cry out at something that, for once, for just this once, had surprised it. But that was wrong, that was impossible. A growing feeling of how wrong all this was, the wrongness shifting swiftly into horror. It wasn't like this, it wasn't—! And the light was all wrong too. Not the re-peated flashes, but just one—fading, swiftly gone like the sound, with only the burning of ice and dying fire left. Gabriel fought for breath, but there was none, only ice in his lungs. Ice sheeting over burnt skin, ice clouding and clotting eyes that could no longer blink or see. He struggled, couldn't move, couldn't—

Gabriel flailed around among the bedclothes for a moment and found that there were no bombs, no ice, no fire, only some-one pounding furiously on his door. And no light. He waved for it, staggered to his feet, opened the door.

There were two other marines there, people whom he knew slightly—security staff with sidearms. He stared at them.

"What?"

"Get dressed, sir," one of them said, as if the word "sir" left a bad taste in his mouth, "and come with us."

As quickly as he could Gabriel threw on his uniform, the everyday duty fatigues rather than the now wrinkled dress blues that he had tossed across the desk. He was slightly annoyed and more than a little uneasy that the two security soldiers stood in the doorway watching him the entire time. When he was ready, they took him by the arms, one on each side, and marched him to the Bridge.

It was not a place where marines went all that often—even Gabriel, in his slightly privileged position, did not make a habit of going there. It was very much Star Force territory, and the two services were careful not to trespass on one another's preserves aboard ship. It was a long narrow room, heavily shielded, since it would be the first part of the ship that an enemy would fire at in combat. A dozen or more officers monitored various screens and holodisplays, occasionally entering commands by datapad or voice relay. Despite the buzz of activity, the entire Bridge was unusually silent, subdued. The few who spoke among themselves did so in whispers. In the middle of the long narrow corridor was the center seat. It was empty at the moment.

The straight slim shape in the Star Force uniform, standing in front of the center seat, turned to him. Elinke Dareyev looked down from the slight eminence on which the seat rested, gazing down at Gabriel with a face as still as that of a carved statue. She looked at him like someone who did not know him, had never known him. It was a stranger's face on the body of a friend.

"Lieutenant Connor," she said, "do you know why you have been brought here?"

"Captain, I-I don't know what you're—"

She turned to her first officer. "Play it," she said and turned away from Gabriel to look at the holographic display platform.

The air above the platform curdled into light, settled into a view of Phorcys, the white-streaked dun of the planet turning beneath. Nothing happened in that view for a while. Then a streak of silver dropped into it. The view zoomed in closer to the gleaming shape. It was a dull white rectangular box with a wedge-shaped cockpit attached to the front. One of the Star Force shuttles, heading for the planet's surface. Down and down it dropped, sliding into the haze of atmosphere—

—and then came the bloom of light, sudden and eye-hurting even against the new planetary day.

Glitter. Bright sparks suddenly spangled Phorcys's dun and

white face and tracked on past it, up into the starlit darkness of space past the planet's terminator. A tiny but disastrous meteor burned itself out in the cold, reducing itself slowly to tiny glittering points of shattered or molten metal.

Gabriel went first hot then deadly cold inside. A slight ringing started in his ears and his knees suddenly felt weak as the significance of who had been on the shuttle dawned on him.

"There were no survivors," said Captain Dareyev as the hologram faded. "The dead include Ambassador Lauren Delvecchio, Second Ambassador Areh Wuhain, diplomatic assistants Elle Masterton and Enrique Delrio; Marine Lieutenant Hal Quentin Rostrevor-Malone—"

Gabriel would have sunk into a crouch on the floor, if he could have, but his muscles would not obey him, not even as regarded something as simple and desirable as collapse. Even his weak knees seemed to have locked. Hal. What were you doing there? *Hal!* And the ambassador!

"You are known by the command of this ship to be affiliated with Concord Intelligence," said Elinke. "Various members of this ship's crew have confirmed that you were asking many questions regarding the shuttle crew and passenger dispositions this morning while such assignments were being made. Other members of the crew have confirmed seeing you delivering unspecified materials to personnel involved in the ongoing treaty negotiations."

"Captain," Gabriel said. Could she really be suggesting what he thought she was? "Please, let me explain! This is all a—"

"Lieutenant," said Captain Dareyev, "Second Lieutenant Lemke David was aboard that shuttle, performing as navigator."

Oh no, Gabriel thought, but his mouth was too dry to let the words out. His mind was suddenly blank. There was nothing to say. Again and again he saw the flash of light, the streak of white-hot fire descending into the atmosphere. Again he heard Delvecchio's surprised scream, then silence.

"Remove him to custody," Captain Dareyev said. "He is to be held on suspicion of murder, pending the conduct of the investigation. Phorcys has claimed trial rights since the crime occurred in their atmospheric space. Since law begins with atmosphere, we have ceded trial rights to them. You will be transferred there tomorrow," she said. "The investigation is already under way. The trial will begin within three days."

She turned her back, standing very straight, very still. Her normally fair complexion was deathly pale in the dim lights of the Bridge.

The guards, other marines, hustled Gabriel away with the firm hands of men who are furious with shame, shame of their own, wishing they could rub that shame out . . . and unable to.

Gabriel understood the feeling well enough, though from the inside.

* * * * *

The next few days shaded into one another in that strange kind of fugue experience that sometimes follows a great shock. Gabriel had undergone a similar experience after Epsedra: days in which time seemed either to slow down to an imperceptible crawl or in which it suddenly advanced in lumps that Gabriel couldn't remember. And there was no way to tell when a day started or ended. He had gone from the barely perceptible "day" of Concord shipboard life with its light- and dark-cycles, to a permanent day inside a bare, white-walled, windowless cell deep within the bowels of some Phorcyn law enforcement facility.

Even contemplating escape was no particular comfort, for Phorcys was a cold, cheerless world, and Duma, the capital city, exemplified this. The few buildings that Gabriel had seen during his escort from the landing shuttle to the holding facility were all crafted from rounded, brown stone and black steel, all of them designed to be easily accessible and to retain heat. The architects had not taken beauty into consideration. The entire city had seemed to hug the ground in an effort to avoid the stinging, freezing curtains of sleet that sheeted down from the leaden roof of the sky. The streets were straight, narrow, and in need of a serious cleaning. The few ash-colored trees that he had seen were squat, leafless, and altogether bedraggled.

With nothing but a comfortless pallet and a sanitary bowl for company, Gabriel sat or lay about for those first few hours and did his best not to think. Whenever he tried to work things out in his mind, thought became suddenly drowned in a repetition of that bright flash of light, the scream suddenly silenced forever, and the strangely beautiful sparkling motes of debris as they dispersed into the upper atmosphere. The only other image he could conjure was Elinke's accusing, hate-filled stare.

Everything within his cell was glarelessly but brilliantly lit, making restful sleep almost impossible. Food arrived in the cell fairly regularly, and Gabriel ate it more out of a sense of the need to keep himself nourished and alert than from any kind of enjoyment.

What also arrived fairly regularly were interrogators. Some of them were male and female officers from Star Force, some of them were marine, and some of them were Phorcyn. At first he had waited for them eagerly, looking forward to the chance to defend himself. Later, when he'd had some experience of how little any of them let him speak during any given session, Gabriel lost a lot of the eagerness. It was all so wearing, and they all asked the same questions over and over again. After the first day or so of giving the same answers over and over again, Gabriel started to realize that there was going to be no trial . . . at least not one with presumption of the defendant's innocence. The civilized practices of the Orion League, with its rigorous upholding of the citizen's rights, seemed a long way off now. He began to realize how much he could miss something that he had formerly taken for granted. Gabriel was on entirely the wrong side of the stellar nations for this case.

At least he had counsel, though he wasn't sure about what that was going to be worth. When he first saw the little man, all bundled up in the swathings of silk that were Phorcyn business wear, he was somewhat impressed. Dor Muhles looked smart, spoke well, and seemed like he might be of help. But Gabriel soon found that mostly what Muhles intended was to help

Gabriel plead guilty. He was convinced of Gabriel's guilt and considered his defense a waste of time and taxpayers' money, though he avoided saying so directly. There was apparently some ethical constraint against it.

At least Muhles brought word to Gabriel once a day of the evidence against him as the investigation unfolded. The merely circumstantial material was sifted through first while the forensic work was still going on. Gabriel began to understand with a sinking heart how so many details of his behavior, which with Delvecchio alive would have seemed minor and unimportant, now looked damning: Gabriel's presence on the shuttles, the questions he had been asking, the people he had been watching so carefully. It all looked very suspicious, if one were already convinced that Gabriel had been up to something. The worst of it was that not one of the investigators or interrogators seemed even slightly interested in the interchange with Jake, no matter how many times Gabriel reminded them that this was his Intelligence connection aboard ship. The captain had to know about him.

Then, around the fourth day of the investigation, the forensic data began to filter in, along with eyewitness testimony to support it. The second ambassador had made a note of the chip she received—though not of its contents—in her dispatch to the Grid-based diplomatic network. Her last dispatch, as it turned out. What its contents had been, the dispatch did not say, merely that it was in her possession. Meanwhile, sweeps of the area of space with ramscoop-based "sniffers" had picked up traces of clathrobutinol, a high-yield explosive used in some mining and manufacturing processes. Taggant analysis on the explosion remnants had begun at once, but at the moment the provenance of the explosive was of secondary importance. Much more important was the fact that when searches were conducted, small packets of the same explosive were found in all of *Falada*'s other shuttles, cleverly hidden near their drivecores in such a way as to pass for auxiliary fuel rods. Each of them was carrying a "receiver" chip similar to the message chip that the second ambassador had been carrying.

The implication was clear enough. With *all* the shuttles rigged to explode in the presence of the proper trigger at the proper height above atmosphere, it wouldn't matter which of them the second ambassador—and almost certainly, her superior—were on. The result would be the same. And the trigger was the chip that Jake had given to Gabriel, the chip that Gabriel in turn had given the second ambassador.

Gabriel had been duped into murdering them all. Hal, Lem, Delvecchio, all the others. Despair and rage warred within him, despair at the dawning certainty that he had little hope of proving his innocence, rage in knowing that the true perpetrators of the crime were still out there, still free, and very likely to get away with it.

It's not murder if I didn't mean it, said the space lawyer in the back of his brain. Manslaughter . . .

But manslaughter was bad enough, especially when the slaughtered included his best friend, a good acquaintance, and the ambassador. The question now remained whether the Phorcyns would kill him for it or simply confine him for the rest of his life.

"They gave you the benefit of the doubt," Muhles said as they were preparing to go to court the first day. "They let the investigation go for five days. Originally I thought they were going to stop at three."

"Nice of them," Gabriel said, as they and what seemed a squadron of guards came out of the barren, windowless corridor leading from his cell. After passing through a heavily guarded security gate, they proceeded into a sealed bay somewhere in the prison facility. Waiting for them was a sleek and windowless flitter. Two guards, Muhles, and Gabriel climbed into it, and its door slammed shut. Gabriel could not find another word to say all the way to court. The word *murderer* kept echoing in his brain, blotting other thought out.

The courtroom to which they were finally escorted was unusually beautiful, at least on the inside. High-ceilinged and airy, the room had smooth walls of pale stone and even a thick

rug or tapestry here or there. To Gabriel it seemed most beautiful because it had windows. Four tall, narrow windows faced
each other along the walls, each slightly concave and tapering to
a sharp point near the top. He could look out them and see daylight. The wrong color, he started to think, and then rejected the
thought. The light of any star falling through genuine atmosphere, however pale and cold, looked good to him now. Some
faint childhood memory of his father reading an old piece of
poetry came to Gabriel, a fragment of a line: . . . *maketh the light
of the sun to fall on the good and the evil alike* . . . He sat there,
looking at the thin watery sunlight of Phorcys coming down
through its blue-green sky, and had no particular doubts about in
which category the inhabitants of this courtroom had filed him.

The courtroom was crowded, mostly with Phorcyns. Besides
the various legal personnel that crowded the upper court, a
parade of journalists with their holographic imagers filled the
cushionless pews. They were surprisingly quiet, talking in whispered murmurs amongst themselves. A small group of Star Force
and marine legal officers sat stone-faced just in front of the
crowd of journalists. In front of them, a cordon of braided ropes
hanging between brass stands separated several rows of seats
behind both the prosecution and defense tables. Upon these seats
sat the witnesses who had been called to testify for the proceedings. Behind the prosecution sat a crowd of Star Force and
marine personnel, some of whom Gabriel knew, but who nevertheless refused to look at him directly. Sprinkled among them
were four or five Phorcyns whom Gabriel thought he recognized
as members of the delegation from the peace talks. The area set
aside for witnesses for the defense was empty.

Three judges looked down from the podium, a stark affair
with three steps built of stone of different colors—symbolic, his
defense counsel had told him, of guilt, innocence, and uncertainty, the last being the "initial state of the universe" according to
some old Phorcyn myth. That was about the most useful information that Gabriel received from his defense counsel that day.
Muhles seemed perfectly content to sit unquestioning and listen

as the Phorcyn prosecution counsel, a tall and handsome woman
with short, shaggy golden-red hair, called her witnesses one after
another. The forensic evidence was presented, and various eye-
witnesses were called. This included many marines—Mil and
others from the party, and numerous Star Force personnel who
had been assisting Hal with the work on the shuttles and the
piloting of them on the day of the final negotiations between
Phorcys and Ino. All, though some of them very unwillingly,
admitted that Gabriel had been on numerous shuttles during the
day, that he had had time alone in each of them over the course
of the day, and that he had seemed eager to get on all the shuttles
he could. Then excerpts of Gabriel's testimony to the interrogators were read, page after page. It seemed that Phorcyn law did
not allow the accused to make a statement until the end of the
trial, the rationale for this apparently was that no one could rebut
until all the evidence had been presented. His own testimony
seemed to Gabriel to have little effect. By the day's end it
seemed obvious even to Gabriel that he must have been up to
something. And right through everything, Muhles sat quietly and
just let it all unfold.

"When are you going to ask them something or cross-
question somebody?" Gabriel demanded on the way back to the
prison.

"Tomorrow, perhaps. It's not the right time yet."

"Yeah, well I'd like to get a second opinion on that. I want
another counsel. What do I do to start the process of getting
one?"

Muhles blinked at that, bemused. "You've already briefed
counsel. Taking the time to do that again would hold up the trial,
and the judges will never permit that. Besides, the court would
never approve the extra expense."

"What price justice," Gabriel muttered to himself and to the
white walls of his cell later that night. The cell where they kept
him was warm enough, even without the shapeless one-piece
coverall the prison officials had issued him—they had absolutely refused to allow him to keep his marine uniform, possibly

through fear of his committing suicide by swallowing the buttons. He was being fed well enough, though the food was desperately tasteless. He longed for one of the meatrolls that he had been so unconsciously stuffing in his face only a week ago. The cell lacked even the minimum entertainment or Grid connections that most enlightened worlds would have allowed a prisoner. Gabriel, though, suspected he was himself most likely the entertainment for someone, somewhere. The room was certainly monitored, though he couldn't see how. Somewhere, he thought, *people are betting on which way this trial will go. Maybe even some of my shipmates . . .*

The thought made Gabriel wince. He rolled over on the hard, white pallet-bed and stared at the bright ceiling. He had heard not a word from any marine aboard *Falada*, or anyone else for that matter, since he had been put on the shuttle and brought down here. Was he being held incommunicado? Or was it simply that no one aboard *Falada* wanted to have anything to do with him now?

Or that Elinke wouldn't *let* them? It was within a captain's powers to approve or deny communications offship to her crew if she felt there was "good and sufficient reason." And from her point of view, there was more than enough reason.

Oh, Lem. Poor Lem. And poor Elinke.

A shiver of sound came from down the hall.

Gabriel's head came up. The soundproofing was not as perfect in here as they thought it was. One set of footsteps he could clearly hear: the usual security guard who patrolled this wing of the facility. But there was also another sound. More footsteps? But the rhythm was strange, and the footfalls were very light.

The door opened. Gabriel stood up. That much courtesy at least he owed whoever might be turning up to see him. Well, not *owed,* but he was a marine, and some habits died hard.

The door slid open. The security guard was visible through it. He was looking peculiarly at Gabriel. After a moment, he stepped aside.

And a fraal came stepping into Gabriel's cell.

The experience was momentarily so bizarre that Gabriel was aware of simply standing there with his mouth hanging open like a mindless thing as he and the fraal looked at each other.

"I greet you, young human," said the fraal in a soft, breathy little voice.

"Greeting and honor to you as well," Gabriel said in passable fraal. His accent was probably hideous, but he and all his classmates had all the basic species greetings hammered endlessly into them in Academy, and no matter how bad his situation was at the moment, it was not so bad that he could not be polite.

She was tall for a fraal, perhaps about five foot four, and very slender-limbed and delicately built. The initial impression of frail age was strengthened somewhat by the look of the single fall of silky, silver-gilt hair that she wore in a tail hanging from the back of her head—it was starting to come in dark at the roots. Slightly incongruous was the fire-blue satin skin jumpsuit she was wearing, a fashion possibly better suited to a First World's capital world rather than a jail cell on a planet in the Verge. But it set off her pearly skin impressively and highlighted her large, pupilless sapphire blue eyes. The overall effect was of elegant old age. Gabriel half expected to smell lavender.

What is it with me and older women lately? Gabriel thought, in some bemusement, then instantly shied away from the thought. The memory of Delvecchio, of that proud fierce life snuffed out, and (however inadvertently) at *his* hands, was too tender to bear much scrutiny at the moment.

The fraal had been looking Gabriel up and down as well for that moment or so. Now she turned to the Phorcyn security guard and said, "Thank you. You may leave us."

"Can't leave you alone with him, madam," said the guard.

The fraal looked at him mildly. "What will we do together, he and I, when you are gone?" she said. "Tunnel our way out? Fly through the ceiling? You have scanned me inside and out and have taken my satchel. You have taken everything from *him* but his garment, which I much doubt he will remove to hang himself with while I am here. I think you might go off to the surveillance room and listen to our every word from there, where you can sit in comfort and have something hot to drink at the same time. Now depart, and return in ten minutes."

The guard blinked at that. He opened his mouth to object, and the fraal tilted her head and gave him a look that suggested to Gabriel (and perhaps to the guard) that this was in the nature of an intelligence test. After a moment the guard shrugged and went away, and the door slid shut.

"Will you sit down, lady?" Gabriel said, standing up rather belatedly.

"I will stand for the moment," said the fraal. "At my age, I do not sit down unless I intend to stay that way for some time."

"Uh, all right," Gabriel said and sat down again, not arguing the point, though there was something in the tone of her voice that made Gabriel think this fraal might be joking with him.

"I have come, young human," said the fraal, "with intent to do you a service, perhaps. If you will allow it."

Gabriel looked at her, shook his head. "I don't understand."

"Understanding is overrated," said the fraal mildly. "Much useful information is missed by those who seek answers too assiduously, at the expense of what else they might find along the road."

"If understanding is overrated, then I should be going way up in your esteem right now," said Gabriel. "But how can I help you?"

"The turn of speech is human-cultural," said the fraal. "I know what is more on your mind at the moment is that *you* are the one in need of help."

Gabriel had to grin ruefully at that. "It does seem likely that I am about to be convicted of either murder or manslaughter," he said.

"Are you guilty of either?" said the fraal.

Gabriel looked at her in shock, such shock that he could say nothing.

"Wise," she said. "Silence holds more than merely secrets. Young human, tell me: when you leave here, what will you do?"

"*Leave* here!" Gabriel shook his head. "At the rate things are going, I doubt I will, except for a larger facility of the same kind, for a long stay or a short one."

She tilted her head, looked at him thoughtfully. "You mean you have no further plans?"

"No, I—excuse me." Gabriel felt his manners beginning to wear a little thin. "What exactly do you *want* with me?"

"Another four minutes," said the fraal and blinked slowly, twice, a meditative gesture. After a moment, she said, "Tell me why you think you are here."

"Because a lot of people died," Gabriel said, wondering why he was even bothering to answer her questions. Who was she? Where did she come from, what did she want, what was she *doing* here? "And they think I did it."

"You have killed people before," said the fraal.

"In the line of duty," Gabriel said, "yes. I am a soldier. Soldiers often kill people." He paused for a moment and said, "Honored, I don't know a lot of the fraal language. But does that language distinguish between 'killing' and 'murder'?"

She looked at him for a few moments. "Yes," she said.

"I have murdered no one," Gabriel said.

She made the slow side-to-side rocking of the head that Gabriel knew from the fraal who had lived near his family on Bluefall meant "yes," or "I understand."

Footsteps outside.

"Ah," said the fraal.

The door opened. There was the security guard. "I thank you," the fraal said to him, and turning back to Gabriel, she made a little bow to him. Sitting, completely confused, he bowed back.

"Perhaps again," she said, and pursed her thin little lips in a smile. Then she went out the door.

The door closed.

Gabriel sat there, opened his mouth and closed it again, trying to make something—anything—of the past few minutes. Finally he gave up, trying to accept it as an interesting interval in what would otherwise have been a miserable evening.

All the same, when he finally got to sleep, the sleep was more uneasy even than it would have been, for the darkness that watched him in his dreams had an unnerving sense of sapphire blueness about it.

Chapter Six

HIS COUNSEL CAME to pick him up the next morning, and together they went back to the courtroom. Gabriel prepared himself for another long and uncomfortable day of little jabs of pain, one after another, as friends and acquaintances testified against him. What he had not been prepared for was the first name called after the court came back into session.

"Captain Elinke Dareyev."

She walked to the little separate platform where witnesses stood and stepped up, looking out at the judges and nowhere else.

"Captain Elinke Dareyev," said the prosecutor, stepping up to stand before her, "do you swear by your oaths of office to tell the truth?"

"I swear," Elinke said.

"Thank you," said the prosecutor. "You have heard the transcript of the testimony of the accused, concerning his claim that he was acting on the instructions of a fellow Intelligence officer, one Jacob Ricel."

"Yes," Elinke said.

"What is your reaction to that testimony?"

"That Jacob Ricel is not known to me as a Concord Intelligence operative," Elinke said.

Gabriel flushed hot and cold and hot again. His first thought was, But she *has* to have known. She's the captain. Is she lying because I killed Lem? Is this simply revenge?

No answer to that one, but the other possibility also had to be considered: that she was telling the truth. I knew I'd been duped.

I plainly haven't realized how thoroughly I've been duped.

But now his brain was spinning with questions. If *he* wasn't Intelligence, then how did he know that I was? Have I been "sold off" as a slightly used intelligence asset? And who "sold" me, and why, and why wasn't I told, and . . . and . . .

He pulled himself back to the moment. It was hard, nearly as hard as having to look at Elinke, standing there like a statue, elegant in black and silver, speaking levelly, looking at the judges but not at Gabriel. Never at him.

"You're quite sure of that?" the prosecutor said.

"Quite sure," Elinke said.

"Thank you, Captain." The prosecutor turned to glance at Muhles. Muhles made the graceful gesture with his hands that Gabriel was beginning to recognize as meaning "I have no questions," or in his case, "Who cares? Let's just get this over with."

Captain Dareyev stepped down and as she walked out of the courtroom, threw Gabriel one glance, just a single look, like a knife.

She was gone from the room, and it suddenly all became too much for Gabriel. He leaped up out of his seat and shouted at the judges, "I want another counsel! This is a farce, I'm being framed here—"

A restraining field immediately shimmered up around him, glued him in place, and slowly pushed him down onto his cold stone bench seat again. The centermost judge looked thoughtfully at Gabriel and said, "Expression of violent tendencies and sentiments in the court is not permitted. The prisoner will be returned to his cell and may listen to the proceedings from there."

And so it was done. Gabriel went back without even the dubious company of Muhles. He spent that afternoon listening to the testimony pile up against him. When the prosecution had finished, he heard Muhles's voice lifted to address the court for the first time (and the last, Gabriel suspected; as he understood the Phorcyn legal process, sentencing would follow shortly after). It would normally be the time when Gabriel would have been allowed to make a statement, and he was still swearing bitterly at himself for not having held onto his composure for just a few moments longer.

. . . when he stopped, and listened, uncomprehending at first, and then finding himself meshed in a rising tangle of emotion as immobilizing as the restraint field had been, but much more involved and painful. For Muhles was reading into the record the text of his Valor decoration, the record of what had happened at Epsedra.

"—while under extensive enemy bombardment, Second Lieutenant Connor led his men up out of the crevasse in Autun Glacier in which they had been trapped, set up a barrage of covering fire directed at the emplacement that had been mortaring them from the nearby mountainside, and maintained that covering fire while his squad escaped down into the strengthened position occupied by Five Squad and took refuge there. Second Lieutenant Connor might then have followed them to cover, but instead attacked upslope toward the emplacement with mass grenades, seriously damaging it and causing it to cease firing until several minutes before the arrival of the relieving troops under—"

Hearing it read in these circumstances, it was all as if it had happened to someone else. For the first time in Gabriel couldn't remember how long, there was no immediate memory of the fire, the ice, the dripping water and the gnawing cold. Only the words "—and was himself wounded, but continued to attack while—" suddenly brought something he had not felt for a while: the biting pain just under his right ribs. Strange how at the time it had felt more like a gas pain than anything else, and he had dismissed it at first. Only when Gabriel's buddies stared at him in horror and made him lie down did he realize what had happened to him. The shock had hit Gabriel badly, then, and a bizarre sense that to have half your liver blown out of you was somehow intrinsically *unfair.*

"—for courage under fire," said Muhles, and Gabriel was hard put, even now, not to snort. At the time, courage had had nothing to do with it. He was just doing what he had to, and it would not help him now.

—and then Muhles's voice again, pleading for clemency for a man once brave, once a good marine, but now clearly gone insane. Gabriel sat there shaking his head.

"Sentencing," said the judge, "will take place tomorrow." And someone rang the soft-toned bell that meant court was done for the day.

Gabriel sat nearly unmoving in the cell for much of the rest of that day, then lay awake all that night as might have been expected, but possibly not for the normal reasons. Strangely, slowly, those reasons began to change as the bright white hours went by. Once again Gabriel found himself wondering about the ambassador's question, possibly in order to avoid thinking about everything else. But the question still had no answer.

Why have they chosen to settle now?

The immediate answer suggested itself: collusion. *They got caught cooperating in an illegality, and maybe they knew they were about to get caught. So they rolled over, allowed themselves to be shepherded into this agreement . . . "forced" into it.*

But the ambassador's voice came through as sharply in Gabriel's mind as if she had still been alive to make the retort. *That might serve for analysis on the upper decks. I expect better of you.*

He bowed his head, unable to think of anything better . . . for the moment.

See what you've done to me? he said to her unquiet ghost. *Now I will never be able to let it be until I know the answer.*

No answer came.

And there were other questions that he would never let be, either.

Why are they doing this to me?

Either Elinke had told the truth, and Jake was *not* Intelligence, which meant someone had sold him up the river . . . or she was lying. And *she* was selling him up the river.

It's not fair. I only did what I was told.

But by whom?

He let out a small, bitter breath of laughter.

No matter. I did what I was told. And now I'm going to pay for it.

And not one of them will lift a finger to help me.

They were going to let Gabriel take the fall. There was no question of it. And he had nothing but his own stupidity to blame. *What made me think it was safe to give that information to Jake?* he thought. *He wasn't in my chain of command.*

Yeah, but we're supposed to cooperate.

When ordered. Yes. But you *got creative,* you *thought you knew better.* He scowled at the floor. *Too much time spent talking to ambassadors, too much time thinking that you were able to make this kind of decision.*

Wasted. You're sunk now.

It's all over.

He rolled over in the white light, buried his head in his arms, and wished the night of ice and fire had been his last one.

* * * * *

The next morning Muhles, looking subdued, came for him, and they went to the courtroom without speaking a word to one another. They took their seats along with the various court officers and the courtroom teams from Star Force and the Marines. After a few minutes, the judges came in and mounted the three-stepped podium.

"Now is the time of verdicts," said the centermost judge. "Let judgment in the case of the Republican Union of Phorcys versus Gabriel Connor be revealed."

Each of them reached inside his robes, a movement that for one wild moment made Gabriel think they were going for weapons. But instead they came out with short colored rods, and each laid a rod on the stone table.

"Guilty," said the center judge, laying down a white rod.

"Guilty but with mitigating circumstances," said the second, laying down a gray rod.

"Dissenting," said the third, pushing a white rod across the table before him, "not proven."

An intake of breath was heard in the room, and then silence, with some of the Star Force and marine officers looking at each other in confusion or anger.

"The dissension is noted," said the first judge. "A lack of majority opinion means that the case is hung. No resolution is achieved." He looked at Gabriel. "The prisoner is free to go, bearing his weight of guilt or innocence as best he may."

Free to go? How? Gabriel.

"We wish to appeal this decision!" the head of the Star Force courtroom team immediately said.

"You have no right of appeal on this world," said the center-most judge, looking like someone who was enjoying what was now happening. "When you granted us jurisdiction over this case, you accepted our right of disposition as binding and final. This man is free."

"But not innocent," said the Star Force officer, hanging onto his temper, but only just. "We require that he be remanded to Star Force custody to undergo court-martial for the criminal manslaughter of—"

"When this man chooses to leave our sovereignty," said the first judge, apparently enjoying this more and more, "you may seize him if you can. For the time being, this system remains a free system, not directly responsible to any stellar nation or defense force under Concord control. And for the time being, while we remain free—" there was a hint of bitterness there— "we will not extradite sentient beings on our territory to Concord forces without due process. Such due process, under our law, has been undertaken and completed. Gabriel Connor," the judge said to him, frowning, "you may go."

But *where* can I go? he thought. It did not seem like a good time to cry that question aloud, though, no matter how much he might feel like it. He stood up and waited, looking around for someone to give him a cue.

Muhles simply bowed to him and then walked off, leaving him there.

The shock of that was considerable. Gabriel could do nothing for the moment but stand and watch. Around him, with a slight hum and bustle that somehow sounded almost disappointed, the courtroom started to empty. Only one person approached him. A marine officer whom Gabriel did not know separated himself from his comrades and walked very stiffly to where Gabriel stood. He handed Gabriel an envelope, then moved hurriedly away from him.

Gabriel ran his finger down the envelope. It unsealed itself. He reached in, removed his ID, his banking card, and a chit to submit for the return of his personal effects. He then took out the other object in the envelope, a little datacart, and put his thumbnail to the quick-read slot. The words started to flow by across the surface of the cart. Dishonorable discharge . . . forfeiture of pay, forfeiture of pension, forfeiture of travel rights . . . And then another block of text. *On entry to any world or space of full Concord membership, having committed acts for which you have not yet been tried in Concord space, you are liable to seizure and trial on the charges of murder, criminal manslaughter, sabotage, terrorist acts, and transfer of secure or classified information to or from persons not qualified to handle that information, the penalties for which are as follows* . . .

So much for the idea of going home, Gabriel thought, and looked up. He was as good as an outlaw once he crossed out of the Verge. And meanwhile he had some money but not much, and it wouldn't last for long. When you were a marine, you had a family that took care of you, fed you, paid you enough to have something to spend on leave and something to put by, and eventually turned you loose into the rest of the world with skills that were worth something in the employment market. But now that "virtual" family was gone, and there was no hope of his own family being able to help him. If his father would even want to help a disgraced man, a cashiered marine, a possible murderer and traitor.

The courtroom was empty when he looked up again.

Slowly Gabriel walked out the way he had seen the others go: out into a large airy corridor, pillared with stark sleek pillars on both sides, and toward an arch that contained two tall, black steel doors. He pushed one of the doors open, stepped outside.

A cold wind bit into him. Flakes of stinging snow drifted by on it. Reaching down from the doorway was a flight of steps that led to a wide, bare street; small ground vehicles were shooting up and down it, going about their business. On the far side of the street was a broad field, a park perhaps, streaked with old dirty snow. Beyond the park were low-roofed, indistinct buildings stretching off to a murky horizon of cloud and low dun-colored mountains. Cloud was coming in. The lucent blue-green of the sky of days past, glimpsed through a window, was now returning to the leaden gray that he had seen on the day of his landing. A high whine pierced the air off to one side where there was a parking lot that seemed to be doing double duty as a landing pad. He brought his head up sharply and saw a small spacecraft, a midnight and silver Star Force shuttle, lifting into the air, up and away, up and into the grayness, out toward the clean dark of space. Leaving him behind.

It was as good a description of his situation as any. This was going to be his world from now on, a world in which he would have to learn to be alone.

"It's true what they say about marines then, that they're made of stone or steel?" said the soft breathy voice, very suddenly, from behind him. "How you can bear weather like this, otherwise, I cannot tell."

He turned around. The blue-eyed fraal was standing beside him, looking out at the increasingly murky day with distaste.

Gabriel could only stare at her for a few moments. Then, "What *do* you want with me?" he said. Right now, anyone who wanted anything to do with me must have a reason. And maybe not one I'd like.

"To trust me?" she said and then stopped. "No. There is no reason for that. You do not know me. Perhaps then . . ." She tilted her head a little. "I simply ask you to come with me," said the fraal.

Gabriel looked at her for a long time while the wind blew harder and the snow kept streaking by. At last he said the only thing he felt he had the strength left to say.

"Why?"

She looked at him. "Because there is nothing else left for you to do," she said.

Gabriel looked at her, shook his head. "I don't even know your name."

She reached out and took him by the hand. "Enda," she said as she led him off down the street, out of sight of the court building, out of earshot of the diminishing whine of the last shuttle leaving, and away from Elinke Dareyev, the marines, and all the rest of Gabriel's world.

*   *   *   *   *

The office was windowless. Upper Director UU563 56VIW Sander Ranulfsson could have had a real window if he'd wanted one, but there had been times when a view would have distracted him from what he should have been doing. That was not something he could afford at the moment. It would have suggested a desire to be seen exercising his power: a weakness, a self-indulgence, likely to prove provocative to the numerous spy and non-spy underlings who were watching his every move out here so closely. That kind of suggestion was something that, right now, UU563 56VIW did not need.

Later it would be useful and would put exactly the wrong idea into exactly the right heads. Then, in the fullness of time, heads would roll. But right now the suggestion of that particular weakness would be premature and would mean that some other bait would have to be substituted.

So for now Sander sat in the windowless office with its softly glowing white walls and glanced up at the far wall, momentarily showing a view down on the muddy, ruddy splendor of Hydrocus as it turned and shone in the light of the F2 sun Corrivale. The green secondary planet Grith climbed over the limb of its parent, making UU563 56VIW frown. Miserable mudball, Sander thought, eyeing those parts of Grith where he knew the trouble lay. It just went to show you how much could go wrong with even the purest vision of the future, how even the best laid plan could develop complications that no one had ever expected.

Like this last week, for example.

He glanced at the watch on his finger. Another hour until Himself called. Just as well. Sander very much wanted that extra time to get his thoughts in order. The day had been good for him so far, but *this* discussion was likely to be a little rugged, for matters had very much gotten out of hand.

UU563 56VIW stopped himself from even thinking the name. Not that anyone around here was a mindwalker, of course not. "Rogue" loose-mind talents like that tended not to go with the VoidCorp mindset, or if they turned up they were winnowed out, encapsulated, or the contractees' contracts terminated in short order. But some of the new software that was being mooted in the less crowded division meetings, lately—well, it made you think. Or rather it made you stop thinking and start watching very closely what for a long time had been the last bastion of privacy. Well, UU563 56VIW thought as he leaned back in his chair, privacy's an overrated state, anyway. If you're in private, how can anyone check on you to see that the work's getting done?

The Mudball rotated serenely "beneath" him, a virtual view from one of the Company's communications satellites. It had been a pleasure for VoidCorp to see to it, years back, that this system finally got a stable platform for the eyes it wanted to have looking down on Grith and other worlds in the Corrivale system. This also gave the Company its all-important "overhead." You could do very little in this world without adequate intelligence.

Sander began to sweat just slightly, since that was most likely what would be the main concern of this morning's conversation with Himself.

Now it was true that WX994 and so on was probably no more cruel to UU563 56VIW than he was to anyone else with lower digits, better than acceptable performance, and a slow but steady motion upward in the corporate scheme of things. He would normally be watching Sander closely, as Sander in turn watched closely the S's and T's milling around below him in this particular arena of operations. And maybe "arena" was a better word than usual in this context. The only difference from the games of ancient times was that there was no cheering crowd, or rather, no one whose function was specifically to be entertained by the furiously enacted antagonisms taking place in the board rooms or out "in the field." There was some entertainment in watching the mighty above you fall, of course, or the inept below you being torn out of comfortable positions by their own underlings, but you dared not laugh too hard. Between one breath and another, someone might decide to make an example of you, since after all we were all supposed to be one big happy corporate Family. It simply did not do to betray too much division or antagonism where outsiders might just possibly see. Pull together or be pulled apart separately. It was a fact of life, and in some cases, of death.

Sometimes the death did not happen, and that could prove troublesome unless you had a quick excuse ready. Sander had been working on this one for the past several days with the intention of putting old WX off his tail for a while. Others had not been watching their own tails closely enough and were about to pay the price.

He looked down again at Grith as it circled Hydrocus and shook his head. The place had been a nuisance to the company for a hundred and fifty years or so now, since burgeoning powers like the Hatire and the StarMech Collective turned up in the Corrivale system and tried to take its advantages right out from under the Company's nose. As if mere prior claim was good enough reason to exploit something! There had been a more rugged time, when the *CA 319* had come swaggering through the system, first of the great VoidCorp freebooters, and had bombed

the Hatire settlement at Diamond Point on Grith back into the
stone age which it had barely exited. Those were the days,
Sander thought rather longingly. When you could roam the
spaceways and take whatever you were strong enough to take.
Life had settled down a bit since then. With the Concord starting
to walk high and wide all over the Verge, with the great stardriver
Lighthouse likely to turn up at any moment full of Concord
Administrators with itchy gavels and Concord marines with
itchy trigger fingers, and with heavy cruisers of who knew which
stellar nation likely to pop in to see what they might extract from
the local yokels, well, the time of freebooting was done. Now
VoidCorp had to manage its corporate affairs in ways that did not
attract quite so much attention.

It was hard to do this, though, when so many others played
unfair, especially the company's own employees. For no sooner
had the first of the Concord ships, Monitor, come back to this
space a few years ago than the initial surveys found a bloody
great colony of goggly, eight-eyed sesheyans living on Grith.
Worse yet, they claimed that they'd always lived there, brought
there by the alien race whose ruins were still to be found scattered through the moon's jungles.

Now this was patently nonsense, because the Compact had
been negotiated with the sesheyans right back in 2274, and it said
perfectly clearly that in exchange for the benefits of technology
and the ability to leave their own planet, the sesheyans became
VoidCorp Employees in perpetuity. You could not ignore that
kind of language in a contract just because you were a mere
thousand light-years away! It was ridiculous even thinking about
it. But here was a colony of a hundred thousand sesheyans sitting
on Grith and defying their rightful employers. And the Concord
actually bought the ridiculous story about an alien transfer in the
deeps of time. It should have been obvious to anyone with even
the brains of a weren that the Grith-based sesheyans had somehow taken advantage of the chaos of the Second Galactic War to
elope from their contracts and set up here as scions of a fake
alien civilization. But Ari Madhra, the Concord Administrator

ruling on the case, bought into the myth and declared the colony independent, an "indigenous race." It obviously wasn't an independent or unbiased judgment. Sander often wondered who had gotten to her and for how much. Someone should have outbid them, ideally the Company. The knowledge that they had not done so made UU563 56VIW think the unthinkable, that someone at a very high level had messed up.

But now Sander sat looking down at Grith and keeping himself busy with the company's business here, which was to find a way to bring these runaway sesheyans back into the fold. The company's long-term strategy indicated perhaps fifty to a hundred years of slow pressure exerted both on Grith itself and on the planets trading with it, wherever they might be, as well as more concrete pressure on the Concord, on Administrators old and new, and on the higher reaches of power in all stellar nations to rescind the old decision or to "re-evaluate" the situation with an eye to making a new one. Slow and steady would win this race. The point was to do nothing too precipitate, to let the sesheyans toughing it out here learn that conditions were much better for their brothers who were in the blessed state of Employment and that attempting to make a go of it by themselves in this system where there was so much competition from other sources just wasn't going to work for them. Time would make the difference, and the Company had plenty of that.

In the meantime, Sander was allowed some leeway to implement short-term solutions that were estimated to have a better than two percent chance of increasing the speed of the fifty-to-a-hundred year plan without otherwise being of detriment to it. The Company saw no reasons why the non-Employee sesheyans on and near Grith shouldn't experience personally how difficult, how foolish it was, to attempt to take on a stellar nation single-handed, especially when they were in the wrong. The "free implementation" exercises also gave local Employees a chance to demonstrate their usefulness and resourcefulness to the Company.

Or for them to help shake themselves out if they're incompetent, UU563 56VIW thought. Well, that was one thing he definitely was not. This present business was sticky, but he would find his way through it and out the other side. And when he did—

"Sir," his assistant's voice came out of the air, "QI440 76RIC is waiting to speak to you."

"Let him wait a few minutes," Sander said, almost in a growl, as he settled himself back in his chair. "He's lucky I don't have him sent to Iphus with nothing but a pail and shovel and let him find his own beach chair."

His assistant broke carrier without saying anything further. Wise, for Sander was in a foul mood about QI140. It would have been such a subtle piece of work, UU563 56VIW thought bitterly. Subtlety was somewhat out of fashion at VoidCorp, mostly for lack of anyone in the place who would recognize it if it ran up and bit him or her in the knee while wearing a T-slick reading FIRST GALACTIC CONCORD SUBTLETY IDENTIFICATION CHALLENGE. That the work probably would not have been recognized for what it was for a year or two didn't bother Sander overly. He had enough other projects in hand to keep him busy, and then he could have been pleasantly "taken by surprise" by the praise and advancement that would inevitably have followed. Instead he would have to duck and cover and pretend that none of it had ever happened, but that was unavoidable. Nothing was worse than failure, except for the identification of failure and the publicizing of it afterwards.

And why shouldn't he have a little? UU563 56VIW thought furiously. "All right," he said to the air, "put him through."

A human shape appeared in the air before him, standing slightly off the floor. Sander resolved one more time to have the engineering people up to do something about the projector's focus. He was tired of having to compensate for it. The hologram hovered there looking somewhat uncertain. The figure was in shadow, probably in a private booth, and his face was indistinct because of the lighting and its combination with the cryptography programming.

"Well?" UU563 56VIW said. "What have you got to say for yourself?"

"The asset you were concerned about has been neutralized," said the man hanging in the air.

"Will you speak in language that other human beings can understand for a change?" Sander said. "For 'Corp's sake, what's all this hardware and software for if we can't communicate securely? What do you want to do, scribble it on a notepad and send it to me by some passing infotrader? Did you kill the asset, or what?"

"No," said the man, "but he's dead all the same."

"If you didn't kill him, who did?"

"He had an accident."

"I'm not going to tell you again, if you don't just say—"

"That's what I'm trying to tell you, he had an *accident*," the other man said, just briefly furious, or as much so as he dared to be. "Nothing prepared. Something to do with his e-suit."

"What?"

"His e-suit gave out on him. There was an accident aboard the ship, some kind of explosive decompression. He either suited up too fast and missed a gasket somewhere, or the e-suit just failed from lack of maintenance. They're still investigating it."

"Are they?" Sander said, sitting up a little straighter at that. "Any unusual attention to the matter from up above?"

"Nothing that our sources were able to identify."

"All right." Sander sat back. "Maybe it's for the best. Anyway, it might throw them off. It sure throws me off. Meanwhile, what about our others aboard? Any news from the lost lamb?"

"Not a word. He took his discharge chit and walked, apparently."

"Alone?"

"No. He's with a fraal."

"What fraal?"

"No one knows. They're trying to work up some intelligence now."

Sander sat tight-lipped for the moment and considered the likelihood that intelligence was the one thing these people would never work up, no matter how much information they managed to find. "What's he doing? He leave the system yet?"

"Just sitting there at the moment. Probably in shock, they say."

"Huh. He would've been a lot more shocked if he'd kept going the way he was going," Sander said. "No matter. I want to make sure that he stays well away from you know where. In particular, I want to know the minute he leaves the system. One move toward Corrivale and I want to know all about it. It might seem harmless, might be just a transit, but I don't want anyone second-guessing me until he actually leaves Corrivale system for somewhere else. And even then I want him tagged and trailed for a good long time, him and his fraal both. Who *is* that fraal? Has someone sent him help we don't know about?"

"They're working on it."

Sander wanted to growl again, but restrained himself. "There's only one other thing I want from you, and probably I'm not going to get it. Did he actually find out anything useful for us?"

"One thing. Just one. The last thing we sent him for. The first two were no-shows."

"One out of three," Sander said reflectively. "Not that bad for a throwaway, I guess. Did he make anything of it? Did he say anything to anyone?"

"Not that we were able to discover. We got the trial transcripts at the same time everyone else did. Nothing in them made any sense in terms of—"

"Don't say it," said UU563 56VIW hurriedly. "That far, not even I trust the encryption. Well, good. Make sure the poor fool gets out of the system and stays out. These minimal assets," Sander said, "you have to wonder why we acquire them. Still, when the recruitment's stale, or as a throwaway . . ." He shrugged. "All right. Go on, go back to work. Where are they posting you next?"

"The scuttlebutt says Aegis. We have to go pick up some other hotshot Administrator."

"Yeah, well, be more careful with this one." UU563 56VIW

chuckled, more to himself than to the other, and broke the connection.

He leaned back again and sighed. It was very sad in its own way. Subtlety, wearing its T-slick and doing a little dance, was fast retreating into the wilderness. Oh well. Six months' work, what's that? *I'll think of something else. And not depend on* them *this time.*

Meanwhile . . . He waved his hand over the desk to see what it would list and said to the air, "Anything new for me?"

"Those files you asked for."

"All right, bring them in. And get QI140's pay file sorted out too. I suppose he's due the usual pittance for that report."

A few seconds later his assistant came in with a pile of carts and a much smaller one, a 3D crystal "chip" of the kind that the Company used for nondenominational payoffs. UU563 56VIW picked the chip up, stuck his thumbnail in it, read out the past payment codes and amounts and keyed one new one in. Then he tossed the chip back at the assistant.

"You still here?" he said, for now that the moderately enjoyable duty had been taken care of, already the tension was beginning to build toward the one that would not be so enjoyable. "Don't just stand there vaguing out on me like some damned Inseer."

His assistant looked shocked. Sander let her. Officially these days VoidCorp denied the very existence of the treacherous rogue division that had declared its independence and somehow even managed to get itself instated as a stellar nation. After the colossal crime of crashing the VoidCorp main Grids and practically—Sander stopped himself. Too much thinking about what *might* have happened in that terrible hour was potentially dangerous, possibly even heretical. Never mind. The Corporation had survived, but their enemy still lurked out in the dark of space, busying itself with cyberwarfare that was still unfinished, leaping from ambush every now and then to foil some important VoidCorp strategy, or even to do something as petty as kill an executive or two. Their pettiness itself betrayed them. They had no grasp of the importance of the great Company goal, but instead went wittering off about independence and the search for ultimate knowledge and other mystical blather. It was laughable. They didn't have the vaguest idea of what real freedom was. "Service is perfect freedom," one of the ancient sages had said. No matter that he hadn't worked for the Company and probably hadn't even known what he meant. He was right.

"Never mind that," UU563 56VIW said. "Just go sort out QI140's payoff account, and then don't disturb me for an hour."

She went, ducking deferentially to him as she closed the door.

Sander sighed and sat back again, looking up just briefly at the Mudball and the green jewel sailing around it. A slow enough orbit, once every fourteen days. Sometimes the thought occurred to him that one could interfere with that orbit. There were newish technologies that one might exploit. Of course, there was the problem of the Hatire who had been recolonizing the planet. Busybodies. What business had the StarMechs selling them that colonization contract in the first place, anyway? And the various other rogue humans scattered around the place. No. It was an inelegant solution. Better not to waste the time thinking about it.

But what a mess local space and further space both had become. All the stellar nations interleaving and interweaving, all sticking little tendrils of influence into one another's territory. It was all very disorganized and untidy. They needed someone to tidy it up for them.

If the Company got its way, it would eventually see to that tidying, no matter what the other nations might have to say about it. That day would be worth waiting for.

Sander sighed and picked up the other reports, knowing what he would see there before he even looked, the monthly output numbers for Iphus Mining Division and the usual report from RC094 29KIN Faren Reaves. Like its author, the report was unimaginative stuff but reliable. Nothing there was of real interest. But right now Sander's—

His assistant said, out of the air, "WX994 02BIN to speak to you, sir."

Damn! He wasn't supposed to call for another— But there he was, in all his theoretical glory, sitting behind his desk. The hologram wavered a little above the floor, but WX994 02BIN was unconcerned if he noticed it. UU563 56VIW stood up hurriedly. "Sir, I—"

"Am not ready, as usual. I could have told you that." If there was one thing Sander hated about the man, it was his big bluff air of geniality. Behind it, inside that huge bear-like body, was a heart of meteoric iron, well coated with ice. "You know what I want to talk to you about."

"The Thalaassa incident, sir. Yes. The first thing that needs to be dealt with is—"

"Don't get the idea that you're handling this meeting," said old WX, grinning, and the mustache positively bristled with amusement. "What you need to know first is that I am not pleased. The second ambassador was not to have been targeted for any purpose. There were projects in which her hand would later have been valuable."

Specifically because she wasn't as smart as her boss, UU563 56VIW thought. "Sir, that is one of the aspects of the operation that regrettably did go out of control. Unfortunately no one could have predicted that the marine whom the Ambassador had been seeing privately would have—"

"And about him," said old WX, frowning. "Was he possibly working as a double? Genuinely Diplomatic or Concord Security, I mean, as well as an acquired asset?"

"No evidence of that, sir. If we look at the—"

"We haven't looked at half the things we should have," said WX, "and one possibility that disturbs me is that the Concord Diplomatic Service's Intelligence people, or just normal Intel, have somehow undermined our assets in that area. That would be a tragic result, both for the undermined and for you. Ombe would come down on you like a ton of the rock of your choice."

UU563 56VIW swallowed. "Ombe" was the VoidCorp Sector Security Chief QN105 74MAC, a fierce-tempered and small-minded woman who took her job more seriously than anything in the world and had a list of "enemies," or Employees whom she considered failures, as long as a weren's arm. Her enemies tended not to prosper.

"I don't see how that could possibly be, sir," said UU563 56VIW as carefully as he could. Almost certainly this interview was being taped, and if it later proved that he had been wrong . . . "If you look at the results, they suggest that such undermining would have meant the ambassador being tipped off as to—"

"If you look at the results," WX said, his voice getting a little louder, but not unsociably so, "you would notice that the leaders of Phorcys and Ino signed a treaty. Signed their names to it in private. They *had* to sign their names to it in public because the third ambassador, who *would* have been killed if I had my druthers, and the wretched captain of *Falada* held their noses to it and insisted that they go through with the public ceremony on time, despite trying to stall 'in memory of the architect of the peace, blah blah blah.' Now we have useful people dead, useless people alive, and a treaty that, even though it isn't quite a peace treaty, is so bloody tightly worded that these two planets can no longer carry on with their previous business, which I desperately hope I do not have to spell out to you at this late date." WX smiled, a genial expression which ran ice down Sander's spine. "This is *not* a good situation, UU563 56VIW, not in the slightest. Had the ambassador not gained the intelligence jump on us that she did, the treaty would never have been signed. Soon enough matters would have relapsed to the comfortable *status quo* that we have been promoting for lo, these many years. I want to find out how she knew what she knew. I want anyone who seems to have information about how she knew what she knew found, brought in as subtly or unsubtly as you like, and emptied of everything that may be of use to us. I want that done now. Soon. Maybe not before you get up to pee, but nearly that soon. And then I want recommendations on how to get the Phorcys and Ino situation back to the way it was. Fortunately, those idiots hate each other's guts so thoroughly that it shouldn't take much time to think of something. Others are thinking of things too. Let's see

if what you come up with is better." That smile seemed to be suggesting that it had better be. "Attention attracted to them, once
again, will divert it from other things better ignored. How long
will it take you to get a report of present intelligence status on
my desk?"

"Just a few minutes, sir."

"Do it. I'll speak to you again this time tomorrow."

And WX was gone.

Sander Ranulfsson, UU563 56VIW, sat down in his chair and
put his head in his hands.

As subtly or unsubtly as you like, the man had said. They
must have that new software in place, at least in the beta stages.

Whether they did or not, it was *not* a good day any more.

Chapter Seven

THE BAR WAS a dive. There was no kinder word for it. The grimy, crowded room had little light and was further dimmed by the various smokes and fumes emanating from the tables and booths. It was the kind of place into which no self-respecting marine would ever have gone unless it was to help a buddy win a fight. From the booth where they were sitting, Gabriel looked around at the dim, ugly little restaurant-cum-bar with its tacky, dingy furnishings—suspended lamps with fringe hanging down, moving "modern art" wall images that had ceased to be modern two decades ago—and thought, not for the first time, that he had come a long way down from his former exalted place in the world. For the truth was that, right now, even *this* looked good to him.

"You have not touched your soup," said Enda.

Gabriel looked up at Enda with what was fast becoming the usual look: bemusement. " 'Swill' would be more like it," he said.

"That may be so," she said, "but we lost the right to treat it like swill when we paid for it. If you do not eat it, I must."

"I wouldn't put that much strain on a new friendship," Gabriel said as he picked up the spoon again.

On the day that his trial ended, the day Enda had come for him the second time, she made no great demands on him. She merely walked him out into Duma, the brown-looking capital city of Phorcys, and there engaged a tiny two-room suite for the night. Calling the place a "suite" had been nearly as much an act of hyperbole as calling the contents "rooms." There was just enough room to lie down in each of them, with a two meter line

of shelf space above the pallet that nearly filled each "room."
Sanitary facilities were down the hall in which the suites were
stacked. These so-called facilities were exceptionally minimal,
the lights being metered as rigorously as the water. At the time
Gabriel noticed little of this. He had thrown himself down on the
pallet with the unthinking gratitude for freedom of someone
whose most recent sleeps have been in a jail cell, and there he
lost the next twenty or so hours of his life, going blissfully and
instantly unconscious.

His awakening under a ceiling only two feet from his nose
was less than rapturous. There had been that magical moment
when everything was dark and he was still befuddled with sleep.
For a moment only, he actually believed that he was back in his
cabin on *Falada*. It took only a second's worth of light (brought
on when he reached out to feel for the edge of his bunk) to show
him reality, and it was bitter. Not even Enda's gentle voice was
able to do much for his mood on that first morning, or rather
afternoon, of freedom.

It had been Enda's opinion that human physiology was briefly
at fault—specifically, blood sugar—and she had brought him
down a grimy, garbage-strewn street, under yet another dim,
cloud-curdled sky to a banged-up wooden door set in an old
blank stone wall. Inside was the Dive.

The entry was itself uncomfortable enough. Even the gray
day outside was bright compared to this place. It took a good
few seconds for Gabriel to get his vision working. He must
have looked like a gaping hick, standing there blinking into the
darkness for some seconds. When his eyes were working again,
he could see that everyone in the place—maybe eight people,
scattered around the ill-lit booths and curtained-off tables—
was staring at him. None of the looks were friendly, and to tell
the truth, Gabriel would not have wanted any of them to be
friendly, to judge from the general looks of the people. They
were unkempt and ill-favored, and they sat hunched over their
food or drinks like men and women who thought that, as a
general rule, strangers should be shot or—better yet—knifed,

since lanth cells and bullets cost money.

Enda paid them no mind at all but led Gabriel over to an unoccupied booth and made him sit down. It was hard. Gabriel wanted to grab a scrub brush and attend to the table, the benches on either side, and some square meters of the floor before actually coming in contact with them.

"Not now," Enda hissed at him, good-humoredly enough, and Gabriel sat, though he kept shifting and twitching in the seat.

After a little while the food came, and Gabriel had to try to do something about it, though mostly he wished what he had done was to order just bread and kalwine, as Enda had. The soup was highly suspect to the scrupulous palate of a marine—*a former marine*, he kept telling himself, while still finding it somehow impossible to believe—and the atmosphere got worse, not better, as the other habitués of the Dive got used to his and Enda's presence there enough to begin ignoring it. The group over at one of the curtained corner tables in particular got noisily jocular—at Gabriel's expense, he thought, but their dialect was so thick that it was had to tell for certain. Then they got obscene, and finally they began to sing, which to Gabriel's eventual astonishment turned out to be even worse than the obscenity. It wasn't that the song itself was rude. It was innocuous enough—but not one of the entities present had the faintest idea what key they were in.

> "Now my newfound friends
> My money spends
> Almost as fast as winkin',
> But when I make
> To clear the slate,
> The landlord says, 'Keep drinkin'! '
> Oh, Lord above,
> Send down a dove
> With beak as sharp as razors
> To cut the throats
> Of them there blokes
> What sells bad beer to spacers—"

It was a universal sentiment, or at least one that Gabriel had heard before on other planets, in other company, and sung in recognizable keys. The poignancy of the contrast between then and now made his eyes sting. He worked to master himself, intent that whatever else he might do with this soup, he would not cry in it.

Gabriel glanced up at the fraal sitting across from him, calmly crumbling her bread into her plate, and wondered for about the thousandth time what to make of her. She had come from nowhere, given him clothes and guidance, and most bizarrely of all, hope. Even a grain of that was welcome at the moment. Enda was unquestionably a godsend. But questions were a matter very much on Gabriel's mind at the moment, and he was unable to simply let any recent occurrence, no matter which god was involved, go uninvestigated. He had been too trusting about letting other matters of late go that way. As a result, his life was changed out of all recognition. He was determined not to let it happen again.

Enda was at least more somberly dressed than she had been on that first meeting, now in a dark coverall that favored the prison clothes Gabriel had been so glad to get rid of after the "suite." But there was no hiding the blue radiance of those eyes, and it was surely an illusion brought on by her natural paleness that made her seem to glow slightly in the darkness of the Dive. Gabriel was perfectly aware of the glances being thrown at Enda from some of those booths. Here and there a curtain would twitch back, eyes would gaze briefly out into the darkness, then the curtain would fall again. Enda went on with her eating, delicate and abstracted, and paid the watchers no mind—or at least, she seemed not to. She had already often given Gabriel the impression that she was watching everything but making an art of seeming not to.

Of course there was always a slight sense of mystery about any fraal, even though they were the alien species that humans had known the longest. Partly this had to do with their innate sense of privacy. They had long since lost their homeworld and many of the talents and treasures associated with it, but they did not generally trumpet the fact or bewail their fate. They got on with life as they found it, which included humans and other species, and they handled it in the ways that best suited them.

Gabriel knew that by and large there were two kinds of fraal, Wanderers and Builders. The former came of stock that, after leaving the fraal homeworld long ago, preferred to hold to the traveling lifestyle, moving from system to system in their city ships and avoiding too much contact (or, humans whispered, "contamination") with other species. The Builders, even before they came across human beings, were more committed to establishing colonies on planets. After their first official contacts with humans in the 22nd century, Builder-sourced fraal began to intermingle and intersettle freely with human beings. Gabriel often wondered whether any other of the known sentient species could have pulled off this coup so successfully, and often enough he doubted it. The fraal, however, had possessed an advantage. Earlier contact with their kind, in the centuries before human space travel, had made its mark on numerous human societies in terms of myths and images that had come to haunt the "racial psyche" of mankind. The recurring tales of slight, pale, slender people, human but not quite human, longer-lived than human beings and somehow involved with them—for good or ill—had been there for a long time, changing over centuries but never quite going away. When the fraal finally revealed themselves and their ancient settlements on Mars, the response was not the widespread xenophobia that might have been expected, but a kind of bemused fascination, as if the human race was saying to itself, Oh, it's only *them*. There were those, more paranoid than others, who had seen some kind of elaborate plot behind this, who were sure that the fraal had planted the stories or made those earlier clandestine visits to Earth as part of some obscure master plan having to do with domination or invasion. Later history made nonsense of this, of course, but there were still some who found the fraal, especially the Wanderers, too oblique for their liking.

Gabriel had no problem with fraal. There had been many

communities of them on Bluefall and later on his other home.
There had been some on *Falada* as well, though not as part of her
marine complement: a few Star Force officers, one of them
(Gabriel thought) a pilot who did shuttle work.

The thought came before he could stop it, *Not one of those I
killed, thank everything.* He winced, though. Suddenly there
were whole great parts of his mind into which he could not venture without pain. Almost everything to do with being a marine,
for example. The matter of his lost friends, and that last look of
Elinke's, that had outstabbed any knife—

"Brooding at the soup will probably make it no warmer,"
Enda said mildly. "I believe entropy runs the other way."

"Sorry," Gabriel said. "Enda . . ."

"You will still be asking questions," she said, somewhat
resignedly, "and under the present circumstances, indeed I
understand why. But there are differences between the ways our
two species order their priorities, despite our many likenesses.
So I will probably not be able to satisfy you as to my motivations
for a long time."

Gabriel sighed. "I don't want to seem ungrateful or suspicious, but you picked me up in a situation where any sane person
would have dropped me."

"Perhaps that is why I picked you up," Enda said, crumbling
a bit more of her loaf on the plate. "I do not care for littering."

She looked up just in time to catch what must have been a
fairly annoyed looked from Gabriel. He regretted it instantly. "A
resource thrown away," Enda said, as if she hadn't seen the look,
"is in danger of being lost forever, unless it is salvaged quickly.
I know many humans find altruism difficult to understand, but
for some of us it is a lifestyle, one we count ourselves fortunate
to be able to enjoy."

She nibbled at a bit of the crumbled bread and said after a
moment, "It is an error to say too much too soon, but this you
will find out soon enough if our association continues. I too have
known what it can be to be cast out of the society in which one
has lived comfortably for many years. I Wandered for a long

time. Eventually I decided to stop—a decision that sufficiently annoyed some of those with whom my path had lain so that they hastened the process considerably. I go my own way now, but the settled life is not for me."

She cocked an eye at him, an amused look. Gabriel's face must have been showing a great deal of what he was thinking, mostly along the lines of *'If' our association continues?* Peculiar as it was, uncomfortable as it had made and still was making him, he did not want to lose it.

"Uh," Gabriel said, "I don't think I'm in any position to make any judgments about anyone else's lifestyles at the moment."

"That is well," said Enda slowly, and took a long drink of her wine, "which, I suppose, leaves us with the same question we had earlier. What will you do?"

By itself that was a question that had given Gabriel enough to think about. A marine didn't have to do much thinking about it—you went where you were sent, and it wasn't your business why you were going where you were going or which stellar nation controlled the territory. That was your superior officers' business. Suddenly, though, all of space was spread out in front of Gabriel. And he didn't have a clue where to go.

Thirteen stellar nations inside the Ring. Well, twelve actually. The Galactic Concord and its neutralities were shut to Gabriel, at least if he wanted to remain free. But elsewhere lay wide choice, depending on how you defined personal freedom and the ways it was implemented. There was the unbridled profiteering capitalism of the Austrin-Ontis worlds, the robotic-oriented hedonism of the StarMech Collective, Insight's freewheeling information-based mysticism, the Nariac workers' "paradise," the fierce pride of the Thuldan Empire, the ancient wealth and history of the Union of Sol, the competitive corporate wealth and ferocity of VoidCorp, the Orlamu Theocracy's hungry search for the knowledge that constituted the key to its universe. Theoretically, Gabriel might find a spot in any of them, though again he would have to consider carefully how to avoid running afoul of the Concord's ban.

And outside the Ring was always "Open Space," the huge areas that during the Second Galactic War were largely devastated—at least in the direction "toward" the other stellar nations. Out beyond the spaces of shattered worlds rendered unlivable by bioweapons, who knew what possibilities lay? Perhaps it was on purpose that the Concord had made no attempt to do much mapping that way. Perhaps it was a tacit admission that though the Galactic Concord had designated this the last area of human territory, their writ could not truly run so far. The vast distances from the rest of civilization made Open Space, for the moment, effectively ungovernable. Maybe the free spirits of the galaxy who wanted nothing to do with any other races might move out that way, but Gabriel was too gregarious to seek that kind of life, and anyway, it went against the grain in other ways. To find out what had been done to him, he must not run away from the populated spaces but toward them.

And do what?

Gabriel was half ashamed of his own paralysis. *I've been defining myself as a marine for so long that I've forgotten that there's anything else to be. Yet what else am I trained for?*

To fight, yes. Of course. But there are other ways to fight.

"I'm e-suit trained," Gabriel said finally, "to what would be an unusually high level of competence around here. That suggests a couple of possibilities: construction and mining."

"For which you would either have to contract yourself out," Enda said, "or buy your own ship."

Gabriel laughed hollowly at that prospect. "Though it could not merely be a system ship," said Enda. "Or so I would think. Even here, there is only so much belt work to be done and not that many large construction projects. Once work ran out, you would have to look elsewhere, and without a stardrive of your own you would be reduced to hitching a ride with whatever driveship comes along. If, however, one came by whose master thought it would be a good idea to make a little extra money by turning you over to the Concord." She shrugged one hand, a dry little gesture that Gabriel was learning to recognize as one of her favorites. "Unless of course you did genuinely wish to stay in this system, to 'settle' here."

"Not the slightest chance," Gabriel answered, looking out the dive's one window into the evening. Snow was blowing by more emphatically on that stinging wind, now almost invisible in the growing dusk. He could still hear the wind, though, and it was not friendly. Space or the controlled environment of a ship—even if there was hard vacuum just centimeters away—now seemed infinitely preferable.

"At the same time, I would have thought you would have preferred elsewhere," Enda remarked, "to this, the scene of your—shall we say?—fall from grace. No matter. We may have to stay here a little while regardless, for driveships do not fall from the sky merely for the wishing, much less ships which will actually perform the function that you have in mind. Time will be needed for customizing, ordering equipment, installing it. . . ."

And that was another thing. Gabriel shook his head, for plainly she had not gotten the message earlier. "Enda," he said, "there's one big problem with this. I don't have anything like the kind of money even for a *good* system ship. I can afford some kind of banger, maybe, but not a decent one, and certainly not a driver. It's not the best idea, just a dream. The only thing I'm going to be able to do is hire myself on to somebody."

"As what?" Enda asked. Gabriel looked at her mournfully. "Some kind of glorified security guard? 'Muscle,' I believe is one of the commoner usages. I suggest, Gabriel, that you would be wasted in this role."

"Wasted maybe," Gabriel said, "but employed."

Enda made a graceful gesture of negation. "Not in a fraal's lifetime of such employment would you make enough to buy a driveship. And I speak from experience, for I have functioned as 'muscle' in my time, though the way fraal reckon such is a little different from the way such jobs function in the human world." She bowed her head "no" in a thoughtful way. "Other options will have to be examined. Meanwhile, there is a fairly active used ship market in this system, and the lending institutions are occasionally sympathetic to the right kind of inducement."

Gabriel suspected that the inducement in question would also involve interest rates that would cripple anything sentient. "Enda, really, you don't get it. I *can't*—"

"Who said that yours would be the only capital to be called upon here?" she asked. As Gabriel opened his mouth, she lifted a finger. He went quiet. "Now," she said, "hearken. I am nearly three hundred years old, and I have seen little enough of this galaxy in my time. I am getting on in years—"

"You don't look a day over two hundred," Gabriel said.

She gave him a fraal's demure smile, which drew the upper lip down over the lower and made her look like an ineluctably wise five-year-old for just a flash. "Gallantry," she said, "the last refuge of the incurably latent. Gabriel, I am of a mind to see the worlds, or some more of them, anyway, without the vagaries of public transport interfering with my schedule. Not that I have a schedule. Occasionally in the past I have considered buying a small driveship, but either finances were unsupportive or I did not desire to hamper myself with the company of those I did not trust. Now I have both the time and the inclination, and I do not find the financial climate unsupportive. And there is someone else involved with whom to share the ship, someone I trust."

The incurably latent? Gabriel stared at her and shook his head. Never mind— "Why would you trust me?"

She blinked at him. "Because you have nothing left to lose," she said.

Over in the corner, the singing had reached a crescendo from which Gabriel thought it could not possibly increase. He shortly found himself wrong.

> "Now my suit's in pawn,
> And creds all gone,
> And head's too sore for shakin';
> I'll take my chip,
> Get back on ship,

And blast when dawn is breakin'.
Oh, Lord above, send down a dove—"

Gabriel let out just a breath or so of laughter, considering that the song must go back to the Solar Union, to judge by the reference to "creds" instead of Concord dollars. Enda shook her own head, a gesture identical among humans and fraal.

"Just what *is* a dove, Gabriel?"

In his mind he heard the ambassador say, *Some kind of bug that gets in bed with you*, and he winced again. "It's a bird," he replied. "Some kind of predator, I think, to go by the bit about the beak being like a razor."

"So," Enda said after a moment. "A ship. Not freight, you think?"

Gabriel was tempted, but he shook his head. "Doesn't seem smart. Not at the physical level, even. A marginal system like this probably already has most of the freight traffic it can handle. Not the high-margin stuff like infotrading, either. Too many things that could go wrong for a company just starting out."

She nodded, pushing her plate away. "One engine breakdown leaves you with a cargo of stale data and a pile of lawsuits. Not to mention the cost of the encryption software and the purchase price of the first load and the fact that we cannot go near Concord space." She sighed as the singing dissolved into a welter of coughs, hiccups, and at last into silence.

"There's one thing we could certainly do if we had to stay in this system for a while," Gabriel said, looking out into the dusk. The snow had now vanished from sight, but he could still hear it ticking faintly against the window. "Mining."

Enda looked slightly surprised, glancing around her. "I would not have thought you would so quickly start to enjoy this kind of environment," she said. "Typical enough of the miners' bars you will find in the Belt. Many will be even less congenial."

Gabriel shook his head. "I don't care for it in the slightest," he said. "But it's a way to make steady money, if slow, and it will pay for other things."

"Grid access?" Enda asked softly.

He looked up sharply at that.

"Doubtless you could conduct those researches easily enough on-planet," Enda said. "No one needs a ship for such. But at the same time, were I in your position, I would always wonder whether someone was looking over my shoulder—someone with the Concord in mind, for good or ill." She looked at him with an expression of which Gabriel could make little. "There will have been people in this system who will have noticed your connection to the old ambassador, and who would wonder what further use could be made of you in one way or another. I am sure you would prefer not to be stuck here waiting for your door to be broken down by one authority or another."

"Space would be safer," Gabriel said as softly, "and as you say, more private."

"Also," Enda added, "you will be wanting to do some investigation of your own."

Gabriel looked at her, trying to find out what was going on in her head, but there was no point in it—fraal could be astonishingly inscrutable when they chose to be, their pale, slender faces showing nothing at all.

"Enda," he said finally, "I was bought. Or bought and sold. I have to find out by whom and why. Friends died because of it, my career is over because of it, and before I stop breathing, *I will know what happened to me.* I will clear my name, no matter what it takes."

Enda slowly tilted her head to one side, then to the other. "From where you now sit," she said, "that will be a mighty undertaking. Even for a rich human, a powerful human, the kind of subterfuge that you wish to investigate would be difficult and dangerous. The more you discover, the more attention you will attract . . . attention from those who wish to see you tried in Concord space, or simply dead in whatever space is most convenient."

Gabriel looked around him. "Does this look like life to you?" he said. "Maybe death would be better."

"There pride answers," Enda said, "but perhaps it would be unwise to chide you for the characteristic for which you were originally selected. That and the courage."

"In any case," Gabriel said, "I don't want to move on too far from here until I get a clearer sense of just what happened to me. The scene of the crime."

"The crime, if there was one," Enda said, "was perpetrated on a Star Force vessel that is by now very likely some starfalls away from here. That is a crime scene you will now have great difficulty examining."

"But it *happened* here," Gabriel said. He had been stirring this issue around in his mind for nearly as long as he had been out of that jail, a place that had made thinking difficult at best. "And I keep getting the idea that somehow it has to do with this system, with something the ambassador had found out or was about to find out."

"Other information that is going to be hard for you to come by now," Enda said, though not without some sympathy. "Are you sure you this is something that you can realistically investigate? Or are you letting stubbornness interfere with reason because the stubbornness is more comfortable?"

It was a thought that had occurred to Gabriel, and one that he had tried to examine closely rather than simply chucking it out of his mind at first impulse. "I don't think so," he replied. "There were a lot of things that the ambassador said to me over the space of the last few weeks that I heard and forgot about or half forgot. I can't get rid of the idea that at least one of them is important. I took a lot of notes on the things she said. I don't have them now; I won't get them back until the marines restore my personal effects, if they don't in fact just confiscate them. But I can't get rid of the idea that something she said is going to help me make sense of this."

Enda bowed her head. "May it be so," she said. "Even at best, I fear you will have a bad time finding out what you need to know. In the meantime, you must do other things, because if you follow this trail too quickly, surely whoever tried to kill you once by the legal pathway will try it again by means less formal. If you are right—if the person or people involved are in this system—they are watching you now."

"So I'll be 'broken' for a while," Gabriel said and glanced around him. "Not that that's going to be a difficult illusion to maintain if I keep hanging around places like this."

Enda looked philosophical, an expression at which most fraal seemed to excel. "The food is not expensive," she said, "and probably will not kill us."

"Speak for yourself," Gabriel said, already beginning to wonder about some of the suspicious sounds coming from his stomach.

"The clientele may prove to be useful. Don't look that way! Some of these people are very likely involved with the used ship trade."

"Not in any way I want to know about," Gabriel muttered. "They all look like pirates to me."

"I would think it would be protective coloration in a place like this," Enda said mildly. "It is we who stand out here, not they. But this too will redound to our favor, tomorrow or the next day, when we walk into a used ship foundry and find that we're known."

"Who wouldn't know me?" Gabriel asked, only slightly bitter.

"You would be surprised," said Enda, "and though many people on Phorcys certainly will know you from the news coverage of the past days, in most cases it will work to your benefit. Many of the people we are most likely to deal with will be watching the transaction with great interest to see if there is a way they can use the information to their advantage. At the same time they will be eager to tell their less savory connections that they sold a ship to Gabriel Connor." She smiled again—a wicked five-year-old look. "They will of course also tell their connections how they cheated you."

Gabriel had to laugh just once at that. "The price of notoriety," he said. "Oh, well . . . if it means better service . . ."

"I do not know about 'better,' " Enda said. "But certainly rather more attentive. Are you finished there?"

"I wish you could find another way to phrase that," Gabriel said as his stomach growled again, more loudly this time. It was suggesting pointedly that the material he had just offered it did not meet its present needs.

"We will work on my phrasing somewhere more private," said Enda, rising gracefully, "as well as on specs for this new . . . joint venture. Neither of us would want to discuss the specifics in front of the dealer. Let us find out who to pay and make our way back to the small palaces that await us."

Gabriel got up and escorted her toward the door, where the proprietor was waiting for them with a tallychip in hand. Eyes rested thoughtfully on them as they went out. No knives, Gabriel thought, as they went out the door. Not this time.

But maybe sometime soon.

* * * * *

Perhaps twenty light-years away, or several starfalls, depending on how one chose to reckon it, a man sat alone on a low couch in a room with rose-colored walls. One hand held a datapad in his lap, and he looked down the list written on it with a practiced eye. A two-meter-long tri staff, the signature weapon of a Concord Administrator, leaned against the wall next to him.

His room on board the light cruiser was plain, undecorated, and seemed scarcely above the quality that would have been found in a medium-grade officer's quarters. The man remembered how there had been complaints about that at first. There were people aboard any ship who could not cope with the idea that someone of his stature should not have a room to match it. He let them worry about that and not about what he was doing. It was less trouble to him that way.

Lorand Kharls was now seventy years old, and he took the Verge very personally. He had not been here, of course, for the earliest expeditions. That wave of exploration had begun when the StarMech Collective's ships first broached these spaces after the First Galactic War, colonizing the planets of the star called Tendril. Neither had he been here for the later colonizations of Aegis system by the Orions, or the Hatire's first seizure of Grith, or the settlements of Algemron system by the Thuldans and the Austrins. Kharls had been born more than twenty-five years after the Battle of Kendai, well into what the burgeoning nations of the Stellar Ring called the Long Silence. All through his childhood, during his schooling when he had first fallen in love with the concept of history as something that was happening *now*, and later as a young man starting his formal adult education, that silence had come back to haunt Kharls. What was *happening* out there? There had been no way to tell, not until the restoration of the stardrive-based communications relay near Hammer's Star had brought the desperate cry for help from the colony at Silver Bell ringing across space, seven years delayed. The ships of the stellar nations, and then those of the Concord, had gone out to find what had happened, and they had been unable to discover anything.

Long before that, still deep in the Silence, Lorand Kharls had gone into the Concord civil service. At first his intention had simply been to find out what he was good for. The numerous batteries of aptitude tests through which he had suffered had given his teachers some indication. Soon, rather against the odds for someone born on a third world, he had found himself at the Administrators' College on Ascension. Ten years he had spent there, then another ten years of field work at Senior Cadet level, before taking his first assignment as a Deputy Administrator in the Aegis system. They had told him it was difficult work, but he had hardly noticed. He had been enjoying himself too much, and besides, his eyes had already turned to other things. Kharls had become aware that if he did his work well he might finally be allowed to live in and investigate the great mystery that had haunted his young life: the Silence, and the places where it had fallen.

It was silent no longer in the Verge. It had stopped being silent by the time he was first assigned here, four years ago, as an early System Administrator for Corrivale. But two years after that he was detached to more advanced duties as a Cluster Administrator, traveling among the stars within a ten-light-year diameter from Corrivale and watching the intricate interlacing of their cultures and governments—advising when he could, intervening when he had to, acting in his "final judicial" role no more than three times over the years since. When he was young and new to the job, he doubtless would have tried and executed that many criminals out in the backwaters of this or that star system in perhaps half a standard year. Now his job took him to places where the criminals were usually of high enough standing in the community that simply trying them and shooting them would have done little good. He had learned a lot of patience and a fair amount of wile moving among the politicians, and he had not had to shoot one yet. Usually there were more effective ways to intervene. Mostly they had to do with arriving in very large Star Force vessels with very large guns. A gun's vocabulary might be limited, but once it spoke there was some tendency for people to listen very carefully to whoever spoke next.

Now a part of the Verge that Kharls took more personally than usual appeared to be having some teething troubles in its neighborhood. There were not that many other star systems in the immediate region of Corrivale. Corrivale itself had once been nothing all that important, that is, until the discovery of the sesheyan colony on Grith, the resurgence of the Hatire, and the inroads since made by VoidCorp. The place was getting crowded. Most specifically, it was getting crowded with power players. Their actions cast shadows a long way, often over people who did not deserve to have their lives shadowed. That was where, when possible, a Concord Administrator might step in and see what could be done.

That time had now come to Kharls, so he would uproot himself from here (which would cause talk), resettle himself in another ship better suited to the duty he would assign it (which would cause much more talk), and then finally start "meddling." Like any good artist, he had not arranged all this without first studying carefully where to go to work. If you wanted to drop a rock on someone's head, for example, you could spend a lot of time trying to push the rock up to the top of the hill to produce the maximum result. Or you could get a lever and a map and push the rock off from right where you were, assuming that the person you wanted to hit with it was presently standing in the right place.

Lorand Kharls's work for a long time now had been inducing the people who needed to be hit by a given rock to go stand under it themselves. The best occurrences of this sort were always when such people started the rock moving under their own power and without realizing what they were doing. You couldn't always count on that happening, but it was always something to shoot for.

And now it was happening, though he wished he understood why.

Phorcys and Ino. They had been a fruit ripe to fall, ready for peace, despite the best efforts of others in the Thalaassa system and elsewhere. Lauren Delvecchio had come along and plucked the fruit with her usual skill, but that skill had availed her no further. The job, or something associated with it, had killed her and numerous others.

That by itself was tragic enough, but rumors had been coming to Kharls's office of something else that might or might not be happening out in the Thalaassa system. Concrete resources on which he could call, at least without stirring up unwanted trouble, were thin out that way. He had sent out feelers to see what the rumors said closer to the source of the problem. He had received no answers back. Somewhat after the fact, Kharls had found that one of the sources he had meant to question had been sold to another bidder quite some time before.

This discovery left him with a whole new box of questions, ones to which he could find no immediate answers. Events began to take their course, and Lorand Kharls sat and watched to see what would happen. The temptation to intervene had been considerable, but Lorand knew that there was no quicker way to lose the formidable reputation of a Concord Administrator than by routinely dashing into planetary legal processes and overturning them. Besides, there were questions about the young man as well. What had he been up to with Delvecchio? What else had he been up to? Whose side he was on? This led to the even more important questions of whether he was still on that side after the disgrace that had befallen him or whether he had turned coats again. The answers to those questions would determine what other questions needed to be asked next—or whether any needed to be asked at all, except the kind of question to which the simplest answer is a corpse. There was some time yet to see what action was required in that area.

Meanwhile, he had set other interventions in motion. The most obvious of them would culminate today, within the hour, Kharls thought. It would cause a great deal of talk, for normally Concord Administrators did not venture too far out of their perceived ambit. The trouble was that the ambit, the Administrator's area of responsibility and power, was still being determined out here in the Verge by trial and error. Worlds not specifically affiliated with the Concord might bridle at the sudden appearance in their space of an Administrator with his or her sweeping powers, but they never seemed to argue about it too loudly when the job was done correctly, and when the spaces in question were left cleaner, more peaceful, or more crime-free than they had been when he started.

When the job was done correctly, Kharls thought. There were always chances that things could go wrong. And this job looked rather more touchy than usual.

He looked at the pad one more time, sighed at being able to find nothing else that needed to be added to it, and dropped it on the couch. That pad was his chief weapon at the moment, his shopping list. He would turn it over to his aide in a little while and then check the execution of the more delicate items in a day or three after he and his staff were settled in the new venue.

There would be the inevitable feeling-out, checking-out period. There were ship captains who felt their authority threatened by the presence of a Concord Administrator who was empowered to act as judge, jury, and executioner. It sometimes took them a while to realize that no Concord Administrator had much interest in playing shipboard politics. Their playing field was much wider, whole systems, whole clusters of stars. Their one duty was peace, and they went through ferocious training to ensure that their personal feelings and emotions would not mar their judgments on the large scale or the small. As a result, their decisions were usually honored, and the solutions they crafted stuck in place.

For a while at least, Kharls thought, getting up and stretching. Time passes, situations change. Then you build new solutions.

For the meantime, this particular problem was coming to a head. He had been watching it from a distance for some time, before the word came down from Julius Baynes, the sector administrator for the Verge, that it needed prompt attention. The problem was large, difficult to manage, and spread over a goodly section of space even as the Verge reckoned it. It was also politically touchy, ethically difficult, and morally something of a morass.

Kharls loved the look of it, but handling it correctly would take some time, possibly too much. If it was allowed to just trundle along at its own pace, there would be no guarantee that this problem would be solved at all—or wouldn't blow up prematurely and wreck its solution half-executed. No, he would have to force the pace, which suggested a detail for the other of the two interventions that were to be enacted immediately. One of them had already been set in train, and not with too much difficulty, since the personnel he wanted were up for reassignment as it was. Conveniently, their immediate superiors had decided that after the traumatic events associated with the deaths of Delvecchio and her party, a change of venue—in this case, a change of commands and ships—would be advisable. The other intervention he had been considering since this morning, since he had finished his packing. Now, as he stood, he decided to go ahead and do it.

He reached down for his pad and stylus and made one more note, emphasizing exactly how he wanted the tiny mission carried out and how the surveillance should be set up. The devil, as one of his instructors had always said, was indeed in the details. Turn your people loose when you delegate, and don't micromanage them, but don't fail to describe the detail of an implementation to them either. You sharpen your own mind by doing so, and your subordinates learn as well. In turn, the thing gets done as you want it, which in other parts of life may merely lead to pleasure. But here, in an Administrator's work, such a result might make the difference between life and death, peace and war, for many millions.

A tap came at the door. Kharls went to the door as it opened. On the other side of it was his aide, a tall young man named Rand, who more or less automatically reached out for the pad Kharls was holding out for him. "The gig's ready, sir," said Rand, "and Captain Orris is waiting to see you off."

"That's very kind of him," Kharls said. "This has been a pleasant stay, a very successful stay. I regret having to move on."

No you don't, said the back of his mind, unrepentant, as they made their way down the halls to the shuttle bay. Any problem solved immediately lost its gloss for Kharls. The pleasure of his superior's praise lasted some while longer. What then began to shine for him was the prospect of the next problem at the end of the next starrise or the one after that—a big, knotty, knobby, horrible difficulty, just made for the kind of training they had given him. *To every cat a fine rat,* the old saying went. Though Kharls had only rarely seen cats and never a rat, he knew what it meant. His enemy, his mission, the thing without which his life had no meaning, was out there waiting for him to come and start working on it. Everything else paled before that. But this truth was one he kept to himself as he made his farewells to Captain Orris and his staff and got into the gig. Only a few moments after buckling in, the engines softly hummed to life and they were off.

The gig itself was small, looking as if someone had taken the cockpit off a standard shuttle and stretched it out by a few meters, but it was immaculately clean and well-maintained. Its cerametal white skin glowed red with the light of Hydrocus beneath. In contrast, the Heavy Cruiser *Schmetterling* to which he was moving, loomed over the planet like some great steel-gray sea beast. Turrets and missile bays dotted much of its surface like angry little barnacles, though "little" was only an illusion brought on by distance. Some of those turrets were considerably larger than the gig in which he now sat.

The ride over to the new ship was uneventful enough. Kharls looked down on Hydrocus, turning there underneath him, the reds and browns sullen near the terminator, brightening toward the limb of the planet where day was coming up with a ruddy flash of Corrivale through the planet's upper atmosphere. Somewhere on the other side, Grith slipped smoothly toward its primary's horizon, bearing its own old problem that no one had been able to solve for this long while now.

Soon enough, Lorand Kharls said privately to the briefly invisible moon hiding away there in the darkness. Your time will come. But meanwhile . . .

The gig docked, and Kharls's aide got out to see that all the people scheduled to meet them were there. A moment later Kharls stepped forward into the shuttle bay and advanced to meet the fair young woman in Star Force black who was waiting for him.

"Good afternoon, Administrator Kharls," she said, "and welcome aboard *Schmetterling.*"

"Good afternoon, Captain Dareyev," he said. "A pleasure to make your acquaintance after having heard so much about you. Shall we go where we can discuss further what *Schmetterling*'s mission will be?"

Chapter Eight

THE NEXT MORNING when they went out in search of breakfast, Gabriel found the package waiting for him at the front desk of their hotel. It was pitifully small, considering what had once been in his closet aboard *Falada,* but much of that had been various versions of uniform, to none of which he was now entitled. Gabriel stood there on the doorstep, unwrapping the package: some paperwork, notes—not the ones he thought he had kept from the ambassador. Some security-conscious person had probably confiscated them; a couple of plastic books, quite old, that had been presents from his father; a couple of laminated solids of his old home on Bluefall, that particular shot of the way the lake looked in the afternoon; and the little, dark, matte-finished stone.

He dumped it out of the wrappings into his hand, and it glowed only very dully. "Too much light out here, I suppose," Enda said, glancing at it incuriously. "By night it must be fine. Will you want to leave the rest of that here?"

Gabriel nodded and dropped the stone into his pocket. He then went back into the hotel, paid an extra couple of dollars for access to his "room" out of hours, and locked the bundle up. After he came out again, he and Enda found their way up to the main boulevard of the capital city, hailed a flycab, and made their way to the first of several used ship foundries.

As with many other planetary capitals where physical registration of a ship would normally be handled, there were at least ten or eleven of these facilities, doing everything from part-time salvage to breaking to "almost new"—basically, just relicensing work for pilots who had one reason or another to want to swap a ship for another of nearly equal age and quality. Usually this had to do with trouble with the law, and the quality of the ships was more than offset, for Gabriel, by the almost unavoidable suggestion that a ship bought under these circumstances was almost certainly somehow tainted, and that possibly you were as well.

The first shop was one of these, not much more than a "swap shop," and the salesman who came out to show them around the yard—a huge space of stained concrete, blindwall force-reinforced fencing, and rolled back no-fly nets—looked as if he had just been unwound from around a driveshaft. He was covered with grease that smelled faintly of electrical equipment, and he wore an expression that suggested he didn't think either Gabriel or Enda could afford anything in his place.

"Whatchalookinfor?"

"Something in the line of a Lanierin Four Forty or a Delgakis," Gabriel said, this being the opening line on which he and Enda had agreed. Their whole "script" went through many permutations and could go on for hours if necessary, depending on whether one or the other of them thought that something suitable might be hidden in the "back room."

The man shook his head immediately and almost with pleasure. "Nothing that new here," he said. "We got Orneries, Altids, some StarMech stuff pretty used."

Those would have been the best of the lot, but they were plainly the exceptions. Gabriel looked around and could see nothing standing on the landing pans but ships mostly less than three years old, bigger than they needed, more expensive than they needed. He would have shaken his head and walked out right then, but Enda said, "Show us what you have. Some of these look big for our needs, but if the other equipment is right, we might be convinced."

They let the man take them around the various ships. He was a little reluctant at first but he soon gained energy and interest as he got the sense from both of them that they were both actually interested in buying and were not simply "timewasters." When the two of them had a thorough poke around and in and through the twelve or so ships that were remotely of interest, Enda thanked the man politely and headed for the gates, making for the street that led to yet another shipfounders' yard perhaps a kilometer away.

They walked on down the grimy road, Gabriel looking with some slight weariness at the relentlessly industrial quality of the land all around them. Weed-patched vacant lots, scarred concrete, bare fences and walls, and many many junked ships seemed to stretch for some miles away from them, toward the horizon where (it being clear for a change) the dim shapes of distant mountains were visible.

"This is going to take us a while, isn't it?" Gabriel asked.

"At least twenty minutes to walk to the next place," Enda answered.

"No, I mean to get off here."

She looked at him wryly but with understanding. "Your life has been lived very fast, I think," Enda said. "Now you feel a different pace and are uncertain whether you like it."

"No, I'm certain," Gabriel said. "I don't like it."

Enda chuckled. "We will see how long that lasts. Meantime, there will be time for the people back at Joris's Used Ship Heaven to make some commcalls."

"Warning every other founder's in the area that there are a couple of hot ones coming."

"And what we are looking for. We have just saved ourselves some time, I think."

At first Gabriel was not so sure. The next lot was almost identical to the first one except that its ships were older, and the woman who came out to meet them was in a slightly tidier coverall. The main problem from Gabriel's point of view was that almost all those ships were too small. Some of them had been runabouts, just pleasure craft, and while they were drive-capable, they either weren't roomy enough or well enough shielded. It was much on Gabriel's mind that stars with good asteroid belts had a tendency to flare. The nearest good mining system, Corrivale, had problems of this kind. A ship without enough shielding would cook all its contents during a flare. Your remains would be sterile, but that would be all that could be said for them.

Enda noticed the lack of shielding and the size problem, and once again they thanked the woman and moved on down the road to the next founder's yard. Rather to Gabriel's astonishment, the sun actually came out as they reached its gates. He looked up, half tantalized and half saddened by the memory of the first sight of that pale sunlight through the tall windows of the courtroom, then he shook his head and went in after Enda.

This founder's was, if anything, dirtier and more chaotic than the first two had been. But the man who came out to meet them, rather to Gabriel's surprise, was clean or cleanish. At least his coverall seemed to have been in contact with some washing surfactant in the recent past. He actually took Enda's hand, which neither of the other founders' people had when it was offered, and shook Gabriel's as well.

"Heard about you," the man said. "I'm Gol Leiysin. Come in and see if we have something that fits you."

They followed him into the big yard, weaving their way around the piles of conduits and scrap metal that seemed to be piled every which way with no sense or solution to it. "Spring cleaning," Leiysin said. "Don't let it frighten you."

"You do this every spring?" Gabriel said, just avoiding tripping over some more conduit.

"Spring on Lecterion, sure," Leiysin said and laughed between his teeth. "We're not fanatics. What are you looking for?"

This time Enda began the recital while Gabriel tried to remember how long Lecterion's year was. It was a gas giant in orbit around Corrivale, that much he remembered, and that Omega Station, a Concord base, orbited one of the planet's moons. If he and Enda were indeed going to Corrivale in search of work, they would have to steer clear of Lecterion simply to prevent him from being arrested. But the planet's gas-giant status suggested that it was a good way out in its system and should therefore be easily avoidable.

"Got some older Delgakises," said Leiysin. "We don't get much call for the Lanierins; parts are too hard to get out here. There's no source for them much closer than Aegis system. Delgakis has a service depot on Grith, though. Handy. Take a look here."

The ships he showed them were old workhorses, not one of them much less than a decade in age, some pushing two. The age itself was not that much an issue. Delgakis was one of those makes of ship known to be "long runners," with thousands of starfalls in them if their service history was good. These, though, were far enough along in their lives to make you think. Gabriel put that matter aside and just examined the ships for a few minutes. They were all the right size for mining work—about sixty meters long, ample space for crew quarters—meaning room for the crew to get away from each other. All of them had good hold space. One of them even had clamps for an extra hold. It was the oldest of the lot, a D80. It amazed Gabriel that they had even been building this ship that long ago. Its lines were surprisingly clean looking, its hull was in fair shape, and the drive bay had held a good-sized stardrive in its time.

"Family ship," said Leiysin when he saw Gabriel looking at it. Enda was busy with one of the others. "They had it from new, apparently, to go by the service record. They did cargo at first, then went for mining afterward. Then they changed again and used the augmented hold for data. A lot of hauls out by Aegis and back into the Verge just after the new drivecomm relay went in to replace the old one lost during the war. By then half the planets in the Corrivale neighborhood were setting up their new Grids now that there was something to link through. Finally the owners did something unusual: they retired. Sold out, went somewhere in-world, found themselves a little cottage up a mountain, and didn't go to space no more."

Gabriel nodded. "They retired the drive too, though."

Leiysin shrugged. "No matter how kindly you treat a drive, twenty years is too long. We've got some here that will fit this module. A Speramundi, a Bricht. The Bricht wouldn't be a perfect fit, though."

Gabriel shook his head. The Bricht would be less expensive, but a jury-rigged stardrive was nightmarish to maintain. That much he knew from many late-night horror stories from Hal. "Let's see the inside," he said.

Leiysin took him through. It was a surprisingly roomy ship, especially as regarded the sanitary fittings. This occurred to him as a possible reason why a family who had blasted in this ship for twenty years were able to retire, all alive, rather than having murdered one another for reasons having to do with hygiene. Gabriel knew a lot of people joked about such things, but marines knew better than most how important it was to success-ful human function when cooped up in a small tin can to be scrupulously clean about it. There was a tiny "sitting room" with a couple of surprisingly comfortable-looking fold-down chairs. Next to the chairs was a modular built-in Grid and entertainment access, possibly another reason the family had not killed one another. The living quarters consisted of three quarters-cubbies, two convertible for storage, and a well-equipped pilot's cabin with room for two to be there without having to be stuffed down one another's jumpsuits.

He came out of the ship to find Enda peering into the main hold. "Commodious," she said. "Should I look inside?"

"Do," Gabriel said, and Enda slipped up the steps and van-ished. Gabriel walked around the ship, trying to do the kind of walk-about that Hal used to tell him about, looking for scratch-es, strange welds, riveted patches that changed color within the patch, other peculiarities. The problem is that I'm not absolutely sure what I'm looking for yet, he thought. I know the symptoms, but not what they mean. But he kept at it anyway.

The ship was shaped like a long, moderately wide box with various sensor relays and system drive equipment extending out of the main hull. Triangular wings jutted out from the rear of the craft. They were obviously intended to stabilize the craft in atmospheric flight, but they also seemed thick enough to be able to accommodate at least one weapons bay in each wing. The com-mand compartment that housed the cockpit was a ten-meter-long cylinder that extended from the front of the ship and tapered into a round nose. Two rectangular bays jutted out from each side of the command compartment. Both of them had been gutted for salvage but could easily be refitted to house either a sensor bay or even a small weapons compartment. The ship's escape pod had also been salvaged, but its housing bay seemed in good shape. Like all of the ships in the yard, the craft's dusky cerametal skin was in desperate need of a good cleaning, but Gabriel could find no exterior damage or unexplained patch work. By the time he had come all the way around the ship, Enda was coming down the stairs and looking severely at Leiysin, who was watching this whole performance with interest.

"It badly needs a cleaning," she said. "I wonder that with so much attention to the technical end, you had not seen to that by now."

"Detailing," Leiysin said and shrugged, "usually comes last." He gave Enda a thoughtful look.

"Well," Enda said after a look of her own at Gabriel, "your decision."

He stood there with his mouth hanging open. Marines were not used to being given decisions of such stature, at least not marines of his rank.

Then Gabriel realized that he was not a marine any more, of any rank, and that other people, normal people, *did* get to make such decisions . . . and maybe it was time he started. Both Enda and Leiysin were standing there staring at him, awaiting his decision.

"What the drik," he said. "Let's do it."

They turned together to Leiysin, who nodded, looking satisfied. "Then let's go into the office and start the process. Sir, honored madam, will that be cash, or shall we investigate other payment options?"

"That depends," Enda said mildly. "How much of a discount do you offer for cash?"

Cash? Gabriel was thinking while concentrating on not allowing his eyes to bug out. Leiysin shook his head regretfully.

"Unfortunately the traffic in the system is light enough that it is not cost-effective to give cash discounts. No business here could—"

"Spare me your tales of woe," said Enda. "May the time come soon when you find yourself enough closer to civilization that you are dealing a little less close to the edge." Gabriel blinked, wondering what that meant. "Are you offering contract work for mortgagees?"

This time it was the dealer's turn to blink. "Phorcyn law forbids that kind of transaction—"

Gabriel's ears perked up at that. The man had not *quite* said that he didn't offer contract work. But he finally said, "No, I don't want anything to do with that at this stage."

Enda nodded to him. "Then we will examine the competing interest rates."

"Competing?" The dealer looked at her in surprise. "Honored, unfortunately the only bank offering ship escrow on Phorcys is—"

"You must think I was born only a hundred years ago," Enda said, and Gabriel grinned. "Flattery. Of course there are more banks available than just the one. I can arrange finance clear back in the Solar Union if I so please, and perhaps we should. Gabriel?"

He nodded to her and turned to go.

"No! No, honored, wait, I'm sure we can come to some agreement—"

Gabriel paused, and after a moment nodded again. The remainder of the financial discussion went by with merciful speed; apparently Leiysin was so terrified of the possibility that this particular transaction might walk away from him that his spirit was nearly broken, and he sat there nodding and agreeing to everything Enda said. It was an interesting development, but as with so many others lately, Gabriel found himself wondering what it meant.

Other details took rather longer to sort out. Verifying the ship's condition came first. One of the independent examination companies had to come out and certify the ship's spaceworthiness—that could be done tonight. Then there was the matter of fittings. A mining ship, even the smallest, required better than usual shielding (since ores are likely to be radioactive), specialized assay equipment, and a fair amount of weaponry—since the work was lonely and the space in which it took place were not much frequented by others except asteroid miners, there are plenty of people willing to take advantage of you. There was also the matter of the installation of the new Speramundi drive. Also, the kind of modular shielding that the ship had once borne and that had been removed for data haulage would now need to be reinstalled. Enda also seemed unusually concerned about the type and quality of the weaponry Leiysin had to offer them. Gabriel supported his end of things by making it a point to be unusually picky and difficult about the mining equipment. What poor Leiysin was making of the whole transaction, Gabriel had no idea.

They signed the initial "commitment" chip after about an hour of detail work. Enda put down the deposit, five percent of the vehicle's full price with the rest scheduled to follow according to the loan repayment schedule that would be arranged with one of several banks tonight or tomorrow. They walked out of there well into the beginning stages of ownership of a Delgakis D-80 "Orindren" driveship, with only a few hundred things like system registration and victualling and drive fueling to handle. For Gabriel it was an exhilarating feeling, the only one he could remember having in some time: the beginning of a new life or rather, the beginning of the long process of finding out what had gone wrong with the last one and fixing it.

* * * * *

Later he started having second thoughts. "Do you ever have first ones?" Enda asked, teasing somewhat.

They were back in the Dive for this discussion, the noise level there at this time of night so horrific that no one not standing directly between them could have managed to overhear them. As for the mere fact of the sale, probably everyone here knew about it already, but anyone wanting to get close enough to hear the details would have to come to grief first. Gabriel ate his soup, which was only marginally better than it had been the other night, and shook his head.

"I'm not sure I like it," he said.

"Well, would you rather go out without weapons?"

"Hardly! But the level of stuff we bought. Look at the numbers! Whoever installs those is going to talk. Word is going to get out. It always does. And someone's going to come after us, wondering why we need such big guns and thinking that we must have something really worth stealing—"

"On the contrary, we will have better weapons yet," Enda said, "but we will not install them here, nor anywhere without posting the customary bribes. Even here, it is possible to make various arrangements in the documentation associated with the weaponry."

"You mean you're going to try to get them to forge the end-use certificates? Do you know what the penalty for—"

"Yes," said Enda, "probably better than you do. It's done all the time, Gabriel, as you know. Or you should know. I sometimes wonder whether the great concentration on producing spotless young entities for the Service does not shelter you too much from the . . ." she trailed off. "Well, let that pass for the moment. In any case, our gunnery will seem ordinary enough by the time we are through fitting the ship, and there are ways to buy off the actual installers as well, ways to ensure that they stay bought. Other matters . . ."

" 'Other matters'?" Gabriel said. "I noticed something about the final bill."

"Yes?"

"It was larger than what the total should have been by about five percent."

Enda blinked. Gabriel gave her a look and said, "Just because I'm a marine doesn't mean I can't count."

"Well, you are certainly right to notice. It is after all your money too, some of it. Quite a bit of it, in fact." She reached around her back and for a moment toyed with that silken fall of pearly hair that normally she kept bound out of the way. "It occurred to me that some slight extra speed might be desired."

"Speed?"

"In departing."

Gabriel put the spoon down in the soup bowl again. "Are you telling me that the delivery date on the manifest is—"

"Inaccurate?" she said. "By some days."

"When will it be—" Then he stopped himself.

"There are those who can read the lips of even fraal," Enda said and smiled that slight smile. "Perhaps we will let that wait."

Gabriel nodded and finished the last couple of spoonfuls of his soup. He thought Enda probably meant "tomorrow," but she was not going to say it. Probably with reason, he thought as he glanced around him. All around was a darkness full of smoke, drink fumes, and oblivious people shouting or singing at each other. Yet who knew what technology was hidden away in quiet corners, recording chance words that might be sold to a willing bidder?

He sighed, pushed back in his seat, pulled out the little pocket-stone, and began fiddling with it while letting the food settle.

"One thing we must settle by tomorrow morning," Enda said after a moment, glancing up from the wineglass that she had been refilling, "is the matter of the ship's name. They will not let us lift without something." She saw Gabriel pause and added, "You could always simply let them generate a letter and number combination, if you prefer. Something meaningless and non-connoted. Certainly there are species that are suspicious about such things."

Abruptly, Gabriel got the shudder. It had been some time since he had felt that: what his mother, when he was very young, had called "somebody walking over my grave," and then laughed and shrugged it off. It never seemed to have anything *specific* to do with something bad happening, but the two sometimes came together.

He raised his eyebrows, put the feeling aside for the moment, and said, "No, it can have a name, there's no problem with that."

"What, then? I have no gift for this kind of thing," Enda said. "You will have to choose."

Gabriel leaned forward on his elbows and thought, twiddling the stone idly as he did so. The image came to him, abruptly, of that thin patch of sunshine that had shone down on them as they walked through the gates of Gol Leiysin's place.

"Sunshine," he said.

Enda tilted her head at him. "Simple, perhaps childlike. No matter. Naming the light is always a good thing. It attracts its attention. 'Sunshine' let it be. We will both have to sign title, but you may as well take care of making the actual registry application, or rather completing it, at the spaceport in the morning. I will take care of the last of the victualling, and when I get back I will go over the final parts manifest with the people from Leiysin's to make sure the inventory is complete. Can you think of anything else that needs doing?"

Gabriel tried to think but couldn't. It was possibly understandable. This had been one of the fullest days he'd had in ages, and he felt much more tired than he should have. He began to wonder whether the trial had taken more out of him than he would have otherwise suspected.

"Not a thing," he said at last. "Though as a second thought, sleeping would be nice."

Enda chuckled. "I thought you might come up with that one eventually. All right. Let me finish this, and then we'll go."

She drank her wine, and Gabriel gestured through the singing for the bartender to send someone over to collect what they owed. Drink was cheap enough here, and Gabriel was glad to get rid of his last few pieces of Phorcyn hard currency. Only bills were left, and the people at the spaceport would readily enough put credit on his chip in exchange while they left. When the bill was paid, Enda got up and headed for the door, Gabriel coming after her through the noise and the smoke.

"Here," he said, "let me get that for you." It was an old habit, but one he should begin to rediscover, he thought. Enda gave him a dry look as Gabriel opened the door for her, then she started past him.

The sound was what hit him first, that low buzz.

His hand shot out almost before he knew what he was doing. He grabbed Enda by the shoulder and snatched her violently back. As she staggered backwards into him, a slug trailing superheated plasma went by directly in front of her, not more than a few centimeters in front of her nose. The slug slammed into the door frame, spraying splinters of wood and stone into their skin.

Gabriel pulled Enda past him, thrust her behind him back into the Dive, and dove out of the doorway. He hit the concrete in the dark. Good thing we've been this way a couple of times before, he thought as he rolled and broke out of the roll sideways. As the charge pistol's fire stitched the concrete behind him, he heard the shuffle of footsteps made brighter than normal by their echo against the nearby wall. He targeted that sound, rolled again, came up and dove straight at the dim shape he saw heading just a little to the left of the dim pink light of the weapon's aiming eye. *Wham!* His head hit something that should have been softer than it was. A battle vest maybe but not full attack armor. Too bad for you, buddy, Gabriel thought as he came down on top of the man, grabbed his head, and banged it on the ground with one hand while feeling with the other for the outstretched arm. Just out of reach, yes, there it was, an M12 charge pistol, full clip. Nasty. Didn't plan to leave much of her, did you? He pushed up and away from the momentarily inert body, grabbed the pistol, twisted the lanth cell's safety out of its socket, and paused as he heard something. A rustling sound came from the other side of the wall. Oh really, he thought. He immediately selected for "overcharge," then chucked the pistol over the wall after its safety, hard.

Motion underneath him, then a groan. The man probably had

some internal injuries and certainly was bleeding badly from the back of his head. This briefly became much clearer in the flare of sudden light from inside the wall. The exploding charge pistol lit everything like a sheet of lightning for a few seconds and rocked the ground. There was a scream from not far away, and the wall shook as something, several somethings, impacted into it with a slightly wet sound.

Gabriel stood up. Enda was standing just outside the doorway, looking with some bemusement into the Dive, from which not so much as a nose had so far put itself out, nor seemed likely to in the near future.

"Somebody here doesn't like you much, I think," Gabriel said as he dusted himself off and stood up. "Any thoughts as to who?"

Enda shook her head, looking around. The street in which the Dive was located was very dark, very quiet, and to Gabriel's senses getting darker and quieter by the moment. Even the barroom was deathly silent. He felt oddly elated. That was it, then. Marines had a sense of when trouble, physical trouble anyway, was going to break out. They might take his uniform and throw him off the ship and out of the Corps, but the instinct was still there. Gabriel produced a rather wolfish grin as he looked at the former attacker lying on the ground.

"Should we call the police?" he asked.

Enda gave him a wide-eyed look, and Gabriel thought to himself once more that the illusion really was amazing. If he hadn't known better, he would have sworn that those eyes glowed in the dark.

"Gabriel," she said with some humor, "you are an optimist indeed if you think the police would come *here* at this time of night! Let us be away swiftly before the acquaintances of these miscreants come for them. For tonight the hotel will be secure enough. In the morning, swiftly with us to the spaceport where the ship will by now be lying in bond. We have business to finish, perhaps a whole day's worth—but I for one want to do every bit of it under official eyes, even the last of the shopping, even at field prices. Then we lift."

"But what if the ship's not ready?"

"Then we sleep in her, in bond. We could not get much more secure—and we are paying so much at the hotel that there would not be much difference!"

There was a faint sound of footsteps in the distance.

Gabriel raised his eyebrows. Their fighting instructor at Academy had always said, "Gentlemen, after dealing with the baddies, do not depend on the local constabulary or anyone else to understand that you were only defending yourself. Have it away on your heels, and live to fight another day."

He grinned at Enda. Together they ran, and the shadows swallowed them.

* * * * *

The next morning they called a flycab to come and get them. Gabriel was in reaction and knew it, but he was unable to do much about it. He felt almost uncontrollably jumpy and couldn't understand why.

"I can think of a couple of reasons," Enda said to him in the cab. "One having to do with where I found you. The other . . ." She shrugged a little and plucked at the sleeve of the pilot's smartsuit that she had insisted on buying him after the sale was initiated yesterday. "Your uniform has changed."

"Oh." He nodded. "Yes, the old one was protection of a kind, I guess."

"But the talents cannot be taken away as the uniform was," Enda said as the craft leveled out over the public access pad to Phorcys's main spaceport and began to sink toward it. "About that at least you may now rest assured."

"I just wish I knew why—"

"So do I," Enda said, "but I would wait for somewhere quieter to discuss it." She gestured with her eyes at the roof of the cab and above. Space, Gabriel thought, and his heart jumped a little in him. He was going to be so glad to get off this planet.

They landed just outside the port's land-access gates, paid the cabbie, went through the spaceport's standard security screening, showed their initial ship-owner's "papers," and then caught a little open tug to take them the three kilometers or so over to the bond yards where ships and goods in transit were laid up. There, off to one side by itself with the port seal obvious on its doors, lay the little ship that would be *Sunshine*. Gabriel looked at her with some satisfaction, for she had been given a last polish by Leiysin's people. Even in the early morning clouded sunlight that was typical of this part of Phorcys during this time of year, she gleamed. Whether she would be clean enough inside was another story, but Gabriel would have plenty of time to take care of that once they were off-planet.

They showed their papers to the port official who showed up as soon as the tug left. This worthy, a sesheyan in coveralls who wore heavily tinted *gailghe* even against this early light, broke the seal and opened the ship for them. After giving them the two flat electronic keys that controlled the cargo lift and the doors, he took himself away without much more conversation. Gabriel and Enda got into the lift together, rode up, and came into the utility room that lay directly behind the pilot's cabin . . . and immediately the signal chimed to tell them someone was outside.

"Now there is terrible timing," Enda said, slipping forward to look out the cockpit window. "It is the supplies delivery already."

"I'll start cleaning," Gabriel said, looking around him. Enda gave him a bemused look, then went off.

He had just started on a really good scrub of Enda's quarters when she came back, looking somehow somber as she shut the outer air lock door behind her and opened the inner one. Gabriel looked at her with some concern. "Problems?"

"No, by no means," she said and slapped the control to bring the small in-hold lift chugging up into the ship's body. She and Gabriel both stopped for a moment to listen to the sound of it. The lift wheezed and hiccuped as if something was wrong with its hydraulics—yet on examination neither they nor the "evaluation" mechanic sent over from the field had been able to find anything the matter. "No," Enda said and reached into her satchel, coming up with a small cube-shaped data solid. "The logbook and revised service history, and the licensing paperwork, will be along in a couple of hours, they told me up front. We could leave bond as early as this evening. And all the groceries are here." The lift snugged into place, and Enda made her way down toward the cargo hold.

"Did you get everything on the list?" Gabriel called after her.

"No," Enda's voice came floating back, "and if I had, we would have had to pay for another float to get it all over here, and at port prices!" She sounded exasperated. "Most things I got. The useful bulk foods, certainly, and the concentrates. But Gabriel, you are going to have to stop eating like a marine, I fear. We simply do not have cargo space for that much food."

That annoyed him slightly. *And I thought I was being so frugal when I made up that list.* "Did you get the sugar, anyway?" he said.

"Of course I got the sugar," Enda said. "Am I an alien, to drink my chai black?"

He grinned, then stood up and looked out the cockpit window. Down on the field, someone was walking toward them from the direction of the tower. "Company," he said.

"Possibly the papers—" Enda said. "Go see to it."

It was the papers. A man in a coverall that was still in the process of ridding itself of a splash of lubricant strolled up to the passenger lift as it came down. He offered Gabriel a package studded with an impressive number of official seals, ties and fastenings.

"Your partner must sign as well," the man said as Gabriel took the stylus from him.

Partner. He found that he liked the sound of that. "Fine. Enda?"

Gabriel scribbled his signature, came up with his ID chip and held it against the authenticating seal. The seal blinked and chirped once to verify that the chip's information had been internalized. After a moment the lift ascended again and came down bearing Enda. She too signed and produced her chip, touching it to the other affixed seal. The man snapped off half of each seal, then handed them back the completed registry package.

"Thank you, sir, honored," said the man. "Please file a flight plan as soon as possible, since Phorcyn law forbids unscheduled or unfiled craft to sit afield for more than three standard hours—"

"Thank you. We will be filing directly, won't we, Gabriel?" she said as they both stepped into the lift.

"Uh," Gabriel said, "I should be ready in about half an hour." The man nodded and walked away.

"Good," Enda continued as they began to ascend back into the ship, "because the timer is running now. Every minute we sit here, we pay nearly six Concord dollars' worth of landing tax. If we take off in prime time, which starts in an hour, it costs us three times as much as if we do it when you said."

"Everything costs, doesn't it?" Gabriel muttered. The lift ground to a halt and they stepped out. "Leaving, arriving, sitting still . . ."

"Everything costs," Enda said as she shut the airlock behind them, "some things more than others." She looked around them. "My, you have been busy."

"Doing what I know best."

"Well, what you know less well is needed now. Normally, I would have told you what those who knew about such things once told me," Enda said. "Never lift without work or the promise of work and make sure the promise includes refund of your fuel costs." She made that small smile and added, "But these circumstances are not normal, and for a while, where we're concerned, I wonder whether there are likely to be any. No matter." She shrugged. "Let us file that plan and lift right away. The sooner we lift, then the sooner you can also learn to manage the ship in both drivespace and normal space. Where will we go? You will have been thinking about that."

Gabriel nodded. "Eraklion," he said. "The mining cooperative there doesn't have enough of its own ships to move everything they produce, and also, they're a fairly small outfit. You don't have VoidCorp all over the system, apparently, the way they do in Corrivale. No heavy cruisers hanging over your head here."

Enda tilted her head "yes."

"It seems sane enough," she said, "though much of our gear is arranged for nickel-iron work instead of ore. We will have to do some rearranging in the processing area. When do you want to start collecting and on what kind of contract?"

"Whoa," Gabriel said, "I hadn't worked that out yet."

"But you *had* worked out," Enda insisted, "that one of the actions about which your ambassador had intelligence, one of the actions involved marginally with her death, took place there at Eraklion."

Gabriel looked at Enda. "Are you sure you're not a mind-walker?" he asked.

Enda pulled her upper lip down in that droll smile. "I don't read minds," she replied. "The news is quite sufficient most of the time, and the rest of the time faces are usually plenty to go on. Well, at average system speeds you will have a day or so to consider the details. Let us get busy and see if she does what we bought her to do."

She went forward and sat down in the pilot's seat. Gabriel made one last turn through the ship to make sure that everything was secure, pausing briefly to look in at the empty cargo hold through its little fish tank window. If everything goes well, in a couple weeks that'll be full. And if it's not, we'll be broke.

"Gabriel, I cannot lift while you are not strapped down!"

He went forward and strapped himself in. I still don't get it, he thought, while under and behind him the engines hummed softly into life. I should feel great right now. We have a ship. We're going to find out what happened to me. At the very least, we're going to make some kind of living for ourselves . . . and begin an adventure. But he felt much less than elated at the moment. Maybe it's just that I've been through a lot lately.

Enda eased the controls forward, and the ship slipped gently upward, the stained concrete of the Phorcys landing ground dropping away beneath her. As if in salute, or just an accident of their rise toward the cloud cover, a final ray of sun broke through, stabbing down onto another part of the spaceport a kilometer or so away. Gabriel looked at it and smiled. A few seconds later they were through the cloud, and all that dismal landscape vanished beneath them, not a second too late for Gabriel. He slipped his hand into his pocket, felt the luck stone warm slightly under his touch as he lifted his eyes to the view above the cockpit and saw, amazingly, the sky already going black. Oh, the stars, he thought in a sudden flood of near-impossible relief, the stars.

And he shuddered at the memory of screams.

Chapter Nine

THE STARLIGHT OF open space might now haunt Gabriel somewhat, but over the next couple of days he began to suspect that the reaction would soon start to fade. He now had a whole new set of things to worry about. Any marine had some basic piloting courses as part of his training, but that particular piece of education was one that Gabriel had mercifully forgotten about as quickly as possible. After all, there were pilots for that kind of work. Marines concentrated on fighting, and Gabriel kept yearning toward that part of the control panel that managed the weapons array.

"Not just yet," Enda said. "Some basics first." She had revised their flight plan so they would not be expected at Eraklion for another five standard days. "We can well use a little more shakedown time in space," she had said, "not to mention a little time for both our sets of nerves to quiet themselves after the last week." And shaking down did happen. The Grid-based communications and entertainment system threw some interesting tantrums while they both attempted to configure it for the kinds of entertainment they preferred, not to mention initially refusing to accept any of their payment details. That sorted itself out, but by the time it did, Gabriel found himself spending more and more time with the piloting manuals. It was mostly stubbornness, Enda claimed. Well, if it is, it's not a bad thing, Gabriel thought more than once.

But making sense of the documentation, the first time out, was a daunting business. The ship-building companies had long since resigned themselves to the fact that their clients had neither the time nor the patience to master hundreds of different proprietary control arrays, so a ship's piloting cabin was more or less the same no matter from whom you bought it. However, no matter how simple they made the controls, there were still too damned many of them for Gabriel's liking. Right in the center of the console lay what was the most important part of the system for Gabriel's present purposes, the controls for the stardrive. And they scared him witless.

The basics were straightforward enough. The drive was a combination of the fraal-sourced gravity induction engine and the mass reactor, a human invention. Combined, the two engines, when activated, opened a small "soft" singularity through which the vessel containing the stardrive dropped. It then spent a hundred and twenty-one hours there, eleven-squared, no matter where it was headed or how far it intended to go. Gabriel had been wondering Why eleven squared? for a long time, first absently, as a child when hearing about it at school (in exactly the same way a lot of people had), but now a lot more urgently. There were no answers, though many guesses. The best one he heard had suggested that this universe was one of a sheaf of eleven, so that the heritage of that basic symmetry ran through everything, including gravitational fields. Another suggested simply that the number was a product of primes, and thereby somehow inherently "nice."

Not half nice enough for me, Gabriel thought, sitting there and going through the manuals one more time, for that was merely where the trouble started. During that time, just a shade over five standard days, you could travel a long distance, a short one, or not at all, depending on the gravitic coordinates you set as your destination. Here, as elsewhere in life, size mattered. A big stardrive would take you further in that one jump—or "starfall"—than a smaller one. Their own ship's drive was no bigger than they could afford, which made it not quite the smallest, but small enough so that its maximum distance per starfall was about five light-years. For their present purposes, that was more than enough. Corrivale, for example, was four point three light-years out, convenient enough for the kind of work they were going to be doing. To go further, you merely had to starfall more often.

If you're comfortable with that, Gabriel thought, turning over pages in the manual again. If you simply dropped into the cooperating void and came out somewhere else five days later, that would be wonderful. Unfortunately the ripples from your initial starfall and your planned starrise at the other end propagated merrily through drivespace for the whole five days. Everybody with detector gear or access to a drivespace communications relay could "see" and "hear" all the starfalls and starrises for about a hundred light-years around.

At least Enda knows how to do basic drivespace work, Gabriel thought. I'm going to have to learn as fast as I can. It wasn't fair to make her do it all. Gabriel was determined to find more ways to pull his weight on this operation. And still niggling at the back of his mind was the idea that, trustworthy as Enda might seem, it still wasn't really wise to leave all this kind of work to another person.

Paranoid, part of his mind commented, but another part said, rather pointedly, yes, but even crazy people have real enemies.

Gabriel sighed and leaned back in the right-hand seat, staring with loathing at the control panels in all their readout-studded glory. He would have given a great deal to be in a situation where pilots piloted and left him alone to get on with fighting, to have his plain, bare cubby back, and nothing more involved to manage than a powered suit. Though now Hal's voice came back to him too, commenting sarcastically, *Just because this suit makes you look like an ape doesn't mean you don't have to be any smarter than that to operate it.*

He sighed and turned away from the memory, looking at the controls again. For the time being they would have nothing to deal with but system work, which was something of a relief. At the same time, the idea of hanging around this place doing what was unmistakably going to be subsistence work simply annoyed him. Oh well, no way out of it . . .

"Gabriel," said the voice from back in the "sitting room," "where have you put my water bottle?"

"The one that squeezes?"

"Yes."

"Last I saw it, it was in your quarters."

He could practically hear her raising her eyebrows in an "Oh really" expression. After a moment's silence, she aked, "Well, for once this is true, instead of you having stolen it."

She came wandering into the cockpit, looking out past him at the stars. "You never get enough of these, do you?" she said, sitting down in the other seat with her hands full.

"I never will," Gabriel said, looking over at what she was carrying. One hand held a small pot with some dirt-like growth medium in it. The other hand held the water bottle. Gabriel leaned closer, trying to see what was half-buried in the pot. It was a bulb of some kind. "What is that?"

"Ondothwait," Enda said. *"Gyrofresia ondothalis fraalii*, the botanists call it in the Solar Union. It has many other names."

"A flower? A green plant?"

She looked up and gave him one of those slightly mysterious, specifically fraalish looks. "Eventually one or the other, but it will be a bulb for a good while."

"Well," Gabriel said, shutting the manual and putting it aside, "it's good to see you relaxing."

"It is mutual," Enda said, carefully squeezing water onto the bulb, "but why would *I* need so much relaxation? Compared to you, anyway? You have had much the worse time of it."

"You were the one who got shot at," Gabriel said. Both of them still sported small scabs where the shrapnel from the door had cut into the skin of their arms and face.

"That! What makes you think they were shooting at *me?*" Enda said.

They looked at each other for a moment. Then Gabriel said, "Uh. . . 'not proven.' "

"I agree," Enda said, "we are short of data. But why would anyone be shooting at me? I have no enemies on Phorcys and am unknown. You, however, are known, and there was some public sentiment against you. Plus we both suspect from your story that other forces could possibly be lingering about you to see what you would now do. Possibly there are forces acting against them that would prefer you dead." She shrugged again. "I admit it is a long stretch of reason, but better than any that leads to *me* being a target. Soon enough you will find out whether you are the target, for Eraklion is not a very controlled place. Anyone wanting to singe your hide will have his chance. Though, after the way you reacted the last time, I suspect they will either use more accurate marksmen or something of higher energy."

"Don't remind me," Gabriel said. "By the way, I heard back from them finally."

"Them who?" Enda questioned, seemingly startled by the change of subject.

"The officials on Eraklion."

"Oh? What was the delay?"

"Security checks, they said." His voice was a little bitter.

"To see if it was legal for them to deal with you?" Enda said. "Well, I suppose that kind of thing is likely until you clear your name. It will be hard, but you too are hard. When do we start?"

"They'll have a load of uranium peroxides ready in three days for haulage to Ino. Three hundred tons at nine hundred thirty Concord dollars per ton."

Enda knitted her fingers together, a gesture which Gabriel was learning meant she was doing math in her head. "That is travel costs and food plus twenty percent. Not bad for a first time. Did they say anything about the rate going up later?"

"No. I'll want to watch that. Twenty percent is not that much better than subsistence in this business."

Enda tilted her head "yes." "Meanwhile, that Grid program you like comes on in a while."

"Oh." Back on *Falada,* and even before he came aboard her, Gabriel had been an avid watcher of *Verge Hunter*, a serial Grid drama with plots so turgid and unlikely that a lot of the marines Gabriel knew had been watching it just to have a good laugh at the end of the day. The characters were also hilarious, some of the main ones being Star Force personnel so unlike anything that actually lived or breathed that Gabriel often wondered whether the people creating the series had ever *seen* a Star Force officer, let alone talked to one. These characters' adventures as they bombed around the Verge destroying villains and generally barging into everything in their path had been the delight of a lot of service people—including Elinke Dareyev, who in her more lighthearted moods (usually late in some party) would shout, "Not for myself, but *For The Force!*" with such energy that you might have thought she meant it as much as the ditzy second officer of the *Hunter* did.

"No," Gabriel said, "it's okay, I've seen that one before. I'll just get back to this." He picked up the manual again. "It's a pretty good read."

Enda made a little sniffing noise, the aural version of putting her eyebrows up, and went off with her bulb. Gabriel had to smile slightly as she went. The only genuinely good thing he had seen about the manual's drivespace section so far was the reassuring information that if you should make the mistake of dropping the ship into drivespace without setting destination coordinates, you would not find yourself in some *Verge Hunter*-like "lost universe" from which you would never return. Your ship would just bob up again immediately at the same spot, leaving you embarrassed but otherwise no worse off. Apparently this was how the drive-based communication relays worked, bobbing "up" and "down" out of drivespace, sending messages at stardrive speeds while "submerged" and picking up new ones when they surfaced again. Gabriel had been relieved to find that at least he could not kill them both that way. Leaving only about another ten thousand ways to do it.

Soon enough they would be experimenting with those. Mining, at best, was not safe work. It involved a lot of heavy machinery, usually in vacuum or noxious atmospheres, and all kinds of things could happen. Accidents—genuine ones, as well as accidents that weren't. What Enda had said about the shooting was something that had occurred to him before, and there were other matters. He could not get rid of the memory of the ambassador's voice saying, *I wish I knew why this was happening now.* Maybe someday, a few years down the way, we'll find out what it was. Increasingly, though there was no question that his main business now was to clear his name, Gabriel found himself wanting to find an answer to the ambassador's question. *It's almost a superstitious thing.* As if, if I can find out the answer, her ghost will rest quieter somehow.

He sniffed at himself. He was not superstitious, but the idea of somehow paying a debt—*paying it forward*, as she had called it, rather than back; paying it to her service, in her memory—that was not a bad one. He would do what he could. Business would mean that he and Enda would be passing through cities on both Phorcys and Ino every now and then for the next—he didn't know how long. Gabriel wanted to keep his contracts short. But I'll keep my ears and eyes open. Who knows? Maybe I'll even find out why they hate each other so much. If not . . .

The thought trailed off. It would have to wait. He was going to have to learn to be patient. And if he—

From the sitting room, a voice shouted, "Not for ourselves, but *For The Force!*" and an entirely-too-familiar theme song began, playing an overheated fanfare in the trumpets. Gabriel sat there for a moment, looking wryly back in that direction, then marked the manual at the page that began the section headed DRIVE DISTANCE/MASS EQUATIONS. He put the manual down carefully on the seat and went back to see what Enda was finding so funny.

* * * * *

Two days later they were at Eraklion, settling toward the pale brown surface of the planet, and Enda was standing over Gabriel's shoulder, letting him do the piloting. He had resisted this at first, but a few hair-raising experiments during which Enda attempted to purposely crash *Sunshine* into asteroids while the ship was running on autopilot convinced Gabriel that this robust little craft was, astonishingly, proof against even him. With the control supervision center set on "Panic," the ship was ready to snatch control away from him before he did anything terminal, so Gabriel made his first landing outside the opencast facility at Ordinen.

It was nothing more than a gigantic ugly hole in the ground. Once the mine works had been in a mountain, one of many. But the miners had grown expert, and the equipment had grown more aggressive and large, and within the first century or so of mining the mountain went away. Over the next century, as the system's fissionables needs increased, many more of the mountain's neighbors went away, until now the effect was of a tidy and almost perfectly hemispherical crater eight miles deep and fifty miles wide, still surrounded by mountains, though ones that looked very ephemeral. A careless viewer could have mistaken the site for a colossal meteor strike, except that meteors did not usually leave terraced sides in their craters.

The whole landscape there was an odd silvery brown, suggesting that lead ores accompanied the pitchblende that was being mined there. All along the terraces, endless unmanned mechanical diggers went up and down, bringing the mined ore up to massive spoil heaps at the "crater's" edge. From these spoil heaps the ore was transported by old-fashioned human- and fraal-driven trucks, though huge ones. The work of loading and unloading into the six processing facilities was just complicated enough to make AI a little less than cost-effective. The facilities themselves produced prepackaged uranium peroxides and other associated lanthanides, which were in turn containered and loaded into the waiting cargo ships, all very neat, very organized.

But Gabriel, landing and getting out in his e-suit, could only look at that huge hole and think of the holos he had seen of the little ships coming in low and fast over the mountains, and of the great gun-bristling shape of *Callirhoë* coming slowly up from the depths of the workings, big and round and broad-shouldered, but also grim looking, like a monstrous cetacean with a grudge to settle. And how the little ships scattered themselves to the eight directions when the guns went hot—

They landed near the number six packaging plant as requested in the contract. The plant was a big blank-walled facility with several gigantic open doors and no windows.

Someone in an e-suit came out to meet them under the near-black sky and said, *"Sunshine?"*

"That's us," Gabriel said. "Connor. Enda."

"Maxson," said the tall woman inside the e-suit, and they clasped arms, that being more generally accepted as a greeting while suited than handshaking. "Your first time on this run?"

"Yes," Enda said.

"TX, then. Run your ship into that fifth door. That's where your cargo is. Check the manifest after this; it'll tell you which portal to check. You have one hour to load. The next load comes in after that hour and gets dumped right on top of yours if you're not out of the way by then."

"For three tons of packaged ore?" Gabriel said. "That's not a lot of time."

"Machines will help you," Maxson said, sounding and looking tired and annoyed. "Just the way it is around here, I'm afraid. You'll get used to the rhythm or you'll find other work elsewhere. Better get moving. You're eating your hour already."

She moved off, and Gabriel and Enda looked at each other.

"At least it is very organized," Enda said.

"There are worse things than organization," Gabriel agreed. They headed back to the ship.

Fifty-eight minutes later they were nudging *Sunshine* out of portal five, and Gabriel was swearing softly under his breath as the ship made it plain she would answer a lot differently to her controls when fully loaded than when empty.

"I thought she's supposed to compensate for the load," Gabriel muttered to Enda as they gingerly hovered their way of the loading facility.

"She does when she is evenly loaded," Enda said, and Gabriel heard her trying hard not to lay blame anywhere.

Both of them were new at this particular work, but Gabriel got the feeling he was much newer at it than Enda was, and at the business of getting the most out of the loading machines that had been assisting them. The machines could have used a dose of better AI than they had, Gabriel thought. In the event, he and Enda had wound up muscling many of the last half hour's worth of loads into the ship themselves at increasing speed. Processed uranium is not light—it is after all a close relative of lead—and Gabriel found himself trying to do math in his head without the assistance of laced fingers as he got the ship up and out of the processing facility and headed her for orbit. *I'm already aching in places I didn't know I had. How am I going to feel about this time tomorrow?*

Enda was looking down through the cockpit windows at the silvery-brown ground dropping away beneath them. "Is twenty percent," she mused, "really worth all this, I wonder?"

"Hey," Gabriel said, trying to sound confident, "we just got started."

"Indeed," Enda said. "Perhaps we will get better."

The ship got up into microgravity again and immediately began to respond better. The thin atmosphere, hardly there at all, thinned away entirely to leave the view beautifully black again. Gabriel sagged back into his seat and punched in the coordinates for Ino to which the shipment was going. He then engaged the system drive on full and felt the slight subsequent push of acceleration.

"What I can't get over," Gabriel said, looking down, "is that it would have been some of the people from *there* who tried to destroy the mine works. At least, that's what the *Callirhoë* crew thought. The attackers knew the mountains. What could those people have been thinking of? It's their local economy, isn't it?"

"I suppose we could go down to some of the local bars and ask them," Enda said, "if we felt like getting beaten or shot at. It is the kind of question that is not likely to produce an even-tempered response, especially if any of them get a sense of who you are."

Gabriel thought about that. He wasn't Star Force, true, but he would be thoroughly enough identified with it to the eyes of anybody in this system who had been watching the news lately. "Yeah," he said finally, "but Enda, look. We do need the money, don't we?"

She started to take her e-suit helmet off then dropped her hands, changing her mind. "I will wait until we have offloaded and have had decontam. Gabriel, truly it was said that life in space is an open hole into which one pours the currency of one's choice. Until we start doing true meteor mining and stumble across the Glory Rock, or unless some relative unknown to either of us dies and leaves us vast wealth, we will neither of us ever again really have *enough* money." She gave him a wry look through the face plate. "That said, this can be a good life. Let us see how it treats us for a while. Twenty percent is enough to keep us going while we do system work. Should we jump out of system, the expense of running the stardrive will push our margins up to perhaps twenty-five, maybe thirty for long hauls. Beyond that . . ." She tilted her head. "There is no point in planning. Also, you wanted spare time to investigate things here. System work, a steady run, will let us do that."

Gabriel nodded. "I'm going to start spending a lot of time in the Grids," he said, "and I'm going to start doing that gunnery practice now. Don't be surprised if you don't see me much socially."

Enda smiled at him. "I have my own work to do, and were life with you not a surprise, I would not have bothered. Let us get this load where it belongs and get on with things."

* * * * *

They did, and they lasted four more loads over the course of ten days. It was not so much the physical exertion, which was brutal enough. Gabriel was hardly able to move the day after their first load, and Enda was little better—rather to Gabriel's surprise. This was the first time he had seen her betray any sign of weariness. Gabriel moaned at the very thought of a hot bath, once a commonplace on *Falada*, now as out of his reach as some planet's moon on a string for a plaything. They both made do with medicinal rubs that left them smelling like some unspecified alien species, and they sat and moaned, almost too stiff to make themselves something to eat.

The next day they scheduled another contract for the day following, Gabriel having said to Enda, "If we don't start moving again as soon as we can, we're never going to get the hang of this."

They did the run again and suffered even more, but this time they spent three days out of commission instead of two. "Come on," Gabriel said again, and they scheduled their third run and went through with it walking as slowly and stiffly as robots. But they were learning how to work with the machines at last, how to get them into a rhythm that worked, how not to waste a moment of time. Gabriel was getting more competent with the system drive, and the third time he flew straight into the loading portal like a beam from the plasma cannon's nose, dropped the ship in place with a certainty and speed that would have terrified him days before, tottered out, and started loading. Three quarters of an hour later he found another of the shift chiefs, a weren named Detaka, watching Enda put a last couple of small container loads into place while the loading machinery toddled off to do something else. Detaka was huge, even for a weren. Despite the slightly hunched over gait that seemed common among his species, the chief stood at least two and half meters tall, and his e-suit could not hide his thick, corded muscles. His e-suit's helmet, modified to fit his massive skull with its protruding tusks, looked almost comical, but Gabriel fixed his expression into polite seriousness. Detaka was not someone that any sane being would want to anger.

"You grow skilled," pronounced the weren around his tusks, leaning down to look at Gabriel with some curiosity. "You are Connor?"

"*Sunshine*, yes."

"You defy what the others say of you," Detaka said, straightening up and looking toward the portal again. "You are always welcome to work with me." And he was off, heading for another portal to look out and see where the next scheduled ship was.

Enda came over to Gabriel as the last machine rolled out and the cargo hold sealed itself up. " 'What others say of you'?" she asked.

"Word must have gotten out," Gabriel said. "Well, we'll see what happens."

They made their way back to Ino, rubbing their bruised and aching limbs but pleased that they were doing as well as they now were. It was harder to tell what was going on with Enda. Either for cultural reasons or because of some personal stoicism, she was only rarely a groaner and would mostly sit and look woeful. That evening and for the next day's travel toward Ino, Gabriel again did as he routinely had been doing, dividing his time between the gunnery software, learning to use its projected-virtual 3D view around the ship, and afterward spending as many hours as he thought they could afford on the Grid, roaming among the various news resources that covered Phorcys and Ino and other matters occurring in the Thalaassa system. He also routinely checked the news of Corrivale and other parts of the Verge.

Phorcys and Ino were in each others' newscasts and "written" Grid media in a much different mode than they had been while Gabriel was still on *Falada*. Then, as part of his work with the ambassador, he had made it his business to keep an eye on what their planetary media were doing. Mostly they were slagging one another off. One day, for amusement's sake, Gabriel had asked the computer that was ancillary to the ship's Grid management system to do a word count on certain words that occurred in translation in both Inoan and Phorcyn news stories. The clear winners for that week were the two words translating as "vile," followed closely by "machinations," "treacherous," and "enemy." After that Gabriel had ordered the machine to prepare him a new Top Ten list each day, and he began watching that list with interest. To his amusement, when he told the ambassador about it so did she. He had also read and listened to the proceeds of the planet-wide "talkrooms," to which anyone with Grid access could contribute. All the inhabitants were breathing virtual fire at those on the other side of the argument (and sometimes at each other, for not agreeing vehemently enough about how bad the Phorcyns or Inoans were).

Toward the beginning of the serious talks, Gabriel had become very concerned, for the frequency of all the worst words in the media had gone way up. Now, though, Gabriel asked the ship's entertainment computer to conduct a similar survey, and to his complete astonishment, it only found the word "treacherous" once. All the other words seemed to have vanished. There was now a great deal of talk from all the major commentators about "the new era of cooperation," the "improved performance" of the former enemy, the "long view," the "great strides toward closer relations." That was surprising enough. But the planets' Grid talkrooms were still full of the discussion of the best way to get rid of all those devils on the other side. Apparently the Inoan or Phorcyn on the street had yet to be convinced by what his politicians were up to. This left Gabriel shaking his head. Boy, he thought, would Delvecchio have known what to make of this.

But maybe she *would* have known. Either way, it seemed like some kind of good sign. Or was it? There was always the status of the talkrooms. How do you have peace, finally, if the people in whose name it is being made don't believe in it or in each other? Still, he thought, from the outside at least, the news looks slightly better than it did before.

Encouraged, Gabriel went off to check on news on other subjects that were also important to him. One of them took a lot of finding. It was buried far down, not in news native to Ino's and Phorcys's own Grids. He found it in a copy transmitted from the much bigger, older Grid at Corrivale. Down in one of the many sections devoted to shipping, there was a small section labeled FLEET MOVEMENTS—as much of an "official" announcement of its ships' whereabouts as the Concord usually made. It was normally issued for the sake of system ships that might want to hitch rides on capital ships set up for that kind of thing. Also attached to that list were some minor personnel notes, if they were thought to be germane to the movement. Here was just the one line that said: CSS *Falada,* out of Corrivale for Aegis, 5/9/2501, pursuant to R&R, promotions and staff reassignment, Capt. E. Dareyev.

Gabriel sighed and glanced away to the next menu, telling the computer to hunt down the next reference. There she went, back to a more civilized part of the Verge, certainly to a more peaceful one. Good-bye, Elinke. There went the Falada, more to the point. If I was ever going to do any scene-of-the-crime work there, any evidence would certainly be long gone. May as well give up on that one.

But the truth was that any evidence that might have helped his case was probably long gone by the time he went to trial. It would be interesting to find out how much of it had been preserved, if any at all was available, though Gabriel suspected that the only way to find out about that would be to return himself to Concord-managed space and turn himself in. Then he would discover quickly enough what the truth was . . . and possibly die of it.

No, he thought, not just today.

That night he roamed the Grids, and the next day until they made their drop at Ino. From the field there, as he had learned to do, Gabriel called administration on Eraklion to set up their next pickup . . .

. . . and was told there wasn't one.

His mouth dropped open. To be told there was no ore to be picked up at Ordinen was like being told there was a shortage of stars in the sky. But the person at the other end of the connection was most firm about it, if a little embarrassed. It was a grizzled, rather ill-kept woman whom Gabriel had become used to seeing on the comms any hour of day or night. She looked at him from the holodisplay and seemed to be trying to look impassive, but she could not quite manage it.

"Nothing for you, I'm afraid," she said.

"What about later. Next week? Next month—"

"Nothing any more," she said. "Sorry."

She shut down the communication, and Gabriel found himself sitting there and staring at the comms network's "ready" screen. Enda came up from checking the just-finished decontam on the cargo hold and gazed at him with some resignation.

"No hint of why?" she said.

"Not to me."

"Well," Enda said, sitting down by him in the other "sitting room" chair, "this is perhaps the only drawback of short-term contracts. If they had tried to force us out while we still had a contract in effect, we could have taken them through the local labor courts, and they would still have had to employ us."

"Which strikes me as a little dangerous under the circumstances," Gabriel said. "Never mind. Someone changed their mind about us. Or had it changed for them. By whom, I wonder?"

"It will probably be very difficult to find out," Enda said. "It is your choice whether we should spend the time." She did not quite say "waste," but Gabriel caught the inference nonetheless.

Gabriel sighed. "Well, at the very least," he said, "if we're being barred from work here, we're going to have to go somewhere else."

Enda nodded. "Corrivale is closest, I suppose." She tilted her head from side to side, got up, and slowly began to pace. This was something that Gabriel had never seen her do before, which he found slightly alarming. "It is strange to see such happening here, though."

"Why strange?"

Enda thought a moment, then said, "It strikes me as the kind of gesture some people here might think would please the Concord, perhaps. Generally speaking, if I understand this system at all, people here are, by and large, not very sanguine about Concord presence."

"It only takes one," Gabriel replied. "Anyway, there have to be *some* of them who're happy that the war has stopped."

"Do there?" Enda said. "Well, it would sound like a rational response, would it not? From what you have told me, there has been little enough rationality in this system." She paced a little more.

"Well," Gabriel said after a moment, "you could make a case that if there's something odd going on here specifically directed at one or both of us, if we change systems it should follow us."

Enda tilted her head back and forth, looking thoughtful. "It would."

"The only problem then would be working out which of us it was directed at."

"If you were. about to suggest that we separate," Enda said, "that I will not do. My money is in this ship as much as yours is. More to the point, what kind of partnership is it that disintegrates at the first sign of stress? Do you really think I would drop so readily what I 'picked up'?"

Gabriel felt ashamed, then, and hurriedly he said, "No, of course not. I just don't want you to be in trouble too. I have no desire to damage your career prospects."

Enda laughed, just one breath. "I have no career! I am an old fraal with the itch for travel, and that is all. But I too can become stubborn when I am thwarted, like Raitiz in the old story, who bit through the tree that threatened to fall on him." She smiled.

Gabriel put his eyebrows up at that. "So what did the tree do?"

"It fell on him, of course. What else, when he had bitten through it? But it was *his* choice, you see. Joy in life is about the perception of power, and the knowledgeable and compassionate exercise of it. That is one of the possible morals of the story."

"And another would be not to bite through trees?"

"It would seem wise," Enda said, "since fraal have no teeth. Not the kind that would be any good for trees anyway."

Gabriel found himself staring at her mouth, rather horrified at the discovery that even after knowing her this long, he had no idea what she had instead of teeth.

"Corrivale, then," said Enda. "Tomorrow? We will have to file a driveplan, and it will take Central over there a little while to process it—they have thousands of ships each day in and out, not like here."

"Fine. We'll slingshot out, then. No use in wasting free energy," Gabriel said.

"You need not go far to find a place where you may drop into drivespace safely, if that is your concern."

"Yeah, well," Gabriel said, " I don't know for sure when we're going to pass this way again. Anyway, it's polite, if nothing else. We'll go out courteously instead of dropping into drivespace somewhere busy where they would have a chance to complain."

Enda shrugged at him. While it was acknowledged as dangerous for ships to drop into drivespace too close together or too close to a massive enough star or planet (or anything else of substantial mass), generally that was as dangerous as things got, though it was certainly the pilot's prerogative to take himself well out of the way if he chose. "As for you," she said, "I suspect that you merely wish to play with the system drive."

"I am starting to get good with it."

"You are," Enda said, "an apt pupil, much quicker than I was, which is a mercy on us both. But then ships were not as smart two hundred years ago as they are now. And there is also the small matter of the guns."

Gabriel had to grin at that. He was enjoying gunnery practice even more than he had suspected, even though all the firing was simulated. The "JustWadeIn" gunnery management package (as the manual coyly called it) was one of Insight's more popular pieces of programming these days. It was expensive but worth it—designed specifically for beginners at the space dogfighting game and upgradeable directly over the Grid (assuming you had enough dollars handy to afford that kind of thing). It used heuristic and advanced semivirtual programming to "drape" you in a cloak of space that gave you the sense of standing on your feet and fighting your spaceborne enemies as if with guns,

blades, or nets, as your own ship's weaponry dictated. Having
begun there, the program slowly trained you in seeing space
combat no longer in the gravity-bound paradigm of someone
standing in a street, but in the gravity-free, three-dimensional
idiom of intersystem and extrasystem combat. Practical as it
was, it was also a lot of fun to play with, and Gabriel had been
using the basic hand-to-hand and other physical combat skills
taught him as a marine to evolve techniques for fighting their
ship in zero-g. Once again the Delgakis turned out to have been
a good buy. She was quick and responsive, spun deftly on any
one of her six axes without complaining too much about it,
shifted from yaw to pitch to roll and combined the three with an
alacrity and force from which her gravity grids protected her
inhabitants very satisfactorily.

"So I like the guns," Gabriel said, fairly unrepentant. "I've
caught you using them too."

"And enjoying it," Enda admitted, "a little human of me, perhaps? Well, I have been among them for long enough that I suppose some traits are catching. No matter. Let us make for the
outer system then and prepare to remove ourselves to Corrivale.
Do you want to do the plan submission, or shall I?"

"I'll take care of it," Gabriel said.

Enda wandered back off down to her quarters, and Gabriel
turned back to the Grid interface, still in 3D format, and switched
it back to screen—he found it hard to handle text in depth.

Gabriel brought up the starfall-plan template, made sure it
was interconnected with the ship's own computer, and plugged
in tomorrow's date, *Sunshine's* stardrive power constants, ship
mass, and the coordinates of the destination. The computer
immediately supplied time of arrival, a spot map of how many
other ships would be likely to be in that zone at that time, and the
standard request form from Corrivale Central for final confirmation of the schedule.

"Confirm it," Gabriel said, surprised to find that his voice was
shaking a little.

The confirmation flashed up. The ship's computer registered

it as well and began counting down toward it, asking Gabriel whether he would like to lay in a course now. He got up to go to the piloting console for his manuals—then stopped himself and sat down again, requesting the computer to show him a map of the Thalaassa system.

It was displayed for him in the round, not to scale. Gabriel chose a long hyperbolic orbit that would take them nearly out to the orbit of the last planet. Their first starfall—*his* first starfall— would take place just inside that little planet's orbit. He checked the system ephemeris. Rhynchus the place was called. No inhabitants, a thin atmosphere, probably too cold to support life comfortably. Good enough. They would swing by just within visual range, then make starfall and be out of here.

Once at Corrivale, there were all kinds of things that Gabriel would do when they found work. Grid prices would be cheaper there. He wanted to start doing an in-depth background check on one Jacob Ricel. Some of his records, the most recent ones anyway, would be under Star Force seal, but his earlier ones could be dug out if the price was right. There were Grid researchers who specialized in just this kind of search, people who would know places to start where Gabriel would not.

And then when he found out why Ricel had betrayed him and whom Ricel was working for, then he would go to the Concord and lay out his case. He was no murderer. Accessory to manslaughter he might be, but it had been unwitting. If he had known anything of what was going to happen, he would never have become involved. With the right evidence against Ricel, it would *have* to be clear to them what had happened. They would clear his name. He would re-enlist. He would . . .

Gabriel started fully awake again, having started to doze off in the comfortable sitting room chair. The back of his brain said to him, very clearly, Do you really think so? This is hopeless. *They* set *you* up. They went to some trouble over it, and they are not going to let you find out *anything* that will make a difference in the long run. The rest of your life is going to be like this. Working and working toward a chance to find something out, and the minute you start getting close, something will happen to rebuff you. Get used to it.

Gabriel sat up straight and frowned, rather astonished by the sheer rush of bitterness that filled him. Blood sugar, he thought, hoping desperately that *was* the problem and got up to head back to the tiny galley.

"Gabriel," Enda said, "eating again?"

"It beats the alternative," Gabriel answered, grim, and started cooking himself up a meat roll.

Chapter Ten

THE NEXT MORNING was their starfall. Gabriel was up three hours early, checking his settings and checking them again. They were fine, but he could not stop checking them.

"A starfall virgin," Enda said, amused, as she came into the cockpit with her morning cup of chai. "There is no sweeter sight. Where are we?"

She set the cup carefully aside and looked over Gabriel's shoulder at the course schematic showing in the front display. "Eight AU or so out from Thalaassa," he said. "No visual on the last planet, but it's out there."

"Will we be swinging by?"

Gabriel shook his head. "No, I changed my mind. There's nothing there, so why waste fuel?"

"System control must be amused," Enda replied.

"So let them be. I'm being careful," Gabriel said.

She raised her eyebrows and sat down beside him in the non-control chair. "I was looking through some of those Grid-homes and sites that you saved from last night's session," she said. "I had not noticed something about one of them, but it spurred my memory of a name, one that had struck me as strange the first time I heard of it."

"Oh?"

" 'Falada.' You did not tell me that your ship was named after a horse."

"What?"

"But it is true. See here." Enda reached out and changed the view in the control-panel tank to echo that of the one in the sitting room, so that text scrolled by, and Gabriel had to squint a little to get the sense of it. "It is a strange tale from the Solar Union somewhere. A young girl of noble birth is cast out of her home. She takes her 'horse,' a beast that talks and gives her advice. She disguises herself and takes service with strangers. After some odd occurrences, the horse is killed. The girl asks that the horse's head be nailed up over an archway under which she passes each day while doing some job of menial work. When she passes, the head of the horse speaks wisdom to her still. It seems to recite a great deal of poetry," Enda added, sounding impressed by this.

"Where did you get that?" Gabriel asked, leaning closer to the screen. "No, it's just a coincidence. *Falada* is just the weren word for 'wildfire.' "

"Yet how strange," Enda said, reaching out into the tank to "touch" it and stop the scrolling. "There is a story rather like this among the fraal about the Lost Wanderer who goes apart from her own—"

"And I'm the horse?" Gabriel said and grinned.

Enda looked at him with an amused look in those huge, burning blue eyes. "Considering the way you eat—"

Then they both jumped practically out of their skins, for the ship's proximity alarm, a dreadful screeching howl that not even a corpse could have ignored, went off right above their heads. Enda plunged out of the cockpit toward the racks where their e-suits were kept. Gabriel switched the tank into detection mode again and scanned it frantically while bringing up the Just-WadeIn routine.

It took only moments for that to load, but right now they seemed like far too many moments. The alarm was shrilling louder, indicating that the incoming craft were accelerating. "Don't just sit there; give me tactical!" Gabriel nearly shouted at the console, then breathed, breathed again, tried to get a grip on himself.

The fighting software's management implementation draped itself around him. Gabriel did not understand the physics of the implementation and did not care to. As far as he was concerned, every citizen of Insight was some kind of mad genius and worth every penny they were paid if they could do for you what the system was presently doing—make space look like something you could walk on, move around in comfortably, get used to. Courtesy of his marine training, Gabriel was at least far enough along in this particular mastery that he did not need to have a virtual "floor" to work on, though the system defaulted to one angled to match the given solar system's ecliptic. He got rid of the "floor" and saw who was coming. There were three ships. They all glowed red, the system's indicator that they had weapons cast loose. The ships were coming at him one above, two below, more or less—deceptive as it always was to use such terms in space—and they were corkscrewing as they came.

Gabriel wasted no time in casting his weapons loose as well. One after another the ports reported open, and the indicators in the tank for each gun's preheat cycle came up, shading up as the seconds went by from blue through violet, heading for red themselves. *Sunshine* was well armed as cargo ships went: one gun on each major axis and two forward, all of them plasma-cartridge ejectors with self-feed and self-clean. This was where a lot of Enda's "defense budget" had gone, but not all. The ace in *Sunshine's* pocket, the gun that Gabriel would not heat until the last moment to avoid betraying its presence, was the 120 mm rail cannon mounted longitudinally on the ship's "roof."

"Okay," Gabriel whispered as the three ships came in. They had not hailed him, and he was not going to bother hailing them—their intentions seemed plain enough. He shrugged his shoulders, feeling space "fit more closely" around him as the program came up to speed. He drew his sidearms. The program let him think he had only two, for convenience's sake, and it had no problem maintaining the illusion since all six of the plasma cartridge guns had nearly one-hundred-eighty-degree traverse mountings.

Gabriel was dimly aware of Enda hurrying in suited, with Gabriel's e-suit in her arms. "No time for that now," he muttered.

"Get strapped in." In his chair, despite the straps, he did his best to curl into a marine's preferred position for zero-g combat, a bolus: arms wrapped around knees so that opposite and equal muscle movement from any side would push or tumble him hard in the other direction. The program read his intention and fed it to the ship, which tumbled toward the intruders.

Two of them split away toward either side, firing. Lasers, Gabriel thought, not great. But maybe only what they choose to start with. The first impacts came, and the sensors in the ship's cerametal hide read them and fed them to the fighting program as a low moan. Nothing too serious. The CM armor had ablated the beams. Gabriel spun the ship to follow them, looking to the tactical system to handle targeting. It was too dark out here for routine visual, and the ships were small. Their shapes were a little unusual. Each of them was scarcely more than a little spherical bullet with no cockpits, at least none with visible windows. Running entirely on sensors, Gabriel thought. Odd, but he filed that information for later if he needed it.

He flung his arms and legs out to stop his spin and fired. The ship spun, answering, and the two side and forward projectile cannons each ignited its chemical load and blasted it out as plasma with a timed explosive core. At short ranges the weapon could be deadly effective if you got a hit. The problem was that in vacuum and microgravity the projectile's trajectory was perfectly flat, as much so as if it had been a laser or light beam itself, and it could bend no more than they could. This meant taking "windage" with every shot, using what data the computer could glean from the local situation to have the shot turn up where your target would turn up in the next second or so. Once there the plasma cartridge underwent its deadly secondary ignition and blew the hell out of anything with which it had come into contact.

This time the computer hadn't had time to construct an effective enough firing solution. Both projectiles missed and all three ships, now past Gabriel, arced around hard for another pass, all firing together.

He could feel Enda slipping the cloak of space around her now as she settled into the number two seat. The hull moaned again, more loudly this time, as the three ships swept past and lasered the *Sunshine* in several spots. *Again no result,* he heard Enda "say" into the program, the "artificial telepathy" feature of the software making it sound as if the words were originating inside his head where noise or the lack of it could not interfere. *But I think they may have something better.*

Could be. But so do we.

Not yet, Gabriel!

Of course not. The ships were coming in close together, much closer than they should have and still firing. Gabriel picked one, let the computer know it, gave it a good couple of seconds for calculation purposes, and just as the front guns' lights went ready again the computer found an interim solution. Gabriel fired again. The projectiles leaped out, the tracks of plasma blinding even in virtual experience. They streaked away, briefly blotting out even the tactical image of the attacking craft—

—then bloomed into fire. Metal shattered outward, air sprayed silvery into space and froze. Then it was all dark again.

The two other craft immediately broke right and left, one high, one low. *The left one,* said Enda as she fired.

The right-hand craft fired as well, and this time not just a laser. *He's got canister too,* Gabriel said, as the program spread all kinds of warnings over his field of vision. *Solution says the cargo bay.*

He felt Enda nod. There was nothing they could do about it. The augmented shielding back there might do some good or it might not. *Wham!*—and the whole ship shook, the hull screaming in their ears through the program. *Holed,* Gabriel said. *Shit, shit, shit!*

Enda said, *It is a nuisance; that was a particularly good price on the modular shielding.* She fired at the left-hand ship as it swept near and past her.

The computer yelled with delight at the look of what seemed a perfect solution. The projectile screamed away, hit it—

—and blew it spectacularly. Gabriel was twitching, though, at the sight of the third ship coming around, coming hard, and *Sunshine's* hull began to scream again, even more loudly than when it had been holed. Things started to shake hard—

What is *that*, Gabriel muttered, *some kind of mass reaction inducer?* The only thing he felt sure of was that it was about to shake the ship apart, and he didn't have a e-suit on, and though Enda might survive such a situation, he certainly wouldn't. He reached around "behind" him, over his shoulder, knowing what the computer would make of the gesture, and came up with the antique weapon that to him best evoked the way the rail cannon worked: a "shotgun."

The other ship dived closer. The shaking was getting very bad. The connection with the computer was beginning to suffer. Gabriel cocked the shotgun, "felt" the shell rack into the barrel— then took careful aim, for he was sure he would not get another chance. The computer text in the tank was breaking up. It had no solution for him. Never mind that. At this range, barely half a klick and closing fast, Gabriel had the only solution that was going to make a difference.

He fired. The rail cannon came alive and shot several rounds straight at the incoming craft. Gabriel was no good at computing other ship's speed by eye yet, but one thing he did know, as the dark little bullet streaked toward the incoming ship. *Vectors add . . .*

The tortured screams of the hull became deafening. The hurtling masses in front of *Sunshine* collided, their vectors added, and the larger of the enemy craft fairly turned itself inside out in a splash of air and liquid, various gases that froze instantly to iridescent microscopic snow as they splashed and drifted away from the source of the explosion. The terrible shuddering of *Sunshine's* outer shell stopped. Everything grew very quiet.

Gabriel let the ship just hang there for a few moments while he scanned all around him. Beside him, in the software, he could see Enda doing the same.

Nothing. Nothing anywhere. Exactly what had been there before all this started. They hung in the midst of much drifting wreckage in the dark with the stars burning all around and Thalaassa way off in the distance, pale as a tiny moon.

After a long silence in which she completed her own scanning, Enda said, "*That* was interesting."

Gabriel had noticed the fraal fondness for understatement some time back and would occasionally rise to the bait. Now he just made a face and said, "Who *were* those people?"

"Let us see if we can find out."

Gabriel nodded and slowly nudged *Sunshine* forward, not wanting to disturb the debris field too much. For this work, visual assessment was better than the computer program, so Gabriel instructed the computer to lift the "drape" for the moment, but to have it ready again immediately if he wanted it.

They both peered through the cockpit windows into the darkness as *Sunshine* slipped slowly among the wreckage. There was a lot of frozen liquid, a lot of torn metal and plastic, not much else. Out of consideration for Enda, Gabriel would not have come right out and said what he was looking for—body parts— but Enda, leaning forward in her seat, said, "We must shoot a little more carefully next time, Gabriel, or less carefully. We have not left big enough pieces of whoever started the fight."

"After what that last ship was using on us," Gabriel muttered, "*no* piece of that stuff out there is small enough for me." He turned to the far right of the control panel and touched the control that would start the ship doing its own sequence of diagnostics. It had sensors buried in all the important circuitry and every square meter of hull and would report in about an hour on where it felt "sick." Gabriel was sure that, after that, it had to feel sick *somewhere*.

"No sign of anybody else," he said to Enda.

"No closer than Eraklion, no," she said.

"Then that wasn't an accident. Someone was lying in wait for us."

"It does seem likely."

"That does it," Gabriel said and reached into the tank again for the drive controls. "The hell with the drive plan. I'm going to—"

Then he stopped. No more than a few kilometers in front of him, he saw something he had been expecting even less than a little pod of ships attacking him.

It was a starrise.

He sat there frozen with astonishment as the light sleeted all around the shape that was dropping out of drivespace not far from them. Completely astonished, Gabriel moved his hand away from the stardrive controls that he had been about to activate. Instead he brought up the sensor displays again. There right in front of them was the ship, the colors of its present starfall still leaking away into space around it.

It was huge. It was a sickly green hue; Gabriel could not discern if it was metallic or some other substance. The body of the craft was sleeker than a lot of human-built ships would have tended to be, but there were still some structures about it that had that "bolted-on" look so dearly beloved of human engineers, what Gabriel could always remember Hal referring to as "chunky and exciting detail." Beyond that, the chief characteristic that struck Gabriel as worthy of notice was its size. It was as big as *Falada* had been, perhaps even bigger. And much of the chunky and exciting detail was gunnery—guns possessing barrels that Gabriel could have walked down without crouching if he was any judge of such things. If there was a logo, livery or other identifying design on the ship's hull, Gabriel could not find it. There was just too much *ship*.

Beside him, Enda simply stared. "What do we do now?" she breathed.

"I think we sit still and pray," said Gabriel, "because there's no use running away from that, and there's sure no use *shooting* at it."

The last fires of starrise trickled away from the hull of the huge ship. Mostly gold colored, this starrise, Gabriel thought. It was lucky enough as spacefarers reckoned such things, though not as lucky as the so-called "black" starrise that radiated into the ultraviolet and made everything for miles around fluoresce. The question is, will it be lucky for us?

A bare breath later, the ship went into starfall.

It just sank away into nothingness, seeming to attenuate from all sides—a bizarre enough effect when you saw it in proper lighting with a bright star nearby and with starfall's own distinctive light crawling over the body that was leaving real space. In this shadowy reach of the Thalaassa system, though, the ship simply seemed to vanish like a ghost as the lights of starfall traced their way over it. Outlines wavered and effaced themselves, highlights evaporated like water drops under a fierce heat, planes and curvatures melted away. A few seconds later, she was gone.

"That's impossible," Enda said, almost inaudible. "Ships can't reenter drivespace that swiftly."

Gabriel sat and stared. A few seconds later, he reached out for the tank and brought up the stardrive controls again. "I don't know what *you* think," he said, "but I think we need to be somewhere quiet for five days."

Enda simply nodded.

Gabriel hit the control for immersion. The light swept up around them, masked away the darkness of Thalaassan space . . .

. . . and they too were gone.

* * * * *

Five days later the light of a new starrise sluiced along the hull of *Sunshine* and across her cockpit, out of which stared a couple of interested faces, looking to see how the ship took her first starrise under their command. Light that splashed and ran like water sheeted "down" the length of the ship, trailing and trickling away. Normal black space followed in its path, leaving them looking at their first glimpse of the Corrivale system. The primary itself, a middle-sized golden star, burned in the middle distance about two AU away. The other planets were strung out as variously bright or dim "stars" along both sides of their sun's ecliptic. Inderon and Tricus were closest to the primary, then Hydrocus with Grith as a companion spark that it occasionally occulted. The outer worlds, Lordan, Lecterion, Iphus, Almaz, and Chark, stretched out into the depths, too dim to see at all without the guidance of tactical overlay.

The "pen" in which they fell out of drivespace was full of other ships and scheduled starrises and starfalls. It was therefore no surprise when the first communication they received was from Corrivale Central, requesting them to get the hell out of there in short order. Not that this was the exact language used, but Gabriel recognized the tone of it clearly enough.

"So where are we headed?" Enda asked from back in her quarters.

"I haven't downloaded system comms yet," Gabriel said.

He was hoping that there would be at least one answer to the numerous queries he had sent before they left Thalaassa. There was no Grid access while you were in drivespace, and all that time he had fretted and played with the comms like a man who couldn't wait. Now he was half afraid to go near the console.

"Well, wait a few minutes," said Enda. "The system Grid will be speaking to our own system and sorting out billing and so forth for some little while yet. It will call when it's ready."

Gabriel sat there on the hot seat side of the cockpit and let out a long breath. The past few days had been welcome enough time to recover from the attack on them. There was also time for assessment of the damage. They had both been very annoyed to discover that the cargo bay had taken considerable damage in the attack. Both the inner shielding and outer plating would have to be replaced before the ship could legally haul again. Other things had been on Gabriel's mind as well. Chief of them was his dislike not only of being shot at but at the possible reasons for it.

"Come now, Gabriel," Enda said. "This is the Verge."

He had laughed at her. "Oh, come on! The Verge has some reputation as being wild and woolly, but not *that* wild and woolly. I was born here. Not this part, but still this is usually a fairly civilized place. What's going *on* out here?"

Enda gave him a thoughtful look and knitted those long slender fingers together in her working-things-out gesture. "But 'civilization' simply means living in cities," she said. "There are relatively few people here doing that, wouldn't you say?"

"That seems a touch pedantic."

"I would rather say that it strikes to the heart of the matter. The Verge is a fair size, and we are a long way from Bluefall. In the Thalaassa system are two planets with various small cities on them, yes. But most of the other people in the system are living by themselves, working the various mining outposts or living in very small groups, in places that are lonely at best and extremely isolated at worst. Nor, without any centralized Concord presence, is there any really organized means for determining how safely people live in the Thalaassa system." She sat back and put her feet up. "I think that is not your main concern."

"No," Gabriel said. He frowned out into the darkness. "I can still remember perfectly well what Jacob sent me off to 'find out' about. Something going on or not going on 'way out' in the system. We were pretty far out there the other day."

"True."

Gabriel got up and started to pace, then stopped himself, this being one of those habits that could get very wearing for those forced to share close quarters with you. "I don't know, but *someone* was being waited for out there. I'd bet money on it."

"Would you bet, however, that it was *us?*"

Paranoia, the back of his mind said to him again. "I don't know," he answered. "We might just have stumbled into a trap laid for someone else, but who? No other driveplans were filed for that area, or system plans either."

"Many people do not bother filing system plans," Enda said, "considering them a waste of money."

Her look was very demure. "Are you suggesting that we should have done something illegal?" Gabriel said.

"You will wait a long time before you catch me suggesting such a thing to *another* being," Enda said, and the look became even more demure and grandmotherly.

Gabriel chuckled. "But, Gabriel," Enda said, "is it not true that believing the universe to be actively involved in one's persecution is far preferable to discovering that it is *not* so involved, and in fact does not give a good flying damn?"

"Enda! What language!"

She snorted at him. "Still. Gabriel, I believe as you believe, that you have been the victim of some kind of plot. What kind? We shall see, but do not complicate its magnitude unnecessarily."

The communications screen chirped, the particular tone that meant that a message was coming in. Gabriel got up and touched the screen. It cleared and displayed a message. "Iphus Independent Mining Collective," he read, "we have received form 8821, and so on and so on." He read down the message, then said, "Well! We're hired!"

"That is a relief," Enda said. "It would have been annoying to get here and find no work waiting."

Gabriel stood, reading the message again. "Did they check back with the mining company on Eraklion?" Enda said.

"They did. Look here—" Gabriel scrolled the message down. "—Satisfactory work record at Eraklion/Ordinen."

"If we were so satisfactory, then why did they refuse to employ us again?" Enda said, rather dryly.

Gabriel turned away from the screen and shook his head, started to pace again, stopped himself again. "We were too good, maybe? Got somebody riled up?"

"Do you believe that?" Enda asked.

"No," Gabriel replied. "I still think about what that weren said."

"Weren are generally too proud to be liars," Enda said. "I would wonder too what it was that was being said about us."

"Wish we could go back and ask him."

"A little late for that," Enda said, "but believe me, sooner or later, if something bad is being said about us, we will find out. People will rush to tell us, people who will claim otherwise to be our friends. We will find out soon enough."

Gabriel nodded and looked down at the contract. "This is freelance," he said. "They don't want us mining actually on the planet. They want to have us 'skimming' the Outer Belt for high nickel-iron content rocks. Apparently there have been a lot of hits late!.They're looking to see how this pans out."

Enda looked over his shoulder. "What about our fuel costs? That is going to be very system drive-heavy work."

"Subsidy of ten percent for the first ten weeks." Gabriel glanced at her. "If we don't know whether we're making our nut within ten weeks, we can always cut and run. The contract's mutually revocable."

Enda looked at the contract for a moment longer, then said, "Why not? We must get the cargo bay repaired first. Grith would be the place, I suppose. After a few days we can go out and see how the Belt treats us."

Gabriel nodded and sat back down in the pilot's seat. At least now they had somewhere to go. He told the system drive to speak to Central's routine and location computers, ID *Sunshine* to them, and find a course for Grith with a later departure to be filed for Iphus.

REQUEST ACCEPTED, said the drive system. WAITING.

* * * * *

It took a while, for elsewhere in the system, other ships were moving. CSS *Schmetterling* had been in orbit around Hydrocus for some hours since her arrival. There were probably those who suspected that this in itself was a message of sorts. Concord capital ships did not go anywhere without reason, and when they stayed in one spot there was generally a reason for that as well. The longer they stayed, the more important the reason would probably seem to those who noticed such a ship's presence.

There were those who rode such ships who were perfectly content for this to be the case. It was a tool they used, like many another. This particular ship was a tool, its captain suspected, and so was she . . . and she was furious at the thought.

"I see no reason why I should cooperate," said Elinke Dareyev.

"I see several," said the man sitting across from her at the polished hardwood table in her quarters, a deep-carpeted, pale-walled, tastefully furnished and comfortable space that had at the moment, for her at least, lost a great deal of its comfort. "Most of them have to do with your rank, and mine."

There was of course no answer to that, but it would not stop her from trying to change his mind. "Administrator," she said. "If I—"

"Mr. Kharls, please," he said, "or Lorand. It's much preferable for you to damn me by my first name, if damn me you must."

"Lorand," Elinke said, "you have to realize what you're asking of me. If you—"

"Captain," he said, "you're mistaking this situation for one in which you have some flexibility. It is not like that. If I must transfer my business to another ship, well enough, but it's *your* career that will suffer, not mine. Obviously I would have to report any such little difficulty. I must suggest that any captain of a ship of this size caught disobeying a direct order from a Concord Administrator would find difficulty commanding anything larger than a system debris scoop in the future."

Elinke sat there with her mouth stretched in a tight thin line for a moment. Then she said, "Sir, my obedience to orders is not in question here. But I also have a responsibility to point out to those with whom I work, when necessary, that they are in error, or about to make serious mistakes."

The man across the table gave her a look that would have been funny on anyone of less power. The problem was that Lorand Kharls was about as powerful a being as one was likely to run into in these spaces. Even so, Elinke would have liked him under other circumstances. He was not a handsome man, but he was good looking in a big, broad, stony sort of way. You would swear that he had been hewn out of some kind of granite in roughly rectangular chunks, from which an absent-minded sculptor had smoothed off the corners as an afterthought. Little eyes, close-set, intelligent, looked out at you from above an easy

smile, and Kharls wore his baldness with the air of a man who
thought that there were more important issues than hair. The
overall effect was of saturninity, someone who enjoyed life's
pleasures but could put them aside in a second when work
required. The sense of a submerged strength, very hard, very
cold, yet always held in reserve, was there and could not be
ignored by anyone with a brain. Equally present was the sense of
a man who would walk straight over you and never regret it if
you got between him and something he wanted. It was, of
course, Elinke's business as a commander to find out exactly
how much attention she had to pay to the ranking passengers,
diplomats, and dignitaries whom she sometimes carried in the
course of work. It was very annoying to find one whom she
could not flatter, blather, confuse, or sideline just enough for her
to honor both her conscience's demands and his. It looked like
this was one of them.

Why him? she thought, furious, but doing her best to cover it
up.

"Well, Captain," Kharls said, "it's kind of you to be concerned for me. Maybe you would spell out the sources of your
concern in slightly broader terms."

To most people, this would have been a warning, and Elinke
knew it. Nonetheless she said, "Sir, you are relatively new in
these spaces and will perhaps have missed some of the finer
detail concerning matters at Thalaassa."

There. If he wanted to be insulting so could she. Elinke was
therefore both very moved and seriously annoyed when Kharls's
face went quite sad, and the set of it told Elinke that the sorrow
was genuine.

"As regards your partner, Captain, of course I heard," he said.
" 'Tragic' is a word that diplomats overuse for such circumstances, and not nearly strong enough most of the time. Having
lost a partner in similar circumstances, all I can say is that the
Concord often asks much too much of many of us."

She shut her mouth.

Outmaneuvered. Oh, you slick old brute.

"Still," Kharls said, "those of us with the strength must continue to do our duty as best we can. So let's get on with it and see what can be redeemed from the horrible mess that ensued after the destruction of the *Falada* shuttle."

"Redemption is always welcome," Elinke replied, "but I question whether that word and the name Gabriel Connor should properly appear in the same sentence."

"That won't be our judgment to make," Kharls said, "and possibly not that of the next generation either. Nonetheless, there are still some loose ends hanging about the investigation."

"The trial certainly should have made Star Force's position clear," Elinke said. "I wonder that you would question it."

"My business is questioning things," said Kharls easily, "which is probably why you're so annoyed with me, especially when you have your mind made up."

She said nothing.

"Far be it from me to confuse you with further facts," said Kharls, "unless you are already in possession of all of them."

She said nothing again.

"So," Kharls said, "let's say there are still some aspects of this situation that require inspection. Captain, I am going to require you to follow my orders or be reassigned, but that doesn't mean I intend to keep you in the dark. That would be rude. For one thing, take the trial itself. Why did Star Force relinquish the right of Connor's trial to Phorcys?"

Elinke looked at him with some surprise. "They had to. It happened in atmosphere—"

"Yes, that well-known truism. Except if Star Force *really* wanted to try Gabriel Connor itself, it would have fought a little harder over the prospect, don't you think? That fight could have gone on for months. You know how the legal process is, even now. How long did it take the Adjudicator General to come back with a decision on the venue?"

"Well, about an hour—"

"The Adjudicator General couldn't—well, there are a *lot* of things she couldn't do in an hour. Never mind. Does the speed with which that decision came through suggest anything to you? Just play with that thought for a while. Second, what about Jacob Ricel?"

"He's dead," Elinke said rather bleakly. "Unfortunately."

"Yes, and when there were so many people who wanted to talk to him. . .theoretically, at least. An interesting problem, that last one with his e-suit. All kinds of people could have gotten at it. It suggests something about e-suit maintenance security on board Concord vessels, or on your last command, anyway."

Elinke held quite still and concentrated on not breaking out in a sweat.

"In any case," said Kharls, "there was Connor claiming under oath and not under it that Ricel was Intelligence of some kind or another, and there was Ricel denying that he was, and there you were denying it as well."

"Administrator," Elinke said, getting annoyed now, "you know perfectly well how Intelligence assets are assigned and identified to Concord commanders. We must know who they are, but sometimes we are required not to approach them with this information, for reasons that Intelligence finds good and proper."

"Which we lesser beings cannot understand, yes, I know. It annoys me too."

"In Ricel's case, no such identification was ever made to me by Intelligence. This leaves us with some uncomfortable possibilities, one of which is that Intel has begun submerging assets in our commands and not telling us—an action that would be very much against the thread of Concord law in these matters, as I understand it."

"Yes," Kharls said, "it would, wouldn't it?"

Elinke got up and walked around, trying to calm herself a little, trying to look at her mother's oil paintings on the walls, those seascapes that she ordinarily found so soothing, which were doing nothing for her at all at the moment. The very thought that they might be submerging assets and not informing her . . . "The other possibility is that Ricel was telling the truth when they questioned him—that he was not Intelligence, no matter what Connor said—and that Connor was lying to try to save his own skin. That possibility was the one that the prosecution favored at the trial."

"Partly because the other one seemed too far-fetched," Kharls suggested.

"Yes," Elinke admitted, a little reluctantly, because she thought she could see where this might be leading.

"However, Captain, you've missed a possibility . . . as did everyone else at the trial, whether accidentally or on purpose."

"And that would be?"

Kharls leaned back in his seat and folded his arms. "That Ricel *was* Intelligence, *but not ours*."

Elinke paused for a moment, then shook her head. "That would be very convenient for Connor, if it were true."

"And what if it were?"

"You would have to work at it to convince me," Elinke said. "It's multiplying conclusions in a way that would have made old Occam whirl in his grave. Why reach so far for a conclusion when there are more convenient ones that don't require the stretch?"

"Because it might be true," Kharls said mildly.

She could think of nothing to say to that.

"If it were the truth," said Kharls, "it would be worth discovering, surely, whether you like it personally or not."

Elinke looked at the table and said nothing.

"But we'll leave that for the moment," said Kharls. "It doesn't matter whether you like the way this line of reasoning is tending. I intend to investigate various aspects of the *Falada* disaster and of the Connor trial as incidental to the disaster. One more question for you, Captain. Why *did* those two planets come to terms so quickly? Don't tell me about the ambassador's plans. I know what they were, close enough. It *still* happened too fast. Even she was surprised."

Elinke blinked. That was information that not many people would have had, and she found herself wondering how Kharls had come by it.

"Yes," he said. "It comes time to continue in the direction that Delvecchio would have, if she could have—not that she could have remained in this system very long. She knew that, but long enough to put some people in place to ask awkward questions. This I intend to do, and one of them will be Connor."

At that Elinke's eyes narrowed. "I wouldn't have thought you would stoop to using a traitor," she said.

"Oh, I wouldn't," Kharls said, "but it's so hard to find out what makes a traitor. Usually they don't consider themselves such. The judgment is almost always external. And myself, I haven't made my judgments. Though of course you have."

Elinke held herself very still and quiet, for there was something obscurely threatening about the way the man was looking at her.

"Captain Dareyev," said Kharls, "my job is justice. You know that. Justice is not always done in one sweep of the broom. Sometimes it takes two or three strokes, or five, or ten, to get it done right, though I try to make as quick a job of it as I can. Believe me, if after I have gathered the evidence I seek, I find that Gabriel Connor was actively involved in the deaths of the ambassador and your partner and the others, I guarantee you that he will not long enjoy sunlight or starlight or anything else. In the meantime I have other business here as well, which I will be attending to in due course. This is a busy system, and there's a lot here that needs the occasional careful eye turned on it while people think I'm occupied with other things."

He sat back. "Grith," he said. "And particularly the se-sheyans' status here."

"It's stable, surely," Elinke said. "That was what the Mahdra settlement was all about."

"It will certainly be stable while *we're* hanging here," Kharls replied dryly. "My concern at the moment is for the periods when our collective back is turned, so to speak. VoidCorp is still looking for ways to overturn Mahdra. As far as they're concerned, it's a direct challenge to their power as a company. In VoidCorp's case, specifically, there is nothing more dangerous.

Their stellar nation status is secondary to them, and they esteem it less than you might suspect. Their main concern in the world is to *dominate the market*. Completely. They believe they own the sesheyans—from the *de facto* point of view, they do, however repellent it may be to us to admit the fact—and any free colony of sesheyans is abominable to them. That there should be a huge one here, sitting right under their noses in a system where the Company already has such extensive holdings and business interests, is an ongoing threat that is impossible for them to ignore."

"But they have been ignoring it," Elinke said, "or at least if they haven't, they've been keeping very quiet about it."

"Therein lies their only hope," Kharls said, "at least as regards overt action. Covertly there is a fair amount of harassment of Grith-based sesheyan interests: market restriction, shady business practices on the small scale. On the small scale, the Concord has seen fit to ignore that kind of thing. No use taking out the cannon to shoot the gnats. At the same time, it has been entirely too long since VoidCorp has attempted something against Grith, and specifically against the Council of Tribes, which hasn't been more overt. This does not reassure me, nor does it suggest that the Company is getting tired of fighting this particular battle."

"You're suggesting that they're about to try something new?"

Kharls nodded. "The Concord has been putting a lot of subtle economic and political pressure on VoidCorp along many fronts in an effort to get them to back off a little in their demands regarding the sesheyan species in general—and the sesheyans on Grith in particular. There's been no movement, not even the kind of token movement that a negotiator might make to convince the other side that something is beginning to happen when it's not really. The suggestion is that not only is VoidCorp's position hardening but that they may be considering some action to consolidate their position regarding the sesheyans—and not at all to the sesheyans' advantage, or the advantage of anyone else who may be standing in the vicinity. They won't care about that. As far as VoidCorp is concerned, 'free' sesheyans are a bad example to all the rest of the Company's Employees, an example that I think from their point of view can't be tolerated any longer."

"If VoidCorp is contemplating some kind of move against Grith," Elinke said, "they have to realize what kind of trouble this would stir up for them with the Concord—"

Kharls shook his head. "It would take a long time for that consequence to follow," he said. "Meantime, they would have done whatever it is they're planning to do. My concern is to find out what they have in mind—for *something* is going on here— and stop it before it happens. They must understand that, as big as the Verge is, it is not unpoliceable, and they will not be allowed to have their own way by acting against the rule of Concord law and then taking the consequences later. They are going to start learning that, at least in the larger matters, it is impossible for them to act against Concord law. Period. Let alone, to do it with impunity."

Now it was Elinke's turn to sit back and fold her arms. The man talked a good fight, that was true, but could he actually produce the result? Then again, Concord Administrators were chosen not only for their sense of justice and their cleverness in producing it, but for a certain innate ruthlessness, a whole suite of emotional tendencies that made them difficult if not impossible to stop. Though we'll see about that, she thought.

"It's a big goal, Administrator. Audacious."

He smiled slightly, in a way that suggested he knew perfectly well what she meant. "Well, what good are small goals?" he asked. "Aim at the sun, and you're more likely to hit it than if you aim into the bushes. But, Captain, I need your help in this. I can understand that my position here, and my intentions here, do not make you happy. At the same time, we both have work to do that overrules or outranks our personal feelings in the matter. I am concerned about Grith and the sesheyans here. I will do whatever I must to preserve their lives and the peace that reigns here at the moment, however rocky and cracked a thing it looks to be.

"Matters here are not going to stay as quiet as they have for very much longer. My presence here—*our* presence here, for you are part of this too—will start to stir things up. One Concord ship just left, and people were beginning to relax. Now here comes another one, and . . ." He shook one hand gently in the air, mimicking the motion of something liquid in a container. "The ripples begin to spread, and it will be very interesting to see what starts to come to the surface."

"Are you expecting 'shooting' to break out?" Elinke asked, rather cautiously.

"Why, Captain, what a restrained way to put it. I am, but I'm not at all sure what form the shooting will take, or who'll be doing it, or from what quarter. Almost all parties involved in this 'discussion' are entirely too used to acting through intermediaries. I expect to take some weeks more of analysis here before I'm certain, unless the situation is even more volatile than I expect, in which case we may have to move very fast indeed. Make sure your marines are in their best form, because they'll need to be. When the pressure builds high enough and this situation blows, it will blow sky high." He smiled slightly. "So, Captain, is there anything else we need to cover?"

"Only one thing," Elinke said. "Administrator, if you bring that man aboard my ship—well, be warned. This is Concord territory, and I will confine him and hold him for transfer to a Concord jurisdiction for trial. A proper trial."

"Captain," said Kharls, unfolding his arms and stretching, "if you attempt that, I will try him right there with whatever data I have at that point, and then I'll try *you*. Don't be sure you would come out any better than he might."

Elinke swallowed.

Kharls stood up. "Anything else?" he inquired amiably.

She shook her head slowly. "No, Administrator," she said, "I think that about covers the ground for the moment."

"Good. Then let's go up to the bridge and look at some stops we'll be making in the next few days."

He led the way out, and Elinke went after him. For the moment, she thought, but not for very much longer, if I can help it.

Chapter Eleven

SCHMETTERLING'S PRESENCE was indeed causing the ripples to spread. The system Grids were full of pictures of her, and there was speculation all over the planetary media as to what her presence might mean. There was some attention, too, to the sudden reassignment of Captain Elinke Dareyev to duties so close to a system where she had previously suffered tragedy. It was well known that Star Force was normally generous with leave for officers who had lost a family member or partner. Much speculation went on about this and other matters.

"I tell you, he's here," the voice said down the shielded line. It was expensive to make Grid contacts secure over long distances, but it could be done if you paid enough for it. In this particular case, money was not even slightly an object.

"Well, that's hardly our problem."

"Oh, yes, it *is,* or it will be, shortly. If they meet and a few things come out that should never have had a chance to come out—"

"That wasn't our fault either."

"It doesn't matter. The only one who could have really made a difference to the situation is gone now where he can't be pumped, not even with the drugs they say they won't use."

"Well, it's just as well they never got suspicious. We've been very lucky so far, but we don't dare take the chance that the luck'll continue. So look, just make sure they don't meet."

"A lot of chance we have of stopping it if he decides a meeting should go ahead."

"Don't be an idiot. There are about a hundred thousand

possible solutions lying right under your nose. Just pick one and go to work, and make sure you lose it afterwards! Some of them would be only too glad to turn around and admit everything in the aftermath. Disloyal creatures—sometimes I wonder why we bother."

"Because they're there, and we own them."

"Well, I just wish the rest of the nations would give up and admit it. Then we could all get on with life. Look, just get *on* with it. It's not exactly as if he's keeping his schedule or his movements a secret. Makes you think he didn't know what was going on."

"Him? Hardly likely. He's got his own agenda, much good may it do him for the short time he has left."

"Right. Well, good luck, and report back immediately when you get it finished. Himself is eager to start the next phase."

"Right."

* * * * *

They dropped slowly toward the green, cloud-swirled world, Gabriel taking his time at the controls while Enda watched without being obvious about it. Cocky as Gabriel had become with the system drive on Eraklion, that had been over barren ground, a world of few settlements and few people, a place where if you crashed you had a better than ninety percent chance of killing no one but yourself. Here though, the chances went up significantly. Oh, Grith might not be overpopulated—a hundred thousand sesheyans or so, maybe a hundred and fifty thousand Hatire humans and others, various other people of various other species—and they might be scattered fairly thinly over a largish world. It would be just his luck, while stunting in a new ship, to lose control and come down right where someone was standing waiting to be killed.

"It's a pretty place, really," Gabriel said as they dropped through Grith's pale orange-red sky toward the big central continent that girdled the planet. The majority of Grith was vast tropical rainforest. There was no landing in that, of course, except spectacularly and permanently. Nor could one land in the landlocked seas that interpenetrated the forests, weaving in and out of the jungles in intricate patterns that caught the fierce sunlight and gleamed like ribbons of fire as the ship swept northward over them.

Beyond the jungles and the bordering seas toward the pole stretched hundreds of thousands of square kilometers of tidal marsh. Those marshes on Grith's sunward side presently had gone shallow and dark, the tides being almost all the way out at the moment. As the planets turned, tugging at each other with the interacting tidal forces that Gabriel had once heard Hal describe as "too damned close a relationship," huge walls of water would rush back to fill those marshes again. In some places, the girdling seas would change their boundaries by hundreds of kilometers in the course of a day.

Add to this the ferocity of Corrivale and the closeness of the orbit around the primary which Grith and Hydrocus shared, and it left you with a planet where the only suitable settlement areas for humans were at the poles. Diamond Point, the location of the main spaceport and the heart of the Hatire settlement, was set in the great polar savanna, surrounded by plains and grassland where the temperature even now in summer would not get much above 40° C. But even there, where the light of Corrivale was abated, there would not be many sesheyans. They were adapted to the multileveled green gloom of the great rain forests and deepest jungle. They would only appear in the Hatire community covered with heavy protective gear and *gailghe*, the goggles they favored, to protect them against Corrivale's unbearable fire.

That light and heat was bad enough for humans and fraal and others who weren't used to it. Gabriel was glad that Enda had thought to purchase goggles along with the rest of their travel clothing. As it was, the cockpit windows were darkening down to help them cope as Gabriel steered north. This time of year in its northern hemisphere, Diamond Point was already experiencing "midnight sun," and would be for some months yet. There was no hiding from Corrivale's light.

"Have you been here before?" asked Enda, looking down at the green and violet curve of the world as it filled more and more of the cockpit windows.

"Just the once, when *Falada* passed through a year ago," Gabriel said, keeping his eyes on the controls and the artificial horizon. The ship was doing most of the work at the moment, but computers had occasionally been known to fail no matter who manufactured them. "We went down to Diamond Point on leave. It was one of the places where they said we weren't likely to get in too much trouble."

"You? Trouble?" Enda said and somehow managed not to make it sound like the taunt it might have been from anyone else these days. "Surely you do not mean brawling and such behavior."

Gabriel grinned. "Brawling? Us? No, it wasn't that. It was political. The Concord didn't really want us taking leave in the sesheyan indigenous areas, meaning most of the planet *except* Diamond Point. The Diocese doesn't have any jurisdiction outside of the Diamond Point area, and they're the only ones who have a due-process agreement with the Concord at this point. Everybody else on the planet, meaning mostly the Council of Tribes for the sesheyans, and the Aanghel, either has legal systems so complex that a marine could vanish into them and never be seen again—" and Gabriel made a face—"or are simply a bunch of crooks, pirates, and other wildlife. The captain said she preferred to put us down where she would be able to find us again later. Anybody who wanted to go see the 'quaint natives' in one of the jungle cities could wait until they came back in a few years, in civvies."

"Ah. Do you wish to do this now?"

Gabriel laughed at her. "Thanks, but if I want to get dirty, lost, and bug-bitten, I don't see why I should pay a sesheyan native guide for the privilege. I can do it on my own time, somewhere else." He shook his head. "Things are weird enough down there just in the Hatire areas, I think. I'll stay out of the jungle for the time being and keep to where things are simpler."

"It is a complex enough business, just keeping track of the relationship between the Hatire and the sesheyans," said Enda, tilting her head to one side. "The sesheyans are indigenous, said the settlement. But at the same time, Grith is a Hatire colony, except that the Hatire Diocese can exert no authority over the sesheyans." She tilted her head sideways, looking resigned. "I understand in a general way what the Mahdra settlement was trying to achieve, but it can hardly be considered a terribly stable kind of solution."

They were dropping more and more swiftly now toward the north polar region, sweeping around the sunlit side of the planet toward Grith's boreal sea, and the cockpit windows darkened slightly to screen out the ever more brilliant reflection from the planet's surface.

"Even without VoidCorp hanging around, yes." Gabriel eased back on the throttle a little. It was easy to "speed" in Grith's lighter gravity. "There was a lot of pressure being applied by the Colonial Diocese when we were here to try to find some way to reverse Mahdra and get the whole planet reverted to Hatire rule. But that seemed about as likely as Hydrocus being opened up for colonization, so no one seemed to be taking it terribly seriously."

"I take it," Enda said as they dropped toward Diamond Point, "that you were not talking to many Hatires."

Gabriel shook his head and grinned. "You ought to strap down," he said. "I might drop this thing on somebody. No point in you being jarred out of your seat as well."

"Both possibilities seem unlikely," Enda said, but she sat down and strapped in anyway.

The landing was uneventful. They came down way off to one side of the spaceport in the customs and bond part of the field reserved for private craft. Several sesheyans in protective suits and *gailghe* came out to meet them, take the ship's registry information, and conduct the usual cursory search. Another one put port seal on the weaponry and confirmed it through the ship's computer, giving Gabriel a decommissioning chit to return to the check-out crew when he and Enda were ready to leave and free the weapons up again.

The field had its own shopping facility, but Gabriel took one look at the prices in the victuallers' shops and shook his head. "They must get a lot of millionaires in here," he said. "Or else everybody on the planet drinks their morning draft black. Look at the price of the sugar!"

"No," Enda replied. "At my age, heart failure so early in the morning is a bad thing. Let us go into the town center and take our chances there."

The public transport to Diamond Point center was down at the end of a long walkway, amply windowed so that you could look out as you went. Outside, that idiosyncratic butter-yellow sunlight beat down mercilessly onto the tarmac from the fiercely red sky.

Gabriel looked out across the field through the waver of heat haze and muttered under his breath to Enda, "A lot of Star Force traffic out there."

She peered in the direction he was looking. "Shuttles mostly. Is there another of the big Concord ships in system?"

"Something called *Schmetterling* is orbiting Hydrocus," Gabriel said. "A heavy cruiser, I know that much. But I don't know her command. Other than that, the only other reported ships are out around Omega Station."

Enda nodded as they came to the end of that walkway. "It has been rather busy here of late," she said. "This part of the Verge has been seeing a lot of activity, with the systems around it opening up so rapidly, not that the locals are entirely happy about all the action, except in the business sense, I suppose. The Hatires in particular would have liked to be left alone to dominate the system, but I would say VoidCorp has its own plans about that, with all its mining interests here."

She glanced over at Gabriel as they came out of the covered walkway, its doors dilating to let them out onto the pavement where the hovbus waited. The sunlight hit Gabriel like a blow. It was almost as if it had weight, like water.

The air in the hovbus was hot, despite its attempt at air conditioning. Sitting down on the wide bench at the end of the bus, hunched over a little, was a sesheyan in protective gear. The oblong egg shape of the helmet around his oval head was completely opaqued, and he was wearing the extended version of the *ayaishe,* sleeved and breeched, with gloves for the talons, legs, and tail, and edge-sealing coverings for the great, leathery green wings folded around him—the "male" pattern was sketched down the outside of the fastening on one wing covering. The sesheyan still looked uncomfortable. Despite the dimming of the hovbus's own windows that cut the worst of the merciless glare from the concrete outside, it still had to be too bright and hot in here for him.

Gabriel headed for the back of the hovbus and found a spot just in front of the sesheyan, nodding to him as he sat down. "Morning, brother."

The head lifted a meter or so as the hovbus took off. There was no seeing any of the eight eyes through the helmet, but Gabriel felt them looking at him. "Morn dawns too bright in the Bare Places: but even Weyshe the Wanderer knew his brother when he saw him: and the afternoon gives way gratefully enough to the Shadows: but long that time seems to me yet."

Gabriel nodded, thinking he was hearing a variation on "Can you believe the weather we've been having." Then, considering that a nod might mean something entirely different to a sesheyan, he said, "I'm not wild about this heat either. Are you headed somewhere cool? Or into town?"

"The Wanderer's way is laid down," said the sesheyan, "but poor mortals must range more widely: errands remain to be run in the heat of the Point of the Diamond, and the day's work stretches forever: yet kindly inquiry ought be met always with kindly reply: and your path must also run long before you, that you dare the eye of day."

The rhythm was catching. Gabriel was trying to frame a reply when Enda said, "Star-kindred, walker in the cool shadow: we must yet find nourishment under His sky: should any know of a place where Cureyfi the Father of Stars opens his arms to those who hunger: that would be reward indeed for those who must soon now journey again."

The sesheyan nodded. Apparently the gesture was common to his species and humans, for he said, "Where this conveyance first stops his headlong flight, let the traveler alight with care, for the artery with traffic is wild: then let the Wanderer guide your eyes to the first drinking place that stands on the right: turn there and walk, not a long journey, but twenty breaths' worth in the cool of the evening: on your right as you go stands the house of Droun-li the Provider, mighty assemblage of things both needful and needless: there you may find what you seek, though it be not born of this planet:"

"*Anything* we seek?" Gabriel said, very softly. "Can I get my name cleared?"

Enda elbowed him gently, and the air went right out of Gabriel. Fraal have sharp elbows and thousands of years' experience at using them. "Star cousin, kindred in travel," she said, "our thanks for advice well given: may your own errands go as swiftly as ours now will with your good rede: seems this to be the place of which you spoke, where we will go with the Wanderer."

The bus was settling. From inside the cloak of the folded wings one gloved talon emerged to sketch a quick gesture in the air as Gabriel and Enda got up. "In his good way go, being ware of the traffic:"

Gabriel lifted a hand to him in salute as they headed out of the hovbus, coming out onto the pavement at a corner from which they could see that the traffic indeed was worth keeping an eye on. There were vehicles plunging by them at great speed from four different directions, and Gabriel could see no signaling devices or other means of direct control.

"Nice gent," he said, as the hovbus pulled away. He peered around, trying to see where the first drinking place on the right might be.

"That is what we search for," Enda said, pointing. "See the tree sticking out above that door?"

"That's a bar? I assume that's what he meant by drinking place?"

"Yes. The symbol is an old one. Even Earth had it once, I hear. And see—there is the grocery. You can just see its sign. Let us chance the traffic."

They hurried across to see about their groceries, not noting at this distance that eight eyes watched them carefully from the hovbus away down Diamond Point's main street.

* * * * *

They had to spend three days on Grith getting the cargo bay repaired and replacing the shielding. Enda swore softly in one of the older fraal languages, making a sound like angry wind in the trees, when she discovered how much the work would cost them.

"This is supposed to be a major repair depot," Gabriel said, also fairly aghast when they were walking away with the repair bill that they had to approve. "They have to get lots of business here. There's no reason to gouge like that."

"I wonder whether there might be," Enda mused as they walked away along the edge of the repair field to where they would catch a hovbus for the spaceport again. "Surely I would suspect strongly that the Diocese gets its cut of all work done here. A 'value added tax,' you might call it. But then there is another possible reason in this system. VoidCorp."

"You mean, everybody gets charged expense account prices because of the 'big business' in town?"

"Yes." Enda sighed. "Possibly. The galaxy is not the innocent place it was, oh, even *two* hundred years ago."

"When the universe had no tarnish," Gabriel said, "and things were bright and new. Come on, Enda, don't look like that. Let's go out and have dinner somewhere."

"I do not feel like it, even slightly," Enda said as they came to the hovbus stop. "After this bill, I feel as poor as the Queen's last lizard. Much too poor to pay for dinner or to let you pay for it either, so do not ask. Let us just go home to the ship and get some sleep. Tomorrow morning we will be able to lift and start making back the cost of our encounter with those ships in the dark."

Gabriel did not push the point, for he was still thinking about those ships—not to mention the great strange shape that had surfaced from nothing and vanished away again with no indication of its coming or warning of its going. "Ghost ships," the second ambassador had said in a whisper. It was a strange phrasing, but what Gabriel had seen could certainly have passed for one.

The next morning they lifted and headed out on system drive, not for Iphus itself but for the inner asteroid belt. Their contracts and other agreements with Iphus Independent had already been settled by Grid, and there was simply no need to go to Iphus. It was unusual enough for a system to have two asteroid belts, but the Corrivale system was fairly large as planetary systems went, stretching Bode's Law a little in terms of exceeding the "usual" average number of planets, and the ratios of planetary distances. It would have been a scenic enough trip, for the Belt, which most people counted as merely a big sphere of rocks with a rather higher concentration of asteroids in the system's ecliptic, was a sight to see when making for it from inside Hydrocus's and Grith's orbits. From such a distance, it appeared to be a chain of stars, drifting slowly, so slowly that you must be practically into the great sphere before you could see individual motion. The scenic aspect was disturbed for Gabriel by only one occurrence. A large dark shape cruised past them, sunward, one day. Probably a VoidCorp heavy cruiser, venturing inward on some obscure business.

Enda was just coming into the cockpit as Gabriel spotted it, and she stood gazing at it with a surprisingly dark look for her. "It goes to intimidate someone," she said. "Mostly they stay out around Iphus, cruising over the planet by day and night, watching 'their interests,' and bringing fear to the independents." She frowned. "But they do not go so much in-system where Concord forces are more concentrated, not unless they have a reason to do so. They ignore Omega Station as if it were not even there, for no one there could do anything about one of *those*."

Gabriel looked after the ship as it headed on sunward and its shadow blotted out any further perception of detail. "I was looking to see if there was any resemblance to our other friend."

"And your conclusion?"

Gabriel shook his head. "This one looked too human. You saw the general presentation: bumps and ducts. The other one didn't look human enough, somehow."

She walked away and left Gabriel staring into the dark, thinking. *Ghost ships.*

The next day, Gabriel and Enda started work. Their job in the Inner Belt was very unlike what they had been doing on Eraklion. This was old-fashioned meteor mining of a kind that had been carried on since human beings and fraal first went out into their respective solar systems with an eye to commerce rather than just plain old exploration.

As usual with any ancient occupation, meteor mining had accrued around it a sort of crust of nostalgia, romanticism, and adventure. Though the 'nostalgia' requirement might have been fulfilled by the fact that the basic techniques of the work had not changed for four hundred years, the romanticism was ill-placed. Mostly it was based on the media-popularized image of the rugged individualist meteor minor as scruffy, tough, inured to the emptiness and loneliness of the depths of space, bold, fierce in a fight, but potentially heroic. It reflected very little truth of a miner's life, which was isolated, difficult, dangerous—just from routine interaction with the machinery involved, never mind the legendary ore pirates and rock-grabbers—and which, when you came right down to it, tended not to pay very well. Most spacers who had enough money to afford the sophisticated equipment needed for really effective rock assay "on the fly" in space, could also afford to do something else. Mostly they did. Those who genuinely desired the lonely life could have it, of course, but there was no guarantee that they would make enough to keep at it for long.

Gabriel had gone to some trouble over *Sunshine*'s assay equipment, foreseeing the possibility that there might come a time when he and Enda would have to "go it alone" in a belt somewhere for what might be a prolonged period—as much for the sake of Gabriel staying out of the reach of over enthusiastic Concord forces as for that of making a decent living. He had insisted on a small magnetic resonance/X-ray "reader" for the ship's assay array so that they would not have to break open every likely looking rock they came across to see what was inside. The sealed portion of the hold had a full specific-gravity, laser-smelting and "slice-'n'-dice" setup that could reduce an iron-riddled asteroid to ingots within a very short time. The physical work for him and Enda mostly involved going out suited to either wrestle a given rock up to the assay array for testing, or cutting a piece off one and bringing it in. Then if the rock had enough of whatever element they were sorting for—it would be nickel-iron to start with—they would do whatever further cutting was necessary to get it into the hold for processing. Once full, they would make their way to a sales-assay station on Grith or Iphus, dump their cargo, and head spaceside again.

They did this for several weeks, making a steady ten percent profit, but not much other headway. When Enda came in one evening and found Gabriel gazing thoughtfully out the cockpit window, she said just one word.

"Bored."

Gabriel turned, looked at her, and sighed. "I don't suppose the odds are terribly high that we'll find the Glory Rock and get filthy rich so that we can retire?"

Enda laughed and went aft again after the squeeze bottle of water for her bulb. Everyone who had been in space for any kind of time knew the miners' stories about the Glory Rock, that fabulous and mythical rock full of gem-quality diamond or Widmanstaetten-lined iron and platinum. Half the people you talked to would know stories about someone who found it—a friend of a friend of course—and retired on the proceeds. Or another friend of a friend who found it and had it turn into the

bane of his existence, the source of divorce, murder, suicide, and
finally, most unfairly of all, of unhappiness.

"Say we did find it," Enda said, coming back with the bottle
and leaning over the bulb that was presently in the sitting room
where Enda would sometimes leave it in front of a Grid-screen
picture of a sunny field full of other plants. "It would not make
you happy. Or me. What would I do with that kind of money?"

"Easy for you to say," Gabriel said. "You're rich already."

"Hardly," Enda said, sitting down in the number two chair and
watering her bulb again. "But I can do simple mathematics, and I
understand what a lump sum and compound interest will do after
a couple of centuries, assuming you find the right place to bank.
Choosing your banker is like choosing an e-suit. You must be
very careful. Get the best to start with, and be careful with maintenance." She chuckled.

Gabriel gave her a look. "Are you suggesting that people
should bribe their bankers?"

"Not in the usual way," Enda said, smiling slightly, and went
back to watering the plant.

Gabriel sat there trying to make sense of that one and finally
turned back to the charts. He had learned by now that there were
moods in which Enda was thoroughly uncommunicative even
when she was speaking in classically constructed sentences. At
such times she tended to make more sense while she was working—and indeed Gabriel thought he had never seen anyone who
could work so hard.

Among other things, Enda was an expert in an e-suit, as much
so, or more, as Gabriel thought he was. She was also surprisingly strong. She could manage weightless loads, stopping them
while moving or starting them up again in situations that would
have torn Gabriel's arms out of their sockets.

"You said you were a Wanderer," he had said to her one
afternoon as they both stood sweating in the maintenance lock
with their helmets off. "You must have done a whole lot of
zero-g work."

She shrugged, leaning against the plates while her breathing went back to normal. "Oh, yes," she said. "Maintenance on a spaceborne city takes nearly eighty percent of its resources. That's one of the reasons we must travel far. It is an enjoyable lifestyle but not cheap."

"And everybody works like this?"

"Oh, no, not everybody," Enda started undoing her e-suit gaskets, "but those who are good at it. They are much honored among us. They are too valuable to lose."

"Is that why you left?" Gabriel asked, teasing. "Because they made you work like that even when you were pushing three hundred?"

She looked at him in sudden shock, and then came a sound he only rarely heard from her, that soft fraal laugh, barely more than a breath. "Oh, no," she said, "not at all." She undid the rest of the gaskets as if in a slight hurry, saying nothing. She then took herself away so that Gabriel stood there staring after her, the sweat still running down him in rivers, wondering exactly what she meant.

The conversation had been so thoroughly derailed that it took Gabriel several days to get it around to what was on his mind again. Boredom, but also other things. Enda herself brought it up, this time, which relieved him. "You are indeed thinking hard about doing something else, are you not?"

"We're making our nut," he said, "but yes." He looked out the port window, then turned back to see her eyeing him with an expression of some concern. *How many times has she caught me this way already?* "How do you feel about hunches?" he said.

"Annoyed," Enda said, "for normally, when I have them, they are right. But you will have known that training the hunch to run 'on a leash' is one of the mindwalker talents, and naturally there are many mindwalkers among the fraal. I cannot deny some of that heritage, but I do not have the training that some others do. Now tell me why you ask."

"It's just a hunch so far," Gabriel said, but then stopped before continuing, "No, it's not even that focused. Every time I get the idea that it would be really wonderful to get out of here, some part of me remains . . . unconvinced. That's the only way I can explain it."

"Not a very active hunch, then," Enda said. "Passive at best. Well, I would be remiss if I claimed to know anything about the mechanics of human hunchery. But were I in your position and were there no strong forces actively driving me in another direction, I would let matters be. Just ride the hunch for the time being. Certainly it could do no active harm."

Gabriel nodded. "Let's stay here for the time being, then."

The next morning, though, Gabriel wondered about the wisdom of the decision. He had dreamed of Epsedra again, much worse than he had for a long time. He had felt the old wound in his gut and woke up from it, not screaming but with a terrible outward *houfff* of breath that left his lungs unable to get another decent breath into him for nearly half a minute. There he sat, gasping for another couple of minutes. He could think of nothing except, *It's not fair. I'm innocent. When will this end?*

But after a few more minutes, his mood set grim. *I am not going to let this beat me. I may not be a marine any more, but the heart that made me one is still there. I swore to take whatever I had to take to do my job. So I have a different job now. It's still me.*

I think.

*   *   *   *   *

Later that week, when they were full of high-quality nickel iron again, they did an assay and dump run to Grith. They could have taken the load to the Iphus Independent Collective offices, but they had done that the last couple of times, and Gabriel was eager for a change of pace.

"I get sick of seeing those VoidCorp cruisers hanging over the place," he said, "like vultures waiting for a snack."

Enda sighed and agreed with him. Slowly Gabriel came to understand that she was no great supporter of VoidCorp either,

though her reasons for this, as for so many other things, were initially obscure. They might simply have been based in the history of the area, of course, in which she seemed well versed.

"There were many little companies out here once," she told
him at one point, "that were 'left over' during the Long Silence
when all other major powers withdrew or were absent from the
Verge. Some of them had been VoidCorp holdings at first, ones
thatsold out to local companies. They incorporated, became
Iphus United, and were very successful, with all the hard work
they put into these facilities in the empty years. They supplied
ore and fissionables all over these parts: to Algemron, Lucullus,
even as far away as Tendril. Everything was going well for them
until VoidCorp came back all of a sudden—in 2497 it would have
been—and said, 'Oh, by the way, we still own you.' What could
they do, under the guns of *those?*" She glanced into space at the
dark shapes in orbit over Iphus. "Now the Collective is all that is
left of that spirit. Fifty-odd facilities on Iphus, and VoidCorp
owns forty-four of them. The others look up and wonder when
the Company will move against them at last. If the blow fell, they
would survive it. But the waiting, the not knowing, that must be
bitter."

"Did your people come this way?" Gabriel asked.

Enda gave him the demure smile. "Where have we *not* been?"
But the smile faded. "Anything that can conquer this darkness,"
she said after a while, "is a good thing, in my mind. Anything
that can bring comfort or wealth that spreads to people or joy that
makes their lives better, anything that wrings that out of the old
darkness, *that* is worthwhile. When people work hard to do that,
and then some great force drops without warning from above and
takes it away from them, all their hard work . . ." She looked a
lot more grandmotherly than usual. "I do not think much of that.
"Those who do such things should fail and will fail. But better it
is if they can be made to fail earlier rather than later."

Gabriel, while privately in agreement with such sentiments,
thought they were probably better not voiced too near Iphus. So
they went back to Grith, landing at Diamond Point's spaceport

again. They unloaded their cargo, making an eight percent profit on it this time. Then, much to Enda's delight, they did tourist things for the afternoon, going up to the observation platform that had been built to exploit the view from the hundred-meter bluffs on which the city was built. The great black rock cliffs served as the settlement's main protection from the tidal surges of the Boreal Sea. Gabriel was delighted at the chance to be a tourist too. No matter what exotic places a marine may visit, he is aware of being a sort of mobile tourist attraction himself, one that is expected to behave itself impeccably at all times, a situation that precludes him from buying and wearing a loud human-tailored overshirt emblazoned with the words A PRESENT FROM GRITH in six languages and five different wavelengths' worth of ink.

Gabriel did exactly this and wore the shirt until Enda began to complain of her sides hurting from laughter. "Now we'll have dinner," he said, and this time Enda was unable to argue with him. He remembered a nice place from when he had last been here. It was clean, and the food was good. They offered local specialties as well as plain simple things that you did not get a lot of in space, such as broiled meat. He found the bar-restaurant again, down a side street several blocks down from the Bluff Heights, and he and Enda sat themselves down at the beginning of the dinner hour and settled in for a long stay. Gabriel was ravenous. Enda, holding the menu, looked sidelong at Gabriel and bit the appetizer page experimentally. Teeth or no teeth, she made a dent. They ordered, and they ate.

It was in all ways a noble dinner, most specifically because of the company and the talk. It was strange, though the two of them had plenty of time to talk on *Sunshine,* how sometimes long silences fell. Gabriel had taken a while to recognize that there was nothing angry or sullen about them. They were just Enda being quiet. Give her a change of venue, though, and she became positively chatty. That had happened tonight, and Gabriel reveled in it, getting her to tell him stories of the last hundred years' wanderings for her. She was reticent about the couple of hundred years before that, but the glow of the wine brought up the banked blue fire in her eyes tonight, and she told of old history with the worlds of the Orion League, of the way Tendril looks when it flares, of the dark places between the stars when the whole fraal city stops "to hear what the darkness has to say." They drank the wine, talked, laughed, and heard other people's laughter.   And then Gabriel heard a voice he knew, and he froze.

Not until that moment did the colossal folly of this whole operation occur to him. *Oh, no, let's go to Diamond Point,* he had said to Enda. *Hey, I know some good places to eat. This one is clean, and the service was good.* And so he had brought them straight to the place he had visited as a marine. A place that other marines would be likely to visit as well, because it suited their high standards and those of others.

Like that fair-haired, delicately featured woman over there, the short one in the Star Force uniform who was just sitting down with a crowd of friends.

Of all the bars for her to walk into . . .

Gabriel gulped. Never mind her. Of all the bars for *me* to walk into . . . For there was Elinke Dareyev.

The glow of the wine went out in him like a blown-out candle. His first instinct was simple and shamed him. *Hide!* Nothing but trouble could possibly come of them meeting now, trouble for him in one of three major forms. First, he could be beaten to a pulp by Elinke herself—for he would not fight with her. Second, he could be beaten to a pulp by the other marines and Star Force people with her, friends of hers. He was sure he could no longer rely on any of them being friends of *his*. Finally, there was the possibility that something, anything that he might say to her, might somehow harm his case before the Concord when he finally got it into good enough shape to be presented. What if she gets the idea that it would be good to arrest me and haul me back up to—what's her ship's name?—and then drag me straight back to Concord space for trial . . . . With possibly an accident thrown in for good measure: "Shot while trying to escape"

There was no time to act on any of these thoughts, though, for she turned and looked at him.

At first there was no recognition on her face, and Gabriel wondered what was the matter with her. *Then* it came. He realized that he now had that strange protection that comes with being seen by another person when you are not wearing the right clothes, not to mention a haircut grown far past marine regulation and a full beard and mustache that were a new addition. With those, and out of uniform, even those who had seen him every day might not have known him, but now Elinke *did* know. He saw recognition rise in her gaze. Maybe I should have left on the shirt that said A PRESENT FROM GRITH.

She sat there frozen for a moment, while at her table the conversation went on. Then very slowly she stood up. To either side of her, her buddies looked at her oddly, wondering what the problem was. They looked the way she was looking. First one of them, then another, saw Gabriel.

Gabriel wondered if he should stand as well and then thought, No. No sudden moves.

Slowly she eased around the table and walked around it toward him. The others watched her, frozen, none of them speaking a word. Gabriel held very still. Then, as she came closer, very slowly he put his hands on the tabletop where everyone could see them and stood up.

"Gabriel?" Enda said.

"Not now," he whispered.

Elinke walked up to the table and looked him in the eye.

"Captain Dareyev," Gabriel said.

"Connor," she said. He could rarely remember having heard any sound so cold as that one word.

"So what has the big man offered you?" she said.

Gabriel looked at her, trying to feel something besides hurt at that coldness, no matter how well deserved he knew it was from her point of view. "I don't follow you."

"Oh, very cagey," she said. "Very wise." Her expression was sardonic. "Probably he told you to keep quiet about your little

discussions. Well, it won't help you. Sooner or later you'll slip
and circumstances will change and someone will haul you back
to Concord space to get what you deserve."

Meaning that *you're* not going to? Now what in the—? He put
it aside. "Captain Dareyev," he said, wanting desperately to call
her by the old friendly name but not daring to, "I don't know
what you're talking about, though I see you don't believe me."

"Why should I?" she said, very quietly—and the voice was
like that one look had been during the trial. A knife. "When you
killed Lem and lied about that too?"

He wanted to shout, *I didn't kill him!* But uncertainty stopped
him. "I didn't lie," Gabriel said at last. "I told the truth about
what happened."

"Oh, yeah," Elinke said. "The parts of it that suited your purpose. And twisted the judges into letting you live when you were
guilty."

"The verdict was 'not proven,' " Gabriel said, "as you know—"

"Some verdict," said Elinke scornfully. "Not very enlightened
in this day and age. Or too afraid to come down on one side or
the other. There was a lot of political pressure surrounding your
trial—or didn't you know? A lot of people high up on Phorcys
wanted their justice system to give ours a black eye, and it
did . . . about the blackest they could have managed. And *you*
played right along, being the good little prisoner, oh so put upon,
declaring your innocence. The Phorcyns didn't dare declare you
guilty—that would have made it look like they were in the Concord's pockets. But they didn't quite have the guts to declare you
innocent either. The middle road was good enough to put us in
our place and get you off their hands."

Gabriel swallowed. This was all news to him.

"I really wish we were the kind of people who behave the
way you did," Elinke said, "because the few of us here tonight
could remove a blotch from the universe's face right now. I can't
understand why that man would have anything to do with you.
He's lowered himself in my esteem, that's for sure—not that
it matters. Traitors and murderers will never prosper. Sooner

or later, someone will give you your deserts and kill you. I wouldn't cross the street to stop it if it happened in front of me. And when I finally do hear about it, I'll track down your grave and dance on it."

Gabriel simply looked at her, but the motion on his right startled him as Enda slowly stood, drawing herself up to her full five feet and gazing at Elinke.

"Young human," she said, "you make bitter charges against Gabriel, and you are wrong."

"And who are *you* supposed to be?" said Elinke.

Enda looked at her with surprising gentleness. "One who knows," she said.

Elinke looked scornfully over at Gabriel. "You make friends wherever you go, don't you?" she said. She turned to Enda and said, "Watch out for yourself. Don't trust him. He tends to kill his friends."

"Death comes to us all eventually," the fraal said, "and trust is no better than fear at warding it off."

Elinke's eyes widened a little, an old habit that Gabriel knew from of old when she had been caught a little off guard. "Mottoes and mysticism won't do much good either," Elinke snapped and turned away without another glance at Gabriel.

Gabriel sat down again very slowly, acutely aware of glances—some angry, some merely suspicious—from the table to which Elinke was returning. He was equally aware that some of the people there were now sitting in ways that suggested they were carrying sidearms to which they wanted ready access. They shouldn't be armed in port. They *shouldn't* be.

"Well," Enda said softly after a moment, sitting down again beside Gabriel. She reached out for her wine. "So that is Captain Dareyev. She is in great distress."

"She is? What about *me?"* Gabriel muttered. His dinner was now like lead inside him, and the glow from half of two bottles of kalwine had burned in minutes to cinders.

"Do not expect me not to see both sides of a situation," Enda observed, "or as many sides as it has. If fraal have one gift that has both complicated matters for us and made them more simple, that is it. Her distress does not only involve you, though, or the matters in which you are involved. There is something else on her mind."

"I thought you said you weren't much of a mindwalker," Gabriel said.

"I am not, compared to some, but faces are easy to read. Her eyes were not on you for much of the time while she was railing at you. Did you not notice? She was looking at someone else."

Gabriel did not say out loud that he had been having so much trouble looking directly at Elinke that this minor detail could very well have eluded him. "Really? And who would it have been, do you think?"

"I am expert at faces, but not that expert," Enda said. "You will probably find out in time." She looked at him with an expression that was unusually sorrowful, even for a fraal's face that could look mournful with great ease. "Probably we should go. You plainly are not enjoying the evening any more."

Gabriel nodded and looked up to see where the man doing table service had gone. He paid, having thumbed a couple of extra dollars' worth of credit onto the billing card before touching his own card to it, and then stood up. He walked past the marines' table without a glance at them and headed out into the street. Silently, like a pale, drifting fragment of evening mist, Enda came after him.

They walked down the little street in silence, in as much dusk as Diamond Point was going to get at this time of year. It was perhaps midnight local time, and the sun would be up again in an hour or so.

"That was my fault," Gabriel said eventually to Enda.

"Oh, of course it was," Enda said. "You are a mindwalker and read the future and knew she would be there, so you went there on purpose so that your soul would be harrowed and you would ruin your own dinner."

Gabriel paused and looked at her with some shock. Enda kept walking. "Are you making fun of me?" Gabriel asked.

"Ridicule," Enda said, still gliding gracefully along ahead and away from him, "is the Universe's way of telling you that the people around you need a good laugh."

The shuffle of feet on stone from off to the right brought Gabriel around, and he saw two men, both shabbily dressed, coming toward him from the shelter of a doorway that led down to a little alley. They knew they had been seen, and one of the men lunged with his arm stretched out straight.

"Oh, now this is just *unfair,*" Gabriel said, but it was just annoyance. The geography of the situation was grasped in a moment. The first man's arm, the one with the knife in it, was grasped about a second later. Gabriel "helped" the man leftward, in front of him and past him, down onto the stones of the street, *hard*. He then made sure of the position of the arm that still had the knife in it, and he stomped down hard—not on the knife, but on the elbow. "Your assailant can always buy a new knife," he could hear his weapons instructor saying, oh, about a thousand years ago, "but even with our present state of medical science, he can*not* buy himself a new elbow. Or he can, but it will *never* work as well as the original. And then next time he comes at someone with a knife, he'll be that much slower. Do the world a favor, and go for the joints."

The noise the man made was the right noise. Elbows are extremely sensitive, especially when you damage that nerve that makes you hop around and curse from just tapping it accidentally on a door frame. Gabriel felt the crushing of the cartilage and the breaking of the bone beneath his foot. As the shriek died away for lack of air and the man rolling and squirming on the ground concentrated on getting enough air for another scream, Gabriel spun to see what the second man was doing. He had gone for Enda with a knife. Gabriel just saw the glint of the streetlight on it as it flashed in low. His mouth was opening to yell to warn her—

It almost instantly became plain that this was unnecessary and that the man's lunge was yet another of the evening's mistakes. Enda sidestepped him as neatly as a blown curtain sidesteps the wind. She then twisted and bent around behind him, using his own forward momentum to throw him straight at the wall of a nearby building. He crashed into the wall, jerked once as he hit it, and slid down, leaving a stain on the stone.

Enda stood there and *tsk*ed gently. "Knives," she said, "belong at dinner."

She stepped lightly over to where Gabriel's poor assailant lay no better than half conscious with pain. That was when the third man materialized, jumping from the opposite alley at Gabriel. Gabriel glanced at this new nuisance with the expression of someone who has had quite enough for one evening, thank you; he also leaped, throwing himself feet first at the third man in a way he had not tried for a while. It was dangerous to do it on a sloping street like this one, but it was more dangerous to let people put knives into your kidneys. Anyway, it was simply both convenient and satisfying. Gabriel's boots, as much like marine ones as he had been able to acquire on their last shopping trip, went straight into the man's midriff. The breath went out of the man, all at once, *whoooof!*—like an airlock venting. The man went down. Gabriel went down, too, but Gabriel got up again.

Gabriel wiped his hands off on his pants and went over to Enda. "Are you all right?"

"Except that I must now make an apology offering to the gods of subtlety," she said, "I will do well enough. You?"

"I'm fine."

" 'Leave while you can,' " Enda said. "I believe that was your instructor's advice?"

"Yes, and also, 'Don't use wire to strangle someone wearing a metal helmet,' " Gabriel said. "The *noise* when the head falls off . . ."

Together they vanished into the dark as quietly as they could. Neither of them mentioned to the other the dark slender shape in the shadows further up the street, a shape in black with a glint of silver about it, and a glint almost as pale from silver-gilt hair, a shape that watched them go and then turned and left as well.

Chapter Twelve

"NOW THAT TIME," Gabriel said when they were safely back into space a couple of hours later, "*that* time they were definitely after me."

"A condition that did not last."

"That was only because you mixed in."

Enda sat down in the number two seat and looked at Gabriel like a grandmother about to explain something to a favorite but half-witted grandchild. "Why would I *not* 'mix in'? I did not get to be three hundred years old by avoiding fights when they came my way."

"From your technique, I wouldn't argue," Gabriel said, "but there are people who might suggest that if you want to see four hundred, you should hang back a little bit! I was doing just fine."

"So you were. But, Gabriel, you need to be clear on one concept. Just because a fight starts with only you does not mean that you can *keep* it that way by encouraging your friends to stay away. It is entirely possible that whoever is targeting you at the moment is equally intent on whoever might be seen with you, which, at the moment, means me."

That thought made him go rather cold. When they went back to work in the Inner Belt, Gabriel decided to let some of his more aggressive Grid searching, especially for information on Jacob Ricel, go by the boards for a while. He found himself wondering whether his searches were themselves triggering increased interest in him. For his own sake, he wouldn't have been bothered by that, but there was Enda to think of.

Two standard weeks went by while they built up a new load

of nickel-iron. They had hit one of those "sparse" patches that only the Belt professionals know about, the ones you rarely hear about otherwise, since the only thing one gladly discusses are the good weeks and the big hits. After two weeks and a bit they were full, and they headed back to Grith to do their assay and dump. They made six percent profit on the run, not exactly munificent but adequate. After they had given the ship a thorough and much-needed cleaning Enda went out for more groceries, it being her turn.

It was odd, but when the marines suddenly showed up outside *Sunshine*'s hatch, Gabriel found it almost impossible to look at them with anything like concern. He had half suspected that something like this might happen, for he had heard via the news on the Grid that there was a Concord Administrator in the system. Such men and women did not turn up without reason. They tended to appear suddenly in places where justice was reported to be breaking down, and they reinstated it with vigor—sometimes with violence, when necessary. They were walking examples of the old phrase "a law unto himself," except that the law in question was that of the Concord, enforced impartially, in places from the highest to the lowest. They were the modern equivalent of the ancient traveling 'circuit judges,' troubleshooters *par excellence* who often shot the trouble themselves.

The marines had a little gig waiting nearby, a mini-shuttle mercifully unlike the ones in which Gabriel had spent most of his last day of active service. They helped him into it courteously enough and sat opposite him as it took off, not glowering at him as Gabriel would have half expected. Maybe they don't know who I am, he thought, though that seemed fairly unlikely.

He could only wait, considering what might be likely to happen to him. Concord Administrators were people of tremendous power. Just the presence of one in the system would make all the powers moving there pause for a moment and wonder just what it meant. He might be here to try me and have me shot, Gabriel thought. I guess some of the higher-ups in Star Force and the marines might have insisted on something like this, since the trial on Phorcys didn't go the way they wanted. But the more he considered this, the less likely it seemed. By and large, one of the things the Concord did not do was waste energy, and sending a Concord Administrator after *him* would be like hitting a bug with a sledgehammer.

So what is he doing here? Gabriel thought. If I'm an after-thought—or perhaps a minor distraction—what brings him to these parts all of a sudden?

The gig came to ground with a slight thump, and the marines got up and escorted Gabriel to the door that opened for them. He stepped down and saw that they were in the shuttle bay of a ship, enough like *Falada's* to be one of her twins. Right. *Schmetter-ling*, then, he thought as the Marines escorted him down through the clean (and surprisingly empty) white halls.

They turned right suddenly into a doorway that opened for them, and Gabriel found himself looking into a small meeting room. It was a very plain place, table and chairs and nothing else but a window on the stars and a man looking out of it. The man turned as Gabriel stepped in and the doors shut behind him.

The man standing before the window was not very tall, bald on top, a little thickset, dressed in a plain dark tunic and breech-es, standard business wear on many worlds where humans worked. But the strongest of the first impressions was of the eyes. They were close set and small. They were very lively, very acute, and rather chill. The mind living behind them was not a kindly one, Gabriel thought, but neither was it cruel, just pitiless when it knew what it wanted and saw it in sight. The face was one with a lot of smile lines, but any smile appearing there would be subordinate to those eyes and the thought they held.

Right now they were looking at Gabriel with bright interest. The interest shocked him a little. Certainly this man knew who he was, what he had been accused of.

"Gabriel Connor," the man said. It was not a question.

"Obviously," Gabriel said, "and you are?"

"Lorand Kharls."

They looked at each other for a moment. "So you're 'the big man,'" said Gabriel then.

Kharls looked at him. "Some nicknames just seem to stick," he said. "Will you sit down, sir, or shall we conduct this entire interview standing?"

"'Interview'?" Gabriel asked. "Am I applying for a position? I don't recall filling out any forms." He stepped to the table, pulled out a chair, and sat down.

Kharls moved to sit down opposite him. "You didn't," answered Kharls. "Do you have any idea why I asked to see you?"

"My first thought was that you were going to take me back to Concord space for trial," Gabriel said, "or possibly try me now, since as a Concord Administrator where you are *is* justice."

Kharls looked at him with an expression that was more than usually unsettling, mostly because Gabriel couldn't make anything of it at all. "And how would you feel about that?" Kharls asked.

Gabriel opened his mouth and closed it, then said, "I'm not ready yet."

"'Yet'?" Kharls said.

"I don't have any of the evidence I need to clear my name," said Gabriel.

"Ah," Kharls said. "Your claim during your trial that you didn't know what the chip was for."

"I thought I did," Gabriel said, "but I was wrong. I had no idea that it would trigger explosives that would cost my shipmates' lives."

Kharls looked thoughtful for a moment. "Even if that were true," he said, "you would still be guilty as an accessory to manslaughter."

"An unwitting accessory," Gabriel replied, "yes. Certainly not knowing what you were doing counts for something in a court of law." He swallowed and said, "Believe me, I grieve for my shipmates. I'm willing to stand trial—but not before I have enough evidence to give me a fighting chance at acquittal and to find out who the real murderer is."

"You might never collect that much evidence," Kharls said.

"Maybe. 'Never' is quite a while," Gabriel returned. "I'll do what I have to do."

Kharls gazed at the floor for a couple of moments, then said, "What if I were to suggest to you that, under certain circumstances, that evidence might be made available to you?"

Gabriel's heart leaped inside him. He worked desperately to keep anything from showing in his face. "What kind of circumstances?"

"Your knowledge of the Thalaassa system's situation," Kharls said after a moment, "was unusually complete according to Ambassador Delvecchio, and your analyses were unusually sharp for someone brought new to the problem."

Her notes, Gabriel thought, and a great rush of hope welled up in him. "Did they find her notes? Did she—"

Kharls held up a finger. Gabriel fell silent. "There are forces moving in the outer reaches of the Thalaassa system that the Concord doesn't understand," Kharls said, "and that it must understand for the security of the surrounding systems."

"You need intelligence," Gabriel said softly. The images of the little ships that had attacked *Sunshine*, and of the big ship that came up out of drivespace and looked at them before vanishing again, were vivid in his mind.

"Yes," Kharls said. "I'm asking you to serve the Concord with something besides a gun."

The phrasing went right through Gabriel with the same heat and pain that a plasma beam might have. "You want me," Gabriel said slowly, "to do the same kind of thing that got me cashiered? And you're offering—what?"

"A shortened sentence," Kharls said. "Manslaughter, even with extenuating circumstances, requires some punishment, and a limited pardon afterwards."

" 'Limited'? You think that I—"

"Reinstatement of certain privileges," said Kharls. "Your pension rights and so forth. Limited—"

"No."

"Don't you even want to know what you would be doing?" Kharls asked.

"No, because already you're not offering enough," Gabriel answered, glaring at the man. "If you have this evidence you claim to have, justice *requires* that you produce it at my trial. Justice is supposed to be your whole duty as a Concord Administrator—"

" 'Our duty is peace,' " Kharls said. "Justice is never forgotten, but sometimes it may have to wait in line."

"Oh, so you can dangle it over my head and make me jump?" Gabriel said, bitter. "Maybe Elinke's opinion of you was right after all."

Kharls's eyebrows went up at that. "You've seen Captain Dareyev recently?"

"Your intelligence-gathering *does* need help," Gabriel remarked softly. "Just what is it I'm supposed to be finding out for you?"

"I'm not sure that's a discussion we should have until we have an agreement in place," Kharls said.

"Oh. So I'm to do a job I won't be told about until I've already agreed to payment that may be wildly inadequate for the service rendered?" Gabriel said and laughed out loud. "Do you just think I'm unusually stupid or just a glutton for punishment? Sorry, Administrator. Find another fool. This one's busy at the moment."

Gabriel got up and was turning to go.

"Connor," the Concord Administrator said.

There was something odd about the note in his voice. Not quite entreaty—Gabriel suspected that such a thing would come very hard to this man. Gabriel turned.

"You may not be a marine any more," Kharls said, "but when you enlisted, you took certain oaths. 'To protect the Concord and the peace of her peoples against all threats overt and covert, public and private.' "

"As you say," Gabriel said, "I'm not a marine any more."

"The Concord may have the power to kick you out of the Service," Kharls said, "but it has no power to absolve you of the oaths you swore. Only the Power to which you swore them has that authority." He put his eyebrows up. "Heard anything from that quarter lately?"

Gabriel could only stare at the man's sheer effrontery. "When I do," he said at last, "you'll be the second to know. Is there anything else?"

They looked at each other for a long moment. Gabriel watched the man studying his face and very much wondered what he was looking for.

"No," Kharls said, "no, that will be all."

Gabriel went out, hardly glancing at the marines on either side of the door to see if they followed him. Half an hour later, he was sitting in *Sunshine* again, staring out the cockpit windows and thinking.

To whom *did* I swear?

* * * * *

He found it hard to express to Enda when she finally got home with the shopping exactly what had passed between him and Kharls or why he was so upset about it. "Upset isn't really the word," Gabriel said, somewhere in the middle of his third attempt to explain, while Enda went on with quietly racking the bulk supplies into their storage shelves. "But I feel like he did something underhanded."

"So that you now feel there is something you must do?" Enda asked.

Gabriel looked at her sharply. "Like what?"

She closed one of the bulk cabinets and opened another, boosting a big bag of freeze-dried starchroot up onto a high shelf. "I was not making a suggestion," she said, "but I can feel the change in the air." She turned a little and gave him a thoughtful sidelong look. "*Ahhrihei*, we would call it at home: a shift of wind, the mind's wind, though. What will you do?"

"Almost anything but what he wants," Gabriel growled, "would be my first response."

Enda *tsk*ed. "But then you are simply acting according to his wishes regardless. Do the opposite of what a person wants just for the sake of foiling him, and he still runs your behavior. What does the shift in your own mind say to you?"

Gabriel sat in the pilot's chair with his feet up and tried to think about that. "I think," he said, "we might go back to Thalaassa."

"Your hunch suggests this?" Enda questioned, closing the cabinet and coming forward to sit in the number two chair.

Gabriel thrust his hands in his pockets and played with the luckstone and his credit chip. "I don't know. It doesn't seem to think much of staying *here* any longer, though."

"Are you sure that is not simply because of our uncomfortable meeting with the captain of *Schmetterling?*"

"I don't think so," Gabriel replied. He thought about it for a second more, then said with more certainty, "No. It's just . . ." He stopped again, then continued, "The ambassador's question still has no answer."

"About why Phorcys and Ino stopped fighting?"

"Yes. I was involved marginally in her finding the answer to the question. She didn't find it, and she's dead. I still don't know any more about the answer to it, but someone seems to be trying hard enough to kill *me* as well. It's as if someone thinks that I might have some part of the answer that I don't even know about." He looked at Enda, but she only shook her head. "But I keep thinking that if we can find out the reason for these attacks on us, we may be able to find out something about the reason for the sudden peace."

"It is a stretch," Enda said, "but truly I cannot think of any other angle from which we might profitably attack. So then. Thalaassa. What will we do there?"

"We could do what we did before, if we had to."

"Though not at Eraklion. Well, let us depart tomorrow, then. Though we must make one stop first. Our medical supplies are not what they should be. The prices here are bad at the moment, but they were much better at the Collective's supply station on

Iphus. We should stop there tomorrow and pick up new supplies for the phymech."

This was the automated emergency medical system that was installed at the back of the living quarters nearest the cargo bay. It had a fairly sophisticated AI system in it, the rationale being that your partner might not necessarily be able to get to you in time if you had an accident; but if the "medicine cabinet" itself had a brain and manipulators guided by it, your chances of surviving an accident in space might be much higher. The system required fairly specialized medical supplies—skinfilms, bandages, antiseptics, painkillers, and so forth—and while a basic supply came with the system when it was installed, even Gabriel had to admit that that basic supply was rather bare.

He nodded and turned to speak briefly to the ship's computer regarding the prospective flight plan, then stopped. Enda was eyeing him.

"Yes?" he asked.

"Nothing at all," Enda said. "Where did you leave my water bottle?"

"It's sitting right next to your bulb. When is that thing going to *do* something?" Gabriel said as Enda headed out.

"It can be so difficult to predict outcomes." Enda's voice floated back to him.

Gabriel turned to the computer again and decided not to input either a flight plan or a starfall plan. *Let's see who finds us this time*, he thought.

* * * * *

Iphus was unusually busy when they got there. The VoidCorp-based facilities there appeared to be undergoing some fairly large-scale personnel transfers. Big ships were coming in and out of orbit around the system almost on an hourly basis, and the sky around the planet was alive with starfalls and starrises.

"Bloody nuisance," Gabriel said to himself as he piloted *Sunshine* in toward the main transit docks of the Iphus Collective, the main mining facility of the planet and one of the few not completely owned by VoidCorp. The big dark VoidCorp ships, huge stylized spheres and teardrops, were all over the place, lounging around local space with the kind of quietly threatening insouciance one would expect of a small neighborhood's resident thugs. Traffic at the Collective itself was light, as if people were purposely avoiding the area. Gabriel had no trouble docking at the most central ring, and after finishing the docking and refueling formalities, he and Enda headed for the main trading dome.

"It's like a desert in here," Gabriel said as they walked through the empty corridors. "So empty."

Enda was looking around her with that pursed-lipped expression Gabriel had learned usually concealed some measure of concern behind it. There were very few people other than themselves in the corridors of what was normally the access to a busy shopping and entertainment area. They saw a few fraal and some humans who looked as if they were on their way to somewhere else as quickly as they could get there. The emptiness of the place accentuated something Gabriel had not really noticed there before—a kind of "hard up" look to facilities and fittings, a suggestion that the place was beginning to fall on hard times. Until now, the vitality of the place had distracted Gabriel from picking up on this. The slight shabbiness had looked like "atmosphere." Now it simply looked run down.

The fraal running the information desk at the center of the main dome shook his head. "Explanations are many, but certainty is scarce," he said to Enda and Gabriel when, after getting directions to the medical facility, they asked casually about the presence of all the VoidCorp vessels in the area. "I have heard it said that VoidCorp is in the midst of a mighty corporate purge, but who from the Company would come here—" he gestured at the dome above them— "to tell us the truth of the story or give it the lie? This place is abomination to them, and outside the Company, who could truly say? They are no lovers of letting their secrets out where others may perceive them. There has been nothing in the news to shed light on the matter, but what would make us think there would be?"

Gabriel and Enda thanked him and walked away. Enda's lips were looking more pursed than ever. "Not a lot of help," Gabriel said.

"More than one might suspect," Enda said. "Corporate purges at VoidCorp have produced turmoil enough in the past. Wars have been fought over them—or as a result of them, but I would not willingly say more about it just now."

They made their way across the space under the echoing main dome and down into one of the many tributary corridors on the other side. That sense of general emptiness and desertion, lost briefly under the dome, returned here in force. Any spaceport that has vacuum or an inimical atmosphere on the outside may acquire a scruffy feel after much use. No amount of maintenance will ever restore that just-new feeling. This place, though, had plainly been missing out on even fairly basic maintenance for a while. The hallways were dusty, walls and panels were smudged, and here and there were sooty smoke trails stretching upwards from where wiring or other components buried inside the panels had combusted themselves.

"It's a mess," Gabriel said softly. It was the kind of appearance that led you to wonder how tight the facility was as regarded its atmosphere. "Maybe we should bring breather packs with us when we come back."

Enda merely pursed her lips again and headed down the corridor, looking for the medical facility. There were two of them at the Collective, but the other was closed at the moment, its medical practitioner apparently away on leave. This one they had not visited before, and Enda raised her eyebrows in satisfaction when they came around a curve in the corridor and saw the frosted glass doors with the numerous species-specific insignia of the medical profession emblazoned on them.

The doors slid aside for them as they approached, and Gabriel and Enda walked into a wide white space that contained nothing except a diagnostic chair in the middle of the floor. They paused.

"Hello?" Gabriel called.

"Nonspecific greeting," said a computer voice out of the middle of the air. "One moment, please."

Gabriel blinked then as everything changed around him. Suddenly they were standing in a forest at morning. Beams of dusty sunlight stabbed down all around them through the trees, and birds sang high up somewhere in the canopy of green. The ground underfoot was covered with a carpet of fine brown needles. The diagnostic chair remained where it was though, amusingly incongruous among the pine needles. A small brown bird dropped down from a branch somewhere above, lit on the back of the chair, eyed Gabriel and Enda, and began to sing at them with great sweetness and (Gabriel thought) a fair amount of territorial aggression.

From behind one of the trees, then, slipped a mechalus. Gabriel looked her with interest. The mechalus was about two meters tall and had precise muscle tone as was usual for that people. She wore the typical *rlin noch'i,* the utilitarian everyday garment that mechalus favored, little more than a simple soft-booted bodysuit covering the body to the neck. The skin of her hands and face was very dark, almost olive hued, and had small veins of circuitry complementing the smoothness of her complexion.

"Introduction: Doctor," the mechalus said, looking at them out of large, dark eyes that had a slight epicanthic fold. She bowed slightly to both of them. "Gender female, in case of treatment matter in which gender affects result or cultural stance. Assistance?"

"Not with a treatment matter," Gabriel said, nodding to her. "Gabriel Connor."

"Enda," the fraal said and bowed slightly as well. "A pleasure, honored one."

"Delde Sota," said the doctor. She was extremely handsome, even by mechalus standards. The genetic engineering the mechalus had done on themselves over many centuries seemed to have selected for what humans considered good looks—high cheekbones, dramatic faces with prominent noses, high foreheads, and large eyes. This mechalus wore her long hair back in a kind of shaggy mane that began to be braided below shoulder level. The neural-net fibers and hair wound together in an elaborate pattern that Gabriel realized, when he got a closer look, somewhat reflected the pattern of the Sealed Knot, the mechalus version of the lifestar or squared cross which many human medical practitioners wore. Many other implants and mechanical augmentations were doubtless woven into and through the doctor's body, engineered there at the molecular level by her ancestors and born with her as part of her normal heredity. Many mechalus even had further augmentations later in life by choice and design, but what these might be there was no telling at first glance.

The doctor came toward them, glancing around her as she paused by the diagnostic chair. "Species-specific comfort system selection is idiosyncratic," she said as the small bird on the chair stared at her and began to sing even more piercingly. "Query: this environment comforting / relaxing / providing relief from stress of visiting medical practitioner?"

"The forest is very beautiful," said Enda, "but I would think this small creature would raise my stress level somewhat if I had to listen to it for very long."

Delde Sota made a slightly annoyed face and waved one graceful hand. The forest disappeared, though a faint echo of the small bird's voice lay on the air for a few seconds after the trees were gone. "Garbage software," she said, "debug process requires millennia, not worth the medium in which produced. Warning: value judgment. Query: nature of assistance required?"

"Phymech supplies," Gabriel said. "Better than the basic pack. Anything you have."

"Query: *anything?*" Doctor Delde Sota said, with a look in those big dark eyes that was suddenly rather mischievous. "Whole-body transplant kit? Special this week. Eight hundred thousand Concord dollars."

Gabriel swallowed. That was maybe a tenth of *Sunshine's* entire cash value, if such a thing as a whole-body transplant kit actually existed. "Uh, no thank you."

"Just the usual second-level augmentation package, I would

think," Enda said mildly. "Traumatic amputation, crushing wound, extremity suite, pneumothorax, and explosive decompression intervention package."

"Query: take original basic package in trade for reconditioning / resale?" Doctor Delde Sota asked.

Gabriel raised his eyebrows at that. "How much would we get in trade?"

The mechalus considered. "One thousand Concord."

"Oh, come on," Gabriel said. "Two at least."

Doctor Delde Sota looked at him with a wry expression. "Statement: this facility medical intervention, break even plus five percent, not charity. Subsidies zero. One thousand two."

"One thousand seven."

"In new condition?"

"Seals unbroken," Gabriel said.

"One thousand five."

"Done," Gabriel said and reached out a hand. The braid came up from behind Doctor Delde Sota's back and wrapped itself around his wrist in agreement, then let go rather quickly. Delde Sota looked at him curiously.

"Unusual 'personal magnetism,' " the doctor said. "Query: planet of origin?"

"Bluefall," Gabriel said, wondering just what her sensors had noticed.

Delde Sota shrugged. "Statement: electrolyte balance may need adjustment. Dietary intervention possibly useful."

"Yes," Enda said, "he does eat like a . . . well, never mind that. Do you have the replacement packs in stock, or will you need to reorder?"

"Statement: all equipment in stock, inventory software fortunately less than garbage," Doctor Delde Sota said and gestured. A panel of the white wall slipped aside. "Conditional query: alternatives: cash and carry; or make purchase, arrange transport and installation?"

"Purchase and have transported and installed, please," Enda said as they followed the doctor into a surprisingly large storage area full of shelving and "secure" cabinetry, impervious to rifling except by the person whose hand prints, or even brain wave patterns, were programmed into the protective circuitry.

"You sure we couldn't save a little money by taking 'cash and carry'?" Gabriel said to Enda.

Doctor Delde Sota gave him that slightly wicked look again. "Statement: savings plus minus ten percent, installation extra, certainty of success of self-installation plus minus forty percent."

Gabriel swallowed again, not much liking the image of sticking a broken arm or half-amputated leg into the phymech and getting a response along the lines of "Installation error, cannot find programming module A458, terminating run."

"No," he said hurriedly, "you go ahead and have the usual installer do the job."

The doctor whistled. A floater pallet came from down behind one of the long racks of shelves and levitated up to where it was wanted. The doctor's braid reached up to touch the pallet and instruct its onboard computer which film-wrapped component packs to select. Manipulating arms whipped out of the pallet and started plucking packs out of the shelving.

"How long will we have to wait for installation?" Enda asked, reaching into her satchel for her credit chip.

"Reply: installation immediate, this module will perform," said Delde Sota, patting the floater pallet with one hand while it finished loading itself. "Self-trained AI with direct oversight, most reliable."

"You don't seem overly busy here," Gabriel remarked after a moment, as the pallet finished its packing.

Doctor Delde Sota gave him a slightly peculiar look. "Meaning of query?"

"Uh," Gabriel hesitated, since he wasn't sure himself exactly what response he had intended to elicit. "I mean, there doesn't seem to be the usual number of people around today."

Delde Sota nodded. "Speculation," she said, "politics, local disruption, possible intervention of outside powers. Instability. Bad for business."

"Outside powers as in the stellar nations?" said Enda. "There has been no indication of such in the news services."

The doctor waved her hands in a gesture that Gabriel thought might have been a shrug. "Statement: nonspecialist, politics; specialist, medicine. Speculation: disruption periodic, especially of powers normally present in this system."

"The Concord," said Enda softly, "and VoidCorp."

Doctor Delde Sota turned away from the pallet, now done loading and levitating down to floor level again. She reached out to take the chip that Enda offered her. "Payment received, thank you," she said as her braid's cyberfilaments brushed briefly over the chip's surface. She handed the chip back, adding, "Statement: VoidCorp traffic in vicinity much increased. Speculation: major disruption. Speculation/analysis: other neighboring star systems very pleasant this time of year."

Gabriel grinned a little. "Noted," he said.

The doctor walked them out to the entrance again. "Instruction: locate ship, open/release phymech module and computer controls. Carrier will implement installation routine. Estimated time for completion one hundred sixty minutes plus-minus ten minutes."

"Thank you very much," Enda said and bowed slightly to the doctor. "May your healing go well."

"Request: ultimate principle probability response your sentiment greater than fifty percent," said the Doctor. She smiled and showed them out. As they went, Gabriel turned to raise a hand to her in farewell and caught, he thought, just the hint of a look at him of—interest? Curiosity? But the doors slid shut on the expression, and Gabriel shrugged at his own sensitivity. *I'm beginning to see hidden motivations in everything,* he thought. *A few days' quiet between starfall and starrise will do me good and stop me from thinking the whole universe is plotting against me.*

They got back to *Sunshine* and spent not a hundred and sixty minutes with the phymech installation, but nearly two hundred and twenty. The installer found a fault in the phymech hardware, one that was reparable with spare parts the installer had handy.

Gabriel got the shivers at the thought of what might have happened had they activated the phymech in a moment of need. There was no telling what kind of chaos the machine could have caused.

"After this," Enda said while putting away some of the other phymech spare supplies in a nearby cupboard, "you will not think quite so hard about saving money."

"You always do."

"Not at the cost of life," Enda said.

She lifted the last few packages of the "basic" phymech supplies onto the pallet that was just retracting its arms after having run one last set of diagnostics on the phymech. She made sure that the supplies were secured in place under the flexible lid that covered the upper portion of the machine, then patted the machine in a friendly manner on one side. She was vaguely astonished when it put out a tentacle and patted her back.

Gabriel chuckled as the pallet made its way down in the lift to the docking bay floor. "Some AI program," he said. " 'Direct oversight' indeed."

Enda too looked after the pallet with amusement. "It might be more direct than we suspect. After so many centuries and generations of being one with machines, the mechalus most likely have modes of consciousness regarding them that we can barely understand. There are mechalus who have so mastered that oneness that they need not even touch a machine to interface with it. Some of them can even meld directly into the Grid without direct or 'mechanical' access."

"It sounds like magic," Gabriel said as he called the lift back up and locked the outer door seals in place.

Enda shrugged. "Doubtless mindwalking in some of its aspects seems like magic to them. To each species its own mysteries. They are what make our lives of interest to one another. Meanwhile, are we ready? Is the computer programmed?"

"We're as ready as we're going to be."

"Then let us leave," Enda said, "not with undue haste. Moving too quickly can attract attention. This many VoidCorp ships in the vicinity make me nervous, and I would as soon be away from here with five days' starfall time between them and me."

"No problem with that," Gabriel said. "We'll head for the Outer Belt and do our starfall there. No point in making our whereabouts too obvious."

* * * * *

They headed outward at a seemly speed. Gabriel twitched somewhat as he lifted *Sunshine* up out of the Iphus Collective's docking ring. As they cleared the atmosphere a few moments later, they saw no less than four of the big VoidCorp cruisers hanging there, overshadowing the planet and matching its rotation exactly to stay perfectly in place. It was intimidation of the plainest kind. *We're here. We could roll in right now and take you over if we wanted. Maybe we'll do it tomorrow, or the day after, but meanwhile, it's fun to watch you just lie there and be afraid.*

Gabriel frowned and kicked in the system drive, aiming for an area of space about forty thousand kilometers past the Outer Belt. There would be very few watching eyes out there. The Concord's Omega Station was there, to be sure, but its eyes, Gabriel was certain, would be turned to the sudden presence of all the VoidCorp cruisers at Iphus. Outbound traffic, especially a small mining vessel, would attract no attention at all.

Enda was busying herself about the cargo storage area again, rearranging things to her liking. This was a job that Gabriel had long learned to leave to her. Enda's grasp of spatial relationships was extraordinary, and she could find ways to fit things into other things that would have seemed impossible at first glance. "It is simply a survival trait when you live in space," she had said once or twice, "whether you will control your environment or allow your environment to control you."

Gabriel stretched in the pilot's seat and told the computer to mind the store for a while. There was no need for his attention for another ten minutes or so, until they finished transiting the Belt and came out the other side. At first he had been nervous about such transits, imagining a storm of stones, every one of which was intent on smashing *Sunshine* to pieces. Now he knew that even the Inner Belt was more like a sea full of widely dispersed islands that you had to go out of your way to hit. The Outer Belt was more sparsely populated yet—or rather, it had about the same number of asteroids as the Inner Belt, but they were spread through a cubic volume of space perhaps a hundred times greater. There was little danger of anything happening that the ship's collision system couldn't handle, swerving it around or over the obstacle even as it was letting you know about it.

He got up and wandered back to see what Enda was doing. "Why are you repacking that again?" he asked. "You just did that storage the other day."

"True, but the new phymech supplies take up less space, and some of the spares can now go in the dedicated cabinet rather than in with general stores," Enda replied, shutting one storage unit and opening another. "You might as well ask why you scrubbed the ship three times from stem to stern during that last starfall."

"It needed it."

"It," Enda asked, "or you?"

He knew the bantering tone well enough now to snicker a little when he heard it. "Well, let's just say that I wouldn't—"

They both jumped as the proximity alarm started to howl. "Some damned rock," said Gabriel, annoyed, turning back toward the cockpit. "I swear I'm going to reduce the sensitivity on that—"

—*thing*, he was about to say, but never had a chance to, as the line of laser light stitched itself across the cockpit windows, half blinding him.

Gabriel swore and threw himself into the pilot's seat, slamming down on the controls that took the ship out of auto. An instant later he punched the second set that would start up the JustWadeIn software. It took too long, it always took too long—

Another flash of laser light, this one not so blinding. The ship was in passive response mode while the weapons came up, and the cockpit windows knew that laser light was bad for its pilots and was blocking anything cohesive. Small blessings, Gabriel thought, as the interactive field fitted itself down over him again. Enda threw herself into the seat beside him, not even bothering to go for their e-suits this time.

It was the same little ships again, the greenish colored bullets. There were more of them, though. Five, Gabriel counted, or thought he counted, as they peeled away from him and around again, already having made one pass. Why didn't they use something deadlier first? he thought as he reached down and drew his "sidearms," felt them heating in his hands. *If they'd hit us with a plasma cannon first, they would have—*

Wham! He went blind as the first jolt of plasma hit him. Ranging, the first one was just ranging, Gabriel thought, staggered, staring around him sightlessly as he tried to get some kind of reference from the program. While he asked for diagnostics from it, Gabriel fired around him blindly with his own plasma cartridges, just two or three times. "Better not to feel helpless even when you are," his weapons instructor had told him. But he did not have unlimited armaments. *Enda!*

I cannot see—

Gabriel's own "vision" was clearing a little. Tactical at least was coming back, showing him the widely divided shapes arcing around to have another pass. Diagnostics were showing some hull damage—microcracks and stress fractures in the hull shielding, but mostly in the aft section. Fortunately atmosphere was not leaking out—yet, anyway—though through the JustWadeIn software, the hull was moaning like a beaten animal.

Show me which one hit us with that big blast, Gabriel said, and the computer obligingly highlighted that ship. It was another ball-bearing shape, a tumbling sphere, the farthest one away from *Sunshine* at the moment. It seemed to be slightly larger than its companions. Watching its almost erratic tumbling, Gabriel thought that perhaps its weapon left the craft with a bigger energy consumption curve than the pilot might have wished. *That's something to play with. Concentrate on that one,* Gabriel told the computer. *Work out its trajectory. I want plenty of warning before the next pass.*

Enda?

It is better, she said and then paused. *Ah!*

WHAM! Another huge impact. A few seconds later something bounced hard off the cockpit windows and left a white smear that froze instantly to opaque ice. *What the heck was that?* Gabriel wondered.

Ah-ha, Enda said, and there was another WHAM!—but no impacts this time. Tactical showed them two of the ships gone with various large fragments left spinning about.

Interesting, Enda said, sounding very satisfied indeed. *I did not notice that this software had a specifically fraal-oriented implementation.*

Didn't read the manual before this? Gabriel said. *Shame. Look out, here they come again. And here comes that big one. I don't want to take another hit from that.* He felt behind him briefly for the "shotgun." He would not power it up just yet, preferring to save it as his ace in the hole.

Here came the larger ship again, finishing its big slow swing away and starting to slide back toward them. *Recharging, I would say,* Enda said. *Let us see what it has in the way of passive defense.*

He got a sense of Enda stitching down the length of it with her own plasma cartridge weapons, but Gabriel had his own problems and could not spare her much attention. Another of the little ships was diving in close, and his own plasma cartridges shot out toward it—and missed as it jumped abruptly sideways. *What the—* It was not specifically a nonrelativistic type of movement, but it was not one likely to be produced by any drive Gabriel had ever heard of. Jump!—and it went sideways again, missing another cartridge. *Analyze that,* Gabriel said hurriedly to the computer. *Give me a hint on how to do "windage" for that kind of motion.*

The computer signaled acquiescence, but Gabriel began to wonder whether it was going to come up with an answer in time to do him any good. He began firing slightly scattershot, thinking, No use conserving ammunition if we're going to be too dead to use the leftovers next time. The ship arrowing in toward him jumped again sideways, and Gabriel suddenly thought, The other way!—and fired to one side of it.

The ship jumped, bloomed into sudden fire, then sudden darkness as air and liquid sprayed away, spattering *Sunshine's* cockpit windows as the wreckage plunged by.

"Now," Enda said.

WHAM!

Sunshine rocked and wallowed, and both of them were blind again, virtually and tactically. Desperate, Gabriel felt around behind him for the "shotgun," determined not to go down without one last shot. But he felt someone pull it out of his hands, taking control of the system, and then he felt something he could not understand, a great peculiar roar, like blood in the body shouting defiance before spilling itself or being spilled. And a faint echo of that cry from somewhere else, he could not tell where, but it froze him with a sense of great age and fear—

—and after that came a strange sudden silence in the software, as if the computer had come up against some response it had not been expecting.

Slowly their vision cleared. Gabriel looked around hurriedly to determine the location of the remaining craft and caught sight of nothing but one hasty starfall off in the distance, red-golden fire sheeting over the surface of another of the little ball-bearing craft. Then it was gone.

"I really must send a nice note to Insight about that software," Gabriel said softly.

"You might want to wait," Enda said, rubbing her eyes. "Void-Corp has been known to monitor drivespace comm relays before this, and they routinely scan for mail that is intended for their enemies."

"So it can wait. How many hostiles was that?" Gabriel asked the computer.

Six, the computer replied.

Gabriel swallowed hard. "Did you count six?" he said to Enda. "I thought there were five."

She told the computer's virtuality field to lift from around her, and she sat back in her seat, tilting her head from side to side. Not, Gabriel thought, as a gesture of negation, but because she was wondering whether she might hear the brains slosh when she did so. His own certainly felt wobbly enough, and there were other parts of him that might need drying off as well.

"Five, I thought," Enda said. "Obviously we both missed something in the heat of the moment."

Gabriel rubbed his face and looked again at the computer's diagnostics. "You're not going to like this," he said, "but I think the cargo bay may have taken another hit. Look at the stress schematic back there."

Enda glanced at it and made an annoyed face. "One more problem," she noted, "but there is another that interests me more. Our shooting was better this time."

"Just barely," Gabriel said. "Yours was what saved us."

"Leaving that aside," Enda said, but Gabriel noticed that she did not contradict him, "look out there. Bodies."

They both bent closer to the computer tank, looking at the slowly spinning outline. "Body, anyway," Gabriel corrected. "At least I don't see more than one. And it looks more or less intact. Human?"

"So it would seem, but you were the one who suggested you wanted to see who or what had been shooting at you."

"So let's go get it and take a look."

Gabriel brought the system drive back up from standby and nudged *Sunshine* toward the floating shape. "Probably won't be recognizable," he said, "after explosive decompression."

"Are you expecting to see anyone you recognize?" Enda asked, getting up to go aft and check the seals between the main section and the cargo bay.

"Hard to say at this point, but no one knew we were going to be here. Or at least no one should have known."

A brief silence. "You did not file a starfall plan, then? Or an insystem flight plan?"

"No," Gabriel said as he inched *Sunshine* closer to the spinning, tumbling form. As they got closer, the tactical display in the tank was better able to show a shape. Definitely humanoid, Gabriel thought. There was something odd about the head though. Even an e-suit helmet would not be quite that big, as a rule.

Enda looked out into the darkness. "Well, we knew there was surveillance of some kind going on, did we not? Now we know that it is not merely random or casual. Something quite sophisticated is being used on us."

"My money says we're carrying some kind of tag or tracer," Gabriel said as they glided very close to the body. He eased back on the throttles and brought up the external spotlights, instructing the ship to train them on the body as they got close enough for them to do any good. "I really love the prospect of tearing this ship apart piece by piece to find out where the tracer is when we don't know what it looks like or where it's been put or even when . . ."

Five hundred meters away, they could now see, just as a speck, the faint reflection from the spotlights on a spread-eagled humanoid form. Gabriel nudged the ship ever so slowly closer to it.

"Who would have put such a thing on us?" Enda asked. "And why?"

"Someone who wants to see us dead of an 'accident' in far system space," Gabriel answered.

"Or in a street on Grith, late at night," Enda said.

Gabriel thought about that for a moment and shook his head. "On-ship surveillance wouldn't help anyone who wanted to do that. The people with the knives and the guns—that's some other kind of surveillance working, I'd say."

"So there might be two different parties tracking us," Enda said.

Two hundred fifty meters now. Gabriel sighed, "I was kind of hoping to avoid that particular conclusion."

"But you have not been able to?"

Gabriel shook his head. Two hundred meters.

"On the other hand," he said, "it's possible that if we removed whatever surveillance device was presently on the ship—"

"—assuming that we could find it in the first place—"

Gabriel nodded. "—that its removal would alert whoever had put it there, and they would get even more annoyed with us than they are."

"I would suggest by present indications that they are already fairly annoyed," Enda said, looking over the computer's diagnostics again and sighing. "More hull repairs for the cargo bay, I fear, and the damage may possibly be well up into the superstructure as well. Well, riches are a burden, they say."

"I thought you said you weren't rich." One hundred meters. The shape was slowing, losing its spin. Gabriel thought he could see something like tubes curving out stiff from the body as if frozen that way. A very big dark head section.

"I was speaking figuratively," Enda said. Together she and Gabriel peered out the cockpit windows as they came up to about fifty meters. Gabriel slowed *Sunshine* down to the merest crawl.

"Have you ever seen an e-suit with a headpiece like that?" Gabriel asked. It looked like solid metal, though the light was poor and certainly there were enough metallic coatings for visors, gold and platinum for example, that could fool you into thinking the whole helmet was polished metal. The shape was peculiar, too, oddly elongated toward the sides.

"Someone with very large ears?" Enda inquired.

"That large?" said Gabriel, and shook his head. "If it's a new species and that *is* for their ears, they're going to have to put up with a lot of teasing."

He reached into the computer's tank and told it to bring up the exterior handling software that controlled the grapples and configurable cables. Gabriel continued to nudge the ship's nose a little to one side of the body to bring the lift access close to it.

The ship inched around and came to rest relative to the body, which was simply drifting now, no longer spinning. Gabriel let the tank's manipulation field snug in around his hand as the grapples extruded themselves from *Sunshine*'s side and snaked out gently toward the body. The grapples were "negative feedback" waldo-hands with sensor-augmented faked sensation so that your hand could "feel" what the grapples felt through the software as they engaged with a solid object. Gabriel felt his way toward the body, opened the fingers of the grapples, and closed them carefully around it. The sensation was peculia, slightly squishy.

Slowly he pulled the body closer and flicked one thumb to open the lift access, then he pushed the body carefully into it and closed the access again. Gabriel put on light gravity in the lift and instructed it to come up to ship level while filling with par-asitic air siphoned out of the main cabin.

The lift clunked into place. Gabriel watched the lift's pressure gauge in the tank until it matched exactly with that of the cabin. Finally he was satisfied of a perfect match and touched the con-trol to open the lift door. Enda was already up out of her seat, heading aft. He went after her.

They stood and looked down at the body on the floor of the lift. Despite its short time out in space, it seemed already well frozen, the arms flung out forwards, one of the legs oddly bent. There was the large glossy headpiece, cracked but otherwise intact, glazed inside with a silvery metallic compound. The e-suit covering the body, though, was most peculiar. It looked like greenish plastic—but the green of the plastic was not even. It looked lighter in some areas, darker in others. Enda knelt down beside it, reached out a hand toward one of the slits that the explosion had apparently torn in the e-suit, then took the hand back again, glancing up at Gabriel.

He put one booted toe out and nudged the body slightly. Over the greenish e-suit were shoulder pads and shin coverings and a breastplate of what might have been some kind of dark armor. It was faintly ribbed and looked less metallic than chitinous, as if it had been wrought from the wing casing of some large beetle. The armor was by no means complete, though, and much of the body was left uncovered. It appeared to have been partially blown away from the lower left leg, and splintered bone was visible. There was little blood, even clotted blood, but from underneath the plastic material of the e-suit where it had been torn, something pallidly green was oozing.

"The suit's filled with something," Gabriel said. "Not air, either." He too put a hand out as if to touch that strange e-suit, then thought better of it and withdrew it.

"I confess to having been eager to see who pursued us," Enda said, pursing her lips, "but now I am less eager. I do not like the thought of investigating this being much further without specialized protective gear, which, alas, we do not have."

Gabriel thought about that for a moment. "I bet I know who does have some, though," he said.

"Oh?"

"Doctor Delde Sota."

Enda blinked at that. "You are considering taking this body back to her for autopsy?"

Gabriel shrugged. "Spacefarers going about their lawful occasions are supposed to assist the authorities in investigating unusual occurrences, especially in system space, where the occurrences could cause danger to life or limb." He glanced back toward the cargo bay. "*Our* limbs were pretty well endangered, if you ask me. Legally, Doctor Sota would have to assist us. This is a 'public health' matter. And anyway, what *is* this creature, Enda? A new alien species of some kind? If it is, people should know about it, and that it's fairly aggressive when it gets you alone out in the dark."

"I would find it hard to argue with that." Enda stood up. "Well, we should wrap it up and keep it as intact as we can." She stood up, thinking for a moment—then turned to the nearby cabinet that contained the phymech and stroked its front panel. The panel lit up and displayed available settings. "I thought so," Enda said. "Here. 'Corpse wrapping.' "

"That's going to use up all the disinfectant film," Gabriel said, looking up past her as the machine displayed its materials requirements.

"Yes, well," Enda said, "what would you recommend we use instead?"

Gabriel sniffed the air. It was already becoming sharply rank with the scent of the green gel that was dripping out of various punctures and rips in the creature's protective suit as the air warmed it and the once-frozen liquids began to melt.

"Never mind," he said hurriedly, "I think you're right; we'd better just do it."

Enda told the phymech to put down its handling arms. It extruded them, wrapped them around the strange body and lifted it, preparatory to wrapping.

"When it's finished," Gabriel said, "I think we'd better put it in the cargo bay and vent the hold."

Enda made a little sniff of laughter. "If the hold is not already well enough vented. But, yes, that should successfully stabilize it. At least, we will hope so."

The phymech got on with its wrapping. Soon there was nothing left but an opaque, silvery-sheened, ungainly, and not very human-looking bundle, for neither Gabriel or Enda wanted the body forced into an unnatural shape that might destroy some useful piece of equipment or other evidence. The shape was awkward. They had some difficulty getting it into the airlock between the forward area and the cargo bay, but it fitted at last after some tugging and pushing. When the airlock was closed again, Gabriel activated the secondary grapples mounted inside the cargo bay, the ones used for handling rocks inside the bay, and carefully opened the other airlock door.

"There remains the problem of exactly how we handle this body when we get to Iphus," Enda said.

Gabriel finished up with the grapples and closed the airlock door again, pausing to look at the inert lump lying there in the light gravity he had left turned on. "Probably," he said, "it wouldn't be a great idea to haul it through the corridors."

"No. I would think we might be able to get the doctor to make a house call, though, especially if there was an illness aboard ship."

"Oh?"

"Yes. I was just thinking how unwell you look, Gabriel."

"What?"

"Oh, most unwell. I think you have eaten something bad. Contaminated stores, perhaps."

Gabriel blinked at her, then made a few experimental retching noises. "Maybe there was something wrong with that last batch of meat rolls?" he suggested.

"Certainly there was," Enda said. "I cannot believe the amount of hot spice with which you ordered them made. They are nearly inedible, but perhaps there was some bacterial contamination as well."

"Something that the phymech can't handle."

"Well, it has never been as strong on nontraumatic problems or simple systemic infections as it is on trauma. Perhaps there might be something wrong with the phymech as well. Yes, some kind of error in installation—or better still, another software problem that the installer missed even though it caught the other one."

Gabriel shook his head and turned to make his way back up to the pilot's seat. "I begin to see why fraal are such a long-lived species," he said.

Enda looked after him with some concern. "Why would that be?"

"Sneakiness," Gabriel said. "Come on. I'm going to go sound sick on the comm back to Iphus."

Smiling very slightly, Enda came after him.

Chapter Thirteen

ABOUT FIVE HOURS later they were docking once again in the main ring on the Iphus Collective. Gabriel had been in no hurry to get there quickly, partly because he was "sick," partly because he wanted to give some of those big VoidCorp ships time to go away. Indeed when *Sunshine* arrived, they were all gone, which also made Gabriel wonder slightly. What other part of the system have they gone off to intimidate, and why?

Doctor Delde Sota was there at the docking ring to meet them. She came up in the lift, stepped into *Sunshine*, and held quite still while she glanced around her. It was slightly amazing to Gabriel how her height made the ship around her look smaller than it really was. Equally surprising was the look she trained on him as she stood there, holding what appeared to be a brushed-metal version of the standard doctor's bag.

"Conjecture: faked illness," the mechalus said with an expression that for the moment was decidedly cool. "Etiology: uncertain. Observation: atypical odors for human/fraal habitation. Query: nature of callout?"

"We were attacked in system space by ships, one of which was piloted by an alien we cannot identify," Gabriel said. "We managed to save the body. It's . . . pretty abnormal."

"Query:" said Doctor Sota, "recording of attack and response?"

"The computer has saved it," said Enda and brought up the JustWadeIn software.

Delde Sota stepped up to the pilot's seat and paused there for a moment, looking at the smear that still lay across the cockpit window from the first object that had hit them. "Query: prove-nance?"

"The residue from an impact," Enda said. "You will see it in the playthrough."

Delde Sota's braid reached up over her shoulder and brushed across the cockpit controls, the hair-tendrils finding one pre-ferred spot and infiltrating itself through it into the computer cir-cuitry behind. The tank flickered with images, dark and bright, too quickly for Gabriel to get a clear sense of any individual one.

Delde Sota turned to them then and said, "Observation: lucky to be alive. Query: repeat occurrence?"

"It happened once before, yes," Gabriel replied, "but there weren't any remains we could find."

"Proposal: autopsy," said Delde Sota, moving aft and taking her bag with her while looking around for a place to put it. "Requirements: suitable surface, disinfectant solution—" She smiled briefly. "Body."

"We have a table," Enda said and led Delde Sota down into the "sitting room" area, where she unfolded the table from the wall.

Wait a minute, we *eat* off that table! Gabriel thought, but he didn't bother to say it out loud, for Enda was already making her way down toward the cargo bay with the doctor in tow. Gabriel sighed and turned to the computer, telling the cargo bay to pres-surize itself with air from inside the docking ring access. He then followed the others.

Enda and Delde Sota were standing there in the chill, looking down at the unwieldily wrapped body. "Observation: some haste in preparation, programming in phymech insufficient," said Delde Sota. "Observation: odor immediately noticeable, some haste suggested. Query: computer interface in this area?"

"There against the wall," said Gabriel, "over by the spee-gee apparatus."

Delde Sota's braid started to lengthen itself, wavering out and along to where the computer interface was embedded by the spe-cific gravity and metallurgic assay equipment. "Observation:

table too small. Conjecture: even if right size, not much good for dinner afterwards," Delde Sota said, going over to kneel by the corpse and putting her bag down while her braid insinuated itself into the ship's computer, "even after scrubbing by marine." Gabriel blinked at that. "Suggestion: pathology and food a bad mixture in close quarters. Query: assistance?"

"I'll help," said Gabriel, utterly horrified a second later that such a suggestion had come out of his mouth.

Doctor Sota gave him a look. "Observation: educational. Also: finder's right." She opened her doctor's bag.

—and it opened, and opened, and opened, and kept on opening so that Gabriel had to just stare at it. The bag flattened itself out across the floor into an incredibly complex set of dividers and clearfoam-wrapped instruments and objects that Gabriel couldn't identify. There seemed to be many times more room in it for things than the original volume would have suggested. Finally it stopped opening, and Gabriel was almost disappointed.

"I wonder if anyone does a version of that for maintenance tools?" Enda asked, looking down at the "bag" with what looked to Gabriel like mild envy.

Delde Sota looked from Enda to Gabriel with that slightly wicked look. "Information: special order," she said. "Offer: will assist you in obtaining discount. Suggestion: put ship in escrow."

"*Thank*youno," Gabriel said hurriedly.

Delde Sota raised her eyebrows, looked over the contents of the "bag," and selected an object wrapped in clearfoam. The foam dissolved away as she lifted the object, a long, slender, extremely keen-looking knife.

"Invocation: here death rejoices to teach the living," Delde Sota said and began slicing delicately at the bodywrap film that covered the corpse. It fell away, crinkling dryly, and Delde Sota looked at that with some bemusement. "Observation: already atypical response in wrapping," she said. "Begin recording. Computer, copy to coroner's records, Iphus Collective Medicolegal Authority, Delde Sota recording, this recording under Coroner's

Seal, Concord Medicolegal / Concord Pathology and Forensics SR7269563355209782673."

The last of the wrapping fell away. "Note dehydration or denaturization reaction in standard bodywrap," said Delde Sota, looking the body over. "Report concerns bodily remains resulting from as yet unreported event in Corrivale system space. See attached file recording for details. Initial examination shows bipedal overtly humanoid figure, gender details not specific at this stage, height one hundred ninety centimeters, mass—" she paused to lift the body—"fifty-eight point nine kilograms, atypically low for most humanoid species even without clothing or covering, the subject still being clothed."

She went on for a few moments to describe the strange e-suit verbally. Gabriel noticed that Delde Sota's idiom was growing more human, probably for the sake of the autopsy report. She paused at one point, putting the blade aside—it hovered steady in the air where she left it—and reached for another instrument that she used to sample the slimy substance inside the suit. Her face darkened somewhat as she said, "Interstitial area between e-suit and skin surface is filled with mucus-like substance, colonized to high titer levels by what appears to be mutated bacteria of geni *Orgontha, Salmonella, Escherichia*, numerous others. Purposes of mutation uncertain. Mucus is acidic, already moving through pH 4.2 and increasing. Exposure to air or damage to outer e-suit may be implicated. Sample retained in airtight capsule for later analysis. Images saved for later analysis. See attached files. Now removing e-suit."

The mechalus doctor reached first into her kit and came up with an object that looked like four small spheres welded together. She took hold of two of them and pulled. A thin silvery thread spun out between them until it was about a meter long. She left the first two spheres handing in the air, grasped the other two, and pulled. The thread started to stretch out into a shimmering sheet of thin-membrane polymer, probably no more than a molecule thick, but (Gabriel guessed) probably nearly unbreakable. This surface hovered in the air, and Delde Sota recovered her first tool, the straight-bladed dissecting knife. A clear skinfilm applied itself around her hands and up her arms, and she went to work.

Slice by slice she removed the e-suit, cutting away the softer portions around the armored parts and piling them up with some care on the membrane "sheet" that grew to accommodate them as she accumulated them. The head piece was the last to come off. Delde Sota lifted the dissecting knife, made a small adjustment to a control in its butt, then stroked it up the side of the headpiece, around and over the top, and down the other side. The headpiece fell apart in two neat pieces, the back half first. Delde Sota let the head rest on the floor, removing the back half of the headpiece first. It was full of the mucus-gel substance, and the inside of the headpiece was patterned with neurocircuitry.

She put the half-helmet aside, lifted the front portion away.

The head was human, and it looked very dead indeed.

"Body inside the e-suit appears to be that of a human male," Delde Sota said calmly enough while Gabriel did his best to keep his stomach under control—as much from the look of the body as from the ever-stronger acid smell that was filling the air.

He glanced over at Enda. She was still, looking at the body, and her face was more completely "shut down" than he could ever remember having seen it, even when she would fall asleep in the pilot chair. Gabriel glanced back at the body, forcing himself to it. The face was sunken, shrunken, the eyes fallen in, the bones of the skull all too clearly visible under the pallid, green-streaked flesh, as if this body had not been moving and shooting at them just half a day before. It looked rather as if it had been lying in some dry place for a long time, dessicating in the darkness. Though wet, the flesh still looked leathery, papery, too thin to stay on the bones. The expression was anguished, almost a rictus of paimn . . . and also rage? Gabriel thought, for he had seen men's faces locked that way after dying on the battlefield. The skull was corded with something like tendons that ran down the back and sides of the skull, down the neck to the chest, from the chest over to the shoulders and arms. The tendons looked like cords of greenish-white material, striated the long way like bundles of twisted fibers. The corpse's muscles were wasted almost to nothing, to cords and strings themselves. The middle of the body was sunken in as if its owner had been long starved. In one spot, Gabriel half thought he could see the contours of the spinal bones showing through the sagging papery skin of the abdomen.

"Age of subject indeterminate because of extreme fragility and denatured status of tissue," Delde Sota was saying calmly, but her eyes were dark with something that was beginning to look like anger. "No adipocere, massive tissue wasting in all extremities, atypical cordlike growth or bioengineered network, apparently sourced in the dural layer of the spine and the dura mater, radiating to all extremities and bone/muscle insertions. Exterior appearance suggests all major organs have experienced pathological wasting." She lifted her knife again. "Paused," she said and looked over at Gabriel. "Observation: some entities find this portion of the examination disturbing."

Enda got up and went hurriedly away. "I will listen—" she said as she went out the cargo bay door and shut it behind her.

The mechalus raised her eyebrows at Gabriel.

"Go ahead," he said.

"Resuming," Delde Sota said and made the first Y-shaped cut that laid the main body cavity and abdomen open.

Gabriel watched her, trying hard not to take what he saw too personally. "That's the problem with doing a lot of attack work," his weapons instructor had said once. "You start taking all the physical consequences personally, and pretty soon you're no good at the job any more. While you have to do this work, just remember: you do not have to accept delivery on the emotions and reactions that occur to you. Let them roll over you. Let them pass by. Later when you're retired, if you want to, I guarantee you that you'll be able to take them out and look at them in detail, but for the meantime they'll just impair your function."

So Gabriel watched Delde Sota take out the shrunken organs, a liver that was hardly there, a pair of lungs that were shriveled to nothing, removing them from a body cavity full of more of the pus-like slime, and Gabriel did not take it personally. He watched her dissect one of the tendonlike structures away from one of the arms, watched the tendon seem to try to hang on tighter as it was removed, then watched it "give up" and melt away into more green slime. Gabriel worked very hard not to take *that* personally.

"Biotech matter," said Delde Sota, detaching another sample and this time managing to get it into a sample capsule before it disintegrated. "Apparently self-augmenting, purpose apparently overtly tendonal, duplicating the tendons' function outside the body since those inside the body have been resorbed or have lost elasticity and no longer function. Biotech matter is either contaminated by or purposely perfused with the bacterial cultures mentioned earlier. Possibly a symbiotic relationship. Culture should be done with an eye to understanding the association of the two materials and determining whether one somehow affects the growth or structure of the other." She glanced over at one of her other instruments, raised her eyebrows. She was getting that angry look again. "First diagnostics on mucus indicate presence of high level of proteins and enzymes that in some conditions would function as psychoactives, and other proteins constructed in mimicry of corticosteroids, neurotransmitters, and messenger hormones primarily involved with rage and pain reactions. Endorphin levels zero." She put aside the tissue samples that she had been retrieving from the lungs and liver and reached down for the heart, lifting it and slicing it free. A great gout of the green pus ran out of the aorta, and Gabriel found it almost impossible not to take *that* personally. He had to turn away and concentrate on his breathing for a moment.

"Entire cardiovascular system has apparently been either invasively compromised or devolved to secondary status," said Delde Sota, slicing the heart open the long way and peeling it carefully apart. "No possible perfusion from this system. Possibility that perfusion is being managed by the mucus held around and within the body. Oxygen level however is almost nil, suggesting some other form of transport, possibly ATP-beta or

-gamma, of the anaerobic type." She frowned. "Investigation will be required of the aqueous humor."

Gabriel briefly misunderstood her and wondered what might possibly be funny about this situation. Then he got a look at the long needle Delde Sota had produced, and he suddenly realized where she was planning to stick it. He turned away hastily. To him eyes were *intensely* personal. He winced, unable to stop himself.

After a moment, "Humor is contaminated with aforementioned bacterial melange culture," said Delde Sota dispassionately. "Analysis follows."

She paused, and after a few seconds Gabriel dared to look back again. Delde Sota was simply looking down at the body, her big dark eyes plainly sorrowful; but the frown was also still there, an expression suggesting she was looking for something that she had not yet seen.

Gazing down at the skin of the neck, she reached down to do another moment's worth of dissection, peeling the skin away there and examining the tendons. They were wasted like all the other true tendons in this body, but there was something strange about the tendon strand on the body's left-hand side. Delde Sota leaned close, narrowing her eyes a little, and Gabriel got a feeling that somewhere in there her optical magnification was being greatly increased.

"Traces of an old incision," she said, "cutting nearly straight across and through the tendon, incising the cricoid cartilage as well, the wound stopping three centimeters before the opposite tendon. Much older than—"

Then she stopped, peered closer.

"Unusual finding," she said. "Old sub-sheath cyst. Nodular, but the shape is atypical."

Gabriel had to look at that—and agreed. He was no medical expert, but it did not seem to him that cysts would normally be square.

Delde Sota reached down and started to excise the cyst, then changed her mind, and left it in place. Instead she reached out for another tool, a much more delicate and fine-bladed knife. She wiped the pus-like slime away from around the tendon and began to dissect away the top of the cyst. Very delicately she did it, as if peeling away one layer of thin, wet tissue paper after another.

Gabriel, who briefly found himself regretting having to make do with unmagnified vision, now leaned closer despite the smell, because he saw something.

A chip. A tiny chip about a centimeter square, buried inside layer after layer of tendonal material that had overgrown and encysted it. Delde Sota glanced up at Gabriel, eyes meeting his in a look of alarm, but peculiarly, also of triumph.

"Electronic material," she said, "almost certainly of known-space provenance, dating to ten years before this date, plus-minus one year. Typical of ID chip sometimes used to store medical information for emergency use."

Very delicately Delde Sota exposed it. Then one strand of her neurobraid undid itself and wavered down toward the surface of the chip, brushed it, then sank into it.

She started and her eyes went wide. She stared at Gabriel. Before he could say anything, she put her fingers to her lips in a gesture that most humanoids understood, then pointed to the wall screen.

Gabriel looked at it. It had been scrolling a text revision of her dictation until now. Now, however, the screen showed various binary characters, but centered among them were the words:

DARSALL, OLEG
Born 08 12 2459
Posted Borealis colony, Silver Bell, 01 18 2486

Gabriel's breath went right out of him.
Silver Bell!
The Second Galactic War, besides endless other damage, had caused the destruction of the drivespace communications relays that had connected the Verge with the rest of human space. Time and money and opportunity to repair them had been lacking for

a long time. Not until fourteen years after the signing of the Treaty of Concord was the relay at Kendai restored. With its restoration had come the first message from the Verge for more than a hundred years—a message that had been trapped in drive-space for years, awaiting the repair that would allow it to be heard. "Borealis colony Silver Bell in Hammer's Star, calling any FreeSpace Alliance vessel . . . We are under attack by . . . Repeat, the colony is under heavy attack by unknown forces. Send help. Repeat, send help. It's May 3rd, 2489. We need help, damn it! Please—"

It had repeated again and again. The Concord had immediately sent the fortress ship *Monitor* to investigate, but when it reached Hammer's Star, there was no one left on the planet Spes where Silver Bell had been. The colony had been completely destroyed. Though *Monitor* contacted other Verge colonies, none of them knew what had happened to Silver Bell. The colony's destruction remained one of the great mysteries and tragedies of the end of the Long Silence, but here was one Oleg Darsall, breaking this particular aspect of the Silence at last.

"Does it check?" Gabriel asked Delde Sota.

She looked thoughtful for a moment, then nodded. "Grid access confirms someone of that name on the colonists' active list," she said. She looked down with an expression of terrible pain and confusion. "Is *this* what happened to all of them?"

Gabriel didn't want to think about it—or rather, he did, but not right here, not with the awful truth of it lying half-dissected on the floor in front of him.

"Autopsy must be continued in much greater detail in secure environment," said Delde Sota. "Recording pauses this time and date while transport and security are arranged."

She sat back on her heels and looked down at the creature that had once been Oleg Darsall. "Conjecture:" she said to Gabriel, "this is information that will be profoundly destabilizing in some areas, and it must be disseminated to the Concord immediately. However, all channels here are routinely monitored." Even here inside *Sunshine*, she mouthed "by VoidCorp" at him in such an obvious way that, just for that moment, Gabriel had to work hard not to burst out laughing. But at the same time, something else was on his mind.

Off to one side of the cargo bay was a simple thing for use when you were suited up and your communications gave out, a plastic pad on which you could write and then erase the written words by lifting the top sheet of plastic away from the one underneath it. Gabriel got up and fetched it, then used the little stylus clipped to the pad to write the words "Lorand Kharls." Gabriel quickly showed them to Delde Sota, and after she looked thoughtfully at them he lifted the plastic sheet and erased the words.

"Maybe you would not want to message him directly," Gabriel said, "but he would be in a position to reach the people who should know about this. He should be able to arrange to pick up the body without attracting too much notice."

The two of them looked at the poor creature lying on the floor, and Gabriel once again had to resist the urge to shudder all over. "Response: acceptable suggestion," said the doctor. "Meanwhile, body must be put in cold/stass until pickup." She thought for a moment, then said with just a shadow of the more normal wickedness in her eyes, "Statement: your phymech is faulty. Records confirm that from last visit."

"That was the excuse we gave inbound," Gabriel said.

The doctor nodded. "Opinion: consistency highly salutary. Statement: 'service' therefore will ensue. Expect service pallet in fifteen standard minutes, plus minus two minutes. Pallet will remain forty minutes. Instruction: remove/disarrange spare parts inside pallet to pallet service carry pack. Do not damage, parts to be recycled. Extra corpsewrap will be provided."

"I understand," Gabriel said.

"Will your 'morgue' be a safe place for this body to lie?" came Enda's voice over comms from the forward area.

The doctor replaced her instruments in her "bag" and waved a hand at it. The bag promptly folded itself up into a much smaller size and shape than should have been possible. "Statement:

surveillance cameras 'intermittently damaged'/disconnected in morgue," she said, with some satisfaction. "Death at least requires privacy." She glanced around her. "Query: phymech functioning correctly after installation?"

"As far as we can tell."

"Opinion:" Delde Sota said, "outdated/poor model, replace as soon as possible. Offer: will assist in obtaining discount," she looked at him thoughtfully and added, "should you survive."

Gabriel shivered. "I would prefer to," he said.

The doctor got a slightly concentrated look and then said in somewhat expanded idiom, "Opinion: you have become a target. Opinion: since when you take yourselves out into unpopulated places you seem to court attack, there would seem to be wisdom in staying in-system. Query: will you take advice from me?"

"Why not?" Gabriel said.

"Warning: advice does not always work, despite best intentions," the doctor said. "Meanwhile: opinion follows. Safety perhaps lies for you now best in numbers. Grith is nearest and most populated, also a place where becoming lost will be easier, but before you go there, go to this cafe—" She stroked the wall screen and a map of the docking rings came up. She showed Gabriel a small area, area 14, ring 6. "Present time is local evening, most of the regulars will be there. Look for a sesheyan in a dark *beishen* with a red stripe. It is distinctive. So is he. His name is Ondway. He and I have had dealings in the past. He will be able to recommend a place where you may hide and make inquiries, safe from attack . . . for a while. Outside of that—" She picked up her bag and shrugged. "Other assistance may be provided if possible. Meanwhile, prediction: life may not be quiet for you. Meanwhile, query: diet/electrolyte balance change?"

Gabriel rolled his eyes at her, glad to have an excuse to get up himself and turn his back on the grisly object on the floor. *Man,* said something in the back of his mind, that was a man once. Be careful.

"I haven't had a lot of time to worry about my diet," Gabriel said, heading toward the airlock with her. "Right now there are other things that look more likely to kill me first."

"Warning: do not be too sure," Doctor Sota said. "Opinion: all unwitting, you seem to bear before you great difficulty, great change. Warning: beware, harbinger, how it changes you." She made her way forward, bowed to Enda, and then slipped into the lift and vanished.

* * * * *

The pallet arrived as promised, and Gabriel "showed" it into the cargo bay area with considerable relief. He thought he might have to stay and instruct it, but the pallet extruded its manipulating arms and went to work with such skill and certainty that Gabriel went away feeling quite sure that the "oversight" that he and Enda had discussed earlier was in full use: that it was Delde Sota's eyes that were looking through the pallet's sensors, her hands that were wrapping Oleg Darsall for his next brief journey. After about half an hour, the job was done, and the pallet took itself away with a drape over it and various "spare parts" from the phymech festooning it. All during this, Enda kept herself in the sitting room, not stirring out. When the pallet was finally gone, Gabriel went in to sit with her, rather concerned.

"Are you all right?"

She tilted her head to one side and sighed. "No. Well, perhaps it should be explained. It is not that fraal have difficulties with death. Death is an error. Some of us feel that someday all errors will be put right, including that one. Yet there are some deaths . . ." She tilted her head again, that repeated gesture of negation. "Do humans not speak of the 'smell' of death?"

"Yes," Gabriel said and swallowed. His stomach was not entirely settled at the moment, and the concept she was mentioning was not entirely welcome. "It has one, all right."

"And of the smell of evil?"

"I'm not so sure about that," Gabriel answered, a little doubtfully, "but we do speak of it."

Enda sighed and rubbed her eyes. "Evil. How does one quantify such a thing as if it were a bulk supply, something that came by the dekaliter? Yet indubitably it exists. What we saw there: *that* smelled evil to me. Some mindwalker talent was moving, perhaps, wakening unsuspected. Perhaps a warning."

She shrugged, a very weary and helpless gesture. "I cannot say, but I am glad she did not decide to use the table."

"You're not alone," Gabriel said. "Not even wire brushes and Dessol would have helped it after that."

"What?" She blinked those huge burning blue eyes at him in complete confusion.

Gabriel grinned, if a little weakly, and told Enda the terrible marine joke to which the repeated punch line is "Wire brush and Dessol, ma'am," citing the name of the famous disinfectant and the honorific due to the commanding officer as she did her inspection. When he delivered the punch line for the last time, Gabriel watched Enda carefully, curious to see what the response would be.

She pitched forward with her face in her hands and began making peculiar wheezing noises. Gabriel bent over her, even more concerned than he had been before. But after a moment Enda sat upright again, and he saw that she was laughing so hard that she could not make a sound. Little pearly tears were rolling down her face.

It took her many minutes to recover. "Now," Enda said, "now you have seen a fraal weep, which means great things will happen to all who saw it, or so they say who do not often see fraal weep. And now, if ever, I need a drink, for fraal do not weep often. Let us by all means go to the bar of which Delde Sota told us. There we may meet the sesheyan to whom she recommended us, and there perhaps I may tell this joke and see how many people of other species laugh." She opened her eyes wide and got up, heading for her quarters to get a clean shirtsuit. " 'Wire brush and Dessol'!" She began wheezing again.

Gabriel thought that changing into a new smartsuit was entirely a good idea. After the events of the previous hour or so, he was not feeling terribly clean. There was no time for a scrub. On the station, thought Gabriel, we might stop by the cleanup facility and have a water shower. It was one of those luxuries that, like the rest of marine life, was likely enough gone forever, and that Gabriel badly missed. Unlimited hot water. Such a little thing it seemed at the time. How little we appreciate what we have . . .

They went back into the Collective's dome area, checked one of the maps there, and located area 14, ring 6. They made their way there, quietly discussing what they would do about the cargo bay the next day. Gabriel had made time to run the hull diagnostic programs one more time, and he was less than happy about the damage.

"We should stay at least long enough to get the hull weave-patched," he said.

"I have never been too sure about these patching processes," Enda said, sounding unconvinced. "One hears all kinds of glowing testimonials about them on the Grid, but one never knows anyone who's had them personally. Were I of a suspicious turn of mind, I would suspect this is because no one who has them done comes back."

"Oh, come on, it's perfectly safe," Gabriel said. "A metal reweave: they go in at the molecular level and rearrange the crystal structure of the hull. It comes out stronger than it was to start with."

"So they would like you to believe," Enda said. "I still would prefer to see some testimonials from satisfied users."

"Oh, come on, Enda," Gabriel said. "You're just shy about trying new things."

"So would you be," Enda said, "if you were pushing three hundred and wanted to see four hundred."

They came around the bend of the corridor and found themselves looking at a set of white-paneled doors with only a small discreet see-through panel set midway up one of them.

"Is this it?" Gabriel asked. "Nothing here but the number over the door."

"Let us find out."

They pushed the doors open and stepped in. Behind them, the doors immediately closed, and they found themselves facing a curtain, which Gabriel cautiously pushed aside.

Gloom.

They stood there for a moment and let their eyes get used to it, gloom and the smell of wetness and growing things. It was surprising when you had just come in out of the general aridity of the dome's corridors. Very faint lights, like distant point sources, and a very pale glow as of midnight in a summery place, shone down from the ceiling, partially blocked away by the gently moving shadows of leaves and branches. The leaves were real, not projections or holographic illusions. Trees and ferny, bushy plants of every kind stood around in huge containers, bending up against the surprisingly high ceiling before curving down again. Creepers, here and there starred with pallid flowers, hung down and brushed against Gabriel's face as they made their way into the room. The place was filled with a faint spicy fragrance that he could not identify.

Enda sniffed and said, "Galya. It is a wonder they can get it to grow here. Someone involved with this place must be a very skilled gardener. Can you see yet?"

"Pretty well."

"Then see if you can find us a table."

There was one available not too far away. They sat down, and Gabriel reached out idly to the tiny star-shaped lamp that sat in the middle of the table. The lamp was a little round ornament more like a stone with a light inside than anything else.

Enda looked at it curiously. "Yes, there is a resemblance, is there not?" she said as Gabriel went into his pocket and came up with the luckstone, turning it over in his fingers and comparing it with the table light. "This one is more polished. The beaches of the world from which these come must be a wonderful sight at night if they all glow like this."

From out of the darkness a sesheyan came looming to stand over their table and said, "From out of the night wanderers come:

in His image they seek refreshment: let them but say what that might be."

"Chai," said Gabriel, still feeling some need for something to settle his stomach. "White, please."

"I will have the same," Enda said.

They looked around them as the sesheyan went away. This place was certainly perfect from that species' point of view: dim enough to be easy on their eight sensitive eyes that were used to the deep multicanopied rainforests of Grith or Sheya. Somewhere off to the side, what might have been a bird whistled something very mournful, a minor-key tune of endless variation.

"Bebe bird," said Enda, sitting back in her chair, pale in the dimness of the room, her eyes great dark pools. "And galya. It is indeed a wonderful evocation of the place."

"Is it always this dark down at ground level?" Gabriel asked.

"Darker," said Enda. "And hotter. The one thing they have spared us is the heat, which this time of year would be stifling near the equator. Dimness the sesheyan eye must have for its comfort, but as regards the heat, I think they can take it or leave it."

Their chai came, and they thanked the sesheyan who brought it. He vanished almost without seeming to move, despite the fact that Gabriel's eyes had already become much more night-adjusted. Just a swirl of wing, a breath of silent breeze, and he was gone. Gabriel shook his head in admiration.

"Wish I could have moved like that," he said.

"They are adept," Enda replied. "It is a great wonder to see, down in the little settlements around the forest cities near Angoweru and Uyellin, how one moment a clearing will be empty, nothing but a great dim space roofed over high above with layer over layer of leaves and darkness,.and suddenly there will be a hundred sesheyans there, or a thousand, chanting the Wanderer's Song." She shook her head, looking upward around her. "This is a worthy evocation. All unlike what you will find elsewhere on the planet."

Gabriel had seen the many VoidCorp-owned facilities scattered across the face of Iphus and he felt no great desire to go anywhere near them, despite the frantic way in which they touted their entertainment facilities and so forth on the Grid.

"Not much like this, in other words."

Enda shook her head. "Oh, doubtless there are places that are physically as pleasant, but I would think there would not be many of them. Besides, without the scent of freedom, how much will the galya matter?" She pursed her lips. " 'Slavery is made no more tolerable by cool shadow or birdsong in the trees.' "

" 'Nor is Vec't'lir's wisdom more desirable merely for suffering's sake: or the Hunter's takings more valuable for their scarcity,' " said a voice directly above their heads.

Both their heads jerked up. The tall shadowy form stood there with arms and wings akimbo, his four foremost eyes looking down on them. Gabriel took a long breath before moving, and he noticed the red stripe down the sides of the *beishen*.

"That is how I heard it some time ago from Devlei'ir," Enda said, "though the meaning was likely to change from moment to moment, as always with his stories." She pulled out the third chair at the table.

The sesheyan sat down and looked from Enda to Gabriel. "I could swear I know your voice from somewhere," Gabriel said.

"Yes," said the sesheyan, folding his wings neatly about him and the chair so that he was little more than a blot of shadow. But a glint from the little star-stone and Gabriel's luckpiece caught in and on the front four eyes. "And I remember your voice, as well. You called me brother."

The idiom was perfectly human, and Gabriel blinked. "Not as gracefully as you would speak to me, I'm afraid," he said. "So you would be Ondway."

"That is my name in trees' shadow: under the Hunter's stars I have another," Ondway said. "You will have been talking with Delde Sota, otherwise the odds of your being in this spot are fairly low."

"If I had known of it, I would have come anyway," Enda said. "This is a welcome change from the more ordinary places and general climate of Iphus."

Ondway dropped his jaw in a grin at that. "If an atmosphere-stripped rock such as this may be said to have a climate," he said, "then you are right. Will you tell me why Delde Sota sends you to me? Though I do have some idea."

"We wouldn't mind somewhere quiet to stay for a while," Gabriel said.

Ondway sat back in his chair and resettled his wings, folding his arms over them. "I would need to know something of the reasons for your stay," he observed. "The reasons for needing quiet, I should say."

"Don't you look at the Grid?" Gabriel said. "I'm a celebrity, much pursued by my public."

Ondway chuckled at that. "Should the Concord come looking specifically for you," he said, "I fear we could do little to protect you."

"That's not what I'm asking. It's not the Concord that concerns me at the moment."

"Is it not?" That seemed to take Ondway a little by surprise.

Enda tilted her head to one side, back again. "There seems to be other interest in our doings," she said. "From a quarter that may lie—well, not exactly a thousand kilometers away from here."

Ondway swore softly, and Gabriel's eyes widened a little at the sound of it. It was the same hiss that Enda occasionally used. He had thought it was fraal.

"I take your meaning," Ondway said.

"We have little concrete proof of this," Enda said. "Suspicion only at the moment. But there also seem to be other factions, or fractions, involved as well, and those we do not understand. Some of them are very frightening, and I would not willingly speak of them in a public place."

Ondway waved one finger up at the ceiling. "Their coverage is not as complete as they think," he said. "It is 'off' when they least suspect it. At other times, we stage events for them so that they will think they're getting what they need." That drop-jawed smile again. "Will you want to be staying out of sight for very long?"

"No more than ten or twenty days. Our ship requires some repair, as well, but after that . . ." Enda glanced over at Gabriel.

"We'll be going back to Thalaassa," he said, then tried to hold his face still, because he had no clear idea why he'd said it.

"For what purpose?" Ondway asked, rather abruptly, Gabriel thought.

"Trade," Gabriel replied. "Light electronics, that kind of thing. And possibly some mining after our cargo bay's put right."

"Mining possibly," said Ondway. "There might be some way you might find your way back to Eraklion, but from this system to Thalaassa you would hardly trade."

"Why not?"

"There is no trade with them any more," Ondway said, "not from Grith."

Enda looked surprised. "Why? What happened?"

"The two worlds have forbidden such. Oh, not openly," Ondway said. "Such restriction of trade would be frowned on by the Concord, which those two worlds are presently studying to please, when they are not also studying to please others."

Gabriel wanted to ask what he meant by that, but the glare that Ondway turned on him silenced him for the moment. "We have been trading with them for a good while, and we have been very much the 'junior partner.' That particular trade wind has blown hot and cold without warning before. They are very fearful," he said, more softly, "having occupied, until the Verge began to open up again, a position that is not very well protected. For a long while the two Thalaassan worlds were willing enough for support from whatever quarter it came, even from sesheyans that they counted not much better than either barbarian savages or company creatures. But this time . . ." Ondway shook his head. "The signs are that our trade with them is now done permanently. With the treaty signed, they have new strong friends, the Concord who will protect them from the dark stories, from the things the tales say have been moving out in the dark of the far reaches of the system, things that even we would not feel comfortable with."

The image of that large ship flashed before Gabriel's mind's eye again. He half thought he would mention it, then closed his mouth. *Being too willing to discuss things or taking things too readily at face value has gotten me into trouble before,* he thought. *Better not.*

"And the influence of the governments on Phorcys and Ino has reached a long way," Ondway said after a moment. "Even the smugglers seem to have stopped running the usual route."

Enda opened her eyes at that. "What would one smuggle to Grith?" she asked, as casually as if she were asking directions in the street.

"Not to," Ondway replied, "from."

"It's still a good question," Gabriel said.

Ondway looked a little reluctant. "The Wanderer would rarely speak—"

"Ah, come now, Ondway," Enda said. "You have been dropping your hints boldly enough. This is a poor time to shy away, when you so obviously want us to ask the question, and have doubtless made sure the surveillance is presently shut off."

He still sat silent for a moment. Then Ondway said, "There have been those who have been carrying supplies to and from Thalaassa."

"To Phorcys and Ino? But you said trade had stopped with them."

"I did."

"Then where else? To Eraklion?" Gabriel shook his head. "There's nothing there but a package mining firm. Why would they need—" He stopped.

"Not to Eraklion," Enda said softly. "Somewhere else. Farther out in the system, I think."

"And even the smugglers have stopped going," Gabriel said.

Ondway shifted in his seat, rustling his wings about him. "There have been stories coming back from those spaces," he said, very quietly, "of those who go and do not return . . . or who return . . . changed." He had about him the air of someone who has sworn not to speak of something, but who at the same time desperately wants to and is hoping that someone will lead him around to the subject by subterfuge.

"Changed how?" Gabriel said.

Ondway was silent a while more, then he said, "You do know that you are endangering yourselves merely by being here and speaking with me. Outside these doors and with very few exceptions elsewhere the planet is under constant surveillance by Void-Corp."

Gabriel ran one hand through his hair in annoyance. It was beginning to get rather long for his tastes. "We've had people trying to kill us for days now," he said.

"Weeks," Enda corrected primly.

"Thank you. A long time," Gabriel said. "Too damned long. I never had so many people trying to kill me when I was a *marine* as I have now, and then I was attending wars on a regular basis. I don't know that a little more endangerment would even register on my personal scale at this point."

"VoidCorp," Ondway said, "has started its own wars in its time. The war with its parent company, both nonphysical and physical, nearly killed the Terran Empire in its cradle. To them what matters is market share. A life lost—or ten thousand here or there—make little odds so long as the bottom line improves. Slavery and death mean little to them in the long term. The Company will live longer than any of its component parts, and therefore Corporate immortality—the Corporation's growth right across all known space and its domination of it—is what matters. They will let nothing stand in the way of that. Even the Concord is cautious about how it moves against VoidCorp openly." He looked down at the table, bitter. "We had great hopes that the solution they engineered on Grith might lead to other similar situations elsewhere."

He stopped very abruptly and would not look at them again.

The hint being, Gabriel thought, that it *has* led to a similar solution elsewhere. Somewhere in the Thalaassa system.

He glanced over at Enda. "We've wandered a bit off our original topic," Gabriel said. "Here's our own bottom line. For our health and that of others, I think it would be smart if we took ourselves down to Grith for a little while. A few days—a week perhaps."

"I would agree," Enda said.

They looked at Ondway. "Certainly we could find you a place to stay there," Ondway said. "Down by Redknife, you would attract little attention. Many tourists pass through that part of our world looking for an experience of the unspoiled sesheyan way of life." He grinned. The expression was humorous, but not entirely kind. "Mostly they pay well enough for it and get what they have come for. They do not, of course, pay for the experience of being hunted wherever one goes by a great and inimical force. Some inadvertently get that for free by trying to save on the 'tour guide fee' and going into the jungles themselves." That smile got a little more amused, now. "Mostly they find out about insects, mud, sablesnakes, and gandercats, but that is their business. In any case, the Redknife Tourist Bureau will easily enough manage your needs for a ten days or so. Ask for Maikaf."

"Very well. And as for the Devli'yan—" Enda said suddenly.

Ondway looked at her. "You have been there before?"

"Some years ago," Enda said, "as a tourist. I did not hazard myself among the gandercats, however interesting their calls and what they mean, but I sat with the shamans under the trees and heard wisdom and told what passed for mine. Some months I spent there."

Ondway nodded. "I thought you might have," he said. "The fraal who come tend to remain a while. Who knows? There may be some there who will remember you yet. One at least, though there is no telling whether he will have time or inclination to see you. He spends much time in the forest these days. He too has those whose attention he prefers to forego."

He breathed out, a long weary sound. "Tomorrow, then," Ondway said, "I will depart for Redknife and will escort you. Eight hours, local time. Will that be satisfactory?"

"Entirely so," said Enda, "and we thank you very much."

Ondway got up and slipped away into the shadows again. Gabriel, fingering his luckstone, looked after him and wondered. Ondway had impressed him, but he was less than eager to trust him entirely. He seemed to have meant a lot more than he actually said in his conversation.

"Shall we call for our bill?" asked.

"I have a feeling it will be here shortly," Enda replied.

Sure enough, the sesheyan who had greeted them first and had brought their drinks now materialized out of the darkness, holding a payment chit. Gabriel reached out for it, checked the total glowing on it in the darkness, slipped a thumbnail into the slot to add the tip, and touched his own chip to it. The sesheyan bowed and took himself away.

The two of them headed out into the station hallway and there had to stop and blink; it was blinding even with the dimmer lights of station "evening" now on show.

"In the morning," Enda said with a sigh as they made their way back toward the main dome and the docking rings, "we will see about the metal reweave you were discussing. Perhaps I am mistrustful of a new technology, especially when it seems too inexpensive to be effective."

Gabriel chuckled, then stopped. A shadow had been just visible out of the corner of his eye as they passed an intersecting hallway. It had been moving toward them with some speed and had stopped. It was out of sight now.

"What?" Enda said as Gabriel slowed somewhat.

"Nothing," he said, walking along as casually as he could without trying to look as if he had slowed his gait too much.

His peripheral vision had always been good—a little too good, according to his weapons instructor. "Don't let it make you too confident of what you think you're seeing. Half the time you're wrong anyway." But with just a very slight turn of his head, Gabriel could see a lot more than people normally thought he could. And once or twice, in fights or in battle, that had served him well. As they came around the curve of the corridor toward the main dome, he turned his head just a little toward Enda as if speaking to her and saw that shape suddenly materialize out of the side corridor again, slipping down toward them.

"We have company," he said, very softly, as they continued on around the curve and toward the dome.

"Who?"

"Someone following us. Sesheyan, I think."

"It could be your imagination." Then Enda stopped herself, catching a glimpse of another shadow up ahead of them as it slipped hurriedly away down another of the corridors that spiraled away from the dome. "Another sesheyan," Enda said softly.

"Or someone trying to look like one," Gabriel said. "The *beishen* is right, but as for the rest of it . . . I'm not sure about the way whoever that is moving. It doesn't look right somehow." He swallowed, made up his mind. "Look, when we get back to *Sunshine*, I want to leave as soon as possible."

"But we were to wait for the guide."

"Do you want to wait, just sitting in dock? Really? With *that?*"

The shadow moved again down that long corridor as they came level with it, and was lost again. Enda looked after it, then determinedly turned away. Gabriel turned his head a little to the right to see around behind them. No one was visible back the way they had come, at the moment.

"And his friend," Gabriel said, "out of sight—"

"Perhaps not," Enda said. "So where?"

"To Grith, where else? Ondway told us where to go, who to see. Let's do it, but I don't want to wait here any longer. I'd still like to know where all those VoidCorp ships took themselves off to."

They started to hurry a little more as they crossed the dome and headed for the access to the docking ring. "And the repairs?" Enda asked.

"They'll have to wait. Look, we won't be hauling anything heavy. In fact, if it's all the same to you, we won't be hauling, period, at least until things quiet down a little. Anyway, maybe they'll have repair facilities down there."

"In Redknife?" Enda said, looking doubtful. "It is a Devli'yan enclave, Gabriel. It is not the kind of place where one will find high-technology metal weaving, at any price, or much of anything *else* which can be described as high technology. The most basic repairs could probably be managed, but—"

"We've made it this far," Gabriel replied. "I'll take my chances. We don't have that far to go, and once we're down into atmosphere, the cargo bay becomes less of a concern."

He looked at her intently, wanting her to understand that suddenly this was important, though he himself found it hard to express why. Enda glanced over at him as they crossed the dome into the corridors that lead to the locking ring. Then she glanced away again.

"So it bites you now, does it?" she said. "The hunch."

Gabriel shook his head. "Maybe."

"Then let us go."

Chapter Fourteen

THEY WERE BACK on *Sunshine* ten minutes later, locking her down for space. Gabriel was still swearing softly at the thought of the last towering figure in the *beishen* who had followed them nearly to the boarding corridor that fed down to their own airlock. After Gabriel hurried through the door after Enda, he had smacked his chip against the reading plate with considerable satisfaction, locking the boarding corridor behind them and leaving that dark shape standing and glowering from way down the curve of the docking ring.

"Now are you sure about the hull?" Enda asked.

Gabriel was looking at the diagnostic yet again, liking it even less as he slapped the controls that pushed the boarding corridor free and told station control that *Sunshine* was going free. "It'll keep," he said, and the attitude jets pushed them up and away from the ring.

Ten more minutes saw them out in open space again and making for Grith on system drive. The run was not a long one, though it seemed a little longer than usual to Gabriel, still looking at the hull diagnostic and listening for any suspicious groans or moans—and most carefully feeling for drafts. Still air in a spacecraft was safe air unless you were standing right under a blower. A draft was the breath of serious trouble, and most spacecraft manufacturers went to a lot of trouble to make sure that their air exchange units produced no tangible drafts at all.

"What is the time down there?" Enda called.

Gabriel sighed, banished the diagnostic diagram from the forward tank and replaced it with a globe clock of Grith. He then reached into the tank and spun the globe until it showed the portion of the continent where Redknife lay. "Late afternoon," he said, looking to see the angle at which the terminator was approaching.

"I wonder if we should not spend a few hours more in space," Enda said. "Ondway did say 'tomorrow.' For all we know, his contacts will not be ready for us."

That was when the proximity alarm went off again, and Gabriel's head snapped up. There was nothing to see with the naked eye but the darkness and Corrivale, a bright star visibly getting brighter and larger. But the schematic in the tank, now reverting to local tactical since the alarm had gone off, showed one of those big teardrop shapes going by perhaps five kilometers away, lounging on toward the heart of the system on a course that might shortly intersect with *Sunshine*'s. Gabriel put his hand into the tank again, this time to tweak *Sunshine*'s course schematic and get the courses to display relative to one another.

Sunshine's showed the standard approach spiral down into Grith Control space, but the big cruiser's course line was flashing. "Delta *v*," Gabriel muttered. "He's accelerating. Swinging around Grith to head somewhere else, the computer thinks."

Enda looked over Gabriel's shoulder into the tank and tilted her head to one side. "We can avoid them easily enough if we must."

"I wouldn't give them the satisfaction," Gabriel growled.

They held their course, and Corrivale grew brighter, its disk growing and becoming ever more blinding, sheening the inside of the cockpit with gold until the windows felt the light would be excessive and started to dim it down on their own recognizance. Gabriel sat back and looked at Hydrocus, now a good-sized disk at something like three hundred thousand kilometers, and Grith, a cabochon emerald swinging around it, glinting with red-violet at atmosphere's edge and glazing with the gleam of the sun. Its albedo was surprisingly fierce for a world with so little ocean and not much "weather" showing at the moment. Gabriel shook his head.

"It looks like such a quiet place, from up here."

Enda sat down beside him, gazing out. "So it would have been once," she said, and Gabriel nodded.

For a long time, after the Silence had fallen, no one had been here but miners and pirates. But slowly others began to pass through, saw the one habitable planet in the system—though its temperature made the habitation marginal, at first—and stayed. Even after sesheyans were discovered living on Grith, that alone made little difference.

But when the Hatire had come, things sped up a great deal. VoidCorp came and killed many of them. Now the Hatire were slowly recovering their old colony on Grith, but all the time with VoidCorp looking over their shoulders. The Concord was now here as well, acting—or, as the others would probably see it—interfering. It would be a long time before this became a quiet system, if it ever could again.

The schematic in the tank showed the VoidCorp cruiser now applying more drive and diving rather closer to Grith, apparently intent on using Hydrocus's gravity to slingshot her around on the way to somewhere else. It was a showy maneuver and not strictly necessary, since VoidCorp cruisers would have drive to burn. But at the same time it could also be seen as intimidation of sorts, less obvious perhaps than what Gabriel had seen at Iphus, but still a clear enough statement. *Think of all the interesting things we could drop on you from this height. We won't . . . today, but tomorrow, who knows what we'll do?*

The VoidCorp cruiser swung around Hydrocus's far side and out of sight. Gabriel sighed. "Good riddance," he said, "and—"

He stopped. Something touched the back of his neck and raised the fine hairs on it.

A breath of air.

"Do you," Enda said suddenly, "feel a draft?"

After that, everything started to happen very fast indeed. "Floaters," Gabriel said, "and the e-suits!"

He reached into the tank and tweaked it until it showed the system drive controls. Then very, very slowly he eased the throttle forward. The drive increased *Sunshine*'s speed, and the draft increased. Gabriel looked down at the pressure readings from the seals around the accesses to the cargo bay and gulped. That low a number of hektopascals was unhealthy.

Enda wisely got their e-suits first, and Gabriel surprised himself by launching himself out of the seat and bettering his best e-suit drill time by at least three seconds. The e-suits were a variation on the basic humanoid style that Star Force had designed and that was marketed most places under their subsidiary license. You stepped into it, almost as if into a bulky overcoat, and the sideseams wrapped themselves around you, closed their gaskets down, and would not open them again until your purposeful touch reactivated them. Now Gabriel slammed the helmet down on his head and felt it home into place in its own gasketry, and he then got back into the seat again, strapping himself in and turning his attention back to the tank.

The system drive was still engaged, but the hull, which Gabriel had put on audio via the computer, was muttering. Enda was now sealed in her e-suit, having clocked a time very little less than Gabriel's, and she was already halfway back to the cabinet where the floaters were kept. She yanked the cabinet open with nothing like her usual grace, pulled the can out, pulled its pin, and sprayed the contents in the approved pattern: up and down, side to side, aft to forward.

Thousands of small plasteine bubbles filled with a lighter-than-air gas burst out of the can, solidified, and began drifting toward the back of the ship. They would congregate near any leak, making it easy to identify for patching purposes. Then the plasteine would denature and the bubbles would vanish. Enda had already tossed away the floater can and pulled out the secondary can, the emergency patcher. This would produce contour flexfilm in amounts sufficient to patch quite a large leak, long enough for *Sunshine* to get down into atmosphere. Gabriel's concern, though, was that the entire back of his ship might be about to fall off, a possibility about which not even the floaters and the can would be able to do much.

Via the computer, the hull was now moaning more loudly as they dropped toward Grith.

"Where are you going to land?" Enda asked.

"It was going to be Redknife, but—"

Gabriel reached into the tank and brought up the schematic of the planet again. It zoomed in on the central continent and northward, looking for Redknife, found it, and locked in on it. Gabriel's mouth was going dry as he saw the course the leaking rear end of *Sunshine* was going to force on him—not the leisurely, low-fuel spiral he had been planning, but something rather faster: system drive up full, pushing the ship hard and straight down into atmosphere. It was a more stress-laden landing than he would have preferred, especially when the stresses might open the leaks out further. Might open one of them up big enough to crack the hull wide open and—

Gabriel swallowed, or tried to, and put that thought aside forcefully. It would do him no good. "We're going to have to make this one pretty quick," he said. "I don't want to linger and increase the stresses on the cargo bay. What about the floaters?"

"They were congregating mostly around the seal to the cargo bay," Enda replied, sitting down and strapping herself in again. "I have sprayed patcher all around there, and the floaters began to move elsewhere. But as our acceleration increases, they will no longer be much good as a diagnostic."

"Just so long as they don't get in our way," Gabriel said and concentrated on what he was doing. He increased the system drive a bit and heard the hull moan a little more, but there wasn't anything they could do about that now. They were committed, and atmosphere was already beginning to bite at *Sunshine*'s wings. "Redknife," Gabriel said, "six minutes."

He glanced over at Enda, and even through her helmet's faceplate he got a glimpse of her swallowing hard: another gesture that humans and fraal apparently shared. Gabriel wondered if her mouth was as dry as his.

"It will be just like the ore pickups on Eraklion, I am sure," Enda said, sounding completely calm.

Gabriel rolled his eyes at the thought of how simple flying had seemed then. *Compared to this!* The computer, of course, was ready to take this job away from him—but already Gabriel was enough of a pilot that the last thing he wanted to do was relinquish control, no matter how out of control he felt. Underneath them Grith was swelling, growing bright as they came past the terminator into the light of afternoon shading to evening. Gabriel headed straight down, gambling that the stresses would not increase too severely, that turning excessively would be worse for the hull—

Crack! He felt it more than heard it, and the hull shrieked protest as somewhere in the cargo bay a plate sprang away from its seams. A faint howling sounded from way in back, an increase in the way *Sunshine* was juddering as she arrowed in. Oh, this is fast, this is too fast, cut it back a little, Gabriel thought, but the computer still suggested that this was the smartest speed to hold, and for the time being Gabriel was not going to argue with it. Pressure in the cargo bay was showing 548 hPa, but that was not an unbelievable density for atmosphere. Now the question is, Gabriel thought, will the air currents lashing around in there make something else spring loose and start knocking bigger pieces out of the hull?

There was no way to tell and no time to worry about it now. Grith filled the whole of the cockpit windows, and Gabriel could see the northward-thrusting finger of green in which Redknife and its little landing facility were buried. The howling of the wind back in the cargo bay was getting louder and louder, which in its way was a good sign, but extremely unnerving. The ground was rushing up. The computer course graphic started flashing, suggesting emphatically to Gabriel that he should start flattening his glide path out now, and he agreed. He pulled her up, lowered her speed, and tried to feel for some glide.

Crack! That was something besides the cargo bay. He felt it distinctly through the tank and the control column. Not the hull, Gabriel thought, one of the control surfaces. Oh shit, oh shit!

He fought with the control column, but it steadied down. The computer was compensating for the damage, whatever it was. The computer was now superimposing a graphic for Redknife's landing facility over the very faint visual Gabriel had of it, though that visual was getting clearer, and stronger, and closer by the minute as he glided toward it. This thing glides like a rock, Gabriel thought. Trouble.

Sunshine was suddenly not responding as well as she had been. Gabriel could clearly see the landing flat and had done all the things the computer had told him to—had managed to decrease his speed, had cut his glide to just above stall, was coming down on landing jets. But one of the landing impellers seemed to be arguing the point with him, giving him more impulsion than he needed.

"No, no," Gabriel shouted at it, "cut it out, it's all right, throttle down, *back off!*"

But the impeller was paying no attention. In a wide and graceful curve, *Sunshine* shot right past and over what should have been her landing berth on the plain concrete strip at Redknife, thoughtfully reserved for her by the computer when it settled its course, and headed out into the jungle, losing altitude all the time.

They were over the highest treetops, which could mean anything depending on where you were on Grith. A hundred feet, five hundred . . . Gabriel saw a spot ahead of him that looked relatively empty of trees. He made for it, dropping altitude while counting seconds in his head to estimate by how much he had overshot Redknife. The ship was trying to continue that infernal curve, but he pulled the control column right over and fought with the attitudinals in the tank. "No, no, no, no—"

The hole was right below him. He cut everything but the landing thrusters and held the column in place. "Hang on!"

Crash!

Everything went white for a moment, and Gabriel thought, That's it, I've aced out the system drive; we're both going to be reduced to talcum powder, *radioactive* talcum powder!

Then again, how am I having time to think these thoughts if we *are* talcum powder?

He opened his eyes. They were on the ground. The cockpit windows were miraculously intact. Vague, misty red late-afternoon sunlight was coming in through them. All the computer's alarms were wailing about all kinds of problems, hull integrity, fuel reserves, system drive status—that one Gabriel *did* do something about, reaching out immediately to shut the drive down. But as for the rest of it, they were intact. *He* was, anyway.

"Enda? Enda!"

As he reached out to help unstrap her, she moved. Gabriel breathed again.

"I am well enough," she said. She turned her head to him and gave him a wry look. "Oh, Gabriel, I wonder whether at this rate we are *ever* going to run this ship at a profit."

He laughed, and laughed harder. For a good several minutes he could do nothing else. Finally he was able to stop, unstrap himself, and get up to see what needed doing.

Sunshine was listing slightly to starboard, but there was no harm in that. She was otherwise mostly sitting flat. Gabriel got up and went to have a look at the seals to the cargo bay. They were still intact, but through the little bay-door window he could see daylight where the hull plate had sprung. He could just hear the not-entirely-regretful way in which some smallship repairman was going suck in his breath and say, "Oh, *that's* going to cost you."

"How is it?" Enda asked, working at her straps.

"Not too bad," Gabriel lied. "We're in one piece, anyway."

He got up to the lift, tried it experimentally. It went down and came up again. "Okay," he said, "at least we're not trapped in here."

Enda made her way back to him, undoing her helmet. "Well," she said, "there is a little daylight left. We still might get help today."

They got into the lift together and headed downward. "Maybe," Gabriel said. He found that he was feeling a little light-headed, but regardless, he added, "Remind me to send a mail to the Delgakis people. The ship held up really well."

"Another letter," Enda said, sounding rather resigned. "But you never *send* any of these. You are terrible with letters."

The lift came down to the bottom and locked in place. Its door opened. Gabriel stepped out—and stopped.

Standing all around them was a crowd of extremely annoyed sesheyans, cowled and goggled, many of them staring and pointing at the ship, and all of them glowering at it.

Gabriel looked around at them for a long moment, then said rather hopefully, "I don't suppose anyone here is from the Redknife Tourist Bureau?"

At this a profound silence fell that seemed to indicate that the probability was slight.

"We were told to ask for someone named Maikaf," Gabriel added. The silence got worse.

Finally one sesheyan came stalking up to the door where Gabriel was standing. He was an imposing gentleman, his wings wrapped around him like a cloak. He wore very high-quality *gailghe* against what for sesheyans was considerable glare, even in the swiftly falling twilight. He pointed forcefully at the ground and said, "Though the Hunter comes from nowhere, the guest requires invitation: to invade the hosts' hospitality, few things are worse in the world: and those who come uninvited, they must earn their fruit by the sword:"

His expression did not look promising.

"At best, we have intruded," Enda said softly. "At worst, I fear they must think we are spies, and spies are not terribly welcome here. There is usually only one assumption about where they come from and what should be done with them."

The crowd closed in around them.

* * * * *

Most people who have not been to the single moon of Hydrocus think of Grith in terms of sweeping generalizations: half rain forest inhabited by gargoyle like noble savages, half windswept polar plain inhabited by religious fundamentalists, and very little

else in between. Others think of it from points of view influenced
by sensationalized exposés of the local "pirate trade" along the
lines of *Corsair Planet*, full of corrupt and ruthless tribal leaders,
illicit markets and shipyards, criminal warlords and sleazy
traders on the take. Still others have formed their opinions from
material appearing in over-romanticized documentaries like
Song of the Gandercat, filled with not very informed speculation
about the "cats'" mysterious abandoned cities, and alternating
haunting recordings of what might be ritual songs with images of
creatures that looked like gigantic moss-covered furballs or (just
after their molt) rubbery-skinned sloths not much smaller than a
rhinoceros. Gabriel had seen all those images at one time or
another, and all of them had seemed interesting, even amusing,
at a safe distance. Now, though, Gabriel found himself wondering whether he, Enda, and *Sunshine* were all on the point of
being sold to some corsair lord at a discount—or, equally, wondering what he would do if a gandercat wound up in the tent with
them.

The local environment was much on Gabriel's mind. After he
and Enda were removed from *Sunshine*, they were taken rather
hurriedly and roughly out of the relative brightness of the clearing into the astonishingly sudden and complete gloom of the surrounding forest. The only sight Gabriel saw that gave him any
reassurance was a final glimpse of *Sunshine* being covered up
with great speed and skill, mostly with chopped-down or uproot-
ed giant ferns. Within minutes, no amount of "overhead" surveillance from satellites would be able to see anything on the
spot but a lump of artfully arranged greenery, as natural looking
as any other small hillock on the planet.

About an hour later they were somewhere else in the rain
forest. By Gabriel's reckoning they still could not be much more
than ten kilometers from Redknife, but there was no other indication whatever of where in the world they might be. Night fell
quickly, and gloomy forest corridors and paths were quickly
exchanged for pitch-black forest corridors and paths. The twenty
or so sesheyans who were conveying them suddenly stopped,

and Gabriel stood there blinking, aware of Enda beside him but still completely unable to see anything but shadows against shadow. High above, the uppermost tree-canopy was faintly colored with the light of what might have been, shining above it, the light of Hydrocus at first quarter, or gibbous—an indefinite ruddy glow such as humans see when they close their eyelids in normal light.

Their hosts or jailers took Gabriel and Enda into one of a number of simple dome like constructions of woven ferns and branches, the sesheyan version of a tent. The sesheyans posted a guard outside it and left them there in a darkness broken only by Gabriel's luckstone. There they spent the night, rather wet (for the shelter leaked), but not cold. It is almost impossible to be cold in a rain forest on Grith in the summertime. Even the most unseasonable weather for that time of year would not have taken the temperature below 20° C. Sesheyans, being fairly inured to the wet as a normal part of their environment, were somewhat blind to the human or fraal attitude toward rain inside a tent. However, sablesnakes inside a tent were something Gabriel was not prepared to take with equanimity. After his robust reaction to the first one, a sesheyan came inside to sit with them, concerned that the prisoners should not die untimely. I bet they're not so sure we're spies any more either, Gabriel thought, just a little glumly. Any spy who would be sent here wouldn't react like that. Pity I couldn't find some less humiliating way to convince them.

The morning came after what seemed an interminable night of gandercats' cries through the darkness, and a great deal of itching, almost all of which was psychosomatic. Before they turned in, Gabriel spotted a particularly large bug walking with exaggerated care across the floor of their shelter. For the rest of the night, he'd had a hard time believing that there weren't lots more of them. There's never just *one* bug. But when the dim light came again, things looked less itchy, and their hosts looked marginally less unfriendly. Maybe it was just the change of lighting, which was now a pronounced, green-tinted twilight instead of dead blackness full of pelting rain and strange screeching noises.

"The water here is at least clean," Enda said, coming back into the shelter after spending a few minutes outside with one of their guards.

She looked more radiant than usual, and her hair had been rinsed and wrung out and wound into a tight bun at the back of her head. Her smartsuit was as clean as one might expect it to be after being dragged through jungle slime and mud. It had managed to lose all of the mud and most of the embedded grime already.

Gabriel shook his head, thinking, If I can ever look that good at three hundred, after being chucked into a jungle, I'll count myself lucky.

There was some noise off to one side of the encampment. Gabriel looked over that wa, then stopped, seeing a flash of color that surprised him. His eyes were definitely getting used to this lighting—yesterday he doubted he would even have been able to see it. Other thoughts were also on his mind though, for the *beishen* he saw coming toward them at ground level, its wearer making his way carefully around the boles of the biggest trees, had a red stripe.

Ondway came into the clearing with several others around him. More sesheyans came to meet them, and there was a lot of hurried talk in low voices. Gabriel stood watching by the door of the shelter, and Ondway looked up past his countrymen and saw Gabriel standing there.

He made a sound rather like a roar. Gabriel winced slightly, until he realized that what he was hearing was the true sesheyan laugh, the sound that was meant to ring out under the trees—not the tamed or subdued laugh of some VoidCorp employee within walls.

Ondway strode toward him. "What are you doing here?" he roared.

"This is where you said we were supposed to come," Gabriel said.

"Here? I think not! You were supposed to go to Redknife!"

"We did try," Enda said, putting her head out of the shelter, "but I fear *Sunshine* had other plans. She is not far from here, still largely functional, but she will need some repair before she sees space again."

"You are going to make us haul a smallship from here to Red-knife?" Ondway roared again. "Hunter of night in the forests: what manner of guest behaves so!"

"The same manner of guest that gets rained on all night," Gabriel said, trying hard not to sound too aggrieved about it.

"Yes, as for that, it would not have happened had you waited as I told you! Why did you not wait for your guide?"

"We were being followed," Gabriel said, starting to get angry now. "I've been attacked too often lately to want much more of it. So has Enda—"

Ondway started to laugh. "I thought you said you would hardly notice! But *followed*! Did you think we would offer you sanctuary without seeing that you came to it safely? The one who followed was your escort, your guide! He would have brought you safely here the next day, but instead you fled from him like . . ." Ondway was now laughing so hard that he could barely speak. "Wanderer, you are incorrigible! And I have had to pay your guide faceprice because you lost him and made off without his help!"

"Sorry," Gabriel said, but he wasn't particularly, and he was feeling better already. Sesheyans were famous for their tracking abilities, and if he had managed to spot one and then lose one, even in the cluttered and uncomplicated environs of the Iphus Collective, that was not exactly a terrible thing. "If I should now pay *you* faceprice, please tell me."

Ondway looked at him with some surprise. "That is a noble offer, Con'hr," he said, "but let us put it by for the moment. Let me talk to my folk."

He turned away. Gabriel turned, too, to find Enda covering her eyes briefly. "Are you all right?" he asked.

"Yes," she said very softly, "but Gabriel, Ondway is related to the Devli'yan clan, a cousin of Devlei'ir himself. His faceprice would be easily equivalent to the whole cost of *Sunshine* . . . probably more."

Gabriel swallowed, then said, "Uh. Yes, well." He looked away into the forest, trying to look like someone absently enjoying the morning's beauties, and thought, When will I learn to just not *say* anything?

Gabriel sat down on a fallen tree-trunk, then got up hurriedly, brushed his pants off, and sat down again a little further down the tree. Some of the bugs here were *really* big. What surprised him was that they didn't even seem to mind being sat on.

Recovering, he glanced around him and said, "If I got my counting right, we're not much more than six or seven kilometers from Redknife."

"A long way through jungle and rain forest," Enda said, "especially for those not used to such travel, or those who are unsure of the way." She sounded dubious.

"Oh, I wasn't thinking of escaping," Gabriel said. "I don't think we need to worry about that at the moment, but all these people appeared so quickly after we came down." He glanced at the sesheyans all around them. "There must be a lot more sesheyans living in the forest immediately around the settlement than we thought."

"It would not surprise me," Enda said. "Many have retreated into the forests, not only because they prefer the ancient hunting and wandering lifestyle, but because they prefer not to be easily counted by those who would have less than benevolent reasons for doing so. Here the forest protects them as it would have in the deeps of time, on Sheya the ancient, much to the annoyance of their enemies." She smiled a little, an oddly satisfied look.

After a little while Ondway came back to them and sat down beside Gabriel on the fallen tree, rustling his wings down about him until he was cloaked. "Well," he said, "you have caused inconvenience, but it can be worked around. Indeed it must be, for naturally the central ship-tracking system noticed that you did not arrive at Redknife as scheduled."

"They'll be sending someone to look for us," Gabriel said.

"As to that," said Ondway with a grin, "we, or some of us anyway, are the 'someones' they would send, and if we report that we cannot find you, well . . ." He shrugged. "Wide are the forest's ways, and even the Wanderer is sometimes lost: a weary time to find the ways again, when every fern holds its shadow . . ."

Enda smiled. "And in the meantime, we will have our 'few days' rest.' "

"While your poor machine is prepared to be hauled out of where it rests. No one from Redknife would bother venturing this way until those of us who are forestwalkers told them there was some reason. Even with positive satellite tracking, there would be no point in attempting a rescue until we told them it was safe." Ondway rustled his wings again.

"Safe from what?" Gabriel asked.

Ondway produced that feral grin once more. "From *us*. Why, Con'hr, there are unstable tribal elements even in this part of the world, reckless, uncontrollable sesheyans who do not obey the rule of law and who pay no fealty to Concord or to any other force moving in these spaces—dangerous pirates and criminal types, smugglers and racketeers, and regular savages." The grin gentled somewhat.

"But some of them walk in the cities," Enda said, "under very different guise."

"Well, that is true," Ondway agreed, and stretched his wings out, then let them drop again in a gigantic shrug. "I myself am based in Diamond Point normally, working for a freight expediting company that subcontracts to various system-based firms. Some of them have ties with VoidCorp; some of them are independents. My citizenship is sourced on Grith, so that the Corpses cannot touch me—yet, but I am able to go freely about the system on the expediting company's business, handling various minor details of freight transfers, sometimes doing courier work for sensitive material. I might be anywhere within the course of a week or two, and no one would think anything of it."

Gabriel digested that, knowing he was being told something of substance but not being certain exactly what as yet. At the same time, though, he felt something familiar: the same itch or urge that had been moving under the surface of his thoughts and had suddenly caused him to say to Ondway, not so long ago, "We'll be going back to Thalaassa." It was as if he had heard something, not even whispered yet, but about to be. Something in the air . . .

Gabriel held still and quiet, trying to isolate that itch, that urge, trying to hear the whisper. Enda, noticing none of this, merely nodded at Ondway. " 'Corpses,' " she said, with that slight smile. "Quite. And among your contacts you count Doctor Delde Sota."

"We have been of use to one another occasionally before," Ondway said. "As now."

"Yes. Well," Enda said, "such 'use' is certainly not without its price. Here we are, and you have helped us and are helping us. Well and good. How may we help you in return?"

Ondway looked at them both in a measuring way. "Where had you thought to go after your stay here?"

The air whispered to Gabriel. Something suddenly came together, made sense. The planet no one mentioned, the name no one spoke, even though it was right there in the neighboring starsystem. "Rhynchus," Gabriel immediately said, while Enda was still opening her mouth.

Ondway looked at him in astonishment—and was there an edge of anger on the expression? "Who told you about that?" he said, much more quietly than he had been speaking.

Gabriel was very tempted to say *You did!*—except that it would almost certainly be misunderstood, and he could hardly explain it himself. "What *is* going on out there?" he asked, also more quietly.

Ondway looked at him.

"Come on, Ondway," Gabriel said. "You can't convince me that VoidCorp has listening devices installed in the trees."

Ondway was very still for a few moments. "Though the doctor recommended you to me," he said at last, "she does not, cannot, even with all her resources, know everything about you—and believe me, within minutes of meeting you, she would have known much. Delde Sota was a Grid pilot before she was a doctor. Nor can I know everything, though I know what has been on the news services of late. They say you are a murderer and a spy."

"The accusations are false," Enda said.

"With respect, honored, were you there? No? Then how can you be sure?"

"The wise take their hearts' advice," Enda said, "even when the heart cannot provide hardcopy documentation, but I do see your point."

Gabriel sat there and looked at the ground, while yet another huge bug trundled by. This is what the rest of your life will be like, said that voice buried down in his brain. No one ever again believing anything you say. Because of one carelessness, one episode of—

"Never mind," Gabriel said then and looked up once more at Ondway. "Let it pass. Maybe we'll go somewhere else." But the look he gave Ondway was intended to suggest, And if you believe that, he thought, I have a few nice planets in the Solar Union to sell you.

Ondway shrugged his wings. "Perhaps it would be wiser. Meantime, we will take a few days for the 'search parties' to 'find you.' Then we will arrange transport for your ship back to Redknife—"

"You ought to let us see if she can be made to lift," Enda interrupted. "There was nothing wrong with her drive when we shut it down. Our main worries were about structural integrity, and a short flight to the spaceport should not be beyond her abilities." She glanced over at Gabriel.

He nodded. "There was that control surface problem I mentioned, but lifting her slowly and not trying anything showy, just limping her in—that shouldn't be a problem."

Ondway thought about that for a moment. "Well, it might be wiser to bring her in via ground transport anyway, annoying as that will be. It might look 'more in character' and would suggest that she is worse damaged than she is if you desire to remain here longer."

"It would also be much more expensive," Enda said, giving Ondway one of those grandmotherly looks. "Not that the transport teams would mind, I am sure. But let us at least check the drive and see how the situation looks in a few more days."

Ondway gestured with his wings, a movement like someone putting their hands up helplessly in the air, and then he chuckled. "Honored, let it be as you say. Meanwhile, have you eaten?"

"Only the cold grain porridge that everyone else had this morning," Enda replied before Gabriel could get his mouth open, "and I am sure Gabriel here is wasting away. If you like, we will draw on ship's stores."

"No, not until we 'find' her," Ondway said. "There should be no need. I had never heard that human warriors were averse to roast meat, and Rohvieh who is cooking this morning has an excellent claw with a roast. We may not be certain of you, but we will not starve you." He got up to lead them off to breakfast.

Gabriel followed willingly enough, but he could not avoid seeing the odd look Enda was giving him. And all the while he was thinking, We seem to be guests for the moment, but we could be prisoners again at any moment.

And just what *is* going on up on Rhynchus?

Chapter Fifteen

THREE DAYS WENT by, and they ate well enough. Gabriel even started to become inured to bugs. The morning when one nearly half a meter long ran over his boot and he merely looked down and said "Huh," Enda clapped her hands and hailed him a hero—and all the sesheyans around him had a good laugh at his expense. That, at least, Gabriel was getting used to. It surprised him what a cheerful people they were, down here in the dimness in their own proper environment. Sesheyan laughter that had so startled him at first because he had never heard its like, now seemed commonplace, and when he didn't hear it, he missed it.

The morning of the fourth day though, the day they were scheduled to "find" *Sunshine*, that laughter was missing when he woke up, and this struck Gabriel as very odd. He dressed and got up in a hurry, leaving Enda sleeping, and headed out of the leaf hut to see what was the matter.

The encampment was very silent. Outside it, all the usual morning-period forest screeches and hoots were in full flower, but there were only a couple of sesheyans about. One of them, tending the low smoky fire that was kept smoored except when cooking was about to begin, was sitting on the ground, hunched up with her wings huddled around her, a posture so eloquent of fear or great distress that Gabriel went straight to her and bent down, saying, "Sister, what troubles you? And where is everybody?"

She looked up at him mournfully—at that point Gabriel suddenly realized that she was one of the youngest of them—and said, "The Hunter may widely range, but sometimes the prey hunts him: and fear goes hunting the forests, and the dark between the stars:"

She choked her words off suddenly. It was an odd sound, for sesheyans normally always left you with the impression that the song of their conversation invariably had another verse that they might add at a moment's notice, or a year from now, but that they were never actually done.

"But where did they all go?"

"Under the forest's shelter lie other places of landing:" she said. "News came from one of the nearer that one had returned untimely: he bore a—"

More broken staves, Gabriel thought. Those were evidence of a sesheyan about as upset as one could become. But what in the worlds could have—

He barely heard them coming. That he could hear them at all was evidence of several days in almost exclusively sesheyan company. Gabriel had a few seconds' warning anyway, before the clearing was full of sesheyans, many more than had routinely been using the encampment. Ondway was among them. His expression, as far as Gabriel could make it out, was very grim and dark. Behind him came several more sesheyans, silently carrying something on a plasteine sheet stretched between them.

Gabriel went over to them, then saw what they carried on the sheet and stopped very still.

He recognized certain things about the object immediately. The green-colored plastic e-suit, full, as he now knew, of that acidic gel, the dark armor in plates and patches over the suit, the terrible, blank protective helmet. The shape suggested strongly that there was no human inside. It was too broad in the shoulders and too thick in the leg.

Gabriel looked around at the sesheyans. "Let's get this open," he said. "Does someone have a hard/soft knife?"

Ondway shouldered forward and took Gabriel by the arm with one claw. It was not an entirely friendly gesture. "Do you know what you are doing?" he growled.

"I think I do," Gabriel said softly. "I think you do, to, but it might be less awful if I do it. Don't you think?"

He and Ondway took a couple of breaths, looking at each other. Then Ondway let go of him and turned away.

As they put the body down, Gabriel knelt down beside it. After a moment one of the sesheyans handed him one of the most beautiful hard/soft knives he had ever seen. "As the Hunter says, use it with care: for what the blade cuts, is severed ever:" said the sesheyan.

Gabriel held it up to stroke the blade out and nodded, agreeing. The blade was of so-called "hard monofilament," barely more than a hair thick, but it would pierce almost any substance and slice through nearly anything, slipping along the molecular interstices as if steel or stone was nothing more resistant than cheese. "Thank you," Gabriel said as he bent over his work, taking it slowly and trying not to breathe more than he had to.

He was not going to attempt what Doctor Delde Sota had done, but his dissembling of the armor slowly revealed the body to be that of a sesheyan, a very young one, just barely adult. There were some other disturbing developments though. The wings, every sesheyan's pride, were gone, amputated, their bony stubs all wound about with the biotendon material that had been present in the body that Delde Sota had autopsied. As this became evident, the sesheyans gathered around raised a low moan, and Enda shaded her eyes in a way that Gabriel suspected was ceremonial rather than having anything to do with the light.

"Sacrilege," said the eldest of the sesheyans looking on. "His soul has been taken from him."

Gabriel wondered what else might have been taken from him as he made the last cut, removing the headpiece and revealing the face. The expression of pain and fury it wore was terrible, the lips wrinkled back, snarling, the eyes pinched nearly oblong by the surrounding musculature. How did I ever think of these faces as expressionless, he thought sadly, just because they had an "unusual" number of eyes?

Gabriel stood up after a few moments and turned to Ondway again. "Where was this found?" he said.

Ondway did not speak for several moments. Finally, very reluctantly, he said, "Far out in this system. The starrise detection equipment says that they came in from somewhere in the neighborhood of—" He stopped.

"Thalaassa," Gabriel said, so that Ondway would not have to.

The other sesheyans suddenly appeared to be looking in every direction at once—not that this was difficult for people who had their optical arrangement. Taking a few extra moments to get control of himself, Gabriel thumbed the knife to "clean," then hit the "sheathe" control and handed it back with thanks to its owner. Then he turned to Ondway. "Son of the Hunter, now comes our time to track. Get the ship handled *today*. Get her to Redknife. Swift get her repaired and fueled, for I must go hunting. Well you know where and why—say no more about it!"

He headed back toward the leaf hut, slipped inside and then sat down in a hurry, for controlling his stomach had left him somewhat weak in the knees. In the dimness of the hut lit only by the luckstone that lay off to one side atop a cross section of tree trunk, Enda's blue eyes caught the light and glowed slightly as she leaned on one elbow, looking at Gabriel.

"I smell something," she said.

"Fear," Gabriel said, without entirely thinking and then added, "A cousin to Doctor Delde Sota's autopsy subject, a sesheyan this time. Or rather, it was sesheyan once. What it is *now,* or was . . ."

"Are you sure you want to find out?" Enda said.

"I'm going to make it my business," Gabriel said. "This is tangled up with Rhynchus, somehow, and Rhynchus is tangled up in the ambassador's death and with me. As soon as the ship is 'recovered' and ready to lift—"

"I understand," Enda said.

"Do you?" Gabriel asked. "Enda," he paused, "you don't have to come."

"Ridiculous!" she said, looking genuinely angry. "Why should I not?"

The image of Enda turning up dead or worse than dead in one

of those suits occurred to Gabriel with sudden and stomach-turning force. He opened his mouth, but before he could say anything, Enda sat upright and said, "Now *that* even the most mind-deaf of fraal might have heard. I may be largely mind-blind, but not deaf. Gabriel, first of all, *Sunshine* is half mine. If you think I will allow you to endanger my investment by making any more such idiotic landings without me aboard to certify that they were made necessary by circumstances, you are greatly mistaken."

Gabriel had to smile wanly at that.

"Additionally, there are forces moving here that I desire to monitor. Twice now, by your telling, you may have heard Ondway thinking. Once more and it ceases to be coincidence. This is a matter of concern to me, as much so as any crazy landing. Third—" She sighed. "Here again is that smell of evil that I mentioned. The scent spreads, it seems. Your people have been wise enough to know that one must act against evil before it becomes too strong, before it comes for those who were too lazy or too complacent to act. I will not wait to let it come for me. If you go to see what is to be done, I go also."

"If only to protect your investment," Gabriel said, a little shaken.

"If only," Enda agreed and got up. "Let us find Ondway and lay our plans."

* * * * *

Two days later they were in Redknife. Gabriel's reaction to the place astonished him. Not so long ago Diamond Point, the biggest settlement on the planet, had seemed like a nice little city, but nothing to get too excited about. Now, after a week of living in a hut with a dirt floor, Redknife seemed wildly cosmopolitan to Gabriel, for all that it was little more than fifty or so buildings—many of them mere uninspired prefab—and a landing flat that looked crowded with more than three ships on it. The effect would wear off, he knew, but for the time being Gabriel kept catching himself goggling like the merest hick.

Sunshine went straight to the single sesheyan-run ship repair facility where she would sit for several days while her hull was mended (not by reweave, but the old fashioned way with layered durasteel, cerametal, and rivets, rather to Enda's satisfaction) and various minor repairs were made to her control surfaces and undercarriage. Gabriel, meanwhile, did some shopping with the guidance of Ondway.

"Protective coloration mostly," Gabriel said, as he and Enda sat with him in a little eating house at the edge of Redknife, looking out on the landing pan. "I don't want anyone who might stop us thinking that we have no reason to be in that system. No good reason, anyway. What kinds of things do 'traders' to Phorcys and Ino take?"

Ondway looked at him in silence for a long while before saying, "Light electronics are useful: phymech supplies, tools, spares for tools and power supplies."

These were all categories in which Phorcys and Ino had their own manufacturing base, Gabriel thought, but he did not speak that thought aloud. "All right," he said. "If you can point us to a supplier who can give us a basic load without attracting too much attention, we'll head out of here tomorrow morning."

"Tonight might be preferable," Ondway said, "not that general surveillance of the planet lessens much at any given time. But nightside takeoffs attract a little less attention. In that, as regards the forest cities and other rogue elements here, those shooting at you will have a little more trouble with accuracy."

Shooting? Gabriel thought.

Enda glanced over at Ondway and said, "I take it then that the corsair fleet support people operating out of Angoweru are no less active despite the Concord's somewhat increased presence?"

"Not at all. The Concord's presence ebbs and flows anyway. The new ship has gone off to Thalaassa, apparently."

Gabriel put his eyebrows up at that. The timing was certainly interesting. "Something go wrong with the treaty?"

"The move was described as 'a routine follow-up visit,' " said

Ondway, "but press releases, as we know, have their own purposes to which the truth is often subsidiary."

Gabriel sighed. It was not as if he had planned to yell for help, yet at the same time, the presence of *Schmetterling* would have lent a little reassurance to this situation. Now that would be missing. Never mind, he thought. We'll do without.

"Will she be ready tonight?" Gabriel asked.

"Late," Ondway replied.

They were quiet a while, sitting and drinking cold chai while the hoots of gandercats drifted across the field from the nearby forests. It was hot and fairly bright even for humans. Ondway was goggled, but increasingly Gabriel found that this was not interfering with his ability to guess at the expressions of the eyes underneath the protection. As with humans, a lot of sesheyan expression lay in the face and no amount of hiding the eyes could conceal everything that was going on.

"What *is* going on there?" Gabriel asked at last.

The goggled head turned toward him. "Three times you have asked," Ondway said, "but three hundred would not avail you. I am oathbound in this. Nor can I direct you to another who could say. This also the oath binds. You must go yourself and come again."

"So we shall," Enda said, "and then *you*, perhaps, will owe *us* faceprice." Her look was possibly more ironic than Gabriel had ever seen it. Ondway shifted a little in his seat and hunched his shoulders up under his wings as if the look rubbed him a little raw.

"Perhaps," Ondway said and got up. "I will go to see how the repairs are coming." Silently he took himself away.

The porch where they sat, a place where insects flew idly in and out of the misty sunlight, was empty of staff and other patrons for a few minutes before Gabriel asked, "Who is he, besides a freight expediter's employee?"

Enda shrugged, looking out toward the field. "Certainly a person of some consequence hereabouts," she said, "because of his relation to Devlei'ir. That one in his turn is more than merely a shaman or religious leader. Something has been crystallizing around him here, the idea that perhaps sesheyans have lost too much of their identity as a people to human and other kinds of civilization. Examples of how their relationships with other species have gone wrong are ready to hand all around them: their measured exploitation by the Hatire here, their corporate enslavement by VoidCorp. A great number of sesheyans on Grith have been returning to the forest life, abandoning 'civilization' as a result of Devlei'ir's wry parables." She tilted her head to one side for a moment, looking at her chai in which all the ice had melted. "Now the predictable backlash is beginning. The Hatire on Grith see a loss of power in their own sphere. Where they had been hoping for coexistence with sesheyans in their own area of influence, in and around Diamond Point, now they see rejection. VoidCorp applies its pressure to this world as it can and equally sees no result. Other powers move here, the Concord chief among them, and they also have not been getting the result that they desire."

She looked absently in the direction Ondway had taken across the field, toward the hangars. "The situation is unstable, and instability creates motion. In turn, motion begets movers, those who analyze the situation themselves and do not wait to be led. Ondway is one—though not, I think, the tool of his kinsman that others think him. Possibly he sees wider than many suspect." She turned her cup a couple of times, looking into it. "But he is care- ful to protect his sources and his own position. Hardly anything one might blame him for, with the shadow of VoidCorp hanging over this system as heavily as it does."

That shadow was beginning to rest on Gabriel's mind a lot more heavily than it had. He nodded and said, "Should we go see if the supplies are ready?"

"You cannot wait, can you?" Enda observed, getting up.

"To get out of here? To find out?" He cut himself off. "No," he answered, "I can't."

* * * * *

Matters progressed as quickly as they could, but even so there were a couple more necessary repairs that needed to be done, and not all of the supplies could be found right away. It was another day before they were able to leave, and Gabriel had to endure Enda's look of mute reproach at the repair bill when it was presented at last. She checked it with care and signed off on it at last, but all the way across the field, in company with Ondway, she had a slightly bruised look, as of a fraal who thought she could have gotten a better bargain elsewhere.

"Still," she said to Gabriel after they said good-bye to Ondway and were doing the last of their preflight checks, "one can't choose where one crashes, I suppose."

"I thought I did a pretty good job," Gabriel said.

"Hmf," Enda said and gave the planet below them a rather jaundiced look as they finally rose up and away from Redknife. Gabriel grinned a little ruefully as they got well out of atmosphere. He gave Grith and Hydrocus only one backward glance, then dropped *Sunshine* into drivespace. Starfall light sheeted green-blue around them, obscuring the emerald that was Grith. Then everything went black.

The five days in drivespace seemed unusually long to Gabriel on this run. He tried to spend the first few of them constructively by doing something he had long intended—going carefully and slowly through the ship, examining everything he could open up and peer inside for anything that might look like a bug. It was difficult, since he had so little idea of what a bug might look like. He spent a lot of time with the manuals for various pieces of equipment, studying the equipment's insides and trying to identify anything that didn't belong there. The manuals frustrated this work by stubbornly refusing to identify every single piece of circuitry inside the equipment—and everywhere were small enclosed solids or boxes labeled *No User-Serviceable Parts Iinside* or *Tampering Invalidates Warranty*. Finally, late on the third evening, Gabriel gave up. If they were bugged, they were bugged. After all this was over, he would find time to land *Sunshine* somewhere where there were experts in the subject, and he would have the ship "swept."

If they survived.

The thought had not escaped him that anyone with a drive-space detector could tell where *Sunshine* would be coming out and when. There would most likely be a "welcoming party" waiting for them. Gabriel spent the early part of the fourth day working out with the JustWadeIn software. He was increasingly needing less of the "gunman" mode as he learned to fight the ship properly, as if he *were* the ship, tumbling in six axes, firing along six axes, and anticipating action in three dimensions rather than "on the flat." He was by no means certain of his ability. He was glad enough to know that the "gunman" paradigm was there to fall back on if he needed it and that Enda had been working out with the software as well, sharpening her own skills—not that they seemed to need much sharpening.

"Well, old habits are hard to break," Enda said. "I did gunnery once before I left the city-ship with which I traveled. It was a long time ago, but they say these talents stay with you forever if you learn them young enough. Weaponry has changed a lot, but tactics do not shift much as regards combat in space. If you have a good enough grasp of spatial relationships, and can lose the 'craving' for gravity or a 'down' orientation when you fight, you can be very effective, but practice makes the biggest difference."

Later that evening Gabriel found her in the sitting room, lounging and looking at an image of stars slowly shifting around them. While she listened to a recording of one of her favorite fraal choirs over the audio system, the entertainment system projected what one would be seeing at this point if there were any stars to be seen in drivespace.

He sat down and said, surprising himself somewhat, "Do you miss it?"

She turned thoughtful eyes to him. "Miss what?"

"The cities? The Wandering?"

"Well, I have not stopped, precisely."

"But there aren't hundreds of other fraal with you. Don't you miss that life?" Gabriel asked.

Enda put her feet up and sighed. "It is not that long ago, really, that I should begin to miss it yet," she replied. "Only a hundred years ago now since I left my own and . . . well, not precisely 'settled.' But I wanted something different from the verities and assurances of fraal life, so I have roamed far and wide, but it has been with humans that I have done it. I have had brief partnerships before and seen them break up, never otherwise than amiably. Both alone and in company, I have done many kinds of labor, physical and mental." She smiled slightly. "I have been a rather unusual sort of migrant laborer, I suppose. Well, work is not necessarily an evil."

"Isn't it?" Gabriel said.

"Not if you do it willingly, certainly. If you do it unwillingly—well, that can be bad. Sometimes a piece of work comes that transforms itself from something annoying, even repellent, to something more worthwhile than you thought. That transformation itself works backward and shifts all the other works you have done that led to it, so that a life that once looked useless, or blighted, becomes something much more positive." She smiled very slightly, a look that reminded Gabriel of a piece of ancient artwork he had seen in facsimile—the dusky human lady in question very demure, but the secret of why she smiled hidden most securely behind her eyes.

Gabriel breathed out, a skeptical sound. "Huh. I didn't think fraal went in for religion."

"We do not, generally," Enda said, "for 'religion' is a binding. This is a setting free, if that is even the right idiom. How can one be set free when one has never really been bound? That is the discovery that this transformation entails."

Gabriel shook his head, amused. "You'll be telling me that life is an illusion next."

"Blasphemy," Enda said, and this time she smiled much more broadly. "Death is, possibly, but where life is concerned, there is nothing more real. Of course it all sounds paradoxical, but fraal do not mind that. Humans often have a problem, though."

Gabriel would have laughed, but at the same time he knew

some scientists said that many of the basic paradoxes at the heart of the fraal-based gravity induction engine had never been solved and probably never would. The only thing to do with them was leave them alone, because the laws in which the paradoxes described unresolvable conflicts worked just fine nevertheless. One slightly facetious scientific paper that Gabriel had seen excerpted at the Academy suggested that if enough people started querying the basis of the gravity induction engine, it might stop working. Now he looked over at Enda and wondered exactly how facetious that paper had been.

"You've had this 'transformation' yourself then?" Gabriel inquired.

"Oh, often," Enda said, "and lost it again as many times, which reminds me. Where is the water bottle?"

Gabriel chuckled. "Where you left it."

"You are not helpful," she said, getting up to go look for it. "If you tell me again it is in 'the last place I will look,' I will serve you as I served that poor thug with the knife in Diamond Point."

Gabriel laughed out loud. "That kind of service I can do without," he said.

"It was the service he required of me and the universe at the time," Enda's voice came down the corridor, "and I had little enough choice but to oblige him. I expect a higher level of request from you, however."

Gabriel shook his head and sat looking at the stars shifting slowly on the entertainment system screen. "I don't get it," he said. "What kind of transformation do you have to have 'often'? I thought once was supposed to do it, as a rule."

"Your sources have misinformed you," Enda said. "As regards the kind of which I speak, one must often have it again and again to get it to 'take.' It is not like a software upgrade."

"Or not a very good one," Gabriel said.

Enda chuckled at that from down the hall. "Perhaps the failure is in the hardware," she said, "much upgraded with varying versions of wildly differing code over long periods, applications that get into fights with each other over system resources and bring the whole thing crashing down. Well, never mind that." She returned with the water bottle and bent over the bulb, watering it carefully.

"You're going to need a bigger pot for that soon," Gabriel said.

Enda gave him an amused look. "Your sense of irony is likely to need a larger container, as well."

Gabriel chuckled, leaned back, and looked at the stars again. "Seriously, I've never heard you talk like this before."

"You may have to wait another hundred years," she said. "It would be a poor life-philosophy that kept you thinking about it all the time. The point is to *live,* in the philosophy or around it, perhaps, but not because of it or through it that you miss your life while trying to live it correctly. There would be little point in that."

"What about when you live your life incorrectly?" Gabriel asked. "When you make mistakes?"

Enda did not look up at the sadness in his voice. "There is no such thing as a life incorrectly lived," she answered. "There are lives which lack that crucial transformation. Experienced once or many times they bring perspective and show you the way through and past the pain and error. Without it, yes, there is much pain and evil that one can inflict on oneself and others. With it everything shifts. Ancient pain becomes a signpost. Present error becomes a gateway. The future becomes clean, as the past eventually does. It all becomes one road." She sighed and put the bottle down, examining the bulb. "It *is* paradoxical, and if you try to apply sense to it, it will bounce. I would think it was ridiculous myself, if I had not had it happen to me so many times."

"When you first came to me, I suppose," Gabriel said.

"Yes," Enda said, and then sat down and looked rather bemused. Gabriel blinked, not expecting quite so emphatic a response.

Those long, slender, pale hands knotted themselves together, and her blue eyes looked at him earnestly. "I do not know how it is for humans, not for sure," Enda said, "but sometimes something—not the hunch, the source is more central, I think—something comes and says in your ear, *Do this.* Usually other people are involved. There is some service you must do them, and if you do it, your life changes. You may rail and complain afterward, but eventually the change is revealed to have been necessary, and the service you did turns out to be as much in your interest as in the others'."

"That happened to you?" Gabriel said.

"Yes." Enda looked up at him as if with some difficulty and said, "I wonder if it might have happened to you, too."

All Gabriel could do, for the moment, was stare at her.

"Dangerous to speculate," Enda said. "Only the person at the heart of the action can tell for sure. The danger lies in mistaking the source of the call for something lesser—or for thinking that service is, well, subservient—a disadvantaged state, a state of being 'one down,' somehow. From my people's point of view, there is probably no higher state than service, for all that it can be painful and annoying as well. The greater the service done, the greater the result."

Gabriel shook his head. He too was becoming uncomfortable. It was not that he disliked the abstract *per se*, but that he had trouble with some aspects of it. Politics he could understand quite well, relations among visible things and people, but the invisible made him twitch.

"Look," he said, "there's no question that you did me a service, and I thank you for it."

At that Enda laughed gently and tilted her head to one side. "But it does not end there. It never does. Service cuts both ways. You too are serving me, though I may not understand how, and I think you may be caught up in some larger service as well, though of what you must be the judge."

"You don't seem to have a lot of definite information about any of this," Gabriel said.

"In this regard, that is not my job," Enda said. "Ask the universe. I merely live in it, like everyone else."

She got up and took the water bottle off to refill it, leaving Gabriel to stare at the Grid screen full of stars and wonder whether someone saying, "Find out about this," and setting him on a course of action that involved so many people getting killed could possibly have been some larger force moving.

Ridiculous.

He dismissed the idea out of hand. Just fraal mysticism, cutting loose without warning in the middle of a boring period. Lots of people went off into philosophical reveries while in drive-space. The Orlamu sat around "contemplating the void" for hours on end, hunting through it for ultimate truth. It must take a lot to find it in a world of solid black.

He sighed, got up, and went forward to the cockpit to sit down and work with the JustWadeIn software again. There would certainly be a reception committee waiting for them at the Thalaassan side. Gabriel would be ready for it.

Chapter Sixteen

WHEN THEY MADE starrise at Thalaassa, they were both in the pilots' seats, both suited, both ready. All *Sunshine*'s diagnostics had been run and reported her ready. The program remained running where Gabriel could get at it quickly if he needed it, and the JustWadeIn software was running in standby, waiting for real space in which to work.

Normally Gabriel despised countdowns, having endured too many of them in some armored shuttle while in the marines. But now he watched the clock with fierce interest as the digits in the tank decremented themselves. When the "one" finally slipped into "zero" and vanished, the tank went black and he could barely contain his excitement. Starrise washed upwards around them in something unexpected, the brightest pure white Gabriel had ever seen, with not the slightest admixture of any other color. *Is that lucky?* he said, staring into the fighting field while waiting for it to bring up tactical.

We should hope so, Enda said. *Look.*

The image of surrounding space in the tank and in the fighting field shimmered and resolved itself. There was a whole swarm of small arrowlike shapes, sleek and deadly, approaching them fast on system drive from about a thousand kilometers out.

Those designs Gabriel knew all too well: the Insight-designed software went out of its way to describe them and their fighting capabilities in gleeful and malicious detail. *VoidCorp*, he said. *Sesheyan Employee ships.*

There were a lot of them, too many of them. Sixteen, the fighting software said. But what Gabriel did not fully understand was that some of them seemed to be avoiding the potential fight. They kept on going, heading away, heading out-system.

They think they can take us with just this many, Enda said, sounding surprisingly annoyed at the prospect.

They can! Gabriel thought but didn't say. It wasn't so much a question of massed armaments as it was numbers. When that many people engaged you, sooner or later you would miss someone coming up from behind, move a little more slowly than you should—and that would be the end of it.

Maybe so, he said, b*ut it seems we're not the only reason they're here. Anyway, damned if I'm going to be mobbed by these people when there's someone in the system who's supposed to prevent this kind of thing from happening.* He asked the tank for another view, a wider one of the system, specifically concentrating on larger ships present there. There was some in-system freight traffic, ships that Gabriel had learned to recognize from their previous stays here—but not what he was looking for. *Where the hell is* Schmetterling? he asked.

Not here, apparently, said Enda. *At least it does not show anywhere in system scan.*

They could be anywhere, dammit. Gabriel was fuming as he scanned the software, trying to sort out all the VoidCorp ships' positions in his head. *Bloody Galactic policemen, all over you like a cheap suit when you* don't *want one, and when you do want one, they're nowhere to be found!*

But there was no more time for that. Twelve of the VoidCorp fighters were now moving in on *Sunshine* in a standard englobement, which was nice for the JustWadeIn software—it had intervention routines for that—but there weren't enough guns aboard *Sunshine* to handle that kind of attack effectively, and the software was plaintively asking for more.

This is going to be a problem, Gabriel heard Enda say softly.

Do you trust the software intervention routines? Gabriel inquired.

I trust them to take care of easy shots and point out difficult ones to me, but you will notice, if you read the manual, that the

Insight performance warranty does not extend to those routines. They stopped insuring them when a few pilots' families sued them after the pilots were killed. It was impossible to prove that the software was not somehow at fault.

Gabriel shook his head. *We're on our own, then.*

More or less.

He still could not understand how Enda could sound so cheerful even when they were outnumbered and outgunned. *Do you know something I don't know?*

You mean, do I have a hunch? No, but I am not sure any of us is ever alone.

Philosophy, Gabriel thought helplessly. Well, if it helps you to shoot straight.

The englobement completed itself around *Sunshine*, the VoidCorp ships disposing themselves roughly on an dodecagon's vertices, preparatory for an inward push and firing run. The Just-WadeIn software's fighting field shimmered around them both and displayed best dispositions for gunnery, hit percentages for each gun, suggestions for maximum fire result and optimum firing distance.

Enda ignored it, picked a direction and threw *Sunshine* that way in a spinning, corkscrewing path, then started shooting.

Gabriel began firing too, picking the closest target and trying to get a sense of windage, but the craft slipped aside as he fired and then came in on a line for him again, firing right back. Enda twisted them out of range, hammering again at the first ship she had targeted, trying to break their formation globe and slip through. It was a standard response: get the englobing group to lose their cohesiveness and the value of their attack formation disintegrates almost immediately. However, these ships' pilots seemed not to be even slightly interested in losing their attack's cohesiveness, and as they slipped aside from Enda's attack and reformed, Gabriel began to think that the only thing going to disintegrate was *Sunshine*. The globe came after them as Enda broke through, mostly firing their lasers. Not a terribly effective attack, but bad enough if you blinded out the software or smoked some component that your enemy ship's manufacturer had not thought important enough to shield adequately.

Enda concentrated on putting some distance between *Sunshine* and the attackers. Little ships like those could not have infinite power capacity, and they were often more poorly provided for power storage than a less well-armed but more mundane mining ship might be. They might be able to make the fighters expend enough power for drive that they would have none to spare for lasers and would have to fall back on whatever other armament they had, using it up and forcing an early return to base—wherever "base" might be. In this case, it probably meant a big VoidCorp ship. Though they could have come all the way from Iphus or one of the other VoidCorp facilities back at Corrivale, that seemed unlikely. And if these fighters failed in what they were supposed to do, it struck Gabriel as all too likely that their base ship would come looking for them.

Are we going to keep running forever? Gabriel asked.

Odd that you should mention that, Enda said as she flipped *Sunshine* end for end and began firing at the approaching globe of fighters. They split apart to reform around *Sunshine* as they came back in, but as they split, Enda kicked in the system drive hard and shot straight through them, firing *en passant*. One bloom of fire burst out as she tore through, and Gabriel fired ahead of them at one fighter that seemed unwilling to get out of their path.

It side slipped at the last moment, and sweat broke out all over Gabriel at the nearness of the passage. He caught a glimpse of muzzleflare as they passed, but Enda saw it too and threw them sideways, so hard that the artificial gravity flickered and Gabriel's teeth banged together.

This is not a tactically advantageous situation, Enda said as she spun *Sunshine* around and fired again. Another of the Void-Corp ships bloomed into brief flame and darkness. *We may have to run.*

I didn't come here to run, Gabriel said. *I came here to go to Rhynchus.* The feeling had begun to dog him that something bad

was happening and was likely to keep happening unless he got to
the bottom of the situation on Rhynchus. Gabriel was beyond
questioning the feeling now. *We need to do whatever it takes to
stay here*, he said. *If it takes getting them all—*

Let us be busy, then, Enda interrupted.

They fought. It went on for another fifteen minutes or so
without pause, Enda throwing *Sunshine* back and forth through
the VoidCorp ships' slowly decreasing numbers. They got several good shots and some that were positively lucky. Once the software took over from Gabriel and made a shot for him, blowing
up a fighter, but the pressure was taking its toll. One plasma cartridge missed them simply because Enda made a mistake in the
way she threw *Sunshine*. Otherwise everything would have been
over for them right then. Through the link Gabriel could hear her
breathing becoming labored, and it occurred to him that bril-
liance in fighting did not always mean endurance. How long
could Enda keep this up? Come to think of it, how long can I? he
wondered. Gabriel was sweating terribly inside the e-suit. Even
the suit's cooling equipment could not keep up with the fine mist
of condensation inside the faceplate that was beginning to interfere with his view into the fighting field.

Maybe it was a dumb idea, trying to fight this many. Their
opponents seemed to know it. Some of them were hanging back
while two or three at a time concentrated on attack. *They'll wear
us down sooner or late*, he thought to himself. *Maybe we really
should cut our losses and get out of here, we've been awfully
lucky.*

But if we do leave, they'll go on with—Gabriel was not sure
even now exactly what he suspected, but he didn't think Void-
Corp ships in the neighborhood of Rhynchus could mean any
good. He was torn. *Enda, what do you—*

Another plasma cartridge went off, entirely too close. The
ship shuddered and the hull began moaning in protest. *Oh, not
again!* Gabriel said. *Enda—*

Something else coming in, Enda said between gasps. She was
working hard, and one more VoidCorp ship had just gone down

at her hands, but Gabriel didn't think she could keep it up much longer. *Look at tactical. Not another VC. Different design.*
Gabriel searched in the fighting field for some indication of the other ship's ID, but nothing was showing. The ship was big, though, twice the size of *Sunshine* at least.

"Cutting in, *Sunshine*," said a voice on local comms, and both Gabriel and Enda jumped. It was a gravelly voice, very matter of fact with a slight drawl. Practically as it spoke, that other ship dove in among the VoidCorp vessels and took two of them out with paired blasts from what appeared to be top and bottom mass cannons.

As the other ship flashed past them, the Insight fighting software identified her as carrying weapons the kind and size of which Gabriel had only been able to dream about when they were doing *Sunshine*'s outfitting. *He's an arsenal all to himself!* Gabriel said. *Who is he, where the hell did he spring from?*

I would not care, Enda said, firing again, and another Void-Corp ship spun away trailing fire and escaped air, b*ut apparently we are not as "on our own" as we thought we were—*

"Friend," Gabriel said down comms, "whoever you are, you're welcome!"

"Helm's my name," replied a gravelly voice. "Introductions can wait, but a lady name of Delde Sota suggested you were coming this way—thought you might be able to use some help."

"Was she ever right. Forgive me for not going visual to greet you," said Gabriel, "but we've got our hands full at the moment."

"No problem, plenty of time later after we finish off these Corpses."

I wish I had your faith in your weaponry, or your deity, or whatever! Gabriel thought. "These guys with the plasma cannon," Gabriel said, "I would dearly love to get rid of them."

"We'll just get to work on that right now," said the voice.

The ship executed an astonishingly tight turn, throwing itself back toward the main cluster of the remaining fighters. Gabriel could only stare at the maneuver in astonishment. Even with artificial gravity, there were limits to the stresses a ship and pilot could take. At the highest accelerations, even the artifical gravity would start to fail out, leaving a pilot with the acceleration-associated blackouts and other problems that had beset atmosphere pilots for hundreds of years. This pilot though, seemed not to care about such things, or else he had an iron vascular system. His ship twisted, aligned itself, and something shot away from him.

Wham! Wham!—and two spectacular plasma bolts lanced out of the ship and took the two VoidCorp ships with the plasma cannon out, neat as could be. The ship arced away and "downward," heading toward the oncoming ships.

"By the way, sorry I was late," said the gravelly voice on the other end, "but I'm always late. I was born that way."

Gabriel shook his head, uncertain what to make of that. "You're on time enough for us."

"Just," said Helm. "Looks like you have some more incoming."

Gabriel checked his tactical. Sure enough, there were the remaining VoidCorp fighters coming back fast. "They passed us by earlier," Gabriel said, "possibly on the way to do something else."

"Looks like maybe they don't want witnesses to their embarrassment," Helm said. "All right, we can do a little something about that. Look at that, so nice and tight."

He nudged his ship toward them. It was so unlike the quicker acceleration of a moment before that Gabriel stared. "Are you all right?"

"Fine, no problem," Helm said. "Just waiting for them to fall into the right configuration. Computer wanted a read on their pattern, since the egg I'm about to lay is a little expensive. Saves time, though. They keep trying to englobe. Good."

He was right. They were englobing again. "Too bad for them," Helm said very cheerfully. "Don't get close, now. Mind your eyes."

Something leaped away from his ship too fast to see, mass-driven, possibly. It shot into the center of the approaching globe formation—

Space whited out from the detonation there. Gabriel was blinded. Enda cried out.

" 'Cherry bomb,' " Helm said. "Squeezed nuke. Don't have many of those, but they sure lend a little excitement to a large party. Would use more of 'em, but the damned cost-accounting program screams too much."

Gabriel, gazing into the field and calling for detailed tactical, could only agree. There seemed to be nothing left of the ships that had been attempting that new englobement except drifting wreckage, much of it white hot or molten.

"Uh oh," Helm said.

Gabriel saw what he saw: the last two of the ships fleeing in opposite directions, one of them vaguely toward Rhynchus, one of them away. "He's mine," Gabriel said, indicating the one heading toward Rhynchus.

"Take him. I'll have this boy."

The two of them arced away in different directions. Gabriel threw *Sunshine* after his quarry at high speed. It was necessary. His quarry was running as if gone wild and blind, not even evading, just shooting away like an arrow. Gabriel curved down under him, caught him as he finally tried to change direction, and put a plasma cartridge right into his belly. The ship blew up most satisfactorily.

Panic, he said to Enda, as he brought the ship around and headed back to the scene of the main combat.

I wonder, Enda said.

A blast of light from up ahead suggested to Gabriel that Helm had caught up with his own target. "You all right?"

"No problem," said the gravelly voice.

"That's a relief," Enda said as she let the fighting field up from around her, unclasped her helmet, and took it off. "Perhaps we have time for introductions now?"

The tank lit. "Helm Ragnarsson."

"Gabriel Connor."

"Enda," the fraal said.

"A pleasure."

They all studied each other for a moment. Though it was hard to tell when someone was sitting down, Helm looked short. He was dark-skinned and amazingly heavy-boned. His shoulders were huge, and his waist might have looked narrow enough for his own build, but it was bigger across than Gabriel's shoulders. A build, in all, much too heavy to have grown that way normally.

"Yes, I'm a mutant," Helm said, in a voice that was just faintly weary. "My 'family' went in for heavy planet work. Generation before last, they started working on engineering some specialty genes into our line. Some people don't like it." He shrugged. "We don't care. We take ourselves where the work is, together or singly."

He was casual enough about it, but Gabriel wondered how long that shell of nonchalance had taken to grow. Mutants were very much a minority among the Concord worlds and were routinely seen as dangerously different—peculiar and dangerous creatures at best, outcasts at worst. For his own part, this man had just saved his life, and Gabriel was not prepared to be sticky about it.

"So that's how you managed those high-g turns," Gabriel said. "What an advantage."

The mutant looked at him for a moment, then grinned. "I like you, Connor. First human I've met in a while who looked at the plus side of it first. Pretty rare."

Gabriel shrugged. "Anyway, believe me, you could have eyes at all corners and legs on all surfaces, and I'd still be glad to see you. You saved our butts."

"My fundament too," Enda said, "would no doubt state its gratitude, were it capable. But, Helm, how did you know where to find us? It has been some while since we saw Delde Sota, and we did not even know our own plans clearly when we last saw her."

"Maybe not," said Helm, "but someone else did."

"Ondway," said Gabriel.

"That her fella on Grith? He'd be the one, then. They keep in pretty close touch, it seems."

"There is a great deal going on in Corrivale space," said Enda, "that seems not to show above the surface."

"You'd be right there, lady. Place is getting complicated in its old age. I don't stay around there much any more. It's getting too civilized. Too crowded."

Gabriel was tempted to laugh. "Grith doesn't strike me as overpopulated, exactly."

"No, but 'crowded' can mean people looking over your shoulder, too," said Helm. "Too much bureaucracy, too many people noticing when you turn up, when you leave, wanting to know how much money you make, what you spend it on." He shrugged. "I spend as little time as I can in places like that."

Gabriel thought that he might have a point there. At the same time, his attention was now attracted somewhat by the wreckage beginning to float around them. He reached into the tank and tweaked a control, bringing up a routine he had programmed in earlier.

"You using beams out there, brother?"

"Scanning," said Gabriel.

"Looking for something in particular?"

"Bodies," Gabriel said.

"Should be plenty of those," said Helm. "Sesheyan mostly, far as I can tell. Company types. This a personal kink, or is there a reason?"

"I don't want to get into it right now."

"Oh," said the friendly voice, "a kink."

Enda was chuckling. "Not the one you think, perhaps," she said.

"Well, that's all right then," Helm said. "Those bodies you looking for usually carry ID beacons?"

"*What?*" Gabriel asked.

"Something out there's got a beacon on it. Squawk four-four-five-oh. Take a listen."

Gabriel spoke to *Sunshine*'s comm settings. A moment later they heard the soft repetitive cheeping of the beacon.

"Black box?" Gabriel said.

"On *these* ships?" said Helm. "Not likely."

"Someone signaling for help?" Enda asked.

Gabriel shook his head. "It could be, but it's hard to tell."

"Signal's attenuating," Helm said. "Not meant to play for long, I think."

"Hurry up, we've got to find it!"

The signal ceased.

"I don't believe it," Gabriel said.

"Look," Enda said. "No, not there. Gabriel, look. There is a light."

He peered out the cockpit windows, then doused the interior lights to help him see. "I see it," he said. "Enda, what eyes you have!"

"There is definitely something attached," she said as Gabriel directed the tactical scanners' attention to that one spot. "A small container, perhaps?"

"Not that small," said Helm. "Looks about two meters by three?"

"Nice call," Gabriel said, for that was almost exactly its size, as the tactical display confirmed. "Some kind of escape capsule?"

"No sign of such," said Helm. "No heat sources at the right frequency, anyway."

"How much stuff have you got *installed* in that ship?" Gabriel said in naked envy. "The weaponry is bad enough. But infrared scanners are—"

"Not cheap, but I have a friend in the business." Helm chuckled. "Delde Sota got me a discount."

Gabriel moaned softly. "Please. Her and her discounts."

"Oh, it didn't come that cheap. She made me install some of her hardware in here as a swap. She likes to watch, does Delde Sota."

" 'Watch'?"

"Not *that,* but just about everything else. You couldn't build a nose big enough to match her nosiness. Sensors, an extension of her little braid, you name it. Comes in handy sometimes, but she charges me to use it, the cheap little metal-head," Helm snickered.

Gabriel had to chuckle at that. "Now then," he said as *Sunshine* came up to the object that had the beacon attached. It was a dark egglike ovoid of black metal. Its strobe was still flashing, but the flashes were getting further apart.

"Another five minutes and we wouldn't have found it," Helm said as his ship nosed up to the object too. Gabriel looked at the name, *Longshot,* fused neatly on near the nose. He then looked down the length of the ship in *Sunshine*'s spotlights. The thing was fairly bristling with weapons that it would take him and Enda years to afford. Gabriel became very glad that Helm had come in on their side and not against them. It would have been a very short fight.

"Now what do you make of this?" Helm was saying.

"It might be a bomb," Gabriel answered.

"It might be nearly *anything,*" said Enda, "but why put a homing device on a bomb? Unless it is so rare a one that you want it back if it does not explode. But what kind of bomb *wouldn't* explode?"

"That logic suggests by itself that it's not a bomb," said Helm. "Do you want to take it on board, or should I?"

Gabriel looked at it, and the words "bomb" and "on board" jarred together uncomfortably in his head. Still, it had been through an explosion already and hadn't exploded.

"We've got X-ray gear in the hold," Gabriel said, "for mining work, usually."

Helm chuckled. "Hunting the Glory Rock, huh? Will this thing fit in?"

"It should."

Gabriel spent about ten minutes with the remote manipulators, fitting the black egg into the cargo bay against the X-ray apparatus. The metal of the egg's casing was magnetizable, but Gabriel was reluctant to use the electromagnet grapples on the egg in case something inside that casing should react unkindly to a strong magnetic field.

He activated the X-ray projector and aimed it at the egg, where it sat in front of the imaging screen. He then transferred the image to the tank. "Can you see this?" Gabriel asked Helm.

"Yeah, getting it through comms."

The now-translucent image of the egg appeared in the tank. "Well, at least it is not opaque," Enda said, leaning in and looking at it curiously. "But what *is* that in there?"

It was hard to tell. There were two fairly large compartments, each packed full of some solid substance with what appeared to be minor cavities in it, then a smaller cavity full of a liquid. Down at the "small" end of the egg was a smaller cavity still that seemed empty but might just as well have had something gaseous in it. Finally, there appeared a small black object with circuitry spun through it—a data solid of some kind.

"If it is a bomb," said Helm, "I've never seen or heard of anything like it."

Enda was shaking her head. She reached into the tank and brought up the controls for one of the secondary sensor arrays in the cargo hold. "Only residual radioactivity," she said. "There is nothing fissionable in there."

"Do you want to open it?" Helm asked.

"Not a chance," Gabriel said forcefully. "Leave it right where it is."

They all looked at it for a few moments more, and then Enda leaned back and sighed. "Helm," she said, "you have our great thanks. Did Delde Sota suggest to you where we were intending to go?"

"She said you might be heading out into the system," Helm said, sitting back in his own pilot's seat with his arms folded. "She didn't go into detail, but she suggested that you might need someone to watch your backs."

"I confess I would be glad of that," Enda said. "If you require reimbursement for your time—"

For some reason, Helm looked genuinely alarmed. "Oh, no, no," he said. "This is payback for a favor Delde Sota did me once upon a time. She does these things for people, with the understanding that she'll call the favor in eventually. My dance card's empty for the next couple of weeks. You just tell me what you need."

"Well," Gabriel said, "we're heading to Rhynchus."

Helm looked bemused. "Rhynchus? There's nothing on Rhynchus."

"That's what we hear," Gabriel said. "Let's have our computers cut a course and head on over there."

Helm shook his head, mystified, and bent to his own console to comply. "Strangers well met," they heard him mutter, "with the emphasis on strange."

Gabriel grinned a little and started working in the tank.

* * * * *

Three hours later, without sighting or hearing from any other craft, they were in orbit over Rhynchus. Moving in silent tandem, using visuals and sensors, *Sunshine* and *Longshot* looked down upon the forlorn world.

The planet was mostly barren-looking. It had little surface water—a few lakes—and any water that appeared within thirty degrees of the poles was well frozen. At the equator, matters were slightly better. Here and there were some small patches of some stubborn native vegetation, even a small forest or two, but they were few. Mostly the surface was rocky and uninviting, and the color of the exposed parts of the crust was not such as to suggest much in the way of mineral or metallic wealth.

There was no sign of anything else, nothing built, no city, no habitation. The two ships were in ball-of-yarn orbit, the precessing orbit that covers a planet's whole surface in a matter of a few hours. They had done one whole pattern for mapping purposes, and the computer was working with the maps. But by eye, there was nothing at all visible, and it was getting frustrating.

"They *have* to be here," Gabriel muttered.

"Who would 'they' be?" Helm inquired from over on his ship.

"There's a colony," Gabriel said after a moment. "It's been, uh, misplaced." Enda gave him a wry look, but said nothing.

"Well," said Helm, "my sensors are pretty good. Any idea what we're looking for, specifically?"

"Not at all," Enda said, sounding more cheerful than Gabriel thought was appropriate.

Helm laughed. "Heat be a fair bet, you think?"

"Sesheyans like it between five and forty C, so, yeah, heat seems smart," Gabriel said.

"Setting up now."

Gabriel sat back "What I don't understand is the atmospheric situation," he mused. "There's much more air here than was mentioned in any survey the Concord did. None of the briefings mentioned anything significant in the way of atmosphere—otherwise everyone in the system would have been a lot more interested in the planet."

"Well," Enda said. "I suppose one might be able to understand it. Say the Concord comes into the system a few years ago, and the people on Phorcys and Ino say there's nothing on that planet. It's just a cold rock with very little atmosphere, too far out to do us any good, no resources, not worth terraforming." She shrugged. "At that early date, why would anyone disbelieve them? Then a survey ship takes a quick pass by, finds it as they described it, then goes away again. No one bothers to go back because surveys cost money, and they had already done one and found nothing."

And one small colony is easily hidden, Gabriel thought, especially if it's vital that it stay hidden. "You're probably right," he said, "but what I don't understand is how anyone is surviving there at all, if the place is so cold."

"Domes?" Enda said. "Or some other form of protection?"

"Domes cost a lot of money to build and more to maintain." Gabriel shook his head.

"Looking at temperature now," said Helm. "One pass in three axes?"

"Sounds about right," Gabriel said. "Let's go."

It took them forty-five minutes. When the pass was finished, Helm spent a few moments working with his computer, then transferred the results to their tank where the data displayed on the surface of a "false-colored" rotating globe.

"It's a lot warmer than it should be," said Helm.

There was no arguing that. The first Concord survey, done twelve years ago, suggested an average planetary temperature of no better than 4° C. This map showed it as being more like 12° C.

"Now *how* did they miss that?" Gabriel asked.

"On the second survey? I think it more than likely that they were just looking to see if the planet was in fact there," Enda replied. "Even if they got a record of the second temperature, who knows who was given the information for analysis, or whether it seemed particularly germane to them? They may have thought that the initial survey was in error." She shrugged.

They coasted around the planet one more time, this time with both *Longshot*'s and *Sunshine*'s sensing equipment listening for communications traces of any kind—drivespace relay traffic, even radio. There was nothing.

"Not that I would have really expected drivespace relay," Gabriel said. "There's no surer way to give yourself away."

"There is one thing, though," Helm said.

"Oh?"

"Had the machine do a little more fine analysis on that last map, narrowing down the temperature bands a little. Got a little tiny hot spot down there in the northern hemisphere," said Helm. "Almost lost it. There are little pinpricks of volcanism all over the place. You see 'em. But those are diffuse. This one is clear and sharp."

"A dome." Enda said.

"A dome. You were right," Gabriel said. "I was wrong."

Enda waved one hand. "As if such things matter. That is what we seek, I think. Helm, we must go down there. We have some slight introduction to them, if a shaky one, but you have none such. I would be afraid you might be fired upon."

"Might be fun," Helm drawled, "but never mind, I'll stay up here."

" 'Riding shotgun,' " Gabriel said.

"A good enough name for it. I'll be here. Better off-load your little egg to me. No point in taking it down there with you; you may need the room to bring something back up. Meanwhile, shout if you need me. I'll keep comms open."

"Believe it," Gabriel said. "We'll take handhelds with us if we leave the ship. Any sign of anyone else around here?"

"Neither hide nor hair. Go on."

They made their way down.

* * * * *

The atmosphere proved not to be as thin as had been reported. There was much more oxygen in it than Gabriel expected, and *Sunshine* reported wing bite more quickly than she should have. Gabriel spoke to the computer, directed it toward that one source of even heat, and told her to take them down. He would hold himself ready to take over if necessary.

But it was a standard landing, as straightforward and uncomplicated as if they were landing on a paved field. Rhynchus's surface here was actually pumice or some other kind of light, porous stone. When Gabriel got up and headed into the lift and the door opened, he saw that *Sunshine*'s landing skids had scraped the stone about an inch deep where she had sideslipped a little on landing.

Then, even in the dimness, he saw the other, much older skidmarks there too. Around them were scorchmarks from landing jets—various people's landing jets—and he understood that this was indeed a landing field, of sorts.

And then, hearing a faint humming in the air, he looked up— very slowly, not wanting to alarm anyone—and saw the sesheyans with the guns. All of them held the guns rock steady with sights trained on him.

"The Wanderer walks strange ways," he said, "and company finds, unlooked-for: but hospitality's laws say feed the guest ere you kill him."

The guns did not lower. But the sesheyan holding the biggest of them, the one who had appeared atop a boulder not far from the edge of the landing field, looked at Gabriel with a long, cold, thoughtful look.

"You are not from VoidCorp," he said in perfectly serviceable human idiom.

The lift activated again. Guns lifted all around. "Just my friend," said Gabriel, "a fraal. She isn't armed and she's pushing three hundred, so please don't frighten her. No, we're not from VoidCorp."

"Not at all," said Enda as she came out of the lift to stand beside Gabriel.

"Prove it," said the sesheyan on the boulder, in a tone of voice that clearly said to Gabriel, "leader."

Gabriel started to become exasperated. "That's going to be a little tough to prove, don't you think? Look, it was Ondway who sent us—or rather, he *didn't* send us. He tried every way he could think of *not* to send us, including not telling us anything about you, or even that you were here. He was very careful about it."

"That is possibly what we call a 'negative proof,' " Enda said demurely.

The leader's eyes pinched down narrow at her.

"We've brought you everything we could think of that might be of help to you, considering that no one would tell us anything outright," Gabriel said. "Electronics supplies, mostly. What I don't understand is what you're doing here! This is not supposed to be an inhabited planet."

"Not *supposed* to be," said the leader, and dropped his jaw in that sesheyan grin, possibly responding to Gabriel's aggrieved tone, similar to that of a tourist complaining that the colorful native dancers were not going to perform today, even though the brochure had said that they would. "No. You have come a long way, and we thank you for it, even though you should not have come. But we must get your ship out of sight very quickly. Things happen here at night."

Gabriel looked around him at the scared looks on the faces of some of the sesheyans, at the way they looked up at the sky as if it might suddenly rain knives. "Tell us where to put it," he said, "then we need to talk."

Chapter Seventeen

IT TOOK ABOUT half an hour to get everything squared away. *Sunshine* was tucked into a cave just big enough to take her, and the cave's opening was sealed over with such care that Gabriel might have thought the locals were expecting a police search. Then he and Enda were led through caves and tunnels into a large dim space. The heat they had detected from orbit and assumed to be a dome was actually a substantial network of caves that the sesheyans had very carefully joined and sealed off over the years. The interior was carefully and sparingly lit by powered lights and much subdivided into "apartments" and private areas. The main area, under the highest arch of a huge natural dome of stone, was left open with many wildly assorted pads and blankets and coverings scattered around. Gabriel thought of the encampment on Grith, the floor of the main clearing having been carefully scattered with branches and plant needles gathered for the purpose, and saw here a faint sad echo of the forest.

Food was served out to them with the great care of people who have not been expecting visitors and have little to spare, but are pleased to give them the best they can manage. There were no questions while they were eating. But when the bowls were taken away and the drink was brought out—mostly chai of a vile Phorcyn kind that Gabriel had had too much of while awaiting trial—many sesheyans gathered around them in a circle, and Gabriel got the sense that there would be grilling now. There was some, conducted politely enough in human idiom. Names and ship registries were demanded, along with details about how

Gabriel and Enda had come to meet Ondway and what had happened afterwards. The sesheyans sitting closest to them, many with guns nearby, listened to every word intently. Gabriel got the very strong feeling that had their story diverged at all significantly from what the sesheyans' own sources must have told them, Helm would have had to make his way home alone.

When they were finished, and Gabriel and Enda had detailed what they had brought in the ship and why, the adult sesheyans in the circle began visibly to relax. Gabriel seized the moment and said, "All I want to know is: what are you *doing* here? How did you get here? And how is it that no one knows?"

The colony leader, Kaiste, replied a little wearily, "I would not say that *no* one knows, alas for that. Since you have been kind enough to have come all this way, we will gladly tell you our history, or as much of it that matters. We cannot tell you all of it. That might be an unnecessary burden on you some day."

If VoidCorp got to hear about it, yes, I just bet, Gabriel thought.

"Obviously we have not been here for very long," said Kaiste, "about twenty standard years. We were originally a large subcontracted work crew who were transshipped here as what we think must have been a very early venture of the Company to investigate or perhaps even colonize this part of space. Certainly they sent us out with full colonial packs, though we were told that we would be executing a subcontract, doing subcontracted non-suited mining work."

" 'Ditchdigging,' " Enda said.

"Yes, but something happened. There was an accident in transit. We came a long way—many starfalls—and after perhaps twenty of them, the ship in which we were being transported suffered an explosion that either caused or was the result of some kind of stardrive failure. The explosion may even have been sabotage. The Company"—again he would not say its name—"was not popular on the world from which we had just been removed. I am not an expert and cannot describe the nature of the failure accurately, but the ship came out of drivespace after the failure and could not locate itself. There was a problem with its navigational systems as well, probably due to the explosion—one of the computers involved in the control of both systems was affected."

Kaiste looked a little bleak. "There is no way to put a good face on this, but we took our chance and rose up, killing almost all the Company people on the ship. Even with the chance that we might do nothing more after that than drift and die slowly in space, we could not let the possibility slip past and know for the rest of our lives that, if we had acted, we might be free. Indeed for some weeks there was confusion. Even among our own people there were killings until we established leadership and some kind of plan. Finally though, among the two thousand aboard, including some of the surviving humans, some of us were found who had a very little experience with stardrives and system drives. After many false starts we set course, as we thought, for Corrivale, hoping that surprise would allow us to reach Grith before the Company could do anything. Perhaps it was a feeble hope, but it was the only course that we could get all the people involved to agree to."

"So you set coordinates," Gabriel said, "and made starfall again."

"That we did. But there was either a fault in the coordinates, or another fault in the stardrive, or perhaps the same one. After five days we came out here. We knew where we were in a general way, but everyone was very afraid that if we tried another starfall, we would rise somewhere even less predictable—inside a sun, say. No one wanted to take another chance. So at last we stripped the ship of supplies and spent a month establishing a sealed colony down here. We used the ship's emergency supplies and shelters to seal and connect the natural caves we found here, which hold air nearly as well as they might water. Then we took our last few people off the ship in a shuttle and sent the ship out on her last starfall. No one knows where she made starrise, though as far as we know, the Company never found her again."

"And you've been here for twenty years," Gabriel said, "scratching out an existence."

"It has not been a proud life," said Kaiste, "but it has at least been a free one. A while after we came, we were finally able to make contact with the traders from Phorcys and Ino, and we traded them what few goods we had and were able to mine—we are good at that at least. We did a good business in the carboniferous stones—our rubies and sapphires are particularly fine."

"Surely you don't think to stay here forever?" Enda said.

Kaiste gazed across the room to where some small sesheyans were playing. An older child was scolding a younger one, who was pulling on his wings and rolling around on the floor. "Our children dream of the forests," Kaiste said. "We very much hope they will see them again. Or rather, for the first time."

"But why are you *still* here?" Gabriel said. "You're not that far from Grith. You could have arranged something—not with the traders maybe, but with some freighter firm based on Grith. Ondway would have helped you, or the people who worked with him."

Kaiste's head was bowed in what Gabriel was learning to recognize as the sesheyan version of shaking one's head "no." When he looked at Gabriel again, that distress was back in his eyes, and a chill ran down Gabriel's back, irrational but impossible to ignore.

Very softly, after a moment, Kaiste said, "We have been betrayed once before. I should say, almost betrayed. Ondway had contacted a trader, a freighter captain whom he trusted. He intended to bring us away from here to Grith on this human's ship in two or three quiet runs. The captain came to look the situation over. We made her welcome, ate fruit with her, did our best to keep her safe here in our home. Then we caught her in the very act of attempting to call VoidCorp to tell them of our presence here. So we killed her." A helpless shrug of the wings. "There was nothing else we could do to protect ourselves. Some among us thought to use her ship ourselves, but when we tried to power up the craft, the entire drive and computer system overloaded, frying the equipment. Apparently the captain had installed some sort of fail-safe device to prevent exactly what we were intending."

Kaiste took a small sip from the metal cup he held. "After that we decided that we would have no more such cases of self-defense on our consciences. Ondway tried to convince us otherwise, wanted to keep trying to organize a way out of here for us, but there would have been no way to be sure that, no matter how much he trusted those who offered him help, they might nevertheless have betrayed him and us. The Company is too powerful. The temptation of what they could offer another betrayer would always be too great. We had come too close to being recaptured or killed, and we would not take that chance again—or the chance of again causing Ondway such guilt and pain as he had suffered because of the captain's betrayal. We made him swear by the Three that he would never reveal our presence here to anyone or try to bring about our rescue, though he was sure he had other friends who would not betray him, humans and others who would have helped. Ondway's movements are simply watched too closely for him to retrieve us himself. Since the incident we have worked to find our own way away from here, no matter how long it takes."

Gabriel sat there in silence, thinking that the time involved might be generations if they kept thinking this way.

"You are very welcome for the supplies you bring and the concern you show," said Kaiste, "but we do not think you should stay longer than the night."

"We appreciate your concern for us," Gabriel said, "but—"

"No, you don't understand," said Kaiste. "This is not a safe place. It has never been a safe place, but now it is even less so."

Gabriel glanced around him at the other sesheyans who sat with them. Their eyes were full of a fear less controlled than Kaiste's.

"What is it?" Gabriel asked. "Let us help."

Kaiste hunched up his wings.

After a few moments one of the other sesheyans said, "The attacks started a year or so ago. It was particularly cruel, in a way, for things on this world were finally beginning to work correctly. We had enough food, the atmosphere was finally showing a little change, the heat was increasing—"

"Heat," Kaiste added. "That has been our main problem out this far in the system. But we had been working on it, and we were succeeding. We had enough technical expertise to begin tailoring gases that would increase the heat held in our atmosphere much more swiftly than might otherwise happen."

"Greenhousing," Enda said. "Terraforming worlds do that. Heat the atmosphere up first with a lot of noble gases, that kind of thing."

Kaiste bowed his wings in assent. "There is much activity below the planet's crust here, and we have been using the volcanism to help us. We mine for the gases that are of most help in heating up the atmosphere. Progress has been made even more quickly than we dared to hope, since we also found light oxides that we could 'crack' for free oxygen."

"It was always a temporary measure," said the other sesheyan, the female who had spoken. "There had always been two hopes for us before we were nearly betrayed. We would get away from here somehow—hire ships, or if we had to, build them— and smuggle ourselves that way to Grith. We know the difficulties," she said, lifting one claw before Gabriel could speak, "better than you believe, but we were willing enough to try. Otherwise—we would make this world marginally liveable and then eventually call on the Concord for aid. The people on Phorcys and Ino with whom we had been dealing said they would not interfere, but they would not help either. We would have to do it ourselves."

Gabriel thought of the plump, comfortable negotiators sitting around the table with the ambassador, sitting on this chilly little secret, and he had to immediately start disabling his own fury before it made him get up and start smashing things.

"Ships seemed impossible to come by," said Kaiste, "so for the time being we concentrated on making air that we could breathe, turning this world into somewhere we could stay while we made the tools to build the tools to construct the ships. We knew that sooner or later we would be noticed, but we kept very quiet and worked to keep that notice from happening for as long as possible. And life actually became settled. We had enough food for the first time, enough water, enough hope—just enough."

Kaiste shook his head. *"Then* came the near-betrayal—and after that the attacks started to come. Our people go out suited, to mine the various metals available here, to tend the various thermal caves where we have been providing light for crops and from which we release the greenhousing gases. What became plain was that someone was watching our comings and goings. Small ships began to come down from space and take our people. There is no time when we are safe from them. They come in gloom or dark; it's all one to them."

"Are these little round ships?" Gabriel asked, making the shape with his hands.

All the sesheyans around him froze. Kaiste looked at him with great suspicion, his foremost eyes narrowing.

"Some have reported such," he answered, "but it is very unusual to see them and live afterward. For a long time they were simply another kind of *unhewoi*, something that came and vanished, taking one of us with it."

"Unhewoi?" Gabriel asked.

Enda tilted her head to one side as if shaking her head in regret. "It is a word for the Taker," she said, "the Beast that waits in the shadow of the woods and snatches you away. Bad sesheyan children are threatened with the *Unhewoi* if they don't behave. Many species have such a figure," Enda shivered, "But none expect it to become real."

"For months now we have scarcely dared to go out," said Kaiste. "Our situation was bad enough when the traders stopped coming. We thought perhaps the Company had somehow gotten wind of us, even though the freighter captain had not been able to complete her message to them. Our fear was great, and our privation has slowly been growing. We were depending too

much, perhaps, on what the traders brought us. Then this worse
danger came upon us, and though we need trade, we dare not
expose others to the danger. Others have tried to come, even
from Grith, but we have warned them to stop lest they too be
taken. We live in a prison now, and we do not know for sure how
we will ever escape."

Gabriel's heart turned over in him. It would be a long time
before he forgot his own taste of prison and the possibility of
living in it forever. "There must be something we can do for
you."

"The kindest thing is to leave," said Kaiste. "The attacks are
always worse after people from Outside are here. We are resigned to our fate. We made it ourselves; we must bear it
ourselves." He shuddered. "Worse yet, we would not be able to
bear it if they came and took you."

That image of Enda, dead in a gel-filled suit, the blue eyes
quenched, her face stretched and distorted with rage and pain, hit
Gabriel again—hit him so hard that it was all he could do to keep
from jumping to his feet and heading back to *Sunshine*.

He looked up after a moment. "We'll go tomorrow," Gabriel
said, "but I don't promise not to come back."

Kaiste shook his head. "Your courage does you credit, but
you only endanger us as well as yourselves. Please go with our
good will. You will keep our secret from the Company, I know.
But beware to whom you speak of us. They do not forget."

* * * * *

No one had much heart for conversation after that. The
sesheyans showed Gabriel and Enda to a screened-off cubicle
where they could have some privacy until the morning. There
was no problem regarding warmth—the stone wall to one side of
them was hot, and a pool of hot water bubbled up in the corner
of their cubicle. But Gabriel had no joy of it, though at any other
time he would have stood on his head in a pool half the size and
praised it all out of proportion.

"We have to do something to help them," he said for about the twentieth time, some hours after they had been left there. Sleep would not come anywhere near him, and Enda had given up on it too since Gabriel plainly could neither lie still nor be quiet.

"I wait to hear a plan from you," Enda said rather wearily, "but I have yet to hear anything coherent."

"It's hard to plan coherently when there's still the matter of those VoidCorp fighters to think about."

"They are no longer a problem, I would have thought."

"That's not what I mean. Where did they come from? It's not that they couldn't have had stardrive, but it's not all that usual. It would make more sense for their base carrier to be around here somewhere, yet there's been no sign of it."

"Possibly they're afraid of attracting as much attention as such a large VoidCorp ship would produce should it appear in Thalaassa system without warning," Enda replied, "especially if they thought *Schmetterling* was going to be here to take official notice."

"I don't believe they wouldn't be pretty well informed of the comings and goings of Concord ships," Gabriel said. Still Enda might have a point. Or there might be some other reason entirely.

He sighed and sat down. "I just don't know," he said. "If I could only—"

Both their handheld comm receivers, tucked in their pockets, beeped softly. Gabriel looked at Enda, who shook her head and reached into her pocket to turn hers off.

The air whispered in Gabriel's ear that this was a mistake. He swallowed, then shook his head and took his comm out, thumbing it open for reception.

"You two still awake down there?" said Helm's voice from both their handhelds.

Enda gave Gabriel a rather dire look, for all around them the cavern had suddenly gone very quiet. Gabriel swallowed again, very certain that this was not because everyone had suddenly gone to bed.

"Helm," Enda said, "I fear dawn will have no secrets from either of us. Why are you still awake?"

"Not my night yet. I was talking to Delde Sota."

"Statement: still is," came the doctor's voice down the comms.

"Delde Sota," Gabriel said immediately, "you are an angel with a wire hairdo. I will change your batteries any time, but what are you doing in this system?"

Delde Sota snickered. "Conjecture: thought gallantry was dead. Objective statement: Helm called me earlier, suggested presence here might be useful. Made excuse to Iphus authorities, called in favor, found outgoing transport. Location: Ino at moment, completing 'supply run.' Needed to do some shopping anyway."

"An angel," Gabriel repeated, "but the analysis—can you do that from this distance?"

"Affirm," Delde Sota said. "I am on the Grid. Helm is on the Grid. *Longshot's* computer is on the Grid and connects to my sensor extension—my braid—in his weapons bay. Object is in his weapons bay. Preparing now."

"The braid has one of those atomic-level microporous tendril attachments," Helm said. "All she has to do is touch it to something and it goes right through—"

"I've seen it," Gabriel said. "Slick."

"Request: quiet for a moment please," Delde Sota said. "Interfacing."

Gabriel and Enda looked at each other. The silence in the cavern was even greater than it had been. Kaiste was standing in the opening between their private space and the main hall, looking at them grimly with a sabot pistol in his claw.

Gabriel looked up at him, wondering whether this was something that would have happened whether he and Enda had suddenly started to communicate with someone on the outside or not. Did they ever intend to let us leave, really? Have we been under a death sentence since we got here, no matter how good our intentions were? Not that it mattered now.

"Kaiste, it's Ondway's friends we're talking to," Gabriel explained and surprised himself somewhat with his own anger. "They know you're here, and they haven't betrayed you any more than we intend to. If you're going to shoot us, at least wait until the doctor finds out what you need to know. Then do what you like." He turned his back on Kaiste, rude though it was. His back itched at the feeling of the pistol leveled at it.

And itched, and itched, but he would not turn around again.

"Initial result," Delde Sota said then. "It is a chemical/enzymatic device. Catalytic compounds . . ." She trailed off.

There was something peculiar about her silence, and apparently Enda heard it too. "Doctor, are you all right?"

"Analyzing." A long silence.

"Conjecture:" Delde Sota said then, "device is intended to promote a catalytic reaction in atmosphere. Catalyzation starts high up, near space altitudes. All free or atmospheric oxygen is catalyzed into 'locked' forms, clathrates and other similar structures, using nitrogen and other gaseous atoms to construct the clathrates. Such structures bind the atoms into 'cages' in which they are inaccessible and from which they cannot escape. Over only very long periods the clathrate 'cages' would disintegrate."

"What would happen if you dropped this into a planet's atmosphere?" Gabriel asked.

"All oxygen in it would become sequestered in clathrate form." Delde Sota's voice was getting angry. Gabriel could just see those dark eyes and the anger in them. "Such oxygen is not respirable. It enters the lungs, but oxygen is not able to bond with hemoglobin in human blood cells, cyanoglobin in sesheyan blood, and so forth. It passes out of the lungs again unused and unusable. Breathing does no good. You breathe freely yet die of suffocation within minutes."

"And then the clathrates disintegrate," Enda said softly.

"Leaving the oxygen slowly freeing itself for use again. Months, perhaps. Weeks, more likely."

"So that after everything that breathed oxygen on a given

planet was dead," Gabriel said softly, "the planet itself would be usable again after a while."

"Why waste perfectly good infrastructure investment?" said Doctor Delde Sota, almost in a growl. "Plants remain unhurt since plants use nitrogen, and plenty of free nitrogen is left. Planet surface is cleansed of undesirable organisms— non-Employee sesheyans, for example."

Suddenly Gabriel thought of that VoidCorp cruiser he had seen heading nonchalantly toward Grith in a maneuver that looked like it was simply using Hydrocus's gravity to slingshot around the two worlds. But something else was going on. Such a maneuver might look like an energy saving move at first. For a cruiser like that, though, it had to cost more energy to set up than it would or could possibly save.

What was it practicing for? Gabriel thought. Insertion of something into the high atmosphere . . . Now, only now, he turned to look at Kaiste again. The sesheyan was standing there, the pistol lowered, looking stricken. "Yes," Gabriel said. "Non-Employee sesheyans, and not just these, either."

Enda was staring at him "What?" Helm said. "Who?"

"*The ones on Grith*," Gabriel said.

Enda's mouth fell open. "But there are thousands of humans there as well, and fraal, and other species. All the Hatire settlers at Diamond Point, and the people scattered through the jungles, and . . ." She trailed off.

"Not VoidCorp employees, though," said Gabriel. "Not *real* people." He was thinking again about Delvecchio's rueful remarks about how long it took to turn other beings into people, or at least the kind of people worthy of being treated like Us.

"They would destabilize the whole system," Enda said slowly. "They would start a war here, and it would spread. They might have wiped out a Hatire colony once, but they would not get away with it twice."

"Wouldn't they? Since when have they cared about a war or two?" Gabriel said. "This is *VoidCorp* we're discussing. Their business, long term and short term, is to *win*, and they can't win as long as there's a colony of renegade sesheyans sitting right out under their noses on Grith, flaunting 'their' contract with the Company! So they'll kill them, but they'll make sure their little gadget works here and kill *these* sesheyans first, because two colonies of free sesheyans are even worse than just one."

"The Concord," said Enda slowly, "cannot allow them to get away with this."

Gabriel did not share his immediate thought. Perhaps the Concord did *not* intend to let them get away with this, and he—and to a lesser extent Enda—were the tools that the Concord were employing to this purpose. The issue had come up for consideration before. Isn't a willing tool still a tool? Gabriel was now finding aspects of the question that he had not considered before. He had occasionally spent some time wondering what good he might be doing Lorand Kharls. Now he found himself wondering what good Lorand Kharls might do *him*, and whether the tool might not turn in the hand of its user in ways that even the user might find surprising.

More—and in a more shadowy manner—the idea was beginning to creep up on Gabriel that there were other kinds of service to the Concord than the strictly military ones and that willing service might change the nature of everything that had gone before it.

Enda's getting to me, he thought, putting that thought aside for the moment. "So that's why that thing was signaling," Gabriel said. "It was waiting for the sesheyans in the attack force to lock onto it and give it the signal to go active. Their bosses didn't want to leave it on automatic. There might have been some reason to abort the attack suddenly."

"Like if a Concord ship turned up suddenly," said Enda.

"Yes."

"And when we turned up, some of them went to go ahead with the delivery, thinking there would be no witnesses, until we started to get a little the better of the situation," Enda said, "at which point the insertion must have been called off. The ships detailed to it came back to finish us off."

"With the results we saw." Gabriel sighed. "Did they make that decision themselves, though? Or did someone order them to? Did they have a chance to report to whoever was in charge of the attack?"

"For all we know, the whole thing was being watched remotely by their masters elsewhere," Enda said. "In fact it seems all too likely. I think we must expect them to return, and in short order."

"On top of everything else, they were using Employee sesheyans to deliver this thing." Gabriel grimaced.

"Probably from VoidCorp's point of view, that just made it even more fun," Helm said.

Gabriel put his head down in his hands—then looked up again, looked over at Kaiste. "Kaiste, you've got to leave," he said. "You've got to get out of here. There's no way VoidCorp can have intended to try something like this and fail to carry it through eventually. You have to come with us."

"In two ships?" Enda said, very softly. "There are at least three thousand sesheyans here."

Gabriel shook his head. "Delde Sota, thanks for the analysis. We may need some more help from you before this is over."

"Call when ready," she said, and the line clicked.

"Helm," Gabriel said.

"I'll be up a while yet."

"Stay ready. We may have to do something in a hurry."

"Like what?"

I have no idea!

"I'll let you know before morning," Gabriel said.

He turned again, but Kaiste had vanished from the doorway out into the silence and the dimness of the cavern.

* * * * *

Earlier, the time seemed to be dragging, but now it seemed to be fleeing by, unfairly swiftly, and Gabriel snatched at every moment of it, hoping that the next moment might give him the idea he needed. But every moment that went by without an answer said in his ear, *You blew it.*

Enda sat by the little hot pool with her eyes closed, listening to him. This was something Gabriel had seen her do on *Sunshine.* She often looked as if she were sleeping, but she never missed a word. Now he paced and talked as he might have done with Delvecchio in those far lost days on *Falada.*

"The Concord ought to be here," he kept saying. "Why aren't they here?"

"Indeed," Enda said after a moment, her eyes still closed, "I would have thought that because of the treaty, the Concord's attention would have been turned much more intently toward this system."

"I think that may be why things have heated up here." Gabriel said. For a moment it was as if it was not Enda sitting there but Delvecchio. Odd how he could almost feel that prickly, amused presence nearby. "Enda, think about the situation as it was. Phorcys and Ino hate each other, but neither is averse to doing a little trading on the side with a tiny colony of sesheyans well out in the middle of nowhere. No one else is interested in that colony. It remains the Thalaassan worlds' little secret, though they understand perfectly well what VoidCorp's response will be if it ever finds out about this place. The Company moves in and deals with this little colony, probably terminally. Then, understanding that Phorcys and Ino will have known about this place but never informed VoidCorp about it, the Company moves into the Thalaassa system with intent. Oh, outwardly it's all very much on the up and up. Development, progress, sell us a few of your outer planets—you don't need them. Sell us some of the bigger companies on your worlds, we'll make them work better. Economies of scale, all the usual excuses. So that would happen too. Soon enough VoidCorp would have a major hold on this system, and once it controlled most things, that's when the revenge would start. The Company has a long memory.

"Then all of a sudden the Concord shows up and starts insisting that Phorcys and Ino stop fighting one another, make peace, lay everything out on the table where it can all be seen. Well, on the one hand, the governments on Phorcys and Ino are absolutely delighted. Here's possibly the only force that can keep the Corpses from eating the whole Thalaassa system alive. At the same time, they don't really want to stop fighting, and they also know that if the Concord finds out about this little colony of sesheyans on Rhynchus, there'll be trouble.

"So it's never mentioned, at first. Then the treaty comes close to being ready to sign. Now, both governments know they can't make a treaty 'disposition' of their system without mentioning it. Yet if they *do* mention Rhynchus, one way or the other, they're straight down the hole. VoidCorp will never forgive them if the Concord makes an issue of this the way they did of Grith . . . and they will. There will be two Griths, one of them in the Thalaassa system, a much less well protected system than Corrivale is, and sooner or later the wrath of VoidCorp will fall on Rhynchus—and on Phorcys and Ino as well. Yet if they *don't* mention the colony on Rhynchus, there's trouble as well. The language of the treaty they signed requires both planets to help to 'protect and defend the sovereignty of all inhabited worlds in the system.' That will have to include Rhynchus, even though no one has mentioned it. When the Concord finds out what's going on there, and what's *been* going on, they'll be furious, and they'll probably withdraw their protection, leaving Phorcys and Ino in just as bad a spot."

Gabriel sat down and thought for a moment, reaching for a cup of chai the sesheyans had left him. "So. Here it starts to get iffy. But I would lay money that at this point, VoidCorp suddenly switched roles and offered to be the 'good cop.' Some soft-voiced, well-dressed type at level Q or better turns up in the offices of the lord president of Phorcys and the delegate of Ino and says, 'Don't get all concerned now. We can do you a little favor, solve your problems, solve our problems. Then everybody will be happy.' What they suggest is that they're going to get rid of the colony on Rhynchus. Sterilize it." The anger was building in him again, but he didn't care. "That way, there will be no dirty little secret for the Concord to discover when they come in after the treaty and start doing detailed scans and assessments on all the planets in the system to determine where the assistance programs and so forth will go. Naturally VoidCorp will be very grateful. Probably the gratitude would at first take the form of them not moving to take over the system wholesale." Gabriel grinned. "My guess is that they'd wait for the Concord to finish the assay sweeps, let *them* spend the money to find out whether there's any reason to stay in the place. Resources, whatever. *Then* move in. Or, if there's nothing worth the taking, leave the place alone. Otherwise . . . until there's enough other infrastructure in place in this part of the Verge to come back inexpensively and take over the system."

"The Company," Enda said softly, "has a long memory."

Gabriel nodded. "Revenge." He put his chai down. "There are other problems."

"Yes," Enda said. "Silver Bell."

Oleg's dead face came up before Gabriel's eyes again. Who's doing this? he thought. These—people—well, they were people once. Now they move, they act, but are they alive?

Who takes a dead person and brings him "alive" again, then sends him out to fight and kill?

He shook his head.

"What will we do?" Enda asked.

Gabriel sighed. "I need more time."

"I think there is no more time," Enda said. "It is dawn."

* * * * *

He and Enda stepped out of the caves for a breath of fresh air and to see the new light. Dawn did not make that much difference here. At this distance Thalaassa was only a small disk, just a step up from a super bright star, its light at noon not much brighter than a misty morning or a very bright moonlit night on Bluefall in Gabriel's childhood. Still it was a change from the blackness of night or the closeness inside the caves.

Gabriel stood out at the edge of the landing field, looking up. The sky here was dark, partly because of the distance from Thalaassa, partly because there was still not that much oxygen or nitrogen to refract the sunlight. The early morning was cloudless—no surprise, the planet had shown little weather when they arrived yesterday. High up, though, there was one long streak of cloud, catching the pale sun, burning surprisingly bright.

Gabriel looked at it. "Has Helm been dipping down into atmosphere?" he said to Enda.

"Why would he do that?"

"Well, that almost looks like a contrail—"

They both stared at it, pausing to nod at Kaiste as he came out behind them and looked up to see the contrail as well. Gabriel glanced at Kaiste and got out his handheld. "Helm?"

A pause. "What?"

"Have you been in atmosphere?"

"Me? Hardly."

"Then what's that contrail up there?"

A long silence. Then, slowly, eloquently, Helm began to swear.

"What? What?" Gabriel asked frantically, but he already knew.

"The sensors say," said Helm, "that it's clathrates. Clathrates of nitrogen."

Gabriel's heart seized up inside him. Something up there was changing the way the air reflected the little sunlight it got from Thalaassa, changing the atmosphere's constitution.

"*Aiai,*" Enda said softly. "They had another one."

"Of course they did," Gabriel said, groaning. "No one ever makes just *one* weapon. And they had to use it quickly because their attack force was seen or because their first bomb was found. Helm, *how did they get past you?*"

He was swearing again, but he stopped long enough to answer. "Not impossible, if there's just one ship in orbit and you stay on the far side of the planet from it at all times. If the ship is small enough—"

What fourteen didn't do, one did, Gabriel thought bitterly.

"How fast will the change come?"

"From what Delde Sota said, pretty fast. It's a catalytic process. Maybe only a few hours to sweep around the planet. Another couple of hours to work right down into the lower atmosphere. After that—"

"After that we will start to die," said Kaiste softly. "We do not have machines to make air from stone the way the satellite colonies do. We take our air from outside, concentrate it, filter it, and process it. If within a few hours there will be no more—then a few hours after that, we will start to die."

They all looked at one another in horror.

"We've got to get everyone out of here," Gabriel said. "Now!"

"There is no way!" protested Kaiste. "There are three thousand of us! We have no ships!"

"We have two," Gabriel said.

"Are you crazy?" Helm said over the handheld. "How many people can we fit in our two little ships? What's the use of saving a few when all the rest are going to be left behind?"

"We can't just give it up. We have to save as many as we can. We can't just leave them here!" Gabriel's mind was going in furious circles. They had to have help, but there was no help. Even if he called for help right now and it agreed to come, it would take five days to get here.

Above him, the contrail from the weapon's insertion into atmosphere burned bright. The refraction effect from it was fading somewhat, but spreading. *Only a few hours.* He looked around him at what was about to become a graveyard for three thousand sesheyans. This desperate little colony of caves and tunnels, everything kept so tidy and neat, even the discarded shipping containers and other rubbish from Phorcys and Ino all carefully stacked and stored out of the way and out of sight, because they must not be destroyed since you could never tell when you might find a way to recycle something. Nothing was wasted. Everything used carefully, cleverly, everything—

Gabriel stopped.

"A few hours," he said to himself. "It just might be time enough."

He turned and ran off in the direction of the cave where *Sunshine* was hidden. "Gabriel," Enda cried, "where are you going?"

"I need my imager," he shouted, "then I have a few comm-calls to make."

Chapter Eighteen

IT WAS NEARLY an hour before Gabriel was ready. He made his way through the caves and storage caverns, ignoring the frightened sesheyans as best he could while he used his little handheld portable imager—a leftover from their tourist time on Grith—to get the images he needed and then to prepare the messages that had to be stored and ready to go. At last he got back into *Sunshine*, got onto the Thalaassan Grid, and found the communications networks he needed. He arranged for a dual conversation—ruinously expensive though it would be—and set about getting in contact with the two people with whom he needed to speak.

It took him a long time to get connected with them. He had to start at a certain level of lackey on both Phorcys and Ino—otherwise they would just have cut him off, not knowing enough to understand what he was threatening them with—and then he had to argue with them, one after another. But he would not take no for an answer, and the work became slightly easier when Gabriel began reaching the level of lackeys who recognized him from his presence around the peace talks with Delvecchio. To each of these people, Gabriel said only one word: Rhynchus. Most of them went pale at the sound of it. Some of them blustered, some of them bluffed, some of them he had to show an image or two to get the desired result, but each of them finally passed him up a level, glad to be rid of the uncomfortable presence at the other end of the comm, the set face that seemed to promise somebody was in a world of trouble and if they acted correctly it might not be them.

Finally Gabriel had the two of them on one screen: flat-faced old Rallet, looking not a whit less dyspeptic than when Gabriel had seen him last, and ErDaishan with that mouth like a razor cut stretched tight as usual. Both were annoyed and disdainful—and both looked ever so slightly uncomfortable.

They both started in on him at once.

"I hope you understand the irregularity—"

"—little chance that you would have anything of import to—"

"Rhynchus," Gabriel said. "Regarding the sesheyan colony here."

The two looked suitably shocked, but neither of them said a word.

"I know all about what's been going on here," Gabriel said, "and specifically, I know all about what's *just* happened. So will many others, shortly. I intend to inform the Concord. Lorand Kharls, the Concord Administrator in these parts, has been showing great interest in your system, as you know, subsequent to the signing of the treaty. He will be very interested to see all the physical evidence on Rhynchus of your long trade with the sesheyan colony on that world that somehow managed to go completely unmentioned while the negotiations were going on—as I know very well." Gabriel smiled nastily as something occurred to him. "That was possibly another reason for my 'not proven' verdict, wasn't it? A verdict designed to get everyone to lose interest, to go away and let you be. Either the 'guilty' or 'innocent' verdict might have produced further investigation in the system, and who knew what that might have turned up? All that used Phorcyn and Inoan hardware scattered here and there on Rhynchus, built into the caves where the sesheyans are living, all very incriminating. It could well be badly misunderstood, certainly by the Concord and possibly by others as well."

Neither of the two former negotiators said anything.

"The sesheyans on Rhynchus are now in danger of their lives," Gabriel continued. "If things go the way they're going at the moment, you're going to be parties to a genocidal attack. I think once the investigations start, it'll take very little time for the investigators to turn up all kinds of proof. However, there's another way out of this that is much better for you. You don't want the sesheyans here any more? Fine. We can help you with that. They'll be more than welcome on Grith, eventually, but right now their planet is losing what little atmosphere it has. The sesheyans must leave, but they have no ships, and we only have two. So here's the plan. You send us enough ships to move them all to somewhere quiet on one of your planets—just for a few days—and after that we can arrange clandestine transfer out of the system for them so that VoidCorp won't be in any position to blame you."

"What guarantee have we that they'll leave again?"

"Do you think they *want* to stay in this system?" Gabriel shouted. "Are you *crazy?* After the way you've treated them in the past? After the way you were willing to let VoidCorp 'erase' your little problem for you now?"

"Young man, you will not address me in that tone!"

Gabriel wished he had Delvecchio's cane. He would not have simply banged it on the table, either. It would have come right down on Rallet's head. "You can both stuff my tone right up—" Gabriel began. Both Rallet and ErDaishan paled with genuine shock. "Never mind. I'll start speaking to you like responsible statesmen when you start acting like them and not like cowards or thugs. The minute you earn my respect, you'll be addressed with respect. Meanwhile, I have a message ready for the Concord Administrator right now, and there are people down here gasping for breath. It's not going to go on that way for a moment more. You will give me an answer. *Now.*"

There was silence at the other end. Then Rallet slowly said, "As Minister of State for Defense, this lies most easily in my remit. I will detach a small complement of ships—"

"I need transport for three thousand sesheyans as well as medical relief and food and drink for them," Gabriel said. "I need it in an hour. Before we break this communication, I need relay and comms information for the relieving ships, and when I contact their commanding officers in a few minutes, they had

better confirm your orders to them. Otherwise Lorand Kharls
gets this," he held up a data solid, "*immediately*, with no further
communications from me to you. Granted there will be a delay
in him receiving the message, but it won't matter. If anything
happens to these people because of your inaction, he will come
down on you anyway. But if you save them, you'll be heroes,
and all will be forgiven."

"I can persuade our emergency services to send ships out,"
said ErDaishan. "Much better equipped for an evacuation than
theirs."

Gabriel could have laughed out loud to see the good old
Phorcyn/Inoan hostility coming out here of all times, but he was
too angry for laughter now. "Good. Send them. Send them now.
I want their commcodes and the their captains' names. *Now.*"

He got them. Within ten minutes Enda had contacted the
commanders of seven different ships and was preparing hails for
eight others. "One more thing," Gabriel said, as he finished sorting them out and went back to his connection to the negotiators.
"How many of the ships are drive-capable?"

There was some bemusement at that. "Maybe half," said the
Phorcyn negotiator.

"All of ours."

"We'll be loading them first," Gabriel said. "I'll advise
them."

"But you said you were bringing them to Phorcys—"

"I like to be prepared for accidents," Gabriel interrupted.
"There have been too many of those lately. Get them out here.
Now." And he held up the data solid one more time.

"And when they arrive—?"

"When the sesheyans are safe," Gabriel said, "I will praise
your statesmanlike response to the skies and to Lorand Kharls.
You will look like heroes, shining examples of the newfound
cooperation between Phorcys and Ino, a new era of peace and
reconciliation, blah, blah, blah. I hope one or the other of you
has an election scheduled sometime soon, because you'll do
very well."

He saw the slightly gloating looks cross both their faces. They *both* have elections. Oh my.

"That's all for now," said Gabriel and reached out to cut the comm connection. "I'll speak to you later."

"You might at least say 'thank you,' " grumbled the Inoan negotiator.

"When I've seen the ships," Gabriel said as he waved the data solid at her and cut the link.

* * * * *

An hour later the ships began to drop into the Rhynchan atmosphere. There was already markedly less of it than there had been—less that was breathable, anyway. The sky was getting more pallid, a side effect of the clathrating nitrogen, Enda told Gabriel. When it reached its palest, all the oxygen would be inaccessible. Gabriel did not plan to be here that long.

The problem now was that the capacity of the ships that the Phorcyns and Inoans had sent was not terribly large. "It'll have to be two runs," Gabriel said to the captain of *Orniol*, one of the first ships to load—a drive-capable Phorcyn emergency vessel usually used for medical transport.

"They told us only one," said *Orniol's* captain, a short stocky woman with what seemed a perpetually mournful look. "Out here and straight back to Phorcys."

"I hate to break this to you," Gabriel said, "but that will still leave something like fifteen hundred people down here while the rest of the atmosphere goes bad. It's not acceptable. I'll get on to your upper-ups again if I have to, but I tell you, if I have to do that I won't like it, and *they* won't like it. And I promise you, neither will you."

Gabriel turned and stomped off to supervise the loading of another of the ships, *Glatha,* which appeared from the condition of its cargo bays to have been doing garbage hauling. Beggars can't choose, Gabriel thought as sesheyans with small bundles of their personal belongings started to pile into it. Dear stars, when I think about what Hal had to go through putting fancy toilet seats in the shuttles for the Phorcyn and Inoan delegations. He tried to calm himself. It was not easy.

The loading seemed to take forever, and a couple of the ships were still not here. One more landed while he watched. Gabriel kept looking up at the sky, and finally there came a moment when it seemed to be getting no paler. What was that flicker? he wondered.

"I think night is coming," Enda said softly from behind him.

Gabriel shivered. Something worse was coming. "Get them in," he said. "Hurry! We have to leave."

"What? Gabriel—"

He could only look at her and run for *Sunshine*.

That was when the plasma fire began raining down around them.

Screams and roars of fear broke out. The sesheyans caught in the open dove for the caves. Those nearest the ships crowded into them, and the ships sealed up. Engines began to heat—the ships' captains had no desire to be on the ground for a second longer. Ships began lifting. Gabriel pelted toward *Sunshine* with Enda hard behind him.

As he ran, he yelled into his handheld, "Helm, heads up! The body snatchers are here!"

"What?"

"Ball bearing-shaped ships! Fire on them! Hit everything you can, and for all sakes don't let any of them hit you! Then follow us. We've got to get out of here!"

"Where?"

It's going to have to be drivespace, Gabriel thought, horrified. We're not ready, but there's nowhere else to go. "Grith!" he yelled. "Make for Grith! But we need cover!"

"Can do," Helm said, very calmly. "Boy, Delde Sota's gonna owe me for this one when we're done."

Gabriel and Enda dove into *Sunshine*, strapped in, and closed her up. In the back areas were several frightened sesheyans, all

of them rather young, who had been sightseeing while the loading was going on. Now they were locked in for good or ill.

"Hang onto things, kids," Gabriel yelled as he fastened the
final strap, "and whatever you do, don't let go!" He had to stop.
Sunshine's lifters were shaking him all over the place.

"All ships, all ships, drivespace as soon as you're out!"
Gabriel yelled into the public comms as Enda flung them
upward into the atmosphere. "Make for the homeworld! Make
for the sesheyan sanctuary!" He could only hope they understood. He was not going to mention names or coordinates over
public comms at this point.

A scream and babble of answers came back, terrified, confused. "Affirmative, understood." "—can't do it, we don't have
stardrive!" "—no supplies, we're—" "—stay and fight—"

"Just go!" Gabriel shouted. "We'll lead! Those of you that
can't follow, make for Phorcys, full speed! Don't let them get
you out in the dark. Make them do it in the sunlight where
people can see! Go on, run for it! The rest of you with stardrive,
follow us!"

Sunshine leaped upward into the middle atmosphere. The
swarm of enemy ships was only a few kilometers above them
now. Oh, dear heaven, the other sesheyans— For there were perhaps another thousand of them fleeing back into the caves.
Would they be safe there? Would the body snatchers decide
there was nothing left to lose and simply wipe them out, taking
them all to make soldiers? Cut their wings off, steal their
souls—

Gabriel wiped his wet face and cursed. The JustWadeIn software was already up, and Enda was already in it. Gabriel pulled
the fighting field down over him, picked one of the small round
targets that was hurtling at them, cursed it soundly, and fired. It
sidestepped. He fired again—

He did not remember much of that fight afterwards. Gabriel
kept hearing screams and was uncertain where they were
coming from: comms on the ground, comms in space, perhaps
from the other four ships that had lifted with them, and that

were clustered in very loose order around *Sunshine*, heading into the upper atmosphere. That paling sky was stitched with plasma fire, ships were diving in all directions, and Gabriel fired and fired at small round ships that would not stay still.

Then suddenly a gravelly voice said, "*Sunshine*, I've got one more cherry."

Gabriel ungritted his teeth. "Pop it. When?"

"Ten seconds."

"All ships," Gabriel said down comms, "cluster close on me five seconds, then scatter. Afterwards, head for atmosphere's top and make starfall. Don't wait!"

More screaming erupted. But suddenly the view around *Sunshine*'s cockpit had entirely too many ships in it, entirely too close. Around them, he could see ballbearings closing in. Don't let them shoot, he thought. For them, it doesn't matter if we're dead, and oh, I don't want to be dead that way.

He kept firing. "Now," Gabriel said softly down comms. The other ships scattered outwards, and suddenly he was left surrounded by too many of the spherical ships. Enda held them there. Gabriel glanced briefly at her then said, *Now's the time.*

She wrenched them sideways. White hot beams of plasma scalded past the cockpit windows as *Sunshine* tumbled and dove out from under the crowd of ships. Then Enda kicked the system drive in at full power, the air screaming in protest against her skin as *Sunshine* fled upwards.

Behind them, the world went white.

They were at nearly twenty kilometers. A squeezed nuke shouldn't do too much harm at this altitude, Gabriel thought rather desperately. Nothing that the atmosphere becoming useless in a few hours wouldn't do anyway.

To the thousand people down there that we couldn't get off before they came.

A thousand people!

"Starfall," Enda said to the other ships, *"now!"*

A thousand people.

* * * * *

The next five days were less easy to bear for Gabriel. They were full of fear. Aboard *Sunshine*, there was not that much physical discomfort. They were carrying enough supplies to feed the sesheyans who had been on board when takeoff became imperative, but there was no contact with the other ships to see in what condition they had made their own starfalls, whether the people aboard them were mostly well, or how they were now. Gabriel knew for a fact that three of the four ships that had arrived had only a little food and water on board, despite his demands. Someone had messed up, or there had been no time, or . . . There had been little time for explanations. They would be getting hungry over in the other ships, and thirsty. They would not know what awaited them on the far side when they made starrise at Corrivale.

Gabriel had his own fears about that. VoidCorp loomed large in them. He doubted that the body snatchers would turn up near Grith. They did seem to prefer the dark. Had there been more of them waiting to descend on Rhynchus after the escape? Even if there had not, would the other ships get there in time to remove the remaining sesheyans before the air ran out?

There were no answers. There would be none until they made starrise, and perhaps not for a good while after that. Gabriel, for the time being, could only spend as much time with the sesheyan youngsters as he could, showing them how to play the non-Grid based games on the entertainment system and trying to comfort them when they were afraid— which was fairly often. They did not know where their parents were and without that basic certainty, they would not talk about much of anything else. Gabriel came to recognize the sound of sesheyan weeping, a kind of breathy gasp. It kept him up at night.

Five days, though, eventually passed. Gabriel strapped himself back in and looked somberly looked over at Enda as the digits on the clock in the tank slipped away. Despite the fact that another possible fight loomed ahead, they were both unsuited. Even if they had sufficient e-suits for everyone to wear, their models would not fit the sesheyans in size or design and it didn't seem right to ensure their own safety while leaving their passengers in danger.

"How are your hunches running?" Enda asked. Less than a minute remained on the countdown.

Gabriel shook his head. "Not a whisper. You?"

"Mine have been regrettably silent."

"Do your people think that means something bad?"

"Some of my people," she said, smiling just slightly—a very sad smile—"think it means you are already dead. Granted, those people would mostly be mindwalkers to whom my normal state of mind would be a pitiful thing indeed. So I do not take them too seriously."

Gabriel nodded. "Enda," he said. "If those body snatchers ever get close to us—"

"I will not be a willing participant," she said, "believe me."

"I don't want to be either," Gabriel said.

She looked at him and blinked slowly, hiding the great blue eyes for a moment. "I will see to it," she said.

"Thirty seconds," Gabriel called to the youngsters in the back. "Get strapped in."

"Right," they said, more or less in chorus. They had not been speaking in staves, and Gabriel found himself wondering whether they usually did so at home and whether he was going to have to pay some kind of outrageous faceprice to their parents for teaching them awful habits.

The seconds ticked by. Twenty . . . ten. There was nervous shuffling in the back of the ship. Gabriel tried to swallow, finding his mouth too dry.

Zero.

Light sheeted down around them as they made starrise. It was red, red as blood that light, and surely it was an illusion that it seemed to run more slowly than usual, slicking down from the cockpit windows to show Corrivale's welcome blast of sunlight off to the left. And off to the right—

—darkness.

Massive, an elongated teardrop shape with VoidCorp insignia, lazing in toward Hydrocus. It could not have been more than ten kilometers away from them, and it still looked immense. Gabriel tried one more time to swallow, then gave it up. There were five other smaller vessels with it, gaudier in their livery—reds and golds and gunfire blues—but all of them wore that insignia, and all their guns were shivering with the electrostatic discharge that suggested they were ready to fire.

Around *Sunshine*, first one other of the refugee ships made starrise in a blast of purple, and then a second, mostly green streaked with yellow. The third did not appear. *Timing error? Gabriel whispered in the fighting field. Or did it jump at all? Never mind,* and he cried to the other ships, *"Scatter!"*

They did, possibly knowing it was the only way to save their lives. The smaller VoidCorp ships went off in pursuit of them severally; one held its place, the biggest of them, hanging above Grith, waiting. *Have you got another of your little toys aboard?* Gabriel thought. He watched that ship carefully to see if it started anything like the maneuver he had seen the earlier Void-Corp ship practicing above Grith. *I don't have a weapon that would make a dustgrain's worth of difference against* that . . . but if necessary, *Sunshine* could punch a real good hole in her updecks, possibly destroy her bridge, certainly leave her in no position for any fancy maneuvering. *Enda* . . . he said in the field.

Gabriel, Enda said, *sometimes you are very audible indeed, or rather, your imagery radiates well.* She shivered. *Possibly I am having some contaminating influence upon you. At any rate, if you think you must exercise such an option for the lives at stake, the price is more than fair, I would say.*

Gabriel swallowed hard, twice. *Always nice to have support from a partner,* he said, and as the VoidCorp vessel started to move slowly toward Grith, Gabriel started to choose his target, getting ready to tell the computer what to do.

The fire of starrise broke out not five kilometers away, sheeting down in ferocious blues around a sleek shape that Gabriel knew more than well. *Falada's* twin, with premonitory corona discharge shuddering around her weapons, all primed and ready to go: *Schmetterling.* She rose out of the darkness. Along with her, five other smaller ships, cutters or light cruisers with all their gunports shivering with blue-black fire, ready to go.

Gabriel looked at *Schmetterling* and gulped again, then he said down the comm connection to the other ships in his group, "People, get back here quick! Close up around me in a hurry and don't move after that!"

They obeyed him, coming in on system drive as quickly as they could, and parked themselves around him no more than a few hundred meters away. Gabriel would have been astonished by the skill of their captains at any other time. Now he just suspected that, as for him, terror was making competence unusually accessible. The four little ships lay close together around *Sunshine*, and around them in turn the six Concord ships swiftly arranged themselves into an open tetrahedron and closed in around the refugee ships at less than a thousand meters.

Gabriel breathed out, but not exactly in relief. There might be time for that later, after this all played itself out. "*Schmetterling,*" he said, "are we ever glad to see you."

"Not my idea, Connor," said Elinke Dareyev's voice. "Not my idea in the slightest, but orders are orders . . . and when did a ship carrying marines ever run away from the opportunity for a good fight?" Her voice was grim. "You want a link to incoming drivespace detection, speak to your computer, have it squawk ours on four-four-nine-nine-three. Now shut up and let us get on with saving your hides."

Gabriel swallowed and started hitting frequency controls. "*Schmetterling,*" said a third voice, "you and your companion ships are to withdraw and release the englobed ships to us. This is VoidCorp company business."

"Regret we can't comply, VC ship," said Elinke's voice.

"These vessels are our affair, none of yours. Suggest you withdraw before you find yourself with a situation."

"The situation would appear to be yours, *Schmetterling*," said the voice of the commander of the biggest VoidCorp ship. "You are badly outnumbered and outgunned."

"Outgunned possibly," Captain Dareyev said, "but as for outnumbered, the only way for you to find out is to give it a try and see what happens." There was a cheerful note in her voice that Gabriel had heard often enough before. He found himself feeling almost sorry for the VoidCorp ships. Almost.

"We'll give you five minutes to reconsider, *Schmetterling*," said the voice from the big VoidCorp ship. "This position is untenable."

"Presently," Elinke said, and she would say nothing more.

The thought had been on Gabriel's mind as well, for in the tank he had finally managed to call up the drivespace relay data detector from *Schmetterling*. It was more than active. *There's incoming,* Gabriel said. *It's something big. They* have *to know.*

They are bluffing it out, said Enda, *waiting to see if they can frighten us into resolving this before whatever that is gets here. Starrise detection has a plus/minus five percent time error depending on the mass of the incoming vessel.*

Gabriel knew the equation well enough but he rarely had so much reason to curse it, since the bigger the ship, the larger the on-time error. It had something to do with the way the ship's stardrive interacted with the ship's mass and with drivespace. *Come on,* he breathed.

Why are you so eager to see it? Enda said. *It could be anything. A VoidCorp dreadnought, some other of their big ships carrying someone whom they are eager to have see that this situation was resolved before they got here.*

It's not.

How do you know?

Hunch, Gabriel said, and then he added, *Besides, why would the Star Force ships be here if they weren't expecting help? They knew something big was about to happen, I'm sure of it. And this group is too small to make a difference in a major engage-ment, especially knowing the kind of VoidCorp ships that have been routinely cruising around in this system. The Concord would never send too small a force to intervene. Too small a force would invite failure. Failure would imply that it could happen somewhere else. Therefore there's more help coming—and that's it.*

I hope indeed that you are right, said Enda, *since if you are not, in very short time we will experience the delights of exis-tence as clouds of ions floating about in the noble void.*

And you tell me I *get graphic,* Gabriel muttered, turning his attention back to the tank. *I bet you'll make a terrific bright streak in a nebula somewhere.* The display in the tank remained stubbornly the same, though. Whatever the new ship was, there was no sign of it. Gabriel was much tempted to thump the tank as if it were the uncooperative waste recycler back in the hygiene suite. *Come on, show me something I want to see.*

The VoidCorp ships closed in, the corona discharge around their guns flickering hotter. They're afraid, Gabriel thought sud-denly. They're *afraid.* They don't quite know—

White fire went off so close to Gabriel, out the cockpit window, that for a moment he thought it was Helm again, appearing to drop one last cherry bomb. But this was somehow much bigger. Gabriel turned in his seat to see, not a kilometer from him, such a blaze and fury of starrise as Corrivale had never witnessed. Whole oceans of white fire streaked and rolled around a shape many times larger than even the biggest of the VoidCorp ships. It was tremendous, the kind of size that makes you think it is going to fall over on you even though you're in zero-g. *Sunshine* was a bumble bee beside her bulk, a huge behemoth with six outriggers supporting weapons pods them-selves the size of the smaller VoidCorp vessels. It took some-thing like a minute before the fire of her starrise drained and vanished away.

"This is the Concord dreadnought CSS *Trader Dawn,*" said a calm voice down comms. "We are here to assist the Phorcyn and Inoan ships *Glatha, Orniol, Enryn* and *Meshugga* and the Phorcys-registered ship *Sunshine* with their emergency relocation of the free sesheyan colonists of Rhynchus. We are carrying the final thousand free sesheyans, evacuated just before the last of the planet's atmosphere became unbreathable. Under Concord statute, a disaster of planetary proportions automatically invokes General Order Eighteen, requiring all vessels within one starfall to render assistance. Do you wish to render assistance, VoidCorp vessels?"

The silence that followed the question was eloquent. Gabriel took what he thought might be his last couple of breaths before becoming superheated plasma.

"Concord vessel," said the VoidCorp vessel after a moment, "these ships are carrying sesheyans who are former undocumented VoidCorp Employees. The Treaty of Concord requires that they be turned over to the Company for reassignment or cancellation of contracts forthwith."

Gabriel swallowed, knowing what "cancellation of contracts" meant in this context.

"On the contrary," said another voice, and Gabriel's mouth abruptly went dry. "This is Lorand Kharls, Concord Administrator for this area, aboard *Trader Dawn.* I regret to inform you, Flag Captain NI147 01GBH, that your claim over these sesheyans is unsubstantiated. If you had knowledge of such a group of 'escaped' Employees, you should have previously filed a request with the Council for their recovery and repatriation under the appropriate articles of the Treaty of Concord. Unfortunately you have filed no such request, not so much as a request for the assignment of a fact-finding team, which the Concord would certainly have honored and investigated through the correct channels. Instead, you have merely turned up in this system and begun attempting to bully independent operators from another system who have been engaged in a massive and difficult humanitarian effort organized in response to an appalling natural emergency that will itself require investigation. Perhaps you would like to assist us with *that?*"

Another of those silences. "Administrator," said the voice from the biggest ship finally, "we contest your claim."

"Contest away," said Kharls, "but do so through channels, because, by my oaths, if you attempt to do it here and now, my judgment of all the parties involved is already on file with the Concord. In implementing that judgment, I would not leave one of your ships' atoms sticking to another, or those of anyone *in* your ships, either. Just so that you understand my intentions. I would dislike having to implement a judicial decision on someone incapable of understanding it." You could just hear the cold smile. "Not that I would fail to implement such a decision, I would simply dislike doing so. You do understand?"

A long silence. "I believe we do, Administrator."

Another long silence. Gabriel waited for the shooting to break out.

"Then get out of here," Lorand Kharls said, "and go file your forms. I'll see you in court—if you dare."

The pause that followed was very long indeed, and Gabriel wondered whether someone on board the biggest ship was thinking, Oh, why not? This is as good a day to start a war as any other.

Then the biggest ship made starfall. Slowly it sank into drivespace, the light sheeting violet-blue around it as it vanished, a subdued color of retreat, of defeat.

Not permanent, Gabriel thought. No one would be so foolish as to think that. But right now, even temporary was better than nothing.

"Refugee vessels," said *Trader Dawn* comms, "you are invited to make planetfall on Grith at Diamond Point where immigration formalities will be completed. And welcome."

There was a muted cheer from the backmost sections of *Sunshine* where the young sesheyans were not quite clear what was happening, except that it sounded like they had won.

Gabriel sat back in his chair and breathed out a breath he realized he had been holding for a long, long time.

Enda collapsed her side of the fighting field and got up,

looking out at the great ruddy disk of Hydrocus. "If you need me," she said, "I will be using the sanitary facilities."

Gabriel laughed and turned back to the tank—then blinked, for the symbol for incoming comms from a Star Force vessel was there. He reached into the tank and told it "go."

The tank cleared. A moment later, Elinke Dareyev was looking at him.

Gabriel stood up. Partly from respect, partly . . . He glanced over his shoulder, saw Enda was still standing there. "Captain," she said.

"I see he hasn't gotten you killed yet," Elinke said.

"I do not expect that outcome," said Enda. She bowed politely and took herself away down the hall.

"I just wanted you to be clear about something," Elinke said. "It was none of my intention to save you. None whatsoever, and I wish to God I had had no part in this operation or in saving your lying, guilty skin. If *I* had my druthers, you would be roasting in whatever hell is reserved for marines who betray their brothers and sisters."

"Your druthers aside, Elinke," Gabriel said, "if you're suggesting that you grudge the rescue of three thousand sesheyan refugees just because I happened to be involved, then you are in need of professional help. Better go find some while you still have time." With some satisfaction he watched her bristle, but the satisfaction was sad.

She just looked at him for a moment, then finally said, "From now on, stay out of my way."

"I was doing my best," Gabriel said, "but I can't help it if you keep following me around."

She reached out to cut the connection.

"That night in Diamond Point," Gabriel said. "After the restaurant. You were there in the street."

Elinke stared at him. "So?"

"Thanks," Gabriel said, "for checking to see if I survived."

She sniffed and cut the link.

A few minutes later, Enda came back into the room behind

him. "Well," she said, "I suppose that was unavoidable."

"Maybe so, but there's still one problem."

"What would that be?"

"I *didn't* see her there that night. I see her there now—that is, I remember her being there as if I'd seen her, but that night—I never saw her at all."

Enda looked at him thoughtfully.

"Interesting," she said. "Now just where have you put my squeeze bottle?"

Chapter Nineteen

THE NEXT FEW days were fairly hectic, spent partly in Diamond Point and partly in Redknife. Gabriel finally got to meet Helm in person and shake him by the hand, though he was apparently mortified beyond belief to have missed the final showdown at Corrivale by a matter of minutes.

"Damned drivespace error," he muttered over a drink with Gabriel and Enda down in "the shed" in Redknife.

"Lose some of those guns," Gabriel suggested. "Lighten your ship a little. Less error."

"You were pretty glad about those guns when they saved your hide," Helm said.

Gabriel pushed him in the shoulder in a friendly way. "I'm kidding you. Helm. We couldn't thank you enough if we both had a fraal's lifetime."

"Not your debt," Helm said. "I'm going to take it out of Delde Sota's hide when I see her. Someday you may owe me something else, and then watch out." He drank a long draft of his drink, swore briefly at the heat, and then asked, "Where you going now?"

"We haven't decided yet. Some possibilities have been presenting themselves. Maybe we could go over to Algemron, do some courier work."

"Courier work is crap. Why not come do armed escort with me?"

"We don't have that kind of weaponry."

"You'd make great bait, though." Helm pushed himself back, roaring with laughter, and got up as he saw a sesheyan coming across the field toward them. "You've got more chat to hold with these people, probably. I'm finished victualling. Gonna head out again. You have my Grid code. Call when you know what you'll do, or leave word with Delde Sota if I'm in drivespace. I always check with her when I make starrise again. Enda—"

"Stars light your path, brother," she said.

"Don't you trip, either," said Helm and headed off.

The sesheyan coming toward them was Ondway, who looked after the mutant with a thoughtful expression. "I thought he might stay."

"Said he had things to do," Gabriel said, pulling a chair out for him. "How are they settling in?"

"Well enough. We did not lose too many," Ondway said, "between your departure and *Trader Dawn's* arrival. There is much work to do to decide where everyone needs to be, where they will settle. There is at least one family," he added, "who feel they must spend many months in the forest enclaves now as a result of their children's journey with you."

"I didn't mean to teach them bad language," said Gabriel desperately. "Really, I—"

"Language?" Ondway looked at him peculiarly. "It was the computer games. Their parents are nontechnology-oriented. They do not feel that computers are good for their young. They feel they must now spend weeks teaching them how to enjoy themselves once more without having a machine to help them."

Gabriel chuckled at that. "How much is the faceprice going to be?"

Ondway gave him a rueful smile. "You are a fool even to speak of it," he said. "They and I owe you faceprice beyond anything that can be calculated. When you understand what that means some day, come back and claim it."

"If they leave me alive after this," Gabriel said, nodding upward at where VoidCorp ships no longer hung for the time being, "some day I will. But believe me when I tell you that I had no choice. I just had to do it. Don't make me out to be a hero. Heroism doesn't come into it."

"For the one who does such an act," Ondway said, "it never does." He got up. "Come back again after your travels, and see your people. They are making staves about you."

"Oh please," Gabriel said.

"You will see eventually," said Ondway, "and then you will not blush, for the staves have a peculiarly . . . human taste to them." He made a face, one that crinkled his face under the goggles. It was a smile, Gabriel thought. "But come back. And you, honored, see that he does."

"I will see to that," said Enda. "Under the trees go well, Wanderer: beware what rises from below, and drops from above."

Ondway dropped that huge jaw in a grin and walked off across the field again to the large hangar that had been converted to office space and support quarters for some of the relocated sesheyans.

"Will we come back here any time soon?" Enda asked.

"I think it might be smart if we took a little vacation from this part of space," Gabriel replied. "Algemron is supposed to be nice this time of year."

"A possibility," Enda said. "Well, *Sunshine* will be ready to lift tonight, and after that—the choices are ours."

Gabriel nodded. "I may have a few loose ends to tidy up," he said, "but tomorrow I'll be ready to go."

* * * * *

That night, late, they sat in the darkened cockpit, just resting and listening to another of Enda's fraal recordings while they looked up at Hydrocus. The great ruddy light of Grith's primary was reduced to a crescent at the moment, and small spicules of gas-burst light erupted here and there from the turbulent atmosphere, backlit by the yellow fire of Corrivale.

"At the end of this long 'day,' " Enda said, "we are left with one question whose answers are still lacking." She looked at Gabriel, dark-eyed. *"Why* did they send you to kill the ambassador and the others? *Who* sent you? For what purpose?"

Gabriel shook his head. "Until I find out more about Jacob Ricel—"

"But he is dead," Enda said.

"I wonder," Gabriel said. "*Is* he?"

Enda looked at him as if he might have taken leave of his senses.

"I don't mean the man who died in some kind of e-suit accident on *Falada*," Gabriel said. "I mean the real identity behind that name. Are we sure whoever 'ran' him doesn't know more about this than Jake himself did? Can we be sure whoever 'ran' Jake didn't also run me?"

"There may not be as much hidden below this matter as you think, Gabriel," Enda said.

"There may be more," said Gabriel. "The past few weeks have, well, sidetracked me somewhat, but it's time to get back on track. I have to find out more about the people who got me into the situation aboard *Falada,* Ricel in particular—if that was his name—or whoever was behind him. Once I've found that out, I can begin assembling the evidence that will clear my name."

"Trying to assemble it," Enda corrected.

Gabriel looked at her and frowned, then finally nodded.

"This is going to take a while," he agreed, "but not forever."

"May it be so," Enda said.

* * * * *

Some light-years away, in a white-and-steel office, a conversation was taking place between two men. One was tall, the other was short, and their suits were of the kind approved by their employer. Beyond that, there was not much to choose between them, for both had spent years cultivating the kind of faces that did not stand out in a crowd and that is quickly forgotten even once it has been described. They spoke in near whispers, uncertain whether, even at their level, their offices were quite secure

"The Concord tame bloodhounds can sniff around all they like," the tall one said. "There's no material evidence. They won't ever be able to prove anything. Life on Grith will go on as always."

"That's the problem," his superior muttered. "It's such a shame. We were so close."

Both of them sighed. "Never mind," said the tall man. "We've got plenty of time yet. Who knows? Their star might even flare. F2's like that are so unstable."

He smiled a long, slow smile. "Now, about those third quarter figures . . ."

* * * * *

The next morning, at last, came the call for which Gabriel had been waiting. He was only surprised that it had taken this long, since they had been on Grith for three days, but Concord Administrators were busy people.

The marines who came to pick Gabriel up from the field at Redknife treated him with surprising respect, though they did not speak to him more than necessary. That was in line with their duty. You did not chatter to people on transport even if they invited it, and Gabriel did not invite it.

Trader Dawn seemed even more gigantic from the inside than from the outside, if that was possible. The walk to the office where his questioner awaited seemed to go on for about a week, and numerous people in Star Force uniform stood around to watch him pass by. A few of them saluted him. Gabriel did not return salute, since he was not in uniform, but he bowed his head a little to them as he passed and tried to keep hold of his composure afterward. It was difficult.

The room into which he was shown was almost a twin to the last one. Small and plain with a table across which all kinds of writing implements and notes were scattered, the room would not have been below the station of a mid-level bureaucrat. On the other side of the table, in a chair that seemed marginally too low for him, sat Lorand Kharls. As Gabriel came in, he rose.

"Mr. Connor," he said. "Will you sit?"

Gabriel pulled out a chair and sat.

"I want to thank you for what you did," Kharls said.

"I didn't do it for you," Gabriel said. "Those people down there were reason enough."

"You're right," Kharls said. "That is the just man's response. Nonetheless, you deserve thanks. There are few enough people who would do what you did because it needed doing."

Gabriel accepted that and sat quiet. He had at least learned something from Enda while they had been together.

"How did you bug my ship?" Gabriel asked after a moment.

"I beg your pardon?"

"I am convinced that you knew where I was most of the time," Gabriel said. "Someone else may have had us bugged as well, but I am uncertain as to who the guilty party might be. You, though—of your responsibility for having us bugged or traced, I'm certain."

Kharls looked at him thoughtfully. "You're suggesting," he said, "that I thought you might lead me to something?"

"Proof of guilt, perhaps," Gabriel said, frowning.

"Are you guilty?" asked Kharls.

"We've been through this," said Gabriel. "No."

"But I take it you're not yet ready for that trial."

"I tell you, Administrator," Gabriel answered, "as I told you before: the moment I have the evidence I need, I'll be on the comm to you. Meanwhile, and until then, I view you with the greatest suspicion."

"You view *me*—!" Kharls chuckled.

"It's probably not an isolated sentiment," Gabriel said. "I bet there are people all over this system who'll be delighted to see the back of you. Even when you are doing good, you make them nervous. And me. Where's the bug in my ship?"

Kharls sat back then and sighed. "In the one place where it was felt certain you would neither suspect a device or try to get rid of it even if you did find it—in your registry documents. No ship owner, no matter how mad, would ever try to lose or damage those. The enabling part of the bug was installed in the verification seals of the document. The enabler in turn spoke to your comms system and its Grid link, as well as to your ship's housekeeping computer. We knew where you were at any moment, we knew who you'd been talking to, how much food you had in the cupboards, and who'd been playing which games."

"You knew too damned much," Gabriel said, furious.

Kharls was unconcerned. "You of all people," he said, "should be in a position to agree with me that not knowing *enough* can be fatal. If you had known anything at all about your 'intelligence contact' back on *Falada,* a lot of people, including friends of yours, would not be dead. Yet if that had happened and had not led to the ensuing causes and effects, a lot *more* people would be dead, and a war would probably have broken out here. If not by now, then very soon. Ripples from that war would have spread right back to the Stellar Ring in time, and to all kinds of people in the other stellar nations who, whatever else they might need or deserve, do not need a war right now, not another one. My job is to keep the peace. It is not easy, and I will use my tools as I find them."

"Yes," Gabriel said, "you will, but sometimes the tools may have ideas of their own."

Gabriel stood up. Kharls stood up too. "Where will you go now?" he asked.

"To Hell in my own good time," Gabriel replied, "and without consulting *you.*"

"Have you reconsidered my offer?" Kharls asked.

"What?" Gabriel retorted. "To do some unspecified job for some unspecified reward that may or may not involve the establishment of my innocence? Do I look stupider than I did last time we spoke, Administrator? I suppose I must. Maybe saving people's lives does that to you. If so, I'll take my chances. Meanwhile, I will get on with what life has been left to me."

"That was not the offer I meant," Kharls said. "I spoke of serving the Concord with something besides a gun."

"I have been doing that," Gabriel said, "since we parted company, for reasons that have nothing to do with you. Another

matter that you won't believe, but it's my business. Now if you'll
excuse me, my partner and I have to get our ship ready to lift."

He turned toward the door. "I'll be in touch," Gabriel said,
"eventually, despite your best attempts otherwise. There is more
to life than being a marine, and I intend to find out how much
more. But I will also clear my name, and then all of you will . . ."
He trailed off. "Never mind. Good day, Administrator."

Gabriel went out.

Lorand Kharls stood and watched him go.

* * * * *

That was the last piece of business that Lorand Kharls had to
handle while remaining on board *Trader Dawn*. He took a gig
over to *Schmetterling* as soon as one became available. Soon
after that, he was sitting cross-legged on the sofa, turning over
pages on his writing pad and looking through other paperwork
that had been printed out for him.

So it was not his doing after all.

The debriefing—if that was the word for it—of the VoidCorp
agent "running" Gabriel Connor, had been very thorough. The
accident had been very expertly staged. Not even the people who
brought him to the ship's sickbay, not even the people who bagged
him up for cryo and return to relatives, had suspected what was
happening. The medical practitioner who had attended the
"death" and signed the certificate was one of the Concord's own
and would not be discussing matters with anyone. Afterwards,
when the experts had restarted his brain and put in the necessary
hardware, the answers had come tumbling out. Chief among
them was that Connor had been an innocent dupe, a genuine
intelligence asset sold off as "stale" or otherwise unsuitable, then
finally designated as expendable by some means that would
incriminate him past any thought of other use or further service.

That by itself had been interesting enough, but that interview
had also revealed information linking, if distantly, to more urgent
issues. The "living dead," as a few upper-ups in the Concord had

called them, had surfaced in the Thalaassa system now in greater
numbers than anyone had seen before—well, no one had seen
more than two examples in any one system, certainly not from
two species. But the one specimen that Connor had first found,
the man who had been Oleg Darsall—that one had raised a terrible question to which no one had answers. Silver Bell, Kharls
thought. How long have I been looking for an answer to that? I
thought that any answer would have been good enough. Now this
comes, and it terrifies me. Have we truly been looking in the
wrong direction these past three years? I could almost wish not
to have found it at all.

There had been rumors for a long time of strange forms and
forces walking the outer reaches of various star systems. Never
coming close to the light, never showing themselves except
obscurely, shadows trailing across space, here and gone again
into the cold and dark. Now the rumors were coming true, finally betraying the concrete nature of their terrors. But there were
no further indications of exactly what it was that had been *done*
to these men and sesheyans and fraal who were taken, and no
indications at all of who had done it to them or why.

What might their designs be for the Verge and the inner
worlds beyond? Designs there were. Whatever else Kharls knew
about this business, it was that there was nothing random about
it. The "changed" bodies had appeared in concert with attacks by
the strange little ships they piloted, all along a curvature of space
that more or less defined the outer reaches of the Verge. Idly he
sketched that curve on the pad, marking the star systems on it:
Algemron, Hammer's Star, Tychus, Oberon, and now Corrivale.
The first two had been bad enough, but Corrivale, deep in the
midst of the Verge, was increasingly becoming a crossroads for
trade in this part of the Verge, despite its tensions. In the vibran-
cy of the place over the last few years, the rumors of dark things
moving out at the edges of the system had mostly been swallowed up, drowned out. When word about *this* started to get out,
though, that would not last. The peace of these parts, won with
such difficulty, would once again start to erode, and this time

more dangerously. Although people might hate and fear the enemies they knew—VoidCorp, the corsairs—they hated and feared
the unknown far more.

His duty was maintaining peace. For the time being this information would have to be kept out of the public eye. Soon enough
something would happen that would make that impossible. In the
meantime, they would use what little time they were granted for
frantic analysis. Meanwhile, he would not throw away useful
assets while they remained so.

Kharls looked up from the pad and found Captain Dareyev
looking in the door at him.

"Lorand," she said, "is there a problem?"

He considered her for a long moment.

"No, Captain," he said, "nothing—nothing at all."

She looked at him a little curiously for a moment then walked
away. Lorand Kharls looked after her, then folded that page of
his pad over and looked at the next one, the clean one. He knew
better than most that the image of a Concord Administrator who
ran around meddling in people's affairs, doing things busily, was
an illusion. The most effective Administrators knew when to sit
still and let matters take their course. The information that had
just come to him would be very, very useful indeed—in time.
But just now there was no need to release it and make changes in
the ongoing situation. Besides—he thought of young Connor as
he had been when he left, rebellious, furious—and filled with an
energy that would take him far. Why suddenly remove the cause
of that energy, the force that drove him? There were more important causes than those of one mere man. By leaving him as he
was, great good might yet be done in the Verge, and justice
delayed was not always justice denied. It depended on how fast
justice moved in your neighborhood, and how wise it was for it
to move any faster.

No, Kharls thought. Let him wait. Kharls turned over another
sheet of the pad's writing plastic and began wondering where to
turn this resource next.

* * * * *

It was night on *Sunshine*. Enda was in her bed. Gabriel sat late in the pilot's seat, looking out at the stars that burned beyond Corrivale. They would be making starfall in the morning.

They were victualled, fueled, and re-armed. All farewells, all blessings and curses, were said. One thing only remained to do before they left.

Gabriel touched his combination into the safe-box set in the wall of the pilots' compartment, waited for the click, then opened the door. He reached in and came out with *Sunshine*'s registry papers. He held them in his lap for nearly an hour, looking at the seals. Finally he glanced around him, looking for something heavy.

There was nothing suitable in the cockpit. He got up, wandered back to the sitting room and glanced around, trying to be quiet. After a moment his eye fell on the hardstone pot in which Enda's bulb lived.

Gabriel reached out to it, glancing at the surface of the fold-down table, a good enough spot. He stopped then. He looked at the pot and the seals on the registry document again, and then he looked at the door to Enda's quarters.

He glanced again at the document in his hand, then walked back to the cockpit, put the registry document in the safe again, locked it, and took one last look at the stars.

Then Gabriel Connor went to bed.

Glossary

Aegis - A G2 yellow star. The Metropolitan Center of the Verge.

Ahhrihei - A fraal euphemism that literally means "a shift of wind," but infers a wind of the mind, i.e., a person's decision to make a change.

AI - Artificial Intelligence. Sentient computer programming whose sophistication varies from model to model.

Aimara - A lake on Ino.

Aleerin - see mechalus

Algemron - A G5 yellow star in the Verge. Also the name of the system.

Altid - A model of driveship.

Arends, Lieutenant Colonel - The marine senior commanding officer on board *Falada*.

AU - Astronomical Unit. 150 million km

Austrin-Ontis Unlimited - A corporate stellar nation that is best known as the strongest arms dealer of the Stellar Ring, but whose citizens view themselves as strong individualists with a deep sense of altruism.

Battle of Kendai (2375) - A battle of the Second Galactic War that effectively cut communications between the stellar nations and the Verge for 121 years.

Baynes, Julius - The chief Concord Administrator for the Verge.

bebe - A bird native to Grith.

Bluefall - Capital planet of the Aegis system. Ruled by the Regency government.

Bluff Heights - The cliff face at the edge of Diamond Point that protects it from the tides.

Boreal Sea - The sea of the north pole on Grith.

Bricht - A model of stardrive engine.

Builder - That section of fraal society that believes in integration with other species and cultures.

Callirhoë - A Concord Star Force Heavy Cruiser.

cerametal - An extremely strong alloy made from laminated ceramics and lightweight metals.

chai - tea

charge pistol - A small firearm in which an electric firing pin ignites a chemical explosive into a white-hot plasma propellant, thus expelling a cerametallic slug at extremely high velocity.

clearfoam - A synthetic, transparent foam used to contain instruments in a sterile environment.

CM armor - cerametal armor.

Colonial Diocese - The Hatire government upon Grith.

Concord - see Galactic Concord.

Connor, Gabriel - A Concord marine lieutenant.

Corrivale - An F2 yellow-white star. Also the name of the system.

Council of Tribes - The formal sesheyan government on Grith.

Cureyfi the Father of Stars - A sesheyan deity.

D80 - A model of Delgakis.

Damrak - A planet in the Orion League.

Dareyev, Elinke - Captain of *Falada*.

David, Lemke - A Star Force second lieutenant navigator.

decontam - short for "radioactive decontamination."

Delgakis (pl. Delgakises) - A model of driveship.

Delrio, Enrique - A Concord diplomatic assistant.

Delvecchio, Lauren - A Concord ambassador.

Detaka - A weren shift chief working in Ordinen.

Devereaux, Captain - Captain of *Callirhoë*.

Diamond Point - The capital city of Grith.

Dietmar, Charles - A marine on board *Falada*.

Dilemma - A planet visited by *Callirhoë's* marine complement.

Diocese, the - see Colonial Diocese

dirg - A creature that lives in nests on rocks.

Dorring - A planet visited by *Callirhoë's* marine complement.

Duma - The capital city of Phorcys.

drivecore - The central core of a stardrive engine.

driveplan - A plan filed with a star system's traffic control stating a ship's planned destination, arrival time, and travel intentions.

driveship - Any spaceship that is equipped with a stardrive.

drivespace - The dimension into which starships enter through use of the stardrive. In this dimension gravity works on a quantum level, thus enabling near-instantaneous movement of a ship from one point in space to another.

Drounli the Provider - A sesheyan deity.

durasteel - Steel that has been strengthened at the molecular level.

e-suit - An environment suit intended to keep the wearer safe from vacuum, extreme temperatures, and radiation.

Enda - A fraal.

Endwith - The main city of Phorcys's northern hemisphere.

Enryn - A Thalaassan starship.

Epsedra - The site of a fierce battle involving Concord Marines.

Eraklian - An inhabitant of Eraklion.

Eraklion - An outer world of the Thalaassan system used primarily for mining.

ErDaishan - An Inoan negotiator.

faceprice - In traditional sesheyan society, the restitution—monetary or otherwise—paid to clear a debt or restore bruised honor.

Falada - A Concord Star Force Heavy Cruiser.

Ferdinand, Lieutenant - *Falada's* protocol chief.

flitter - A small transport craft.

floater pallet - An anti-grav pallet.

force curtain - An energy field that keeps the atmosphere in a hangar bay but allows ships to come in.

fraal - A non-Terran sentient species. Fraal are very slender, large-eyed humanoids.

gailghe - Goggles worn by sesheyans to protect their sensitive eyes from bright light.

Galactic Concord - The thirteenth stellar nation formed by the Treaty of the Concord.

gandercat - An enormous arboreal omnivore native to Grith.

galya - A scented flower native to Grith.

General Order Eighteen - A statute of the Treaty of the Concord, which requires all ships within one starfall of a life-threatening emergency to render assistance.

gig - A colloquial term for any ship-to-ground shuttle. Any small craft capable of transporting passengers or cargo from one place to another. Most have gravity induction engines and a fuel range of no more than 100 million kilometers.

Glatha - A Thalaassan starship.

gravity induction - A process whereby a cyclotron accelerates particles to near-light speeds, thereby creating gravitons between the particle and the surrounding mass. This process can be adjusted and redirected, thus allowing the force of gravity to be overcome. Most starships use a gravity induction engine for inner system travel.

Grid - An interstellar computer network.

Grith - A moon of Hydrocus, and the only habitable world in the Corrivale system.

Gyrofresia ondothalis fraalii - A plant of uncertain origin, though general assumption states that it is native to the fraal homeworld, but the fraal themselves are uncertain of this. The plant has three life stages: bulb (during which it may lie dormant for long periods), shoot (a cluster of laneolate succulent type leaves with hypogynous bristles on the "upper" sides), and flower (single quadrangular flower spike with long, narrow panicles of white or cream-colored florets).

Hammer's Star - The outermost star system of the Verge.

Hatire Community - A theocratic stellar nation founded by the generally anti-technology religion of the same name.

holocomm - holographic communication.

holodisplay - The display of a holocomm that can be viewed in either one, two, or three dimensions.

hovbus - A large public transportation hovercraft that is popular on many worlds.

Hydrocus - An uninhabitable planet of the Corrivale system.

imager - A camera that records holographic, three-dimensional images.

Ino - A planet in the Thalaassa system.

Inseer - A citizen of Insight.

Insight - A subsidiary of VoidCorp that broke away to form a separate stellar nation.

Iphus - A planet in the Corrivale system.

Iphus Collective - A mining facility run by StarMech Collective on Iphus.

Iphus Independent - An independent mining guild based on Iphus.

Iphus Mining Division - The forty-four mining conglomerates on Iphus that are a subsidiary of VoidCorp.

Iphus United - A mining conglomerate in the Corrivale system that was absorbed by VoidCorp in a corporate takeover in 2497. Now Iphus Mining Division.

Jaeger - Capital planet of the Orion League; birthplace of Gabriel Connor.

Joris - Owner of a used spacecraft foundry on Phorcys.

Joris's Used Ship Heaven - A used spacecraft foundry on Phorcys.

JustWadeIn - A software program developed by Insight that allows the user to learn space combat at ever-increasing levels of difficulty.

Kaiste - A sesheyan.

kalwine - A wine.

Kendai - A planet on the edge of the Stellar Ring that houses the drivespace relay that connects communications between the stellar nations and the Verge. See also "Battle of Kendai."

Kharls, Lorand - A Concord Administrator.

Lanierin Four Fourty - A model of driveship.

lanth cell - The standard lanthanide battery used to power most small electronic equipment and firearms.

Leiysin, Gol - Owner of a used spacecraft foundry.

Longshot - Helm Ragnarsson's weapon-laden starship.

Long Silence - That period of time when the stellar nations lost contact with the Verge due to the Second Galactic War.

Lucullus - A binary star system in the Verge.

Madhra, Ari - A Concord Administrator.

Mashan - A small mining community on Eraklion.

mass cannon - A cannon that fires a ripple of intense gravity waves, striking its target like a massive physical blow.

mass reactor - The primary power source of a stardrive. The reactor collects, stores, and processes dark matter, thus producing massive amounts of energy.

Masterton, Elle - A Concord diplomatic assistant.

Maxson - A woman who works at the number six packaging plant in Ordinen.

mechalus - The most common term used for an Aleerin, a sentient humanoid symbiote species that has achieved a union between biological life and cybernetic enhancements.

Meldrum, Torine - A marine on board *Falada*.

Meshugga - A Thalaassan starship.

mindwalker - Any being proficient with psionic powers.

Muhles, Dor - Gabriel's Phorcyn legal counsel during his trial.

Nariac Domain - A stellar nation founded on principles of providing equality for all species, genders, and social statuses through superior cybernetic implantation and command economics.

Neshii'en - A sesheyan deity; the Trickster.

neurocircuitry - Cybernetic implants intended to fuse electronic or mechanic systems with a living biological entity.

NII47 OIGBH - A VoidCorp flag captain.

Noumara - A lake on Ino.

Ombe, Mayasa - VoidCorp employee QN105 74MAC. Also the sector security chief.

ondothwait - see *Gyrofresia ondothalis fraalii*.

Ordinen - An opencast mining community on Eraklion.

Orindren - A class of Delgakis driveship.

Orion League - A heterogeneous stellar nation founded on principles of freedom and equal rights for all sentients.

Orlamism - A religion based upon the belief that drivespace is true reality, or as the Orlamu themselves call it, "the Divine Unconscious." Orlamu believe that ultimate Truth will be achieved by communing with the Divine Unconscious.

Orlamu Theocracy - A theocratic stellar nation founded upon the principles of the Orlamu faith.

Ornery (pl. Orneries) - A model of driveship.

Orniel - A Thalaassan ship.

Orris, Captain - A Star Force captain.

Phorcys - A planet of the Thalaassa system.

phymech - An automated emergency medical system with a fairly sophisticated AI system. Most phymechs come with specialized medical supplies—skinfilms, bandages, antiseptics, painkillers, etc.

Pink Death - A highly alcoholic mixed drink made with Austrin gin.

Point of the Diamond - A term occasionally used by sesheyans for Diamond Point.

QI440 76RIC - A VoidCorp Employee.

QN105 74MAC - A VoidCorp sector security chief on Iphus. Her personal name is Mayasa Ombe.

Ragnarsson, Helm - A human mutant.

rail cannon - An electromagnetic accelerator that fires projectiles at high velocities.

Raitiz - A character in an old story mentioned by Enda.

Rallet - A Phorcyn delegate and minister of state for defense.

ramscoop - A hydrogen collector.

Rand - Lorand Kharls's assistant.

Ranulfsson, Sander - VoidCorp Employee UU563 56VIW. Upper Director rank.

RC094 29KIN - VoidCorp Employee Faren Reaves.

Reaves, Faren - VoidCorp Employee RC094 29KIN.

Redpath, Charles - A marine on board *Falada*.

Rhynchus - The outermost planet of the Thalaassa system.

Ricel, Jacob - A marine on board *Falada*. Gabriel's "security" contact.

Rike - A marine on board *Falada*.

rlin noch'i - The common garb of the mechalus. Consists of a multi-pocketed smartsuit and soft boots.

Roscinzsky, Mick - A marine on board *Falada*.

Rostrevor-Malone, Hal Quentin - A marine engineer on board *Falada*. A friend of Gabriel's.

sabot pistol - A small firearm that uses electromagnetic pulses to accelerate a discarding-rocket slug at hypersonic speeds.

Sealed Knot, the - A mechalus symbol favored by medical practioners of that species.

sesheyan - A bipedal sentient species possessing long, bulbous heads, large ears, and eight light-sensitive eyes. Most sesheyans are about 1.7 meters tall and have two leathery wings that span between 2.5 - 4 meters. Sheya, the sesheyan homeworld, has been subjugated by VoidCorp. However, a substantial population of "free sesheyans" live on Grith.

Silence, the - see the Long Silence.

Silver Bell - A Borealin colony on the planet Spes of the Hammer's Star system which was completely annihilated by unknown forces in 2489.

skinfilm - An artifical polymer membrance, usually only a few molecules thick, that is often used for sanitary protection or containment.

sniffer - A ramscoop detecting device.

Solar Union - A common term for the Union of Sol.

spaceport - A planetary landing zone for driveships.

spatball - A sport.

spee-g - short for specific gravity.

Speramundi - A stardrive engine model.

Spes - A planet in the Hammer's Star system.

stardrive - The standard starship engine that combines a gravity induction coil and a mass reactor to open a temporary singularity in space and thus allow interstellar travel. All stardrive jumps take 121 hours, no matter the distance.

starfall - The term used to describe a ship entering drivespace.

Star Force - The naval branch of the Concord military.

StarMech Collective, the - A high technology-oriented stellar nation.

starport - A zero-g, orbital docking zone for driveships.

starrise - The term used to describe a ship leaving drivespace.

Steilin, Dawn - A marine second lieutenant on board *Falada*.

stellar nation - Any of the thirteen independant nations of the Stellar Ring. They are Austrin-Ontis Unlimited, the Borealis Republic, the Hatire Community, Insight, the Nariac Domain, the Orion League, the Orlamu Theocracy, the Rigunmor Star Consortium, the StarMech Collective, the Thuldan Empire, the Union of Sol, VoidCorp, and the Galactic Concord.

Stellar Ring - The systems that make up the thirteen stellar nations, the center of which is Sol.

STG shuttle - Space-To-Ground shuttle.

system drive - Any form of non-stardrive propulsion used for inner system traffic.

Tal - A sesheyan deity; the Hunter.

Tendril - An F1 blue star. Also the name of the system.

Thalaassa - An F2 yellow star. Also the name of the system.

Thalaassan - A citizen of Thalaassa.

Three, the - A grouping of the three sesheyan dieties Neshii'en the trickster, Tal the hunter, and Vec't'lir the brood-mother.

Thuldan Empire - A militaristic stellar nation. The largest of the stellar nations.

Thuldan Prime - Homeworld of the Thuldan Empire.

Tractate - A planet visited by *Callirhoë's* marine complement.

Treaty of Concord, the - The Treaty that ended the Second
    Galactic War and formed the Galactic Concord.

tri-staff - The traditional weapon carried by Concord
    Administrators. It is a two-meter-long staff topped by a
    three-pronged blade.

T'teka - A marine. Captain Urrizh's superior.

Unhewoi - A sesheyan deity. The Taker, or the Beast.

Union of Sol - The hub of the Stellar Ring and the most densely
    populated stellar nation in existence.

Urrizh, Captain - A marine. Gabriel Connor's immediate
    superior.

UU563 56VIW - Sander Ranulfsson, a VoidCorp Employee.

Vec't'lir - A sesheyan deity. The brood-mother.

Verge, the - The frontier region of space originally colonized by
    the stellar nations that was cut off during the Second
    Galactic War.

VoidCorp - A corporate stellar nation. Citizens are referred to as
    Employees and all have an assigned number.

Wanasha - A Concord Star Force Cruiser.

Weyshe the Wanderer - A sesheyan deity.

Wanderer - 1.) *fraal*: A term used to describe that segment of
    fraal culture that prefers life aboard their wandering
    city-ships rather than settling down to mingle with other
    species. 2.) *sesheyan*: see Weyshe the Wanderer.

weren - A sentient species native to the planet Kurg. Most
    weren stand well over 2 meters, are covered in thick fur,
    and have sharp claws. Male weren have large tusks
    protruding from the bottom jaw.

Wuhain, Areh - Delvecchio's assistant ambassador.

WX994 02BIN - A high ranking VoidCorp Employee.

Wyens, Mil - A marine stationed aboard *Callirhoë*.

THE DRAGONS OF A NEW AGE TRILOGY
by Jean Rabe

Volume One:
The Dawning of a New Age
$5.99; $6.99 CAN
8376
0-7869-0616-2

Volume Two:
The Day of the Tempest
$5.99; $6.99 CAN
8381
0-7869-0668-5

Volume Three:
The Eve of the Maelstrom
$5.99; $6.99 CAN
8385
0-7869-0749-5

Krynn struggles to survive under the bleak curse of Chaos, father of the gods. Magic has vanished. Dragonlords rule and slaughter. A harsh apocalyptic world requires new strategies and new heroes, among them Palin Majere, the son of Caramon. This series opens an exciting page into the future.

RELICS AND OMENS:
TALES OF THE FIFTH AGE®
Edited by Margaret Weis and Tracy Hickman

The first Fifth Age anthology features new short stories exploring the post-*Dragons of Summer Flame* world of banished gods and lost magic. *Relics and Omens* showcases TSR's best-known and beloved authors: Douglas Niles, Jeff Grubb, Roger Moore, Nancy Berberick, Paul Thompson, Nick O'Donohoe, and more. The anthology includes the first Fifth Age adventure of Caramon Majere, one of the last surviving original companions, written by Margaret Weis and Don Perrin.

$5.99; $6.99 CAN,
8386
0-7869-1169-7